A STARBOUND NOVEL

THIS SHATTERED WORLD

A STARBOUND NOVEL

THIS SHATTERED WORLD

Amie Kaufman & Meagan Spooner

Hyperion

Los Angeles New York

First Hardcover Edition, December 2014
First Paperback Edition, December 2015
1 3 5 7 9 10 8 6 4 2
FAC-025438-15258
Printed in the United States of America

SUSTAINABLE FORESTRY INITIATIVE
Certified Chain of Custody
Promoting Sustainable Forestry
www.sfiprogram.org
SFI-01054
The SFI label applies to the text stock

Designed by Whitney Manger

Library of Congress Control Number for Hardcover Edition: 2014019419
ISBN 978-1-4231-7122-5

Visit www.hyperionteens.com

For Marilyn Kaufman and Sandra Spooner,
who have always been our unflinching allies,
and will always have our backs in every battle we face.

The girl is standing on a battlefield, and it's the street she grew up on. The people here don't know there's a war coming, and every time she opens her mouth to warn them, the city called November drowns her out. A car screeches past, a siren wails, children laugh, a holoboard starts playing its looped ad high above. The girl screams, but only the pigeons at her feet notice. Startled, they fly upward and disappear into the bright patchwork maze of laundry lines and lanterns crisscrossing overhead.

No one hears her.

ONE

JUBILEE

THERE'S A GUY STARING AT ME FROM THE OTHER END OF the bar. I can only see him because I'm in the habit of leaning forward, elbows on the plastene surface, so I can see past the row of heads. From here I can keep an eye on the whole place by watching the bartender's mirror overhead. And the guy I'm watching is using the same trick.

He's new. For one thing I don't recognize him, but for another he's got that look. Definitely a recruit, with something to prove, like they all do at first. But he's still glancing around, careful not to bump into the other guys, not too familiar with anyone else. He's wearing a uniform T-shirt, jacket, and fatigues, but the clothes are ill-fitting, the tiniest bit too tight. Could be because he's so new, they haven't ordered them in his size yet. Could also be because the uniform isn't his.

Still, the new ones know by the end of their first week not to hit on Captain Chase, even when she's at Molly Malone's. I'm not interested. Eighteen is pretty young to take yourself off the market, but it's safer to send them all the same message from day one.

But this guy . . . this guy makes me pause. Makes me forget all of that. Dark tumbly hair, thick brows, dangerously sweet eyes. Sensuous mouth, tiny smirk barely hidden at its corner. He's got a poet's mouth. Artistic, expressive.

He looks oddly familiar. Beads of condensation form around my fingers as I hold my drink. Scratch that—I'd remember this guy if I'd seen him before.

"All good?" The bartender comes between us, leaning on the bar and tilting his head toward me. It's a crappy bar on a crappy makeshift street, wistfully named Molly Malone's. Some ghost story from the Irish roots claimed by this particular cluster of terraforming fodder folk. "Molly" is a three-hundred-pound bald Chinese man with a tattoo of a chrysanthemum on his neck. I've been a favorite of his ever since I landed here, not least because I'm one of the only people who can speak more than a word or two of Mandarin, thanks to my mother.

I raise an eyebrow at him. "Trying to get me drunk?"

"I live an' dream an' hope, babe."

"Someday, Molly." I pause, my attention returning to the mirror. This time, the guy sees me looking and meets my gaze unapologetically. I fight the urge to jerk my eyes away, and lean closer to the bartender. "Hey, Mol—who's the new guy down at the end?"

Molly knows better than to look over his shoulder and starts rinsing out a new glass instead. "The pretty one?"

"Mmm."

"Said he was just posted here, trying to get a feel for the place. He's asking lots of questions."

Odd. The fresh meat usually comes in herd form, entire platoons of wide-eyed, nervous boys and girls all shuffling wherever they're told. A little voice in my head points out that's not really fair, that I was meat once too, and only two years ago. But they're so woefully unprepared for life on Avon that I can't help it.

This one's different, though—and he's all alone. Wariness tingles at the base of my neck, my gaze sharpening. Here on Avon, *different* usually means *dangerous*.

"Thanks, Molly." I flick the condensation on my fingertips at him, and he flinches away and grins before turning back to his more demanding customers.

The guy's still staring at me. The smirk is not quite so hidden now. I know I'm staring back, but I don't really care. If he really is a soldier, I can say I was sizing him up in an official capacity, looking for warning signs. Just because I'm off duty doesn't mean I can leave my responsibilities behind. We don't get much warning when we're about to lose one to the Fury.

He doesn't look much older than I am, so even if he enlisted the day he turned sixteen he won't have more than two years of service under his belt. Enough to get cocky—not enough to know he should wipe that grin off his face. A few weeks on Avon will do that for him. He's chiseled, with a chin so perfect, it makes me want to hit it. The shadow of stubble along his jaw only emphasizes the lines of his face. These guys invariably end up being assholes, but from this distance he's just beautiful. Like he was put together by an artist.

Guys like this make me want to believe in God.

The missionaries should really start recruiting guys like him before the military can get to them. After all, you don't have to be pretty to shoot people. But I think it probably helps if you're trying to spread your faith.

With my eyes on his in the mirror overhead, I give a deliberate jerk of my chin to summon him over. He gets the message, but takes his time about responding. In an ordinary bar on an ordinary planet, it'd mean he wasn't interested or was playing hard to get. But since I'm not after what people in ordinary bars are after, his hesitation makes me pause. Either he doesn't know who I am or he doesn't care. It can't be the former—everyone on this rock knows Captain Lee Chase, no matter how freshly arrived. But if it's the latter, he's no ordinary recruit.

Some stooge from Central Command, trying to lie low by dressing like us? A field agent for Terra Dynamics, come to see if the military's doing its job in preventing an all-out uprising? It's not unheard of for a corporation to send in spies to make sure the government is holding up its end of the terraforming agreement. Which only makes our job harder. The corporations are constantly lobbying to be able to hire private mercs, but since the Galactic Council doesn't exactly relish the thought of privately funded armies running around, they're stuck petitioning for government forces. Maybe he's *from* the Galactic Council, here to spy on Avon before their planetary review in a couple months.

No matter who he is, it can't be good news for me. *Why can't these people leave me alone and let me do my job?*

The dark-haired guy picks up his beer and makes his way over to my end of the bar. He puts on a good show of eager shyness, like he's surprised to be singled out, but I know better. "Hey," he says by way of greeting. "I don't want you to panic, but your drink appears to be blue."

It's one of Molly's concoctions, which he sometimes gives me for free as an excuse to actually mix drinks instead of filling pitchers of beer.

I make a snap decision. If he wants to play it coy, I can do coy right back. He's not exactly hard on the eyes, and this curiosity is tugging at me—I want to see what happens if I go along with it. I know he can't be interested in me. At least not the way he's pretending to be.

I fish out the plastic sword—it's hot pink—from the martini glass and suck the cherries off of it, one by one. The guy's eyes fix on my lips, sending a brief surge of satisfaction through me. Molly doesn't get much opportunity to mix drinks here—and I don't get much opportunity to flirt.

I let my lips curve in a smile and lean in a fraction. "I like it blue."

His mouth opens to respond, but instead he's forced to clear his throat at length.

"Got a touch of the swamp bug?" I feign concern. "Molly'll take care of that for you. His drinks'll cure anything, from wounded feelings to appendicitis."

"That so?" He's found his voice again, and his smile. There's a gleam behind the *aw-shucks* new-boy persona he's wearing: pleasure. He's enjoying himself.

Well, so are you, points out a snide little voice in my head. I shove it aside. "If you give it a second, we'll find out if it'll turn my tongue blue, to boot."

"That an invitation to make a personal inspection?"

I can see some of my platoon at a table in the background, watching me and the new guy, no doubt waiting to see if I rip off something important. "Play your cards right."

He laughs, leaning sideways against the bar. It's a bit of a capitulation, a pause in the game. He's not so much hitting on me as feeling me out.

I set my drink down on the bar next to a set of initials scratched into the composite surface. They were here before I ever showed up, and their owner is long gone. "This is the part where you'd ordinarily introduce yourself, Romeo."

"And ruin my mystique?" The guy's thick brows go up. "Pretty sure Romeo kept his mask on when he met Jubilee."

"Juliet," I correct him, trying not to flinch at his use of my whole name. He must be new, not to know how much I hate that. Still, he's given me a valuable hint. If this guy knows Shakespeare, he's got to have been educated somewhere off-world. The swamp-dwellers can barely read an instruction manual, much less ancient classics.

"Oh, a scholar?" he replies, eyes gleaming. "This is a strange place to find a girl like you. So, who'd you offend to get stuck on Avon?"

I lean back against the bar, propping myself on my elbows. One hand fidgets with the plastic sword, weaving it back and forth through my fingers. "I'm a troublemaker."

"My favorite kind of girl." Romeo meets my eyes with a smile, then looks away. But not before I've seen it: he's tense. It's subtle, but I've been trained to notice the invisible currents, the ebb and flow of a person's energy. A muscle tic here, a line of tension there. Sometimes it's all the warning you get before someone tries to blow themselves up, and take you with them.

Adrenaline sharpens my senses as I lean forward. The air in here smells of spilled beer, cigar smoke, and air freshener—none of which is strong enough to drown out the invasive smell of the swamp outside. I try to shut out the sound of my platoon laughing in the background and look more closely at Romeo. I can't tell, in the low light, whether his pupils are dilated. If he's new to the planet, he shouldn't have had time to succumb to the Fury—unless he's been transferred here from somewhere else on Avon.

He shifts his weight under my scrutiny, then straightens. "Listen," he says, his voice getting brisker, "let me settle for your drink, and I'll leave you to your evening."

Somehow he's gotten a read on me. He knows I'm suspicious.

"Hang on." I reach out to lay my hand on his arm. It's a gentle touch, but firm. He'll have to jerk away if he wants to leave before I'm ready to let him go. "You're not a soldier," I say finally. "And not a local. Quite the little puzzle. You're not going to leave me so unsatisfied, are you?"

"Unsatisfied?" The guy's smile doesn't flicker a millimeter. He's good. He's got to be a spy from one of TerraDyn's competitors. Nova Tech or SpaceCorp, or any one of the neighboring corporations with space staked out on Avon. "That's unkind, Captain Chase."

I abandon pretense. "I never told you who I was."

"Like Stone-faced Chase needs an introduction."

Though you'd never catch my platoon calling me that, at least to my face, the nickname caught on like wildfire after my first few days here. I don't reply, scanning his features and trying to figure out why he looks so familiar. If he's a criminal, maybe I've seen his picture in the database.

He makes a small attempt to free his arm to test how badly I want to hold on to him. "Look, I'm just a guy trying to buy a girl a drink. So why don't you let me do that, and then we can go our separate ways and dream about what might've been?"

I clench my jaw. "Listen, Romeo." My fingers tighten—I can feel the tense muscle beneath my hand. He's no weakling, but I'm better trained. "How about instead, we go to HQ and chat there?"

The muscle in his forearm under my palm twitches, and I glance at his hand. It's empty—but then he shifts his weight, and suddenly there's something digging into my ribs, held in his other hand. He had a gun tucked inside his shirt. *Goddammit.* It's ancient, a tarnished ballistics weapon, not one of the sleek Gleidels I'm used to. No wonder he's wearing a jacket despite the heat inside the bar. The long sleeves are concealing his genetag tattoo, the spiral design on the forearm that all the locals get at birth.

"Sorry." He leans close to me to conceal the gun between us. "I really did just want to pay for your drink and get out of here."

Beyond him I can see my guys, heads together, laughing and occasionally peeking our way. Though half of them are well into their twenties, they still act like a bunch of gossips. Mori, one of my oldest soldiers, meets my eyes for a moment—but she looks away before I can convey anything through my gaze. Alexi's there too, his pink hair gelled up, looking way too interested in the wall. From their perspective, I'm letting this guy drape himself all over me. Stone-faced Chase, getting a little action for once. Troops cycle in and out of Avon so often that all of those here have only known the past few months' ceasefire—their senses aren't battle-sharpened. They're not suspicious enough.

"Are you kidding me?" My own weapon is on my hip, but we're close enough that he could easily shoot me before I reach it. "You can't actually think this is going to work."

"You haven't really given me much choice, have you?" He glances down at the holster on my hip. "You seem a little overdressed, Captain. Leave the gun on the stool there. *Slowly.*"

I roll my eyes toward Molly, but he's leaning back drying glasses and watching the holovid over the end of the bar. I try to catch someone's eye—*anyone's* eye—but they're all carefully ignoring me, all too eager to tell stories later about how they saw Captain Chase get picked up at Molly's. My abductor shields me with his body as I reach for my Gleidel and set it down where he indicates. He wraps a hand around my waist, turning me toward the door. "Shall we?"

"You're an idiot." I clench my hands, the pink cocktail skewer digging into my palm. Then I turn a little, making a token struggle to test his grip and the distribution of his weight. There—he's leaning a little too far forward. I tense my muscles and jerk, leaning back and giving my arm a twist. It hurts like hell, but—

He grunts, and the barrel of the gun digs more sharply into my rib cage. But he doesn't let me go. He's good. *Damn, damn, DAMN.*

"You're not the first person to say so," he says, breathing a little faster.

"Fine—ow, I'm going, okay?" I let him steer me toward the door. I could call his bluff, but if he's stupid enough to bring a gun onto a military base, he might be stupid enough to fire it. And if this blows up into a firefight, my people could get hurt.

Besides, someone will stop us. Alexi, surely—he knows me too well to let this happen. Someone will see the gun—someone will remember that Captain Chase doesn't leave the bar with strange guys. She doesn't leave the bar with anyone. Someone will realize something's wrong.

But no one does. As the door swings closed behind us, I hear a low sound of whistles and catcalls in the bar as my entire platoon starts jeering and gossiping like a bunch of old hens. *Bastards,* I think furiously. *I'm going to make you run so many laps in the morning, you'll wish YOU had been carried off by a rebel.*

Because that's who this is. I don't know how he knows Shakespeare, or where he got his training, but he's got to be one of the swamp rats. They call themselves the Fianna—warriors—but they're all just blood-thirsty lawbreakers. Who else would dare infiltrate the base with nothing but a pistol that looks like it's from the dawn of time? At least that means there's no danger of him snapping into mindless violence, since Avon's deadly Fury only affects off-worlders. I only have to worry about the average, everyday violence that comes so easily to these swamp-dwellers.

He tugs me off the main path and into the shadows between the bar and the supply shed next door. Then it hits me: I'm not going to be making anyone run laps in the morning. I'm a military officer, being captured by a rebel. I'm probably never going to see my troops again, because I'll be dead by morning.

With a snarl, I jam my hand back and down, sending the blade of the pink plastic cocktail sword deep into the guy's thigh. Before he has time to react, I give it a savage twist and snap off the hilt, leaving the hot-pink plastic embedded in the muscle.

At least I won't go without a fight.

The boys are playing with firecrackers in the alley, stolen from the strings in the temple. The girl watches through a hole in the wall, her face pressed against the crumbling brick. Yesterday it was the Lutheran priest's turn in the temple, but tomorrow is a wedding, and it's her mother's turn to convert the tiny box of a building at the end of the street to match too-distant memories of traditional ceremonies on Earth.

The boys are lighting the firecrackers and seeing who can hold on to the red sticks longest before tossing them away to snap like gunfire in the air. The girl squeezes through a gap in the wall and runs to snatch a lit firecracker from the biggest boy. Her skin crawls with the hiss and heat of the fuse, but she refuses to let go.

TWO

FLYNN

PAIN SEARS DOWN MY LEG, AND MY GRIP LOOSENS FOR AN instant. She's away like a flash.

I have only a split second to act, and if I miss, she's going to kill me. I leap back as she swings at me, and the night is shattered by the sound of a gunshot. *My* gun. She goes sprawling into the mud with a gasp of pain, but I don't have time to consider what damage I might have done. Everybody on the base will have heard the shot, and even with the echo bouncing around the buildings, they'll find me soon enough.

I start to reach for her, but she's already moving; she's not badly hurt, or else adrenaline is holding her together. She kicks out, her foot connecting with my arm and numbing it from the elbow down. The gun goes sliding along the wet ground.

We both lunge after it. Her elbow jabs at my solar plexus, missing it by an inch—I'm left wheezing rather than half dead, dragging in air as I force myself to move. She scrambles ahead of me and I grab at her ankle, scrabbling in the mud to drag her back again before she can grab the gun or shout for backup.

She may be trained, but I'm fighting for my family, my home, my freedom. She's fighting for a goddamn paycheck.

For a long moment there's only the harsh staccato of our breathing as we fight to get ahead of one another. Then my hand finds the familiar grip of my grandfather's pistol. I jab my elbow back at her face; she dodges it easily, but it throws her off enough for me to roll over and end up with the gun pointed between her eyes.

She goes still.

I can only see the dark, furious glitter of her eyes meeting mine. I can't speak, too winded, too shell-shocked. Slowly, she lifts her hands, palms out. Surrender.

I want nothing more than to collapse in the mud. But I can hear the shouts of soldiers looking for intruders, hunting for the source of the gunshot. I've got no time. I need to get her to my currach—if I leave her here she'll be found too quickly and I won't have enough time to vanish into the swamp.

I give the gun a jerk, silently ordering the soldier to her feet. I stagger up myself, then grab for her arm to turn her around and twist it behind her back. I rest the barrel of the gun against her lower spine, where she can feel it.

My fingers are wet and sticky with her blood, but it's too dark to tell how much there is. I know I hit her; I saw her fall. But she's on her feet, so the wound isn't slowing her down that much. I must have only grazed her side with the bullet.

I try to calm my breathing, listening for the soldiers. Getting off the base is going to be a hell of a lot harder now; I wish I had time to camouflage myself with the mud at our feet. Her skin's brown and more difficult to see in the low lighting, but mine's the pale white that comes from living on a planet with constant cloud cover. I practically glow in the dark.

"Well?" She's panting. "What's it going to be? You could at least have the decency to aim for my heart and not my head. I'll look prettier at my funeral."

"There's something very wrong with you, Captain," I tell her, keeping her close. Her black hair's escaping her ponytail, tickling my face and getting into my eyes. "You don't invite a thing like that around here."

"As if you need an invitation," she growls, and though she's completely still, I can almost feel her humming with anger. I can't let her go. She'd never let *me* go. She shoves back roughly, sending pain spearing down my leg.

I shift my grip on the gun, letting it press against her a little harder.

It was easy to get the new recruits talking, but their security clearance is way too low to have any useful information. But trying to get close to Captain Chase for information was another matter entirely. What was I thinking? Sean would laugh if he could see me now: the Fianna's biggest pacifist holding Avon's most notorious soldier at gunpoint.

"I'll recognize your pretty face anywhere now, you know that." There's a smug satisfaction in her tone, underneath her anger. Like winning the point is what matters, even if it means she ends up dead. "You have to get rid of the problem."

"*Póg mo thóin, trodaire,*" I mutter, tightening my grip. *Kiss my ass, soldier.*

Captain Chase lets off a string of what sound like insults in return, though I don't understand the language. She doesn't look like she's got any Irish in her, probably has no idea what I said. But she recognized my tone, as easily as I can tell she's cursing right back at me, speaking . . . Chinese, maybe? She looks like she might have that ancestry in her blood somewhere, but with the off-worlders it's hard to tell. She gives a savage twist and then gasps as the movement wrenches at her wound. It's lucky I managed to graze her, because I wouldn't be able to keep hold of her otherwise. She's even stronger than she looks.

My mind races. This isn't over yet, and I can still turn it to my advantage if I think quickly. The recruits in the bar may not have known about the hidden facility to the east, but now I have a captain, and one who's been on Avon longer than any other soldier. Who better to get me that info than the military's golden child?

That facility scares me too much to ignore. Until I saw it a few hours ago, I'd never clapped eyes on it. I don't know how they hid the construction. It appeared out of nowhere, surrounded by fences and spotlights. From the outside, there's no way to tell what's in there: weapons, new search drone technology, ways to destroy the Fianna we haven't thought of. Until we know why the facility is there, every minute is danger.

I give her a shove and start moving toward the perimeter of the base, keeping to the shadows and away from the surveillance cameras. "Ever seen the beauty of the outer swamps?"

"I suppose out there they won't find my body at all. Smart."

"Does your platoon's psych attendant know about this obsession with your own death?"

"Just trying to be helpful," she mutters through gritted teeth. We're not far from where I snuck in through their fencing. I'm sure on a more high-tech world, the perimeter would light up with lasers and six kinds of alarm bells, but out here beyond the edge of civilization, the soldiers are stuck with wire fences and foot patrols. Central Command spends as little as it can get away with to supply them, and it shows. On top of that, the last few months of ceasefire have made them lazy. Their patrols aren't what they should be.

I can hear the search parties on the other side of the base, but here where it butts up against the town, it's quieter. They always think the rebels will come from the swamp. Like we're not smart enough to walk around to approach from the town, where there's less protection.

I can tell she starts thinking about those search parties about the same time as I do—she draws breath to shout, and I dig the barrel of the gun into her skin in warning. We're both still for a long, tense moment as she decides whether to call my bluff. I'm praying she doesn't. She lets the air out of her lungs in a furious capitulation.

I kick at the wire until the place I wound the severed ends back together gives way, and then we're outside her territory and into the swamp beyond. The marsh stretches out before us into the gloom, mud-flats and bare rock interspersed with a thousand winding creeks and streams. The water's as muddy as the land and half concealed by reeds and rotting algae, so nobody but the locals can tell where the solid ground is until they put their feet down. The floating clumps of vegetation mean the waterways are constantly shifting—deeper, shallower, interconnecting in different ways each week as mud and algae flow sluggishly.

Most of the swamp is a murky black right now, the permanent clouds above us blocking any hint of light from the stars. We were taught there are a couple of moons up there too, somewhere, coaxing the waters to flow this way and that. But I've never once seen them—only the clouds, *always* the clouds. Avon's sky is gray.

My currach is pulled up and beached on the mud by the fence, her flat-bottomed hull of sturdy plastene a battered contrast to the military patrol boats. I don't mind her, though—she can go places they don't even see, without making a sound. I push Jubilee ahead of me, down toward the water's edge, and she growls a wordless protest.

"You know, most people find me charming." I keep talking in her ear, hoping to keep her too distracted to think of a way out of this. "Even you looked keen on me for a sec there, Jubilee." I hear her huff. Using her name annoys her for some reason—good. One more way to keep her off balance. "Maybe you just need to give me a second chance."

I shove her forward into the currach and knock the lid off the fuel can with my foot. The crude gasoline we're forced to use is so toxic, I can smell the fumes from here, but I grab her collar to shove her face down against the can. With an indignant protest she sucks in a lungful of vapor. It takes her a few seconds to push past the pain and work out what I'm doing, but she's inhaled enough that her limbs don't work. When she tries to push me away, her legs give out and she slips, wrenching free of me to thump down into the bottom of the boat.

For a moment our eyes meet in the dim light. Her gaze is furious as she struggles to stay conscious, trying to push up on one elbow. Then she's gone, her head falling back to thunk against the plastene hull. I lean in carefully to peel back her eyelids, but she's out. She'll have a screaming headache when she wakes, but it's better than hitting her over the head. Too easy to misjudge the blow and end up killing her instead.

Without wasting another second, I flick on the safety, stick my gun into my waistband, and shove off with my foot. The currach glides swift and silent through the water. I can't risk a light, not when I can see the lights of the base security forces dancing behind me, still searching for the intruder. I navigate by feel, unclipping the pole from the gunwale and using soft, quick touches ahead and around me to make sure I'm keeping to the channel that will lead me away from danger.

By the time they get searchlights sweeping the stretch of swamp beyond the fences, I'm too far away for the light to reach. I keep expecting to feel a hand on my ankle, or the captain's fist meeting my gut, but she doesn't stir.

As soon as the sounds of shouts carrying across the water begin to fade and I can no longer see the distant lights of the base, I stop long enough to find my lantern and light it. We use algae to coat the glass, giving the light an eerie green-brown wash; occasionally the soldiers spot our boats or our signal lights, and the camouflage can make them dismiss what they've seen as the will-o'-the-wisps so feared in this swamp.

What they don't know is that anyone who'd seen a *real* wisp could never confuse it with one of our lanterns.

I hang the lantern on its spur rising from the bow and turn back to the unconscious *trodaire* in the bottom of the currach. There's no way out of this now. Whether or not she can shed light on what's happening in the stretch of no-man's-land east of the base, she knows my face. She may not know my name yet, but if she manages to connect me with my sister, she'll personally lead the hunt until she has my head on a platter—she won't need their so-called Fury as an excuse for taking me apart piece by piece.

Taking out Captain Chase would be a huge blow for the *trodairí*, and a triumph for us. I know at least two dozen Fianna who would shoot her without hesitation and sleep just fine tonight. If I came back with her body, my people would love me for it.

I let my breath out slowly, and my thumb hovers over the safety on my grandfather's pistol tucked in my waistband. But that way is a pit, one my sister couldn't escape once she fell into it.

I've heard more stories about this girl than any ten other trodairí put together. They claim she's the only one unaffected by what the soldiers call Avon's Fury. Probably because she doesn't need to fall back on that thin excuse to commit violence against my people—according to the stories, she practically embraces it. They talk about how she single-handedly cleared out the resistance cell on the southern edge of TerraDyn territory. How the soldiers under her command are the fastest to respond, the first on the scene, the fiercest fighters. How she skins rebels alive just for fun.

I wasn't so sure about that last one until I saw how she looked at me after I pulled my gun on her. But at least one of the stories is true. My cousin Sean nearly got his head blown off by her platoon a week after she took command, and when I asked him what she was like, he said she was mind-twistingly hot. He had that part right. If only she weren't a murderer-for-hire.

My best hope is to force her to tell me what she knows about the facility—maybe even get me inside for a look around—then split. At least I'll have a head start when the hunt begins.

I tear my eyes away and concentrate once more on the pole. The currach glides true through the water, my path lit only a few meters ahead by my dim green lamp. I ought to feel better, lighter, with every minute I put between us and the bright lights of the base, but I know this is not a victory. The soldier in the bottom of my boat will stop at nothing to kill me and escape when she wakes; and if the rest of the Fianna discover I have her, they'll stop at nothing to kill *her*. Our ceasefire will be over, my people forced once more into a war they cannot hope to win.

I have to work fast.

This time the dream is fragmented, arriving in razor-edged shards that don't fit together and slice at her memory. The girl is on Paradisa, and she's trying to climb a wall. Time's up, yells the sergeant, making her arms shiver with exhaustion as her toes scrabble for purchase against the plastene.

She wants to let go and drop to the ground. But when she looks down, her mother is there, with that always-tired sigh, that soft-eyed hint of disappointment. Her father is there, hands grimy in grav-engine grease, a bullet hole in his head.

The sergeant shouts at her again to give up and this time she screams back, using a word that will later earn her a week digging trenches.

There are too many ghosts down there to let go.

THREE

JUBILEE

I'VE GOT THE HANGOVER FROM HELL. MY HEAD'S POUNDING; how much did I have to drink at Molly's last night? Except that's impossible. I haven't had a hangover since the morning after I was finally accepted into basic training. It was technically three weeks shy of my sixteenth birthday, and therefore illegal for me to drink. But after I tried to get into the military for three years running by lying about my age, they finally caved and bent the rules. What was three weeks? Odds were I'd be dead within the year anyway. Might as well let the cannon fodder have a few beers first.

But once was enough. It wasn't the drinking or even really the hangover that got me—it was being less than capable on my first day of training. There, all it meant was that I didn't make the best first impression on my instructors, and let my sparring partner pin me in less than a minute. No big deal.

But out here, being at less than one hundred percent could mean death. And I've never had more than a few drinks at a time since then.

So why do I feel like tossing the contents of my stomach all over the floor?

The ground sways under me, and I force my eyes open, ignoring the way my eyelids feel like they're lined with sandpaper. The first thing I see is the blank, slate-gray expanse of Avon's unchanging night sky. I try to sit up and fall over sideways, making the floor shudder and sway; my hands are bound and tied to something. A flash of agony rips up my side, carrying with it the memory of a bullet splitting my skin.

"Bad idea, Captain," says an infuriatingly cheerful voice somewhere above and behind me. "If you capsize us, I don't really fancy your chances of swimming to solid ground while tied to a sinking boat."

I lift my head, squinting at the guy standing backlit over me. *Romeo.*

"At least if I drown," I wheeze, my voice sounding like gravel, "your friends won't have the pleasure of stringing me up from the rafters at your little hideout."

Romeo narrows his eyes at me, brows drawing in as he pushes us off a clump of vegetation with one of the long poles the natives use. "We don't hang soldiers," he retorts with exaggerated outrage. "We burn them at the stake. It takes ages to collect the fuel, given the landscape. It's quite a special occasion."

I snort, using the sound to disguise the creak as I test the strength of the boat rib I'm tied to. Despite how shoddy-looking the boat is, the rib doesn't give. But being tied up is the least of my problems.

Avon's perpetual cloud cover means there's no navigating by starlight, the way we're trained to do in survival situations. The swamp stretches as far as the eye can see, giving me no reference points, no way to tell what direction we're going. Even the occasional spires of rock thrusting upward look alike. They're sharp as razor blades; Avon's only had wind and water to erode them for a few generations, barely a heartbeat in geological time. The waterways between islands and floating masses of vegetation shift so rapidly that from day to day, the same patch of swamp can look entirely different. I have no idea where we are. And being lost, on Avon, is deadlier than being a soldier in the middle of a pack of bloodthirsty rebels.

There's a dingy lantern hanging from a pole in the bow, casting a dim light over the water. We must be far enough from the base that Romeo feels safe using light. I strain my eyes, trying to get my bearings, but all I get are spots swimming in front of my vision. My soldiers some-times claim they can see things out here, lights that seem to lead off into the swamp. The rebels call them will-o'-the-wisps, out of some fairy tale from ancient Earth. In all my time here, I've never seen anything but my own mind playing tricks on me—and, I suppose, the occasional rebel lantern bobbing through the marsh. But when you're surrounded by nothingness, your eyes will create anything to keep you from feeling alone. I blink hard to clear the spots dancing in front of my eyes.

"Why do this instead of killing me on the base?" I say finally, twisting my wrists, trying to see how much give there is in the rope. Not much. It's thick from repeated soakings, and stiff with age. "Are you planning some public execution?"

Romeo's lips press together more tightly, but this time he keeps his eyes on the swamp ahead of us as he poles through the clumps of floating algae. "You really are insane."

My mind is racing, taking stock of my injuries. My head aches from the gas fumes, sending spikes of nausea rippling through me, and my side hurts. But there doesn't seem to be much blood, so he can't have wounded me that badly. "I don't see why it's crazy to want to know exactly how you plan on murdering me." I'm not done yet. All things considered, I'm in decent shape. I can still get out of this.

"I don't plan on murdering you at all." Romeo still won't meet my eyes. "That might be your first instinct, but it's not mine. You're going to get me inside the facility you've been hiding from us and show me exactly what you're doing in there."

"My first instinct was to arrest you," I snap. "You're the one who brought a gun to my bar." I keep staring behind us, but there's no sign of the lights from the military base. "What facility?"

"The secret base to the east. It wasn't there last week, and now there's a full setup. Buildings, security fencing, the works. I've seen it, you don't need to pretend. I want to know how you got it set up so fast, and without anybody knowing. I want to know what it's for."

My hands go still, my attempt to escape momentarily forgotten. "Secret base," I echo, trying to quell the dread rising in my gut. It's one thing to be captured by a rebel. It's another to be taken into the swamp by a delusional madman.

"Act as surprised as you want," he replies with a shrug. "But you're getting me inside that facility."

His face is impassive, but he's not as good at concealing his hand as he thinks he is. There's a thread of white-hot desperation in his features, a tension pinching his lips and eyes I've seen before, countless times. For the first time, I wonder if he was telling the truth before, that he really was in the bar looking for information—and not a target for that antique gun of his.

My mind races. There's no base to the east of us—even if the military had the funding to expand to a second base in this part of TerraDyn's territory, which we don't, there'd be no reason to keep it a secret. But he believes it. I can see that as clearly as I can see his desperation. *This is a good thing,* I tell myself. *Even if he's mad, he's still only one guy.* If I'd ended up in their rebel hideout, I'd be dead for sure. But here . . . there's still a chance I could escape. For now, my only hope is to play along.

"So what is it you think you're going to find in this secret facility?"

Romeo doesn't answer straight away, leaving me watching as he poles the boat through the swamp. Though there is an engine hanging off the stern, he hasn't touched it since I came to. This poling technique is one a few of us have campaigned for training on from HQ, but to no avail. We're forced to navigate the swamps with noisy engines that get clogged every five minutes with swamp debris, while the natives slip through the narrow corridors soundlessly. A military patrol could pass not fifty yards away from us and never know we were here.

He pauses, withdrawing the pole and laying it across the boat so we merely drift along with the sluggish current. He's favoring his leg, which has a makeshift bandage tied around it where I embedded that plastic cocktail sword. It gives me a surge of satisfaction to think that he probably doesn't have the tools out here to fish out the broken piece. He drops down onto the bench, letting me see his face more clearly. He still looks oddly familiar, though I'm sure I would have remembered him if we'd met before tonight. "What *am* I going to find?" he asks, reaching for a canteen stowed underneath the seat and taking a long drink from it. "You tell me."

"I can't tell you," I say, trying to hide my irritation. And my thirst, watching him swallow. *Play along,* I remind myself savagely. *Earn his trust, such as it is. Use it to get out of this mess.* "I would if I could, but I've never heard of a facility to the east."

Romeo rolls his eyes. "Right. Well, there could be anything in there. Weapons, maybe. Some new tool to flush us out of the caves, for all I know. It has to be out of the ordinary for you to get it set up so fast, and with such secrecy."

I peer through the fog. It's growing lighter, which means I must've been unconscious for at least a few hours. Dawn is approaching. "That's what you risked capture for, snooping around on my base? We already have weapons that outmatch yours ten to one. We've already tried every state-of-the-art technology to find your hideout. This swamp of a planet makes it impossible."

Romeo grins at me, a smile that would be charming if there weren't something darker behind it. "All that effort to find me, and you say you don't like me?" He winks, holding the canteen up to my lips like it's a peace offering. I could kick at his knees—he didn't tie my feet, and he's within reach now. I could knock him from his seat, have him in the swamp before he knew what was going on.

But then what?

I give in to my thirst and lean forward to take a pull from the canteen. I watched him drink from the same flask, so it's not going to be poisoned or drugged. Avon's muddy-flavored water never tasted so good.

Romeo sighs, setting the canteen back down when I'm finished. "Look, Captain." He regards me with keen, thoughtful green eyes, as casual as if he were chatting with a friend and not interrogating his enemy. "I want a way out of this war for all of us. But first I want to know why Avon is generations behind where it should be on its terraforming schedule. You say that facility out there isn't military; if that's true, then it belongs to Terra Dynamics. I'm tired of them keeping secrets from us. The planetary review's coming up, and if someone's deliberately slowing down Avon's progress, our side wants to know how."

Surprise robs me of any clever retort. "You think there's a secret facility in the middle of the swamp where we're controlling the climate."

His eyes cloud over, and without further warning he gets back to his feet, bracing them against the ribs and reaching for the pole once more. "I wouldn't expect one of their hired guns to care anyway."

Hired gun? I swallow down the impulse to lash back at him. If all I wanted was money, there are about a thousand careers I could have chosen instead of volunteering to get tossed onto this mudball and paid next to nothing to keep the peace. I grit my teeth. "Why would we want to stop Avon from developing, even if we could? What could the military *or* TerraDyn possibly stand to gain from that?"

"If Avon stays like this, too unstable to support a bigger population, we'll never have enough leverage to pass the planetary review and be declared independent. We should be farmers by now, not fighters. We should be leading our own lives, earning wages, trading, able to come and go from Avon as we please. Instead we're stuck here. No voice in the Galactic Council, no leverage, no rights."

He's got a surprising grasp of the politics of the situation, for someone who probably stopped going to school before he was ten years old. "You really think TerraDyn's goal is to sit here and oppress a bunch of backwater terra-trash? They paid good money to create this part of the world. I don't see how they start making that money back until Avon starts producing enough goods to export."

Romeo's jaw tightens. "They must. Otherwise, you tell me why nobody's trying to find out why we're all still algae farmers and water testers."

"Not all of you are," I point out dryly. "Some of you are thieves and murderers and anarchists living underground."

"Why, Jubilee," he says, grinning when the use of my full name makes my cheek twitch with irritation. "I had no idea you admired me so."

I refuse to dignify that with a response, and fall silent. I have no answer to his question. Terraforming experts come and go, but Avon never changes. And it's true that while Avon's lack of development prompts a new investigation every few years, the results are always the same: cause unknown. If Romeo would stop asking so many questions, he and his so-called Fianna would be a lot better off.

Dawn has well and truly broken now, as much as dawn ever comes on Avon. In the thick, cold fog, the edges of the world slip away, leaving only our little boat and the sloshing of the water as the pole dips in and out. Romeo's breath catches with each effort, hitching and stopping as he strains against the pole, then exhaling the rest of the way as he eases back and lifts it for another stroke.

He's not using a compass. Compasses are useless on Avon anyway, which doesn't have the right kind of magnetic field, and Avon's weather patterns make satellite signals as unreliable as our broadcasts on the base.

Even when they do work, with the way the canals shift and vanish due to floating islands of vegetation, the SatNav can get us into as much trouble as a compass would.

But Romeo seems to have an innate understanding of the world he lives in. Like he's got a receiver hardwired into his brain, getting signals directly from Avon. We never run aground, we never get stuck on the floating islands. As far as I can tell, we never have to double back or change course.

I keep watching him, trying to understand how he does it. If I can learn the trick of it, maybe I can find my way back to base if I get free. He turns to navigate around a denser clump of vegetation and I lower my eyes, studying the way he shifts his weight to compensate. I lift my eyes only to realize he's turned back around and is watching me watch *him* with one eyebrow raised.

I'm not sure which would be worse, him thinking I'm eyeing the gun at his hip, or him assuming I'm staring at his ass. I jerk my gaze away and give up on trying to study my captor. We move through the waterways in silence for the next half hour or more, my head pounding and his expression grim.

Abruptly, the bottom of the boat scrapes along mud and reeds and gravel, splitting the quiet with a screech.

"Ah," says Romeo, bracing one foot against the bench and leaning down to clip the pole back to the side of the boat. "We're here."

All I can see is fog. He moves around behind me, brows drawing together in a silent warning against an attack as he bends to untie me. I clench my jaw so hard a line of pain runs up behind my ear to join seamlessly with the throbbing at the back of my skull. I could probably disable him, but we both know that without some idea of where we are, his people are just as likely—more likely—to find me than mine. I have to wait for a better chance. If only he were right, and there *were* a base here, I'd have the advantage. But a base means people—and where is the air traffic, the patrols, the static defenses? There's only silence.

His fingers tug at the rope, warm as they brush the skin on my wrists, and with a sudden release of pressure, I'm free. I press my lips together hard against the bolt of agony that comes as circulation returns. He grimaces in reply, as though he's actually sorry for the pain, and curls his hands gently around my bare wrists, fingers massaging the blood back. I shake his hands off, too irritated to accept any gesture of help. He rolls his eyes and climbs out of the boat, landing on the marshy ground with a squelch.

My fingers tingle with pins and needles as I grasp the gunwale and climb out after him. The fog is too thick to see anything, but he's still acting like he knows where he's going. "So? Where is this place?" I ask.

"It's up here. I was here a couple of hours ago." He's utterly confident as he moves, keeping his voice down. His gun's on his left hip, but he keeps me on his right with a vise-like grip on my arm. I find myself stepping softly, like I really might find myself on the wrong end of a sentry challenge, which is ridiculous—except after surviving this long on Avon, I'd hate to go down under friendly fire.

He leads me forward a few steps, but we haven't gone far when even I know something's wrong. His hold on me is tense, his face void of all smugness.

Then the fog clears, just for a moment. Just long enough for us to see that the stretch of solid land ahead of us is empty, barren of everything but weeds and rocks and untouched mud. The far side of the island dips back down into the water, which stretches on, uninterrupted but for the occasional distant outcropping of bare rock.

We both stare, though I don't know why. I didn't believe him—I never believed him. And yet, standing on this empty stretch of island, my stomach sinking and ears ringing, I'm surprised. I jerk my arm away, stumbling backward with the effort. "Why did you bring me here?" I spit the words, fists clenched against the urge to strike out at him. "What was the point? Why not just dump me somewhere out there in the swamps?"

But he's not looking at me. He's still staring, though the curtain of fog has closed again and there's nothing to be seen. "It was here," he's saying. "This is exactly the place. I don't understand—it was right—"

"Stop!" My shout brings him up short, and he turns on his heel, blinking at me. "I want an answer. Why did you bring me here?"

"Jubilee," he murmurs, one fist relaxing and reaching toward me, palm up. So charming, so open, like we're friends. This guy oozes charisma from his pores—if he'd been born on a legitimate planet, he'd have been a politician. "I swear it was here. I'm not lying to you."

"Your promises don't mean much to me, Romeo," I snap.

"They can't have left without a trace," he says, clearing his throat and striding past me. "There was an entire facility here—fences, buildings, crates, aircraft. Help me look, there's got to be a sign. Footprints, foundations, anything."

While his eyes scan the mud, searching for his so-called signs, it gives me a chance to scan his features. He's frustrated. More than frustrated—he's scared. Confused. He really believes there was something here.

I've got to humor him if I've got any hope of returning to the base alive.

It's a large island, and Romeo drags me through the mist, along the edge of the vegetation. He's too cautious to let me out of his sight, but I'm not stupid enough to make a bid for freedom here. One wrong step and it'll be a long, slow sink beneath the surface, with plenty of time to think about what a pointless way that is to go.

Humor him. Play nice. Talk him into sending you back.

The after effects from that gas can are still with me, long after they should've dissipated. My mouth tastes oddly metallic, like blood, and my pulse rushes unnaturally loud in my ears. I take a deep breath and try to focus. I find myself longing for the stars, the openness of the sky you never see on Avon. The fog has closed in again, and it's impossible to see more than a few yards ahead, leaving me suspended in a world of gray and white. I have to keep my eyes on the ground to keep my balance, because looking out through the fog tricks my eyes into thinking I'm floating.

Luckily, Romeo doesn't seem to have noticed. Maybe he chalks my stumbling up to the fact that he keeps jerking me along by the wrist. We've covered about half the shoreline when Romeo halts and lets go of me, gazing around with confusion.

Abruptly, a light blossoms in front of my eyes. Pale green, swaying gently from side to side, it's no more than a few inches across. It dances there for a moment and I freeze, and as Romeo turns to start moving again, I realize he doesn't see it.

Then the world slides sideways.

My vision flickers, the taste of metal in my mouth growing overpowering. Suddenly I'm not seeing fog and mud and emptiness; I'm not even seeing the wisp. An entire building flashes into existence, and between it and me, a high chain-link fence. And just beyond it, a figure in black clothes and some kind of mask, staring expressionlessly through its visor at me.

I drop to my hands and knees, blinded, choking on metal and flinching as the impact jars the wound in my side. When I lift my head again the vision is gone, but my hand encounters a sharp object digging into my palm. My fingers close around it. All around me rises a quick, frenzied susurration, like the wind through grass, or aspen leaves quivering in a storm. But Avon has no grass, and Avon has no aspen trees.

Everything goes black, and then the whispering is gone as abruptly as it started. Suddenly I hear Romeo shouting at me, his voice urgent. I open my eyes to find his face close to mine, gripping me by the shoulder.

"What's going on? Get up!" He's drawn his gun; he thinks I'm faking.

"Don't know." I slide the thing I found into my boot with a shaking hand. I can't stop to examine it now; whatever it is, it's regular, plastic, man-made. There's no reason this would turn up here on its own.

"Stay here, I'll get you some water." He starts to release me, but I grab at his chest, gripping a handful of his shirt. *The canteen.*

"You drugged me," I gasp, my vision spinning away like the fog eddying around us. My body's shaking, shivering in his grasp like I'm on the verge of hypothermia.

"I—what?" Romeo peers closer. "Why would I— Stop, calm down." He grabs hold of my shoulders again and gives me a tiny shake, my head snapping back as though I'm too tired to lift it.

Something in my mind is screaming to be heard, something— something about his hands, gripping my arms, supporting me. Both hands.

If both hands are on my shoulders, then where is the gun?

There, on the ground by his feet. I flail out for the old-fashioned pistol, only a few inches from my fingertips. My shaking fingers fumble with the grip, clumsy with whatever drug is coursing through my system.

Romeo spots the movement. Somehow, despite drinking from the canteen himself, he's unaffected; he gives an inarticulate cry and lunges for the weapon. "Goddammit, Jubilee—give it a rest for five seconds!"

"Never," I gasp, dropping to the spongy, wet earth, too weak to stand without his support. Whatever he did to me, it's getting worse.

Slowly, the sound of whispering is overtaking my hearing once more. I reach for Romeo, but I don't know if I'm trying to get the gun back from him or hold myself up. He shoves the pistol into his waistband, out of my reach, and my vision clouds again.

It isn't until I feel arms wrapping around my waist and a heartbeat by my ear that I realize I'm slipping out of consciousness, and Romeo's carrying me the rest of the way back to his boat.

She's back in the alley again, holding a burning firecracker, eyes watering with the effort of not letting go.

Beyond the ring of boys shouting and jeering at her, through the shifting clouds of smoke from the gunpowder, she sees a tiny light dancing and bobbing. It winks at her, surprised, hovering just out of reach. The girl stands frozen, staring, until the firecracker explodes in her hands, singeing her fingers. The ball of light vanishes in the flash, and the girl is too shocked and deafened to feel the pain in her hand until her father sprints into the alley to carry her away to the hospital.

FOUR

FLYNN

THE WARM LIGHT OF OUR DOCKING LAMPS WELCOMES ME
home as I coast into the harbor, the rock swallowing me up. Hidden
behind the stone walls of the cavern, the lamps hang along a string, bobbing lazily like a row of will-o'-the-wisps—though these lights lead to
safety rather than danger. A weight presses down on my shoulders as I
ease the currach forward. A weight exactly equal to the trodaire curled
up in the bottom of my boat. Jubilee is on her side, still unconscious, her
hands bound once again. Whatever took her down in the swamp seems
to have passed, and I can't risk leaving her unrestrained.

Her dog tags have fallen outside her shirt, and I see the metal glint
in the lamplight as she lies unmoving. Without them, you might almost
forget she's one of the trodairí. Without them, she'd look halfway human,
like someone who might listen for half a second before pulling a gun on
you. Until she woke up and tried to kill me, that is. But when there's no
hope to be found anywhere, even the tiniest chance is worth taking.

I can't let McBride and his followers find her, or they'll have her head
on a spike before I can blink. But I can't let her go either. She's too valuable. Maybe the military will trade for her and give us resources we need,
like food rations or medicine.

And maybe, just maybe, I can convince her not all of us are the lawless
villains she and her kind believe us to be.

If Jubilee Chase can be convinced to stop shooting, anyone can.

The currach catches the current slowly swirling through our hidden harbor, drifting toward the dock. I stow the pole and let the water carry us the rest of the way, risking a glance away from my prisoner and up at the vaulted stone ceiling stretching high above us, stalactites hanging down. It drives the soldiers mad, trying to work out how we hide so many people right under their noses out here in the swamps.

From the air, this place looks like a couple of rocks no larger than one of their buildings on the base. From the water, only the trained eye can see we've disguised its size with woven camouflage, made it less prominent, rerouted the channels leading up to the base so there's no easy way to approach by boat without knowing the way. You could get here by foot from the base if you were determined enough, but it would mean hours of slogging through mud and waist-deep water. The stone hides us from their heat detectors, and Avon's atmosphere wreaks havoc with imaging drones and search gear. The leading theory among TerraDyn scientists is that the ionization levels interfere with their equipment, but all we know is that it forces them to search for us the old-fashioned way, with boats and spotlights. Though there are pockets of resistance all across the planet, these caves harbor a significant percentage of TerraDyn's most-wanted list.

We call ourselves the Fianna. The soldiers think it has some simple meaning—"warriors" is how they usually translate it. But it's more than that. Blood is forever, and though Earth was abandoned so long ago the generations are now uncounted, we remember our cradle. We remember Ireland, and her stories, and the bands of warriors who defended their home. And we carry on their traditions, and honor them. Avon takes care of us, hides us, and in return we fight for her.

The currach nudges up against the dock, and I yank my attention back to the present when I realize I've heard no challenge. The sentries are gone. The landing is empty where there should be guards, and abruptly my heart's pounding again as panic sweeps through me. The military has discovered Jubilee missing. I shouldn't have taken that detour—they've found our base and beaten me back here to rescue her.

I leave the trodaire in the currach, hands bound, and hurriedly tug a tarp up over her limp form to hide her from view. Then I scramble up onto the dock and toward the passageway. My wounded leg is aching as my mind pulls in a dozen directions all at once, tracing the path the trodairí would take, predicting which caverns they'd claim and which we'd hold, mapping a way to the weapons storage as I pull my gun from my belt.

But slowly one thing sinks in: if the trodairí had found us, this place would be swarming with copters and speedboats outside, not to mention ringing with shouts and gunfire. There's only silence, until I make my way farther in and hear the low murmur of voices coming from the meeting cavern.

The crowd in there's so big I can't see my way to the front, but relief rushes through me as I recognize this noise as anger, not panic. It's only the Fianna inside, and there are no soldiers here today except the one I left in my currach.

Our meeting place is a high-ceilinged bubble in the rock that we've hewn larger over time, stone softened and echoes muffled by rugs hung around the walls and crates of liberated military supplies stored along the edges. It's almost impossible to round us up in the same place—there are always folks on patrol, on guard, asleep—but this is the biggest crowd I've seen in a long time.

They're crammed in, perching on the crates, leaning against the walls and sitting on the ground. The cavern's full, buzzing with tension. Then I hear McBride's voice at the front, and I know what brought them together.

For ten years we've been hiding out in these caves, paying for the bloody rebellion my sister led. Too hungry to get organized, too sick and too bruised to care who was in charge. It's taken a decade to come close to stability again, but the day my people could fill their bellies without fear of where the next meal would come from, there was McBride. He has the age and experience I lack, and his talk of fighting back and finishing what my sister, Orla, started makes my people itch for action.

Victory, to his faction, is beating the trodairí at any cost. Casualties are glorious sacrifices to the cause. Firepower is the only measure of strength. Because, futile though the fight might be, there's a satisfaction in direct action that these people crave. It's the easier path—I feel myself tugged that way too, sometimes. So did Orla. And that's what killed her in the end.

These people remember my sister, and how she fought to the last and faced her execution fearlessly. Her death buys me their sympathy, and thus their attention, but every time McBride opens his mouth, I lose a few more of them. Nobody wants to listen to a teenager speaking for peace when their children are sick and their very freedoms are being bled away by TerraDyn's harsh regulations. McBride knows it. I know it too. They all wish I were more like Orla.

Judging by the air of tension in the crowd, it seems he's jumped on my absence to stir them up and inch ever closer to breaking the cease-fire. Only fear of retaliation and lack of resources has stopped McBride's lieutenants from carrying out their own raids without the support of the rest of us. That, and I've got the key to the munitions locker—and I'm not about to let McBride get his hands on it.

I tuck my gun away and start to work toward the front of the crowd.

He hasn't noticed me yet. His square, shadowed jaw is tense, brows crowding together as he calls out in impassioned tones, "How many times are we going to hide in our caves, watching while they take our loved ones away? How much longer are we going to wait for change?" He's pacing back and forth at the front of the cavern, the nervous energy of his steps infecting the crowd, making them all shift on their feet and itch for action. "On one thing, Flynn Cormac and I agree: violence must only ever be a last resort. We are not the trodairí with their so-called Fury, their imaginary disease, their excuse for the shows of violence supposed to keep us cowed. But I say today we are *past* our last resort, and we are *past* the point of no return."

My own heart beats hard as I listen in spite of myself. He sounds like my sister, except Orla's eyes never carried that feverish gleam. When she spoke of last resorts, she meant it. But these people don't see McBride as I do. They're too desperate for change to recognize the madness behind his words.

"But what about Flynn, you're saying. He wouldn't want this. He'd tell us to talk to them, reason with them—but look where reasoning has gotten him! No sign, no word; I'll tell you where it's gotten him, why he hasn't come back. This very moment he's in a trodairí prison cell. They've got Orla's little brother bound and bloodied, no doubt trying to beat our location out of him. We would betray the memory of his sister if we let them take him without getting an answer from us."

I stop in my tracks. He's trying to lead our people in an attack on the trodairí to free *me*. McBride's only guessing as to where I am, but all he needs is one spark to ignite my people. And what better to win over the reluctant ones, those who've been listening to me, than a mission of rescue? Because rescue or no, once open war breaks out, *all* of the Fianna will have no choice but to fight for their lives.

The anger that surges up in me would impress even Jubilee Chase. I bow my head, letting my fists curl, riding it out. Waiting until I can be sure my voice will be strong and steady before I call out.

"McBride, I'm touched. I had no idea you cared so much."

The heads nearest me snap around, voices rising in shock and relief. I push my way into the free space in front of McBride's platform. He's stopped in his tracks, staring blankly at me for a half a beat too long. Then relief floods his strong features, and he jumps down off the platform to approach me. "You're alive!" he exclaims, and though he claps a hand to my shoulder, the eyes that meet mine are anything but warm. "I'd been imagining the worst."

I'll bet you were.

I reach for calm. "I had an opportunity to do some information-gathering, and I took it. No way to get a signal back without risking discovery."

McBride's brows lift a little. "Taking action, Cormac," he replies, lips curling. From a distance, it might look like a smile. "Glad to hear it. What'd you learn?"

I can't tell them I saw a facility that was gone a few hours later; they'll think I've lost my mind. "Nothing concrete yet." I try not to wince at the weight of his hand on my shoulder. He's a head taller than I am, and strongly built. If he ever wanted to take me out once and for all, he'd have the upper hand and then some. "But as long as we know nothing's changed on the base, we know they're not coming for us. And we can keep looking for a way out of this."

McBride squeezes my shoulder. "Sometimes the only way out is through," he replies, raising his voice a little to make it carry farther.

I turn away, using the movement to wrench my shoulder free of his bruising grip. It's not the time to dance this dance with him, the same steps, the same push and pull. I have a bigger problem in the form of the trodaire in my currach, who I need to move before she wakes up under that tarp and makes a noise. Because one thing is certain: if McBride's people find her, Captain Chase will be dead by tomorrow.

The energy in the crowd has shifted—with me standing here, the immediate need to fight is gone, but they're slow to come down, not sure where to turn. I can't let them latch on to me, not until the trodaire is stashed somewhere safe.

I catch Turlough Doyle's eye, then jerk my gaze toward McBride, who's regrouping and turning back for the platform, no doubt figuring out a way to use my return in his rhetoric.

Turlough steps forward before he can get there. "While we're all here," he says pleasantly, "perhaps we can talk about the sleeping quarters." He uses that same encouraging tone when he's teaching new Fianna how to lay tripwires.

I ghost back into the crowd, slipping out the back to go in search of my cousin Sean.

I find him in the classroom, which is little more than a cavern softened by handmade rugs to sit on and a chest containing some toys and a few precious, battered textbooks from a time when we were still allowed to barter with traders. It's Sean's domain—he teaches when he's not out on patrol or helping plan a raid. I knew he'd be here, keeping the children away from McBride's anger and the talk of violence in the main cavern. He's in one corner with his five-year-old nephew, Fergal, in his lap. He's surrounded by a gaggle of children—and a couple of girls far too old for story time, but the right age for Sean—faces turned up to him.

"Now, as you know, Tír na nÓg was the land of eternal youth, which most people think sounds like a fine thing. But Oisín wasn't so sure. Do you *know* how many times you have to tidy your room when you live forever? His girlfriend, Niamh, lived there, and she was the one who'd invited him to stay. He'd moved in pretty quickly, and a decision like that, well . . . He should have asked a few more questions before he jumped on in. Turns out their gravball teams were arch-enemies, and they both hated doing laundry."

I recognize the tale, if not Sean's unique embellishments. We were told these stories as kids by our parents, who heard them from our grandparents. I bet Jubilee would be surprised to find out we hand down our myths and legends, Scheherazade and Shakespeare and stories from a time before men left Earth. The suits from TerraDyn and their trodairí lackeys think we're all illiterate and uneducated. I only have hazy memories of comscreens and the bright, dancing colors of shows on the HV from my childhood, and it pains me that these children can't even imagine modern technology. We may not have the books and holovids anymore, or the official schools the off-worlders have, but the stories themselves never go. Right now, I want nothing more than to linger in the shadows and listen.

But instead, I step forward and catch his eye before tilting my head toward the corridor. *Wrap it up, I need you.*

His mouth drops open, the relief clear on his face. Even some part of Sean thought McBride might be right and I might be in danger. He nods, and I lean against the wall to rest my leg while I listen to the end of the tale. "So Oisín slips away home on a shuttle to Ireland for a quick visit, and Niamh warns him that if he gets out of his ship and touches the ground, he can never come back. It's the only thing he has to do, is make sure he doesn't touch the ground. So what does the fool do? He might be too lazy to pick up his own laundry, but he can't resist showing off. He forgets—or he wasn't listening, like some people we know, right, Cabhan?—and he jumps out of the shuttle to help these guys move a rock. The second he hits the grass . . ." He pauses, and the kids lean in, then jerk back when he claps his hands. "Bam! Three hundred years catch up with him, and he's dead as a soldier on a solo patrol. So the moral of the story is, never pick up after yourself, and *certainly* never pick up after anyone else. It could be fatal. Now, off with the lot of you, before I ask who's done their homework." They scatter, and he hoists Fergal up into his arms with casual confidence to wade free of them all. He's had him a year and a half now, since his brother and sister-in-law died in a raid.

"I'm almost sure that wasn't the moral when we learned it," I say.

He grins, unrepentant. That's Sean—always grinning, smooth as silk. "Should have been. I take it you ruined McBride's latest tactic?" Fergal reaches up to grab at Sean's face, trying with great determination to inspect the inside of his nostrils.

"For now."

Sean leans down to pick up his nephew's favorite toy, a strange, pudgy creature with wings and a tail called Tomás. I've never been sure what Tomás is, but I know he's sewn from one of Sean's brother's old shirts, and Fergal won't go anywhere without him. Placated, Fergal rests his head on Sean's shoulder as his uncle speaks. "I tried to hail you, but you didn't answer. Figured there was too much interference today."

Our radios almost never work due to Avon's atmosphere, but that wasn't why I didn't answer. "Thanks for trying. Don't worry, I can handle McBride."

"Clear skies, cousin." *Good luck,* he means. There are never clear skies on Avon, no blue, no stars. But we don't give up hope, and we use those words to remind ourselves. Clear skies will come, one day.

I turn a little so he won't see the bloody bandage over my pants leg from Lee Chase's hot-pink souvenir; I'll get him to pull it out later, but for now we've got a more pressing concern. "Forget good fortune. We don't have time to wait for clear skies." I duck my head to catch his nephew's eye. "Fergal, go get into bed for your nap, and we'll come and tuck you in soon. I need your uncle's help."

Sean stares down into the bottom of the currach, voice hushed in horror. "Flynn Cormac, you never did. McBride is going to throw a party and use her head for a punch bowl."

"This is an opportunity, Sean. If the military will ever trade for anyone, it will be her. If we play this right, we could exchange her for medical supplies, perhaps some of our people they've got in their cells—maybe even leverage for the planetary review in a few months."

"Or she could tell everybody who you are, and what you look like, and where to come calling if they feel the urge to visit."

"She doesn't know." I let myself grin. "Fair to say she didn't exactly volunteer to help steer the currach home. She saw nothing, and we can make it that way when she leaves."

"You've got to be joking. That's Lee *Chase,* Flynn. We can't let her go back. You think she can't tell them plenty about *you?*"

"What, you think I let her scan my genetag?" I cut in over him. "I didn't tell her my name."

"They'll never trade for her. They don't trade. McBride would say asking will make us look weak."

Weak. Why is it weakness to want to talk before I kill someone? "McBride won't know."

"You seriously think there's a chance they'll listen to us?"

"I seriously think we're going to ask them. Now help me get her somewhere out of sight, before she wakes up."

We muscle her out of the bottom of the currach together, draping my jacket around her shoulders to hide her uniform. I thought she'd be stirring by now, but whatever dropped her out in the swamp hit her even harder than the fumes from my gas can did. As we navigate the corridors toward the disused caverns below, I keep having to catch her head before it can loll against the stone walls.

Sean huffs softly, shaking his head at me for taking the trouble. This is the guy who has a collection of photos tacked up on the stone wall next to his hammock, women from brightly lit worlds laughing and smiling and pouting for the camera. Wives or girlfriends or lovers, I suppose. Pictures he takes off the bodies of the soldiers and pins up as morbid trophies. This is what the fight does to people. To someone like Sean, who devotes his time to teaching our children, but can't bring himself to see the soldiers as human.

There are a number of caverns at the bottom of our network of tunnels that we don't use anymore. Too damp for living space, and there are far fewer Fianna now than there were during my sister's time. Sean binds the trodaire while I keep watch at the door, scanning the empty passageway, waiting for someone to round the corner and discover us. He's tying her down, looping the rope tightly through a post drilled into the stone that was once used to stabilize shelving. At one time this had been a storeroom for weaponry. "You really think there's any chance this works out at all?" he asks, finishing off a knot and stepping back to inspect his work.

I can hear the doubt in his voice, and the long, exhausting night I've had crowds in on me all at once. I need a moment's respite. I need Sean, of all people, on my side. "Lecture me later," I say, as pain pulses through my leg again. "I need a little first aid before I can take any more."

Sean's initial alarm fades when I unwrap my makeshift bandage to reveal the miniature stab wound in my leg. Leaning close to inspect it, he frowns and asks, "What is *that*?"

I lean against the wall, taking the pressure off my leg. "A cocktail garnish," I mutter.

Sean's head jerks up so he can look at me—my expression prompts a burst of laughter as he realizes who's responsible for the plastic sword in my thigh. The bands of tension around my chest ease a fraction. Sean leaves me there as he goes off in search of a pair of pliers; no sense risking anyone else discovering Lee Chase nearly bested me with a cocktail sword. By the time he comes back, Sean's still grinning.

"You've had worse luck with girls," he points out, widening the rip in my pants leg so he can get at the plastic with the pliers. "Remember that time you tried to sweet-talk Mhairi and she laughed at you?"

I wince as he loses his grip on the remnants of the cocktail sword. "I was thirteen, shut up."

"Or Aoife? Or Alejandra?"

"What are you talking about? Alejandra and I—"

"Poor girl felt sorry for you." He huffs, pulling the thing free and holding it up for us both to take a look at it. It's annoyingly small, the hot pink still visible beneath the darker red of my blood. He starts laughing again and grabs at the wall beside him for support. "No wonder you were able to capture her, if this is all she had to work with."

"Just bandage it up, Sean, before I start listing your romantic failures. We'll be here all day."

By the time he's done, his smile has faded. The laughter couldn't last forever, but it was enough of a rest to let me breathe a little easier. Sean's my pressure valve, my best friend as well as my cousin, but he's as fierce a fighter as we've got. We lean against the rocky wall for a little, side by side, eyes on the unconscious soldier tied up near the far side of the cave.

"What the hell, man?" Sean breaks the silence, his voice quiet. "What were you even *doing* on their base?"

I hesitate. If I tell Sean about the facility I saw, he'll insist we send scouts, and how can I tell him there's nothing there anymore? "I got itchy, I was scouting. Things are getting tense, and I wanted to know what's in the wind."

He groans, tipping his head back to let it smack gently against the stone wall. "You've got to be kidding me. I *know* you know what happens if you of all people get caught. McBride's just waiting for the chance to move while you're off following a hunch. He nearly did tonight, without you there to speak against it. Where does the trodaire come into this?"

"She spotted me. I spotted an opportunity."

"To bring her to our home? To risk discovery?"

"She has information we need, and think what we could trade her for." I grit my teeth. "You think I should've killed her?"

"*Yes,*" he replies, exasperated. "Yes, I think you should have killed her."

"And set them panicking about an assassination on their own base?" I can hear the snap in my voice and I swallow it down, carefully even out my tone. The idea comes so easily to Sean, one of the best, gentlest guys I know. Maybe it seems natural to him because it *is* natural. Maybe I'm as mad as McBride thinks I am, trying to settle a decade-old conflict with words.

Or maybe Sean's good nature, the sweetness in him that's been there since we were children, is fading. Maybe it's one more casualty of this war.

The image of the secret compound is right there when I close my eyes—a wire fence, a small collection of prefab buildings built into the gentle slope of the island. I want to tell him I saw it. I want to tell him I went back and it was gone. But it'll only convince him I'm losing my mind. He's my greatest ally—my closest friend. I can't afford to alienate him.

Sean sighs, eyeing the trodaire again. "What are we going to do about your girlfriend?"

"I'm going to get Martha to send word to the base. Lee Chase is valuable to them; they'll trade for her. It'll show McBride that my way gets results too, without bloodshed."

"And if they refuse to trade?" Sean raises an eyebrow.

I square my jaw. "I don't want her killed."

"You're too soft, cousin. If you were their prisoner, she'd never spare your life."

"I know." Even now, the words stab at my heart. We're both thinking of Orla. "But if we kill her, that's it for the ceasefire. They'll come for us like they never have before, and we wouldn't survive that kind of assault."

"You wouldn't make that argument with McBride, I bet."

"Tell McBride he's not strong enough to beat someone in a fight, first thing he does is find a way to justify punching them in the face." I kick at a loose pebble, hearing it ricochet off the opposite wall of the cave. "He'd find a way to make it about me and how I'm afraid to fight."

Sean hesitates. "You could lead us," he says finally. "If it came to a fight. You could—"

I don't find out what he might have said next. Fergal's voice echoes down the corridor. "Uncle Sean, I need you to tuck me in." He must have followed us.

Sean curses, leaping to his feet and leaving the cave and its unconscious occupant. "I don't want him or the other kids to know about this," he mutters. "You want to keep it hidden, fine. Just don't let anyone find her, because then it's going to get noisy."

Though unspoken, I recognize what he's saying: he'll trust me. For now. "Sean—thanks." We share a beat of silence, and then Sean heads back up the passageway to collect Fergal.

I retrieve the lantern, hoping darkness will make it harder for the trodaire to work out an escape when she wakes, and hurry away before anyone realizes we're down here. The relief at having Sean's support is short-lived; I know it won't last. One of these days even Sean will run out of patience. Already I feel us drifting, sense it in the silences between us. But whenever that day's coming, it's not today. For now, I know he'll follow me, because I asked him to.

I just wish I knew where I was leading him.

The girl is under the counter in her mother's store, her reading punctuated at random intervals by the door chime as customers come and go. She's reading about deep-sea divers in an ancient submarine. There are no oceans on Verona, but the girl is going to grow up and be an explorer.

"Jubilee," the girl's mother calls. "Where are you? Come help me, we're going to make dumplings to sell."

The girl holds her breath. Sea monsters are more exciting than dumplings, especially since the dumplings are always accompanied by a lecture about preserving her heritage. Maybe her mother won't look for her here.

"Relax, Mei." That's her father; she didn't know he'd come home. "She'll come around. As I recall, you spent our whole first date complaining that your dad was making you learn calligraphy. Let her just be a kid—there's plenty of time."

The girl shuts her eyes. No—this is all wrong. Wake up . . . wake UP.

FIVE

JUBILEE

I KNOW BEFORE I OPEN MY EYES THAT I'M IN TROUBLE. I can smell mildew and decay, and I'm so cold I could cry. It's pitch-black, wherever I am, and the surface underneath me is hard and damp. Stone. I'm half propped up on my knees, but when I try to sit up I go crashing toward the ground. My arms nearly jerk out of their sockets and I'm caught a few inches away from hitting the floor. Pain lances through my shoulders, making my eyes water. My gasp echoes aloud in the room, rattling through my parched throat.

My wrists are bound together behind my back. I follow the rope with my fingers to find it tied through a metal post drilled into the rough-hewn floor. The rope is short enough and tied high enough that I can't lie down without it pulling my arms painfully upward. I can't stand, can't even sit properly. Whoever did this knows exactly how uncomfortable this must be.

The memory of a pretty face flashes in front of my eyes. Romeo. After that entire ill-fated journey through the swamp, I still don't know the bastard's name. And I'm probably not likely to, at this rate. Somewhere out there is a rebel with a limp, probably getting two inches of hot-pink plastic pulled out of his thigh as we speak. Either they've left me here to die on my own of dehydration, or they're going to try to get information or resources out of the military in exchange for my life.

But we don't make deals with rebels. And that means I'm going to die. I can't help but think of my platoon, and how they'll manage without me. I know each of them like I know myself. I watch them every day, I keep track of their dreams, I monitor how each of them is coping, living this close to the ragged edge. This close to the Fury. I can tell when one of them is about to snap, when they're done here and need reassignment off Avon before they hurt someone. Who will watch over them when I'm dead?

In the darkness, my mind conjures up the image of what I saw out in the swamp. A flash of what Romeo claimed he saw: a facility where there shouldn't be one, high fences and spotlights and guards. It's impossible for something to be there one moment and gone the next—far more likely I was hallucinating, experiencing some early side effect of whatever drug Romeo used to knock me out.

Though that doesn't explain the thing I found, the thing in my boot that I can't get to now, with my hands tied.

I twist a little until I can get the sole of one of my boots against the post embedded in the floor. Wrapping my hands around the rope to take the pressure off my wrist joints, I pull as hard as I can, straining and trying to feel for the slightest give in the rope.

No dice. It was a long shot anyway.

I let go, taking a few seconds to find my breath again. I can sense no trace of whatever drug he used to knock me out on that island. The whispering sound is gone, and except for a few cold-induced tremors, my body's under control again. No more shaking. No more metallic taste in my mouth.

If the ropes won't give, maybe the stone will. They're not exactly high-tech out here—maybe the hole they drilled isn't perfect. I brace myself the best I can without any slack in the rope and kick back, pounding at the stake with the sole of my boot.

Nothing.

I stay there, panting, grimacing at the floor. I'll have to wait until they move me. Which they'll have to do eventually, no matter what. They could just shoot me here, but it's much easier to move a body by making it get up and walk somewhere than it is to carry it.

Then again, one of them was wandering around asking questions in a military bar like it was a good idea. They're not exactly the smartest rebels ever.

Gritting my teeth, I get to work on the post again. It has to give. Each blow travels up my leg and makes my jaw ache. But better a little ache now than to be stuck here for a week, dying of thirst. I can taste my own fear, sour like bile at the back of my throat.

No. Captain Chase is never afraid.

"It's hammered down pretty hard." An amused voice comes from the shadows, making my heart lurch in fear. But a moment later, I recognize it—and in the darkness, any familiar voice is a welcome change from silence.

"Can't blame a girl for trying," I manage, trying not to pant too audibly as I search the shadows for Romeo.

He unshields a lantern, sending a sliver of light slicing through the gloom. I'm tied to a post in the middle of a cave, its only feature a long tunnel behind Romeo, leading into the shadows. The lamp is burning, not battery-powered. I watch the flame until my eyes water, a tiny part of me glad that at least I'm not going to be killed in the dark.

I didn't expect to see him again, that's for sure. He didn't strike me as the type to do what he's no doubt come here to do. And yet, here he is. Maybe there's more to Romeo than I thought.

He steps forward. "Are you going to kick me if I come in close enough to give you some water?" In his other hand he's holding a canteen.

My vision is still wavering, my head still ringing, and my mouth tastes like swamp mud. "That depends," I say through gritted teeth. "Are you planning on drugging me again?"

"I didn't drug you then, and I'm not going to now." Romeo takes another step forward, and I can't help it—I move backward, the rope rasping across the stone like snakeskin. "And I could clean that graze for you if you let me. I didn't realize how bad it was when we were on the water."

I glance down to see what looks like ink in the lantern light staining the side of my T-shirt. Our struggle in the mud outside Molly's comes flooding back to me, and with memory comes the awareness of pain, flickering up through me like a tiny fire.

He starts to move forward again, and this time I'm snapping back before I have time to think. "You can stay right where you are."

My fingers clench around the ropes binding my hands. It's not like I can do anything to him if he comes. Maybe I could sweep his legs from under him, but it wouldn't be enough to take him out, and even if it was—what then?

But he stops anyway, watching me in silence. After a while he slings the strap of the canteen over his shoulder and crosses his arms. "How're you feeling?" His smile is insulting.

You dragged me out of my bar, shot me, forced me to breathe chemical fumes, took me into the middle of nowhere, drugged me, then tied me to a post in an underground cave. How do you think *I'm feeling?*

But I'll tear my own arms off trying to get free before I'll give him the satisfaction of an honest reply. I smile back at him, giving it every ounce of malice I can summon. "Just peachy, Romeo. How's your leg?"

His smile vanishes, and I see the subtle shift of his weight from one foot to the other. I wonder who pulled the hot-pink plastic out of his leg, and if they gave him a hard time for it.

"It's the least of my problems."

"Your problems? Romeo, you shouldn't have brought me home if you didn't think Mom and Dad would like me."

"I'll know better next time." He tips his head to one side. "Sure you don't want some water?" He jiggles the canteen so the water sloshes audibly. My mouth suddenly feels like it's wallpapered with sand.

I want to tell him to go to hell. I want to tell him to get iced. I want to punch that perfect jaw until the smug assurance falls off.

But I want the water more.

I swallow, trying to ignore how dry my throat feels. "You drink first." *Not that that helped me before.*

He rolls his eyes, like it's unreasonable for me to mistrust him. He unscrews the canteen and puts it to his mouth.

I was expecting him to take a sip. Instead he gulps it down with a noisy *glug glug* of water. When he finally lowers it, he makes a show of squinting into the mouth of the canteen. "Oh, shoot, most of it's gone now. You want what's left?"

Only the pain in my shoulders keeps me from trying to pull free of my ropes again. "You're kind of an asshole, aren't you? The pretty ones always are."

He makes a show of surprise. "You think I'm pretty? Why, Jubilee—I'm blushing. Look, you want this or not?"

He's figured out his devil-may-care attitude pisses me off. My jaw's clenched so tight I'm half afraid it's about to break. "What, do you want me to beg for it? Did you come here to gloat?"

He raises an eyebrow, that smug smile turning wry. "I want you to promise me you're not going to try to kick my pretty face in if I come any closer."

He's actually afraid I'm going to hurt him somehow. No wonder they've got me tied down so tightly I can't even sit upright. "What would your buddies say? Scared of a girl tied to a post in the ground."

"They'd say 'Don't go near her, that's Lee Chase, she eats rebel babies for breakfast.' "

My throat closes a little. *Be proud,* I remind myself. *You want them scared. Might make them think twice before they shoot at your platoon.* I inhale sharply through my nose. Bracing. Cleansing. *You want them to fear you.*

"Don't have enough leverage to kick you anyway," I say eventually.

He takes me at my word, closing the gap between us. He's moving carefully, though, watching me closely for signs I'm about to attack. Maybe I should take advantage somehow, but I was telling the truth when I said I didn't have the right leverage. I can't get him, the way I'm tied down.

"I'll hold it for you," he says quietly, dropping into a crouch at my side.

"My hero." The words pop out, dripping with malice, before I can stop them. *Mock the guy after you get your water,* I remind myself.

He holds the canteen anyway, letting me gulp down the last dregs of the slightly muddy water inside. Their filters don't work any better than ours do. It still tastes like swamp. When I'm done, he lowers the canteen and rests his elbows on his knees, watching me. Backlit as he is, I can't make out his features very well. I can only see his eyes, glittering in the gloom, slightly narrowed.

He really doesn't know what to do with me. And to be honest, I don't really know what to make of him. If he were the kind of guy I'd expected him to be, I'd be dead right now. And he certainly wouldn't be bringing me water.

"So does Romeo have a name?"

He snorts. "I'm going to have enough problems if you take my face back to your base with you. I don't think I'm about to give you a name to go with it."

"I'm not going back," I reply, my voice quiet. It's the first time I've said it aloud. It doesn't make it any easier. "And if you don't realize that yet, you're a bigger idiot than I thought."

"Well, you do think I'm a pretty high-grade moron." There's amusement in his voice, which, now that he's speaking without the smugness, is actually gentler than I would've thought. "You're their golden child, their prodigy. They'll trade for you, I'm sure of it."

"Trade what, exactly?" I shift, trying to get my weight under me, trying to feel a little less vulnerable. "Say we all did what you wanted, what Orla Cormac demanded during the last rebellion on Avon. Say the entire military left, tomorrow, and TerraDyn left you alone. What then?"

"We're not asking for the military to go, not anymore. We just want to live our lives free of TerraDyn's regulations. We want to be independent citizens."

"What would you eat, without TerraDyn's imports? Where would you get building materials for your houses? Avon can't support life on its own, not yet. It's too young; the ecosystems are too fragile. It's not done being terraformed yet. If Orla Cormac had won a decade ago, you'd all be starving to death right now."

"Orla was wrong." I can see it costs him to say it. "And she was executed for it. We're not asking for complete autonomy. All we want is medicine for our kids, food for our elderly. Schools. This is no kind of life, you must know that."

"What I know is if the military weren't here to keep order, TerraDyn would pull out and abandon the settlement, and then we'd see how far you got eating algae. Hate us all you like, but the military's what's keeping you alive."

His jaw tightens as he looks at me, and I know I've scored a point. But he doesn't give up, saying quietly, "Orla Cormac no longer leads us. Not all of us want you dead. I want to talk, not fight. I want someone to find out *why* Avon's not progressing through the terraforming stages. This is my home, and it's broken. There has to be a better way."

I lean back, the ropes chafing at my skin. I have no quick reply to that—I'd expected him to snap something stupid and noble, like most idealistic young rebels. Logic is harder to dismiss. In some other place, not tied to the floor, I could've spent hours debating with this guy. I lift my chin, squaring my jaw. "If you wanted to talk, then kidnapping an officer off the military base probably wasn't the best way to go about it."

"It's hard to think of a way this ends well," he admits grudgingly. "You should've let me walk out of there."

"I let a potential threat walk away, it's my fault when my soldiers go home to their families in boxes." Already my throat's becoming dry again. I can tell I'm dehydrated. "If you weren't there to hurt anyone, you should have let me take you to HQ. If you weren't doing anything wrong you had nothing to fear."

"Bullshit." The gentleness in his voice is gone as he pushes up to his feet. Why does he still look so familiar? Where have I seen him before? "I was just *talking*."

"You had a gun!"

"Which you didn't know about until you tried to arrest me."

"You *shot* me, Romeo." I give a savage jerk on the rope, but all it does is send a jolt of pain through my shoulders.

"You jumped to the conclusion I was up to something." Romeo glares down at me, jaw tight. "Same way everyone assumes we're up to something. That's exactly why we have to hide out here. I'd rather die than trust myself to TerraDyn's laws or the military's idea of enforcing them."

"I may have assumed, but I wasn't wrong. And I'd rather die than let you or any of your terrorist friends hurt anyone on my watch." My mouth twitches to a smile, humorless and cold. "Looks like one of us will get our wish, at least."

"I'm not a terrorist." Romeo steps back, lit once more as he stoops to retrieve his lantern. His handsome face is hard, his voice thick with hostility. The humor, the wry sarcasm—completely gone. "All we want is what belongs to us. I was only after information about that hidden facility. If I wanted to blow up your stupid bar, I wouldn't have wasted time flirting with you."

"For all I knew you were flirting with me because you'd been sent to kill me."

He's silent, breathing hard in and out through his nose. I don't have much power—I don't have *any* power, tied down like this—but at least I can make him angry.

"This is getting us nowhere," he says, his voice low.

I try to lean forward, constrained by my bonds. "All I did was my job. You're the one who got us into this. And if you stop and think about it, I don't really think I'm the one you're mad at."

He makes a show of thinking about it, then snaps, "No, I'm pretty sure it's you."

And then he's gone, stalking back up the tunnel and taking the light with him. I was right—he doesn't have the stomach to kill me. He's going to make someone else do it. So much for having some company before I die.

I should keep trying to work the post free, but I know I'm not going anywhere until they decide I am. I know it like I know the truth: they're going to kill me. Romeo might not know it yet—he might think the military will give these people something in exchange for my safe return. But Base Commander Towers follows procedure to the letter, and that includes captured soldiers. We don't work like that. We don't make deals.

And they're not coming for me.

I've just managed to doze a little, chin dropped to my chest, when the scrape of footsteps and a light playing against my eyelids rouses me. I push away the flicker of warmth it brings, the sudden stab of relief that he hasn't left me here to rot alone after he left so angry.

Romeo, can't you see I need my beauty sleep?

I open one eye, and my heart sinks.

It's not Romeo. It's someone I've never seen before, a tall, burly man twice Romeo's size. Most of his face is covered by a kerchief, which is the only good sign I've had since I woke. Concealing his face means he isn't here to kill me—or he hasn't made up his mind yet.

"So it's true." The man is staring at me with a burning intensity that lifts the hairs on the back of my neck in warning. He steps into the cavern from the tunnel slowly, deliberately. "Captain Jubilee Chase."

His voice is quiet, almost genial—yet on his lips my name sounds like a curse.

I draw myself up slowly and say nothing. I know how this plays out, and there's nothing I can say that will change what's about to happen.

Romeo, where are you?

"Hard to believe our resident pacifist thought he could capture an enemy officer and keep her hidden in our base." The man paces to one side and sets his lantern down on a shelf of rock. He pauses there, eyes scanning me slowly, raking over my body, dwelling on the bruised, welted flesh beneath the ropes binding me. "And I thought it was too good to be true."

Despite his calm voice, his eyes carry a fevered hatred in them that freezes my blood. Whoever this man is, he's not entirely sane. I've seen that look on other planets, in other rebellions. This is the kind of person who walks into a school and blows it up to make a point. This is what keeps me awake at night—what keeps me questioning every strange face, enforcing every new security measure. Men like this are why I'm here.

My gut tightens with dread, and I look away, fixing my eyes on the ceiling and running over my training like a litany. *Don't engage. Don't give him what he wants.*

"Perhaps you can settle an argument for me," the man murmurs, crossing over toward me and dropping to a crouch not far away. "My wife used to say the military doesn't open its hospitals to civilians because it'll remove the motivation to develop our own. I always told her it's because you're a bunch of sadistic bastards who want to watch us die."

We don't let civilians into our hospitals because these "civilians" are as likely to walk in with weapons as with wounds—but it'll do no good to explain that to him. I'm not sure he'd hear me if I did.

"Too good to talk to me, trodaire? Look at me." The man reaches out to grab my chin, wrenching my face into the light. I clench my jaw, and his own face tightens. "You people," he whispers, his voice shaking a little. "If you had the tiniest shred of human decency, you never would've turned away a six-year-old boy from the treatment that would've saved his life."

My eyes dart up, meeting his before I can stop the impulse.

"Ah," he says quietly. "There it is. You think my son would've compromised base security? Still think you're better than us, condemning children to die?"

Shit. He's lost family. That explains the look in his eyes. I don't answer, staring through the gloom. It's so easy to see an angry eight-year-old girl there looking back at me, like the space between us is a mirror, like the last ten years of my life never happened.

"I asked you a question." The man lets go of my face with a jerk that sends me crashing to the ground, rope jerking at my arms and my wounded side wrenching. I let out an involuntary cry of pain, the rebel's face swimming dizzyingly in my vision. "Do you think you're better than us?"

I try not to choke, try to calm my breathing, but that fever's burning openly in the man's eyes now. His bloodlust is stirring, firing in response to my pain. "You think ignoring me will make me go away. But I'm a patient man, Captain Chase. Your people taught me that. Be patient. Beg for every scrap of food, every dose of medicine." He leans forward, and I can feel his breath on my face when he speaks again. "I'll teach you how to beg, trodaire."

His hand shoots out and slams my head down to the stone, the flat of his palm hitting me in the eye. He lurches to his feet, and then his boot connects with my rib cage with a sickening thud—my vision clouds, the air groaning out of me before my mind registers the pain.

"That's the difference between you and me," I gasp finally, fighting for consciousness. "I don't beg."

This time his snarl of rage is inarticulate, wordless, as he surrenders to what he came here to do, falling on me with all his rage and pain and grief. Even through the pain, through the sound of my own bones bruising and cracking, I can see his thoughts. Because there's no difference between this man and the grief-stricken eight-year-old girl I used to be. He'll keep beating me, keep kicking and punching and screaming at me, until he can't see his son's face anymore.

Which means he won't stop until I'm dead.

"You were thirteen last year, you think I don't remember you? Go *home*, kid."

The girl is on the street now, outside the recruitment office, watching as they shut off the lights and lock up the doors for the night. She throws the forged ident card into the gutter, swearing under her breath at the techhead who sold it to her.

"They don't believe you're sixteen, huh?" It's one of the recruits she saw while she was waiting, and two of his friends. He saunters closer, eyes traveling down from her face. "I can help prove it to them." He reaches out, but the girl jerks her arm away.

"Don't mess with me," she snaps, ignoring the hot tang of fear in her mouth. "Think I can't handle you?"

One of his friends laughs and moves toward her, but before she can react, the other friend grabs his arm. "Come on, leave her alone. She's just a kid."

They move off, grumbling protests. The third guy glances back at her, and his face is familiar; handsome, with green eyes and a charming smile as he winks at her.

But that's wrong too. She hasn't met him yet.

SIX

FLYNN

"ANYTHING YET?" I STEP INSIDE THE RADIO BOOTH AFTER checking Martha's still alone in there. I could tell she wasn't happy about sending my message to the military base, and less happy still about doing it in secret. But she's the best operator we've got, and no one else would be able to coax a clear transmission.

She jumps at the sound of my voice and starts to turn, but then catches herself. She hesitates halfway around, one hand on the dial, the other fluttering down at her side. "Flynn," she blurts, flashing one brief, agonized look my way. Brief, but telling.

I grip the door frame. "What is it? Did they respond?"

"No." She shakes her head, a touch too quickly. "No, no reply. I don't even know if the transmission went through."

"What's going on?" She shouldn't be this nervous. "Martha—look at me."

She resists, keeping her eyes on the floor even when I reach out to turn her toward me by the shoulders. Ice creeps down my spine.

"Martha, who did you tell?"

She swallows hard, draws a shaky breath, and then, like every inch is torture, lifts her gaze toward me. The guilt there tells me all I need to know.

I throw myself out of the radio booth and take off across the main cavern, not caring anymore who sees. I can hear Martha's voice calling after me, wailing, "She's a trodaire, Flynn! *She deserves to die!*"

I sprint past Sean—he doesn't know what's going on, but he can see my panic and after another heartbeat he starts shouting for backup. I hear him break into a run, along with Mike and Turlough Doyle farther back; Turlough is cursing, Mike stumbling behind his husband, hampered by his perpetual limp. I ricochet off the stone wall of the tunnel, throwing myself around the corner toward the unused caves. The air grows thick and wet as I stumble down the corridors into the oldest part of the cave system, but I know where the steps are slippery, and I can't afford to waste a second.

If Jubilee's dead it'll be my fault.

When I round the corner, I can hear the thick sounds of fists and feet on flesh; not a sound from Jubilee, only inarticulate sounds of effort and rage from McBride. My heart stops, but my feet keep going—I burst into the cavern to find McBride slamming his boot into her ribs over and over. Using sheer momentum I slam him against the wall a few meters behind her. The air goes out of him with a grunt, and I twist to look back at Jubilee—that's my mistake. With a heft of one arm, McBride sends me flying. I crash down beside Jubilee, the world spinning as my head cracks against the floor. She doesn't move.

Then the others are there, and as Sean, Mike, and Turlough put themselves between McBride and me, Jubilee cracks open one eye to take a look at me. Her throat moves like she's trying to swallow, and her cracked lips part, trying to make the shape of a word.

Romeo.

My breath comes out in a rush, hot relief flashing through my veins. She's alive.

McBride gasps for air, and with Sean on one arm, Mike on the other, and Turlough pushing against his chest, he tries to surge forward. His gaze doesn't waver—I don't even think he's realized we're here, except as obstacles to what he wants. I hear Mike shout in pain as his bad knee gives, and I scramble to my feet, my back burning and my vision blurring for one dangerous moment. Before I can reach McBride, he's grabbing for the stolen military Gleidel he carries, yanking it from its holster and spinning toward Jubilee. I leap for him again, shoving him back against the wall, so when his finger jerks at the trigger, the bolt dissipates harmlessly off the stone.

Sean wrestles the gun from his hand; the soldier crumpled at our feet didn't so much as flinch in response to the sound of gunfire. McBride shoves me away, though he stays sagging against the wall, sucking in great lungfuls of air, grief etched all over his face. "You thought you could bring that—that *thing* here, to our home, and no one would find out?" McBride wipes a hand across his reddened eyes, all signs of the orator gone. If only the others could see him like this. See the insanity, the violence, lurking behind his calls for action. "Good thing Martha's more loyal than you, you goddamn coward."

"Get out." My voice low with anger, I sound nothing like myself.

He shakes Sean's grip off his arm, then lets Mike and Turlough guide him toward the tunnel. "Make sure McBride stays out there," I tell them, my voice shaking with adrenaline. Sean stays to help me with Jubilee. We can't leave her here, now that McBride knows where to find her. Sean wouldn't condemn even a trodaire to that fate.

Jubilee is barely conscious as I untie her hands, and she's murmuring incoherently—maybe in Chinese again, I can't tell. There's a storage room up closer to the harbor that's been a cell for a long time now, for use if anyone got too trigger-happy and needed to cool their heels overnight. It was too exposed, too easy for someone to wander by and discover her, but now I wish I'd locked her there and left her unbound. No matter who she is or what she's done, she doesn't deserve to be tied down, unable to defend herself against a man half mad with grief and anger.

With Sean's help I move her up to the storeroom, ignoring the faces that watch us go. They all know now who we've captured—there's no point hiding her anymore. There's a ratty mattress in the corner, and we lower her down there. Sean shoots me a long look and, without another word, vanishes again. I know he's going to make sure that McBride stays where he is.

I pull a blanket over her still form before crouching beside the bed to study her face. The cavern's bathed in the soft, eerie green glow of bioluminescence—the wispfire that grows all over Avon likes to cluster in these damp caves. But despite the poor light, I can tell her face looks ashen, her dark hair a wild tangle, so out of place on such a perfect soldier. My fingers twitch, wanting to reach out and smooth it back. Instead

I run my hands down her side, keeping my fingers light. Her ribs are broken—that much is certain when her voice tangles in a sob at my touch. Her breathing is steady, so I think her lungs are okay, and she's not coughing blood. The beating's opened up the wound from my gun, though, and she needs treatment as soon as I make sure no one else gets the bright idea to take their rage out on her.

My gaze lifts to find her watching me through my examination, her brown eyes grave.

I was wrong, I want to say, my lips frozen. I scan Jubilee's bruised face, her lips parted and brows drawn. All she'll care about now is that the Fianna tied her down and beat her. In a single stroke, McBride has managed to destroy any chance I might have had at convincing her, at convincing *any* of them, to listen to me.

I push to my feet in silence, ignoring the lead in my heart and setting the canteen down beside the bed for her. I have to get out there and try to limit the damage—I know what McBride will do if I'm not there to counter him. The light of the wispfire is dim, but at least she won't be trapped in darkness again. Then I shut the door behind me and double-check the lock before I walk away.

They're already fighting in the main cavern when I walk in. Sean and McBride stand toe to toe, two dozen others crowded around.

"And if they say yes to a trade, and we don't have her alive?" Sean's demanding, heated, ready to start shoving. "What then, genius?"

But McBride's no fool. That's exactly what he's hoping will happen. Standing in the doorway, I ache for my sister. She'd know what to say to them. But she's gone, and it's left to me.

"We can't kill her." I stay in the doorway, fists clenched. "There are people here who have family in town. The last thing we need is for things to get worse, for the trodairí to start using them against us. We don't want to break the ceasefire."

McBride's gotten himself mostly under control again, but his gaze when it swings around to me carries murder in it. If he hated me before for not being my sister, he despises me now for standing between him and the trodaire.

"What use is a ceasefire when we're dying out here anyway?" He turns away from Sean, and the ring of onlookers parts so he can pace away a few steps. "How has our situation gotten any better in the last ten years? We never should have shied away from direct action."

"This isn't just any prisoner," I point out, forcing my voice to stay low. "She's Captain Lee Chase. Until we know what they'll trade for her, we have to wait."

"They won't trade." McBride's voice is heavy with cold certainty, and I see more than a few heads nodding in response. "They'd rather see her dead than us getting what we ask for."

"You don't know that for sure. We've never had an officer captured alive. We've never tried this." I step forward and they part for me, letting me walk toward him. "What if they'll trade medical supplies, or send back prisoners? Kill her now and we lose those options."

"Always dreaming. They're not your friends, Cormac, they never will be. The trodairí are TerraDyn's lackeys, and TerraDyn wants to hide Avon's pain, their failure, from the rest of the galaxy. Nobody's coming to help us. We have to help *ourselves*."

"And we will, by . . ." My voice dies in my throat. Behind him I can see Martha in the doorway, and I know she's come from the radio room. The tight lines around her mouth speak for her. One by one, the others follow my gaze, and she waits until silence has fallen. There's an apology in her eyes when she looks at me, but she can't change her message.

"Well?" McBride's voice is rough. "What did they say?"

My gut twists, and all the aches and pains and exhaustion of the last day come rushing back at me, so I barely hear her reply.

"We don't negotiate with rebels."

One of her eyes is swelling shut, and the rise and fall of her broken ribs is painfully shallow. She's awake when I ease open the door, but she doesn't speak. I push it closed and cross over to sink down beside her on the stone floor. Her shirt is wet with blood where the wound in her side has opened up again.

My heart thuds as we stare at each other. The wispfire growing all over the ceiling washes her skin with blue-green light. Her dark eyes are wary, but not afraid. I'm beginning to think she doesn't have that in her. "We're keeping this door locked." I break the silence, my voice rusty.

"I've got the key, and I'm going to keep it with me at all times. That shouldn't have happened."

She shifts, trying to sit up a little straighter where she's leaning against the wall, but says nothing in return. If she's relieved, she doesn't show it, gaze skittering away from mine to fix on the door. "You called him McBride." Her own voice is hoarse.

I flinch. "Yes." And I know why she's asking. McBride's been at the top of TerraDyn's most-wanted list for the last decade. To someone like Jubilee, getting her hands on him would be like . . . well, like us getting our hands on *her*.

"He's got one of our guns."

"He likes the poetry of it." Killing soldiers with their own weapons. She speaks through clenched teeth. "He's mad."

No kidding, I want to say. Instead I stay silent, reaching for the meager first aid supplies I've brought with me. She flinches when I reach for the bottom of her shirt, but she lets me ease the bloodstained fabric up and away from her skin. The gash my bullet made when it grazed her side is oozing, and above it I can see the beginnings of the sharp, dramatic bruising across her ribs. I wish I'd brought a lantern, but I don't want anyone to catch me using our precious first aid supplies on a trodaire. Safer to work by the dim blue light of the wispfire. I clean the worst of the blood away with a boiled rag, then reach for a small tin in the first aid kit.

"What's that?" There's an edge to her voice as I prize the lid free and sniff the brown muck inside to test its freshness.

"Microbiotic mud from TerraDyn's seeding tanks." I'm trying to concentrate on the wound, and not Jubilee's bare stomach as I run my fingers across her skin and test for the heat of infection.

"Mud." Dubiousness cuts through the pain in her voice; she's eyeing me like I've lost my mind. *Maybe I have.* Her face is flushed—with anger, no doubt, or pain.

I pull my hand away and scoop out some of our makeshift antiseptic. "Mud," I echo. "It'll help keep infection away." I carefully start to smooth it over the wound as she flinches and hisses with pain. Her skin twitches under my touch, and when I glance up, she's staring intently at the ceiling with her lip caught between her teeth.

"The light," she says finally, voice tense with pain, but softer now. "How do you do that?" Her eyes are on the bioluminescence lighting the cavern.

Though her face betrays little except that she's braced against my ministrations, her gaze is softening, eyes sweeping across the ceiling with something like wonder. In this moment she could be one of us. I don't think I've ever seen an outsider admire any part of Avon before.

"It's a kind of mushroom or fungus," I say, trying to focus on what I'm doing; it's hard not to watch her face. "We've always called it wispfire."

She's silent for a long time. "It's like a nebula," she murmurs, almost to herself. I risk another glance at her, and though her eyes are glazed a little with pain, she's still gazing upward.

"A nebula's something in the sky, right?" I reply, keeping my own voice low. The distraction is making this process easier for her, and I want to get through it as quickly as possible. Or—and I can barely admit it even to myself—perhaps it's because this softer, quieter version of Jubilee is fascinating. "I've wondered before if that's how starlight looks."

She blinks, refocusing with some difficulty on my face. "You've never been off-world before." It's not quite a question—but she's surprised.

"How would I get off-world?" Despite my good intentions, I can hear the bitterness in my voice. "Avon's my home, anyway. Clouds or no clouds."

I'm bracing myself for a snapped retort, but it doesn't come. I wipe my fingers clean without looking at her face, replacing the tin in the kit and reaching for the bandages instead.

"I've always thought nebulae were beautiful," she says finally, her voice still quiet. She sounds tired, and I can't blame her; the injuries I'm treating make my own side ache in sympathy. "When a star dies, it explodes; a nebula is what's left behind." She's still gazing up at the blue-green swirls on the ceiling. "Eventually new stars grow inside them, from what remains of the old."

"A pregnant star." I smooth the adhesive bandage over her side, grimacing when she flinches. "I like that."

The strangeness of the conversation seems to strike her at the same time it strikes me, and she cranes her neck to look down at her freshly bandaged side. "Look, why are you doing this?"

"Because not all of us are like him," I reply, keeping my voice carefully even. "Some of us realize that just because it's easier to pick up a gun and shoot than it is to talk, doesn't make it right."

"And yet you work with men like McBride."

"You think I don't know we'd be better off without him?" As though patching her up was keeping my frustration at bay, now it comes surging back. "If it were as simple as taking him out into the swamp one night and ending it, maybe it would already be done."

She's recovering from the pain, her voice growing a bit stronger now that I'm done with my work. "So why don't you?" she challenges.

"The alternative to fighting will take years," I reply, suddenly feeling the weight of it, the exhaustion from trying to keep what little control I have over my people from slipping away. "McBride has got them thinking that if they fight hard enough, they can change Avon tomorrow."

"That'll never happen. You're outnumbered. Outgunned."

"No, really? I hadn't noticed." I toss the bandage wrappers back into the kit and lock it shut with a snap. When I turn back, she's still watching me. Her eyes are bright with pain, but clearer now—thoughtful. I sigh. "McBride's waiting for something, *anything*, to give him an excuse to fight."

"I noticed." Her voice is flat.

"Anything happens to him, or he finds a reason somewhere, and his people would blame your people, and that'd be the end of the ceasefire. Your nightmares about bombs in your hospitals would become a reality."

She tries to sit up again, hissing between her teeth but managing to lift her head enough to look at me squarely. "Funny how kidnapping doesn't seem to bother you, but bombs do."

Irritation kindles once more, too quick and sharp to be ignored. "You lock me up, and there's nobody standing between McBride and all-out war. Look, there aren't just two sides to this thing."

She doesn't respond right away, but when she does, her voice is quiet again. "There are never just two sides to anything."

They're not words I would've expected from a soldier—especially not one with Jubilee's reputation. I tear my gaze away from her face and look up at the ceiling, cast into uneven shadow by the bioluminescence. "Listen. Your people won't deal with us for you. If I can't convince the others you can offer something in return for your passage out of here—"

"I know," she whispers. "Are you only just now working that out?"

My temper snaps. "What are you *doing*? You're not even going to *try* to save yourself? If you want to be a martyr, this isn't the way. They'll dump you somewhere, nobody will know. Nobody will remember you for it."

She lifts her chin, stubborn, her eyes flinty hard. It's like she doesn't understand what's happening—like she doesn't understand she's signing her own death warrant.

"Listen, don't you have a family?" I can hear the desperation in my own voice. "You should at least try to get out of this alive, for them."

"Everything I do is for my family." Her voice is sharp—I've hit a nerve, and it costs her. One hand presses to her side as she gulps air against the pain of her broken ribs. Looks like Captain Lee Chase has a weak spot after all.

I don't know what I expected her to be like, but it wasn't this. The stories about her say she's made of steel—she volunteered to come to Avon, the planet that drives men mad. She never runs, never hides, never loses. Stone-faced Chase, inhuman and deadly.

But she's lying here, half-curled up on the bare mattress, her eye swelling and her lip oozing blood. She doesn't look like a killer—she barely looks like she's going to survive the night. I know some of what they say about her is true. Deadly, certainly. Made of steel, probably. But inhuman?

"Jubilee, please." She looks at me, her jaw clenched, lips pressed into a thin line. "Just give me something. A tiny, insignificant thing. Something I can bring to them to show you're working with us. Something to keep you alive."

Jubilee swallows. I can see her throat move, see the way her fingers curl more tightly around her own arms. And in that moment I know I was wrong. It isn't that she doesn't understand. She knows she's going to die if she doesn't give in. She knows—and she's choosing death. Her gaze is steady, fixed on mine. Her mouth relaxes, trembles the tiniest fraction. Even now, with that deadly grace muted by her injuries, I could watch her for hours. I was wrong, when I thought she couldn't feel fear. She's terrified.

She lifts her chin. "What's your name?"

I have to clear my throat, my voice rasping. "I—told you. I can't tell you—"

"Romeo," she interrupts gently. For all her flippant remarks about death, I can see it in her face, her dark eyes, her lips as they press together. She's afraid. "Come on."

The silence of this cell is oppressive. It's separated from the rest of the base enough that you can't hear the sounds of life—it's as though this tiny hole in the rock is all there is. This hole, the ratty mattress, and the girl looking death in the face. I know why she's asking. Because it won't matter if I tell her.

"Flynn." It comes out as a croak.

She lets her head rest against the stone at her back, one corner of her mouth lifting a little in a smile.

I try again, and this time my voice is a little steadier. "My name's Flynn."

"Sit still, it's your own fault you have to wear these bandages."

"Mama, are there ghosts here in November?"

"Where did you get that idea? Did your father tell you that?"

"I saw one. Right before the firecracker."

"There's no such thing as ghosts, love. You saw the flash from the explosion, that's all."

"Then why make firecrackers to scare them away?"

"Because—because our ancestors did. Because lighting the fireworks helps us remember everyone who came before us."

"If I was a ghost, firecrackers wouldn't scare me."

"Why were you playing with them in the first place? You could have been very badly hurt."

"The boys were doing it. I'm braver than them."

"Letting yourself get hurt isn't brave, love. Brave is protecting others from hurt. I'm disappointed in you."

SEVEN

JUBILEE

THE CELL THEY'VE GOT ME IN ISN'T THAT BIG. ONLY ABOUT
two meters by three, and most of the floor space is taken up with a saggy
mattress that smells like mildew. The door is steel, no doubt salvaged
from commandeered military equipment. When I can make it to my feet
I try forcing it, hard enough to make me gasp from the pain in my ribs,
but it doesn't budge.

I spend a while stretching, testing out my muscles. I can't do much
about my abdominals, what with the broken ribs and the gunshot wound,
but my arms and neck and legs all still work. Romeo might think I've
given up, and that's fine. When they come for me, I'll be ready for them.
Because the last thing people will say about Lee Chase after she's gone is
that she just rolled over and died without a fight.

The bioluminescence—the wispfire—washes the cave with an eerie,
soft light. Unsettling, but beautiful too. When I tilt my head back, my
vision is flooded with blue-green stars, filling me with a strange, sweeping
vertigo. It's been so long since I've seen the stars that these seem brighter,
more real. But at least I remember stars. At least I've seen the sky.

I jerk my eyes away. I should be trying to find a weapon. The madman
McBride was sporting a military-issue Gleidel, no doubt looted from a
fallen soldier; if my hands had been free, maybe I could've gotten it from
him. With one shot, I could've gotten justice for the murders he's committed over the years since the last open rebellion. But since they haven't
fed me yet, I don't have so much as a spoon to work with. I ease down

onto the mattress, too exhausted to think. It's only then that it occurs to me: mattresses have metal springs.

I let myself have a minute to sit there, unmoving, gathering my strength. Then, muffling the sound of tearing fabric with my body, I rip open the corner of the mattress farthest from the door. Before long my hands are aching, cramping, but the sharp spring I'm trying to work loose is moving more freely. If I bend it back and forth enough, the metal will fatigue to the point where it snaps.

I'm stretching my fingers when I hear footsteps. I slide onto the mattress and put my back to the wall, facing the door. I interlace my fingers behind my head, making my ribs burn in protest.

Nothing to see here, assholes.

"You're not going to try and kill me through the grate, are you?" Romeo. How familiar that voice is becoming. I wonder if it'll ever *not* make me long to punch him—though I have to admit it's better than isolation.

"Can't make any promises," I call back. A lantern abruptly casts light into my cell from the grate, and then his face is there. His eyes look so familiar—even more so with the bottom half of his face concealed by the steel of the door. I've seen those eyes somewhere before.

"Still alive?"

"For the most part." I lower my arms carefully. Hurts too much to keep them up. But I don't really want to give away how badly I'm aching from McBride's attack. "You can come in, you know."

"Trying to lure me in so you can hit me over the head and steal the keys?"

I wonder if I'm as irritating to him as he is to me. Maybe it's easier to feel charitable toward a dead girl walking. Abruptly I'm too tired to make another joke. "Maybe I don't want my last words with another human being to be spoken through a prison grate."

The amusement in his eyes dims. His humor is just like mine. A defense. I let mine down, he responds in kind. If only I'd learned it sooner, maybe I could've gotten more out of him, information I could use in the future back on base.

What future?

He continues to hesitate, though I hear him take a step closer to the door. "Fine. I brought you some soup anyway, hard to feed you through the grate. Stay back there, will you?"

Part of me finds it funny that he thinks I'm in any shape to do anything to him at all. "I'm not going anywhere."

The lock slams back and the door screeches outward, awkwardly set on its hinges. Romeo hovers in the doorway, carrying a bowl in one hand and a lantern in the other.

Even knowing his name, I can't think of him as Flynn. His first name feels too strange, too intimate. I'm not going to be one of those prisoners who starts thinking of her captors as anything other than enemies. This is the guy who's killed me. Whether he delivers the final blow or not, he's the one who dragged me here, made it impossible for there to be any other outcome. I have to keep telling myself that.

"So, Romeo." I lean my head back, waiting for him to make some move farther into the cell. "Why do you keep coming back here to see me? Can't get enough, huh?"

"Never," he replies easily enough, stooping to set the bowl down on the floor inside the door. My heart sinks a little, ready to watch him retreat now that he's delivered the soup. Instead, to my relief, he straightens and leans back against the wall. "I suppose I keep coming back because you're my responsibility."

"Your responsibility as in, you're gonna be the one to bash my head in when the time comes?"

His face shuts down, muscles tensing. He really doesn't like it when I mention violence—an odd trait for a rebel. "You really are screwed up," he mutters.

"You're the one who knocked me out and carried me off into the swamp. If that's not screwed up, don't know what is."

"I don't know why I'm bothering." He pushes away from the door, pacing the few steps from one side of the cell to the other.

I look past him at the hallway. It'd only take a few seconds to rush him. A few seconds of agony, with my ribs, with my gash, with my spinning head and rebelling stomach. But then I'd be free. And alive. Just rush him. *Just do it.*

But one body can only handle so much abuse, and I can only ask so much of it. Maybe I could have done it when my anger was fresh. But I'm tired. I'm so tired, and there's no one here to know it if, for one moment, I rest.

"Listen," he says, coming to a halt between me and the door. "I'm talking to them. I'm trying to convince them it's not worth military retaliation if they kill you. Some of them are listening to me, at least hesitating."

"Sure." I snort. "You're going to single-handedly convince the whole rebel base *not* to kill such a high-profile prisoner?"

"Yes." He speaks simply, his eyes on me.

That brings me up short. The smug assurance is gone, the mocking half smile, the arrogant set to his jaw. Instead he looks determined. Resigned. Oddly strong, for someone so goddamn pretty.

Then it hits me.

"Flynn," I echo. "Flynn—*Cormac*? Orla Cormac's brother?"

Orla Cormac, leader of the Fianna during the last uprising on Avon, long before my time. Orla Cormac, the woman responsible for organizing and establishing the base, the one who gave the townie criminals a place to hide. Orla Cormac, executed ten years ago by military personnel acting on behalf of the Galactic Council.

Survived by her only remaining family member, a little brother ten years younger. A boy named Flynn, who fled to the swamps to avoid being shipped off to an orphanage off-world.

And I'd recognize Orla's face anywhere—we all learned about her in basic training. How to stop someone like her from ever happening again. No wonder I thought Romeo looked so familiar.

He's quiet, watching me put it all together. "A pleasure to meet you, Jubilee Chase," he murmurs.

I haven't just been captured by an idiot with a charming grin. I've been taken by the only surviving family of Avon's most infamous martyr. My hand itches, my hip aching with the absence of my gun against it. If I could have one shot, just *one* shot, I could put an end to this revenge cycle right here, right now.

Except if what he's saying is true, and he's the only thing stopping McBride from whipping the rebels into all-out war, then killing him would solve nothing.

"I'm talking to them," Cormac continues when I say nothing. "But you need to give me some time."

"I'm supposed to believe that you, the brother of the woman we executed, actually want to get me out alive?"

"*You* didn't kill her," Cormac replies quietly. "I'm not saying you and I are ever going to be friends, but even if you had signed her death warrant, this isn't the way toward justice. It didn't work ten years ago, and it's not going to work now. I know we need a different way."

I swallow, the muscles in my jaw tightening. Somewhere inside me, the pain stirs, straining against the bonds of control that lock it away. If I came face-to-face with a member of the group responsible for my parents, I'm not sure I'd hesitate before I blew them off the face of whatever sorry planet they ended up on. In fact, I know I wouldn't.

"So what now?" I ask finally, my voice sounding papery and thin.

"We wait. And you stop trying to figure out a way out of this cell, because I definitely can't convince them to let you go if we have to shoot you while you're fighting your way out of this base."

"What? How could I—"

"Please." Cormac lifts his jaw, pointing with it toward the torn corner of the mattress. "The last thing I need added to my list of credentials is 'stabbed by a mattress,' in addition to a cocktail skewer."

Shit.

"Fine," I say through gritted teeth.

He eyes me for a long moment. "Fine."

I give him a few minutes to get clear, listening to his footsteps retreating down the corridor. Once all traces of lantern light and footsteps are gone, I slide off the mattress again and get back to work on the spring.

The door bangs open and I jerk awake in confusion. The movement jars my ribs and I gasp aloud, too befuddled to hide it. *When did I fall asleep? Shit—what do I—*

"Get up, we don't have a lot of time. Can you walk?"

"Romeo, what's—"

"*Now.*" Cormac's voice is urgent, utterly lacking in its usual lazy insolence. "Take my hand, come on."

I let him help me to my feet, choking back the groan that tries to escape. It's only after he starts pulling me toward the door that it hits me. *He's taking me to be killed.*

My muscles tense. It'd be smarter to wait, let him think I'm going willingly, use the element of surprise. But I'm still half asleep, and my body's acting on instinct. I wrench my arm back with a twist, ready to pin his against his back.

"Will you stop doing that?" He escapes me, barely, jumping backward. He's got a lantern with him, but it's mostly shielded. Only slivers of light escape to break up the blue-green illumination of the wispfire. "I'm getting you out of here, you stupid trodaire."

My brain feels like it's running on a treadmill in a pool of tar. "Out of here," I echo stupidly. "Your people changed their minds?"

"Not exactly." To his credit, he doesn't try to manhandle me again, keeping a cautious distance.

I stare at him, confused. I've seen his hideout—granted, not much of it from the inside of my cell, but I'll see a whole lot more of it while he's leading me to safety.

My mouth opens, and I find myself asking, "What're the other rebels going to do to you when they find out you helped me?"

"I'm hoping it'll look like you escaped on your own. But I'll cross that bridge when I come to it. Now, are you coming?"

A flicker of admiration courses through me. Going against his own people takes guts. Of course, if he were on our base, he'd get handed a court martial for insubordination. "You're insane," I point out, trying not to shiver in the clammy chill.

"Then I'm in good company." He shrugs off his jacket and holds it out. "Coming?"

This time I don't hesitate. I turn and let him put the jacket over my shoulders, and together we slip from the cell and out into the corridor.

"Where are you taking me?"

"Oh, I thought maybe dinner and a nice boat ride to see the wisps. Somewhere quiet and romantic, then maybe drinks afterward before I drop you home."

This is costing him, going against his people in order to get me out. He's covering, and not doing a very good job of it. A thousand cutting retorts flicker through my thoughts, but the words don't come. We lapse into silence as he leads me through the corridors.

After a time he slows, lifting a hand to warn me to do the same. Then he strides around the corner like he owns the place. We must be into more heavily trafficked areas now, where people would notice if he was skulking around secretively. After a second he gestures for me to follow. All clear. It's only a few seconds later that footsteps echo back toward us, and Cormac's hand reaches out to jerk me into an alcove.

This nook is barely more than a crack in the rock, with only enough room for us to squeeze in out of sight in the shadows. Our bodies press together, my ribs aching in protest, the gash in my side burning. His head turns a little, the light sandpapery stubble along his jaw brushing my cheek. I try to concentrate on something I know, training that comes easily to me. This close, I could so easily overpower him. I could use him as a hostage. They wouldn't fire on one of their own. I've got no weapon, but I could probably break his neck if I had to, if I got the right leverage. His hand tightens around my wrist. I could—

The footsteps grow louder and louder. I catch a glimpse of movement out of the corner of my eye. Someone heads past our hiding spot— doesn't pause. The footsteps continue, growing fainter this time.

He eases out of the alcove first, then tugs on my wrist to get me to follow. "There are families here," he murmurs. "That was someone's mother who just walked by. Think about that before you lead any of your people back here, okay?"

I pull my hand away, making him grit his teeth. In another lifetime, I think I could learn to enjoy pissing this guy off. In this lifetime, though, I don't have the luxury. Instead, I gesture for him to lead the way—I'm not about to walk in front of him. If he were smart, he wouldn't let *me* walk behind *him*. But either he trusts me, or he's just that foolish. Probably both. He'd certainly have to be foolish to trust me.

I try to make a mental map as we go, but with the flickering, deceptive shards of light and the twists and turns, it's impossible to keep track. No time to think about what it'll mean for Romeo if I hand over whatever I *can* remember to my people.

If? *If* I hand it over? I need to get out of here. *Now.*

An endless series of corridors and crude staircases later, there's a shift in the air—the slightly stale dampness turns fresher. We're near the exit. This place is huge, far bigger than we'd guessed. I don't understand how we could've missed it on our sweeps. Sure, their being underground would mean infrared wouldn't pick them up, but surely a landmass this big would've been searched right away. They must have it camouflaged somehow.

Cormac peers down another corridor, then leads me into a vast underground harbor. A T-intersection of docks houses a small fleet of the little two-man boats the locals favor, and the sound of water lapping up against the sheet metal reminds me sharply of how dehydrated I am. At the far end of the cavern is the inky darkness of Avon's overcast night sky.

After checking again that no one's on our heels, Cormac heads for the boats. Each one is numbered, corresponding to a matching number along the dock. Easy to tell when one's missing. I never would've found this place on my own—even assuming I could've somehow gotten out of my cell. If he hadn't come for me . . .

Who cares? It's his fault you're here in the first place. Go. Just GO.

I find myself staring at him. "You're really letting me go? This isn't some kind of trick?"

"No tricks," he replies, voice darkening a little as he drops his gaze to look over the boats. His shoulders drop, as though the weight of this choice is a tangible force threatening to crush him. "I'll take you back to the base."

"And what will you do when your people find us gone? They'll know you helped me."

"I'll handle it." He crouches down by the mooring lines before tilting his head back to look at me, his gaze thoughtful, almost troubled. "What do you care?"

He's going to get himself killed by his own people, and though he's the reason I'm in this mess, I can't discount his risking everything to get me out of it. I won't let him do something this stupid. I find my smile, realizing at the back of my mind that it's not hard to locate, looking at his face. "Good luck, Cormac."

I see the recognition dawning in his eyes, but he doesn't have my instincts. I bring my knee up into his chin—not hard, but enough to knock him off balance. Enough for me to take my time, give him a more measured blow with the heel of my hand that sends him down onto the dock, motionless.

It's a moment before I register the pain in my side from my ribs and my gash, the price paid for such quick movement. With a grimace, I stoop and feel for Cormac's pulse. Strong, steady. I stifle my relief and straighten. I could so easily roll him off into one of the waiting boats, bring him back to base, and force him to answer for the crimes of the Fianna. Orla Cormac's brother would be a powerful bargaining chip. Maybe powerful enough to stop this war without having to rely on Romeo to stand between his people and McBride.

I swear under my breath, hating myself for my hesitation. I drag him a few feet back away from the edge of the dock so he doesn't roll off and drown. I scan the three boats tied to the post he was kneeling by and choose the one whose gas gauge is highest. I don't know where I am, but I'll pick a direction and get as far from here as I can, and pray I hit a patrol from the base.

Unable to resist, I sneak one last glance at Cormac, sprawled on the dock. I peel off the jacket he gave me and drop it beside him—I'll miss its warmth out in the swamps, but if I do get recaptured, the jacket will be a dead giveaway he helped me. Cormac's arm is outflung, like he's reaching for something, and the genetag tattoo there is unmistakable now with his sleeves rolled up. The coded spiral of data would match his sister's in the database if I scanned it. And yet, it's clear they're not the same person. Orla would have killed me in the alley behind Molly's.

Voices down the corridor interrupt me, and I grab for the boats on either side to start pulling myself toward the exit.

Sorry, Romeo. You'll be glad when you wake up and you're still a part of your gang.

Revving the motor, I turn the boat and speed out toward the channel.

He helped me—it's the honorable thing to do, not turning on him and bringing him in. Honor, payback. He saved my life and I'm doing the same for him, just this once. And if anyone's voice should be heard among this rabble, it should be the voice of someone whose first instinct isn't blood and violence. His place is here, and he shouldn't be cast out for helping me. I keep trying to tell myself it was the logical move.

But I'm struggling to convince myself that logic had anything to do with it.

"Don't watch that show." The girl's father jabs the power button on the holovid, his dark eyes stormy and his jaw tense. "I never want to see you watching that again, you hear me?"

"But Daaaaad, the other kids watch it. Their parents watch with them. It's just cartoons. And Mom would like it, they're all Chinese stories."

"Our family doesn't." His voice is sharp, frightening the girl. Her father looks at her again and sighs. "You don't have to understand, Jelly Bean, you just have to do as I say on this, okay?"

The girl waits, ears straining, until she hears the chime of the shop door opening as he leaves. Then, her little heart dancing with daring, she crawls over to the set and hits the power button. But when the HV comes back on, suddenly she's not in her parents' shop anymore. She's on a military base on Avon and she's being made to watch interrogation footage. The rebel leader is young, with a long black braid over her shoulder and a proud, unremorseful bearing. She's been permitted a visitor on this, her last day before execution: a little boy with green eyes and dark, tumbly hair. He doesn't let go of the woman in the cell for a single second of the ten minutes they're allowed together. She's whispering something to him that the microphones can't pick up.

"Turn it off!" shouts the girl, but she's the only one there, and the HV is too far away to reach. The video keeps playing.

EIGHT

FLYNN

MY HEAD IS POUNDING. EVERY SHOUT REVERBERATES INSIDE my temples; every lantern beam slices through my vision. I'm sitting against the stone wall of the harbor, cursing this concussion, waiting to be able to stand without dizziness.

As I fight a wave of nausea, two versions of Sean run past, moving perfectly in sync, their edges blurred. He'll have two dozen children to watch, their parents all out searching. Jubilee is gone, and with her, whatever chance I had of keeping my people in check tonight.

That fool of a trodaire—this didn't have to happen. If she'd just waited, just let me take her, I'd have had time to come up with—hell, I have no idea what I'd have done, but at least I'd have had a chance to think. Instead, this. She's spared me any suspicion from my people that I helped her escape, but at what cost?

By now signal lights, our answer to Avon's radio troubles, will have spread throughout the swamp, inviting the boats of our allies to peel quietly away from the docks in town to come and help. Half the time when people report seeing wisps dancing in the swamps, it's actually some distant signal light trying to speak to us. The other half the time . . . well, not even TerraDyn's scientists have an answer there.

We have search grids for times like these, with a level of organization that would surprise the soldiers. We know the places the swamps can channel a boat, and we know where they send you if you're lost. What I wish I knew is how long a head start Jubilee has, and whether she *is* lost.

All around me the Fianna are pairing off and climbing down into currachs, the first wave of searchers already gone. The shouts that set off bursts of pain behind my eyes are urgent, but disciplined—there's anger, but no panic. I press two fingers gently to the side of my head, finding the lump there as the O'Leary brothers cast off, their boat vanishing into the dark of the night. *Damn her.*

"Well?" I look up and find the last wave of searchers standing over me, lanterns in hands. It's Connor Tran speaking. "Do you remember anything yet, Cormac?" There's a frustration in his tone echoed in all their faces, and I'm pinned to the wall by half a dozen pairs of eyes. "You must have seen something. You must remember some part of getting up here."

I start to shake my head, then think better of it when the room starts to spin. "I don't know what happened," I murmur. I know it sounds weak, but the truth would be worse.

"He knows nothing." McBride pushes his way through the crowd to look down at me. His voice is calm, cutting through the others with an easy authority, but his gaze is for me and holds nothing but contempt. "It's not his fault. He's young; no one could expect him to defend himself against a trained fighter. What matters now is whether she makes it back to her base and, if she does, whether she's got our location."

And just like that, I'm sidelined from the discussion.

"We're trying to get an update from someone at the base," Tran replies as all eyes swing toward McBride. "We radioed Riley, but he doesn't have a shift on the base for another two days. They'll look at him too closely if he tries to get in before then."

"Who else, then? Forget the janitors, maybe someone who does deliveries."

"Davin Quinn." That's Mike Doyle at the back. "He's got a new job in the warehouse on base."

Davin's weathered, grinning face flashes up before my eyes. He has a daughter not much younger than me, and he wants nothing to do with our fight. I refuse to drag more innocents into this. I brace myself against the wall as I ease up to my feet, raising my voice before McBride can approve Doyle's suggestion. "Quinn's too old to move fast enough for us. Speak to Matt Daly. He sells his *poitín* to the trodairí. They'll let him onto the base if it means more of his moonshine. There's a chance she was too injured to keep track of where she was. She might not know anything."

There's a quick murmur of agreement from the group. I start to straighten, and Tran's hand comes out to steady my shoulder as the concussion threatens to send me staggering.

When I turn my head, McBride's gaze is waiting for me again, still burning. But the idea's a good one, and it's not the right time to speak against it—against me. "Try him," he agrees, and like that, they scatter. Back to work.

And hours pass. Search teams report in with no luck, and I can't escape the thought of Jubilee, broken ribs and all, lost in Avon's ever-shifting waterways. The thought shouldn't stay with me the way it does—I shouldn't care whether we're empty-handed because she drowned or made it back to base. Her words are still echoing in my ears. *There are never just two sides to anything.*

We all work through the night. My concussion proves minor, and as my eyesight starts to clear, I focus on the maps, handing out new coordinates to tired teams. As each reports back, I dread hearing they found her, and I dread hearing they didn't. On my breaks I help load currachs for those evacuating, afraid she'll lead the trodairí to our door.

If she hasn't found her way back to the base by now, then she's probably dead. Avon's waters are treacherous, and if she ran out of gas and ditched the currach she stole, then the bog most likely swallowed her. And yet, every time I hear the sputtering of an engine returning to the harbor, I have to swallow the bitter fear that it's her, and that she's brought an army with her.

She knows my face now, too. Nobody says it, but it's in their glances, their pauses. She knows my face, and if they catch me in town after she reports back with my identity, I'll be lucky to spend the rest of my life locked up.

McBride's out with the search parties most of the night—if he's the one to find her, it will cement his leadership for good, and he can't miss that opportunity. But he returns now and then, ostensibly to refuel. I see him mingling, moving among the people left behind, dropping the right words in the right ears. Talking, reassuring, quietly fueling their anger under the guise of sharing their concerns. His tone's always calm, but I can't forget the contempt I saw in his gaze, the venom. He's not finished with me. I wish I could guess at his next step—figure out what speech or trick he'll use to win the rest of my people to his cause.

When he lays his hand on my shoulder, I lose my patience, shrugging him off and turning away from the table where I'm standing to stride away down a hallway. I can hear his voice behind me, but my head's pounding, and the words I'm biting back will only make things worse. Letting him take a jab at my receding back is the lesser of two evils. I brought her here, I let her get away, and if I want a chance to be heard at all, I know it won't be tonight.

I turn right, away from the main cavern, automatically making for Sean and the classroom. He's got the children sleeping in there, little mattresses lined up, their bodies small lumps under the blankets. He's standing silent watch over our innocents as they sleep, his expression unreadable. I wonder if he envies them.

Then he spots the shifting shadow as I pause in the doorway, and he turns to make his way over to me. "How's your head?" No hint of his usual tease, his gaze searching.

"Sore, but thick-skulled as usual. Takes a harder hit than that to kill me."

Sean's voice remains low, thoughtful. "I've spent all night thinking it over, trying to work out how the trodaire escaped. Doesn't make sense, especially since you had the only key to the door."

A heavy weight settles inside me, and when I look up, his gaze is waiting.

He speaks again, almost inaudible. "If I figured it out, how long do you think it'll take McBride and the others to get there?"

"Sean, I—"

"You've signed our death warrants, Flynn. All of us." The note of betrayal in his voice cuts me far deeper than the anger.

"This is how we start to find common ground," I reply, hoping my face doesn't show how guilty I feel. "She's not what you think. She's different from the others."

"Different?" Sean's jaw tightens, eyes shadowing abruptly with horror. "God, you *like* her. Flynn, please. Tell me you don't think—"

"Of course not," I snap, then lower my voice with an effort when a few of the children behind my cousin stir in their beds. "But if there's a chance she'll help us, I have to take it."

"She's a *trodaire*."

"I don't think that means she deserves to die for doing her job."

"Her job *is* to die," he hisses. "Or make sure we do."

"She didn't kill me when she escaped, and she could have."

He watches me for a long moment, and I can feel my heart thumping to count out the seconds. "Give me the key," he says finally.

"Key?"

"To the cell she was in." He holds out his hand, gesturing with his fingers for me to hurry up. "They find it on you, and you're done."

My breath rattles out in an unsteady sigh, and I fish around in my pocket for the key I used to let Jubilee out. Sean takes it and shoves it into his own pocket, scanning the corridor beyond me before moving past to head up the tunnel.

"Sean." My voice makes him pause. "Thank y—"

"Don't," he interrupts. "Just—stop." Then he's gone, no doubt to find some place to stash the key where no one will find it.

I walk slowly down the corridor and take a left, ducking away from the noise, the people. Except as soon as I find quiet, I can hear Jubilee Chase instead.

Now what, Romeo?

I make my way down a set of stairs, into the darker, quieter parts of the cave complex. Somewhere I can think.

Here, the rough surfaces of the rocks aren't smoothed back, and stretches of plastene cover holes to other caverns that would let in drafts. It's only when I round a corner that I figure out where my feet are taking me—toward the munitions storeroom, where thick metal doors still stand between McBride and outright war. To look at a solid, physical reminder that he hasn't won yet.

The fear Sean was right thumps hard in my chest. If he worked out I helped Jubilee, how much longer can it be until McBride does? Still, he lacks the proof, and while I have breath, I can keep fighting.

I just wish I knew what I was fighting *for.* What the world I want would look like. The fear and anger in the air tonight make clearer than ever that any chance of peace is vanishing right before our eyes. McBride's gaining followers, and soon the tide will turn.

I pull a lantern from its hook on the wall, turning the last corner.

There's a twisted hole where the lock used to be on the munitions storeroom doors, jagged edges burned and blackened by a blowtorch. All I can hear is my pulse pounding.

My hand flies up to my neck, scrabbling there for the chain that holds the key. It catches against my fingers and I haul it out, the edge pressing into my skin as I grip it. But now my brain's translating what it sees, and I realize nobody needed the key to do this.

McBride isn't waiting for the tide to turn, not anymore. He's not waiting to win over the hearts and minds of all our people.

I acted alone, and now he's done the same. The cabinet is empty. All our guns, our explosives, everything he needs to provoke the trodairí into all-out war—they're gone.

She's hiding under the counter again, and the green-eyed boy is there too. They're listening to the girl's parents fight.

"If we just give them what they want, they'll leave us alone." The girl's father speaks in a tight, sharp voice. His fear calls to the girl's fear, and she swallows, her palms sweaty.

"Let them win?" Her mother is afraid too, but her anger is stronger. "Let them use our shop, our home, to stage their rebellion? What about our daughter? Do you think she should help them with their plans?"

"We could go to Babel, visit your father. He hasn't seen Jubilee since she was a baby, I'm sure he'd take us in for a few weeks."

"I'm not letting them turn our home into a war zone."

The girl shuts her eyes tight, trying to block out the voices. The boy reaches out and grabs her hand, making the girl stare at him in confusion.

"You're not supposed to be here," she whispers. "You were never in November."

"I'm not your enemy," the boy whispers back. "And you don't have to do this alone."

NINE

JUBILEE

THE PRIVATE ON PATROL WHO FINDS ME A FEW KLICKS OUT from the base isn't one of mine, and I don't know his name. With soldiers coming and going every few weeks, there's no way to know them all. We try to study photo rosters, to keep rebels from taking advantage of the base's high turnover rate, but we still can't really keep up.

I'm bustled onto the base, greeted by a blur of shocked and relieved faces, shoved into the hospital. I hear words like *exposure* and *fractures* and *signs of internal bleeding*. I'm surrounded by concern over my ribs, the gash in my side dressed with mud, the knot on the back of my head. I want to protest that if I wasn't dead after spending the better part of a day struggling through those damn swamps, a few more minutes probably isn't going to kill me. But I'm too tired.

I get about five minutes of silence when the medics retreat before a horde of my soldiers come through, all shouting and saluting and reaching for my hand. They don't know whether to be relieved I'm alive or furious that I'm so damaged. If I had the energy, I'd tear them a new one for letting their commanding officer get abducted right under their noses, but I can barely even follow the conversation going on around me.

You get to know one another pretty quickly out here on the edge. As my old captain used to tell me, "Learn fast, or don't." For a moment I miss him, his practicality; I miss having someone I trust blindly to tell me what to do. As officers, we're tasked with tracking our soldiers—with monitoring them psychologically as well as physically, to make sure we catch them before the Fury kicks in. It's only our vigilance that keeps this base operational.

But as well as I know my guys, it goes both ways. They know me too, and they can tell that I'm not okay. They can tell I'm barely staying afloat.

It's Mori who realizes I'm falling apart, and she starts pulling the others out of my room. A few seconds later Alexi comes through, his shock of neon hair jerking me from my daze. He finishes clearing the room and then shuts the door on the crowd outside.

"Thanks, Lieutenant." My voice sounds weak, and I'm relieved it's only Alexi there to hear it.

"No problem, sir. Commander's orders, though. You're not to be disturbed until she can debrief."

That makes me pause—Alexi's rarely so formal. Avon's particular corner of the military has an odd assortment of rules, and one is that not all the same formalities observed in the populated planets apply. Another has to do with the dress code, though even Alexi strains the boundaries of that one. His hair—hot pink this week—would be enough to make even the laxest commander look twice.

So if Alexi's talking like a desk colonel—with me of all people—something's up.

"Should I have stayed lost?" I try to make it sound like a joke, but there's a ripple of fear through my gut that I hope doesn't come out in my voice. Could Commander Towers somehow have found out I had Orla Cormac's brother in my grasp and let him slip?

But Alexi just grins at me. "You know the commander. Wants to make sure no one messes up your memories, that we get an official story first."

"Someone's been giving her psych textbooks again." I swallow. "Where are the shrinks, then?"

Alexi shrugs. "She's insisted on doing it herself. I guess it's a delicate situation."

I try not to show my sudden stab of anxiety; I hadn't anticipated being interrogated by the commander herself. That's not standard procedure by any stretch, and Towers is not one to break protocol.

Alexi drops into the rickety folding chair beside my cot with a groan, leaning back enough to make the plastene composite creak ominously.

"You had us pretty spooked, Captain. You all right?" Alexi was one of the soldiers who saw me leave with Cormac from Molly's bar. His face is quiet, his gaze frank. I know what he's asking.

"I'm fine," I reply, meeting that gaze. "A few scrapes and bruises, nothing more."

He presses his lips together, frustrated. "I should've seen it. I just thought you liked the guy . . . but I should've realized he was one of the swamp rats."

From Alexi, the slur's half a joke. Even so, I find myself looking away, smoothing down a wrinkle in the blanket covering my lap. "You didn't know. Neither did I."

"I see him again, I'm not waiting to hear his side of things." Alexi's eyes are on the X-rays of my ribs hanging next to my bed.

I have to bite back the desire to correct him, to tell him that the guy in the bar isn't the one who beat me. But what difference does it make? If Cormac's smart, he won't show his face here again.

Alexi leans closer. "You look . . . unsettled. You're sure you're fine? No blackouts, no . . . dreams?" His voice drops for that, as though he doesn't dare come too near that idea. Doesn't dare imagine this ordeal will be the one that finally turns the unbreakable Captain Lee Chase into a blank-eyed, violent madwoman.

"None." I reach for a smile with dubious success. "You know I never get the dreams, Alexi." *I never get any dreams.* I haven't since I was eight years old. Since Verona.

"Hey, even you're human." Pause. "I think."

"Thanks for worrying about me, LT."

He opens his mouth, but before he can frame any words, the comms unit clipped to his belt crackles to life, making us both jump. A thick, gravelly voice—I recognize it as Captain Biltmore's—summons him to the security office.

Alexi lifts his head, flashing me an apologetic look. "They had us all reporting to other officers while you were . . . gone. Temporarily. As soon as you're up again, we'll be back with you."

I don't bother to hide my smile. Alexi's one of the few I trust enough to smile at like this, anyway. "Don't worry, I'll swallow my jealousy for a day or two."

The comms unit crackles again, but Alexi clamps his hand onto the mute button with a grimace. "Make it quick, Captain."

I grin as he gets to his feet. Biltmore's the asshole of the month, and everyone on the base knows it. No wonder Alexi's anxious for me to get back on my feet.

Alexi reaches down to lay his palm against my shoulder. "Lee," he says quietly, his grin fading to something quiet and private and grave. "If you ever do need me, you know I'm here, right?"

My throat dry, I can only nod.

Alexi nods back and then slips from the room, shoving his hands in his pockets and dropping into his habitual slouch.

I exhale slowly, letting my eyes settle on the ceiling. Alexi hasn't touched me, with the exception of sparring and handshakes, since we first served together on Patron over a year ago. He was the one who taught me I could never under any circumstances become close with someone posted alongside me. Our fling was discovered right after I was promoted, and suddenly every time Alexi got assigned some duty someone else wanted, it was because I was playing favorites, not because I was doing my job.

Alexi requested a transfer, and then I moved on to Avon with my old captain and the rest of my platoon. No one here knows we ever did more than serve together once—now, he's simply one of my oldest friends. He's mine, but only in the way all my guys are.

Still. Knowing he's there—my throat tightens. I wish I could talk to him. I wish I could talk to him, to *anyone*, about the Fianna boy and his talk of peace, so unlike what we've always known to be true of the rebels. But not even Alexi would understand why I didn't take him prisoner to face justice for his crimes.

Hell, I don't even understand it myself.

There's a hospital gown draped over the back of the chair, but I'm not quite willing to face Commander Towers in a dress that doesn't close in the back. Still, I push myself up into a seated position with a groan and reach for the laces on my boots. It's not until I've tossed one into the corner and am reaching for the other that something loose shifts inside the lining, and I remember the thing I found half-hidden in the mud on Cormac's island. With everything that happened—the rebel hideout, McBride, my escape—I'd forgotten it.

I tug the boot free and upend it. A small rectangular bit of plastic drops out onto the blanket. It's definitely man-made, covered in foil circuitry on one side. My fingers reach for it and turn it over. The other side's got a scan bar on it.

It's an ident chip. Low-tech, compared to the flashy things we get nowadays, with holovid images of our faces and DNA samples and fingerprints built in. This is one of the models from ten, twenty years ago. Outdated, but simple. Doesn't require much technology to produce— but the advantage is that it can't be read without the right scanner. And I'll bet anything that if I tried to scan it, the identity of its owner would come up encrypted. There's no telling who this chip belongs to.

Except it wasn't a soldier, because we've got different chips. And it wasn't a townie or a rebel, because their genetag IDs are all tattooed on their forearms and verified via DNA scans, so they can't be forged or lost. This isn't the tech TerraDyn uses—they have all their own in-house systems.

It's someone else. Someone who isn't supposed to be in TerraDyn's territory. Another player on Avon.

Before I have much time to process, there's a knock at the door. I shove the ident chip deep into my pocket and lift my head. The door swings open, and Commander Towers appears.

She's the only other female officer on the base above a lieutenant, but we couldn't look more different. She's willowy and lean, with sharply defined features and blond hair she wears in a bun at the nape of her neck. Less experienced than the base commander she replaced four or five months ago, but far more competent. She's a lifer, like me. We're the ones who progress quickly through the ranks, who devote our lives to these fights. Most recruits who show up are only passing through, enlisting for a few years to earn enough to start their real careers or go to school, or to see a bit of the galaxy before they settle down somewhere. But with Towers and me, one look is all you need to know we'll be soldiers until we're done.

"Chase," she greets me, stepping through the doorway. "How are you feeling?"

I pause, as though considering my answer. "A bit hungry, sir."

Her lips twitch into a small smile, and then she sinks down onto the same chair Alexi occupied a few moments before. Though instead of dropping into it heavily, she alights on the edge, hands folded over her knees.

"You know why I'm here. We need to know what happened out there, Captain. Are you up to talking about it?" Her tone makes it clear she isn't really asking me. This debrief is happening now, whether I want it to or not.

Truthfully, I still feel as though I'm being squeezed through flat rollers, stretched out and held to a hot iron. My ribs itch and throb as the fractures knit in response to the medics' treatment. Every movement makes my head ache with exhaustion, and all I want to do is go to sleep.

"I'm fine, sir," I say instead of the truth. This, at least, is a lie I can deal with. "Truly. No long-lasting trauma." *Except, you know, going mad in the swamp and seeing a secret facility that's no longer there.*

The commander nods, her posture relaxing a fraction. "In that case, we can handle the official debrief process now." She reaches into her pocket, pulling out a recorder about the size of her index finger and snapping the top open so the green recording light flashes at me. She sets it down on the medicine cabinet beside my bed. "Debrief interview, post-incident with Captain Jubilee Chase, recording for transcript by TD-Alpha Base senior officer, Commander Antje Towers. Galactic date code 080449. Let's begin, Captain. Can you tell me what you remember, starting from the beginning?"

I take a slow breath, testing the point at which my healing ribs twinge. *A boy named Flynn Cormac abducted me and then saved my life and let me go again.* I think of the first moment I saw him in Molly's, nursing his beer and watching me in the mirror over the bar. My mouth opens—but nothing comes out.

Commander Towers is studying me expectantly, her fair eyebrows slightly raised, hands still folded over her knees. The clinic is quiet, the silence roaring in my ears.

Then, a strange voice says, "I don't remember much."

I clear my throat, pressing my palms down flat against the blankets. I'm committed now. I've lied.

"There was a guy at Molly Malone's, and he had a gun. It all happened so fast, I didn't get a good look at his face. He knocked me out when we got outside."

"Tell me what you do remember about him. Young or old? Strong or weak? Any dominant racial traits?"

"Strong," I say, picking the most harmless of the questions to answer.

"Did you learn anything at all about who he was?"

My stomach lurches. If I tell her that Orla Cormac's brother is out there, alive and among the Fianna, they'll never stop searching for him. "Not really, no." My voice sounds steady. "He and the others were careful not to use names."

"Is the one who took you responsible for your injuries?"

My gaze wants to drag itself across to the winking green light on the recorder, waiting to catch me out. I force myself to focus on Commander Towers. "No, that was later. I think I was in a cave. One of them beat me." I move my arm so I can rest my hand briefly over my ribs. "They kept me a few days, until they decided for some reason to move me. I figured that was my only chance, and I got the jump on the guys escorting me. Stole a boat, managed to get it most of the way back before it ran out of gas, and I walked the rest of the way."

"Slow down. Is the cave the next location you remember?" Her gaze is intent. "Take me through it chronologically."

My head's aching, and it feels like wading through syrup as I rifle through the options. Every lie I tell carries me deeper, makes it harder to think of all the ways they might be able to catch me. They might have had a visual on his boat leaving and know which way we went. This is what I get for lying for a rebel. "No, before we went to the cave he took me east."

"Did he say why?" Now she shifts her weight forward in her chair, and I know I'm not imagining the fact that she's more alert, focused on the smallest shift in my face.

I try to shrug, and my ribs send a lance of pain up my side to protest that idea. "He thought there was some kind of military installation out that way, but I didn't know of any."

The risk of what I'm about to do makes my head spin like I'm doing an air-drop without a chute. But if there's even a chance she'll answer the questions churning in my brain, I have to take the leap. "Though my platoon's never been assigned patrol in that sector—maybe there is something out there that I didn't know about." I can almost feel that ident chip in my pocket, burning a hole against my thigh.

Commander Towers hasn't moved, eyes still on my face. I school my expression, trying to remember what polite inquiry would look like. Am I too blank? Should I raise my brows? Smile? My heartbeat is too loud, and I'm nearly as dizzy as I was when I collapsed on the island. The moment stretches into an eternity, me gazing at my commander and her gazing back.

Abruptly she reaches out for the recorder, switching it off but keeping her eyes on her fingers.

My heart stops; she's caught me. She's turning off the recorder because she's about to call for security to haul me down to lockup. "Commander—"

Her head snaps up, lips twisting into what's clearly meant to be a reassuring smile. "Thank you, Captain. I've heard enough."

I blink, trying to sit up despite the dull, painful protest of my ribs. "But the rest of my account?"

She gives the recorder a little shake, her half smile turning wry. "There's enough here to satisfy the higher-ups. You need rest more than you need a debrief." Her cheek twitches minutely, a sign her jaw's carrying some tension. "Rest up, Chase. We need you back."

I ought to feel relieved. No more questions, no more chance my actions will be discovered. But Commander Towers has been here nearly as long as I have, and I know her well enough to see she's troubled.

She misinterprets my expression and reaches out to lay her hand on mine. Her skin is cool and dry, and I know she's going to feel the flush of betrayal and lies the moment she touches me. But instead she just gazes at me. "You did good, Lee. I don't think most soldiers would've made it back. Take some time off, get yourself together—and then get back to work."

When she's gone, I let myself melt back against the cot, trying to find a comfortable position, listening to the fibers creak as if in answer to my creaky ribs. I can't remember the last time I disobeyed orders, much less outright lied to my commanding officer. And yet, I'm not the only one. It can't be a coincidence Commander Towers shut down my debrief when I mentioned the sector to the east.

But believing that would mean believing Cormac's insane conspiracy theories. Might mean believing I actually saw more than a hallucination in the moments before passing out.

My thoughts turn in frantic circles, the room spinning away around me as though all laws of gravity and physics have abandoned me along with my principles.

I can't afford to lie here, letting uncertainty overpower me. Captain Lee Chase doesn't *get* confused. She doesn't hesitate, she doesn't think twice.

I force myself upright again, swinging my legs over the edge of the cot and swallowing down the nausea pushing bile up in my throat and making it burn.

A light breeze wafts in through the window, carrying with it the earthy, peat-sulfur smell of the swamp. One nice thing about Avon: it's too young to have a thriving insect population. No screens on the windows. The hospital is more centrally located, but I'm in a halfway house, one of the temporary buildings erected to deal with the greater numbers of minor illnesses and collapses that afflict newcomers to this environment. On this side of the building, the small, square windows overlook the swamp, only the perimeter fence between it and the wilderness.

I find myself straining to pick up the scent of rock and damp that pervaded the rebels' underground cave system. All I want is for everything to get back to normal. Hopefully I'll never see Flynn Cormac again— because if I do, it'll probably be on the other end of the barrel of my Gleidel.

It's a few days before the medics clear me to leave the base, and though my ribs still ache a little, that's not enough for me to stay cooped up. I'm not quite ready to go back to Molly's yet, so instead I'm walking down this town's sorry excuse for a main drag with a few of my platoon.

There's not much to do on the base; our comms aren't much better than the ones the rebels have cobbled together out in the swamps. The

HV signals are so bad, it's not worth watching unless you're truly desperate and willing to watch shows that are ninety percent static. We have retransmission satellites for official business, but unless Towers is in an uncommonly good mood, we never get to use them for anything as basic as entertainment.

But it's a nice night for a walk. As nice as any on Avon ever is. The air is still close and cold, clammy with damp. There's no fog, so the meager lights along the packed-dirt road disperse most of the shadows.

It's always sobering to go into town, though. Caught between the military enforcing TerraDyn's claim to the land here and the rebels protesting the conditions, the townspeople bear the brunt of the strict rules and curfews. Most of them work in the algae swamps or as surveyors of the surrounding ecosystems—necessary work if Avon's ever going to stabilize and support life on its own. But as many rebels as there are living out in the swamp, there are plenty of sympathizers living quietly here in town. And all it takes for a sympathizer to become a rebel is one irresistible opportunity.

Things have been quieter since the ceasefire started a few months ago, but even though we're off duty, we can't relax, not completely. We have to watch every passerby and monitor every shift in the air. And, knowing how close the Fianna are to open rebellion, I'm more jumpy than anyone.

I'm sure the walk was Alexi's idea. He and Mori showed up at my door after I left the mess hall. Of everyone, I think he suspects most that I'm not being honest about what happened to me out in the swamp. But he can't know the truth. He's being careful, keeping me close. My ribs are healing well, and thanks to the boosters the medics gave me, the bruising's almost completely gone. But it's not the visible wounds and symptoms that Alexi's worried about. And he doesn't know what to do about it.

I try my best to show him I'm okay. Mori's telling some wildly inappropriate joke that's so offensive to everyone involved—officers, terra-trash, and more racial groups than I can count—that it goes straight through offensive and out the other side. I laugh and threaten to make her clean latrines for a week, then climb up and walk along a fence post for a few yards. I jump down again as soon as I can, though. Still too dizzy for that. Still too unsettled.

Most of the buildings in town are residences, some of which have had their front rooms converted into shops or trade rooms of varying kinds. We're headed for this one house where the husband will take folks' grain allotments and give them baked goods back in return. We'll trade some of the military ration bars for some of the locals' homemade bread. The bread tastes a little like the swamp, but eat enough decade-old shelf-stable meals at the mess and you're willing to put up with some swamp in your bread.

We round the corner of the house and Alexi collides headlong with someone. They both go stumbling back, but the other guy recovers first, rocking forward on the balls of his feet.

"Watch it!" He's not much older than we are, but his face bears as many scars as any soldier.

"Hey, man, sorry." Alexi's quiet, calm. He's the best man possible in a crisis. "Didn't see you. Where you headed?"

"Like I have to tell you?" There are people like this all over the place on Avon. They were all over Verona, too. Angry about everything and willing to take it out on whoever comes through their line of sight. The ceasefire between the military and the rebels doesn't mean the townies like us any better.

Mori steps forward, putting herself between Alexi and the kid. "Actually, you do." Mori's not big, but she's strong and competent, and in this moment, she looks it. She casually rests her hand on her holster, where her Gleidel sits. "Curfew's in half an hour."

The boy spits to the left of Mori's shoe. "You're just gonna have to wonder, trodaire." The way he throws the word at her is more biting than any insult.

"Let's go," Alexi suggests with a roll of his eyes. "If we want bread, we've gotta scramble."

Mori doesn't move, doesn't even acknowledge Alexi. Her eyes are on the townie boy—all the animation has left her face. The hairs begin to rise on my arms, on the back of my neck. Something's wrong.

"You'll tell us where you're going," says Mori. Her voice is cold. No way this is the same girl who minutes before was joking and laughing. "And roll up your sleeve, we'll need to scan your genetag."

"Corporal," I interject. "Leave him. Let's go."

The townie's noticed the shift in the air. He doesn't know Mori like we do, but he's no idiot, not living where he does. He can read the change in a crowd. He takes a step back, glances over his shoulder. There's a small face pressed to the glass of the window in the house. With a jolt, I realize the boy's looking back at his little brother, who's watching the whole thing. No wonder he's trying to act tough.

I can see the boy fighting the urge to back down, to play it safe. I will him to go home. *Walk away.*

Then his jaw clenches. "Yeah, well you can suck my—"

Gunfire rends the quiet, and for a half second I'm blinded by its laser flash. I launch myself backward, my own gun leaping into my hand. I'm searching for the shooter for what feels like an eternity before I see the townie drop to his knees. Before the sound of the brother inside screaming hits my ears. Before I see that half the boy's face is gone. Before I realize Mori's hand is holding the gun, and it's pointed at where the boy was standing.

The next few seconds are a blur. I leap for Mori, Alexi throws himself down by the townie's body as the townspeople nearby start to run—some toward us, some away. Somewhere there's a woman screaming. I can smell burned hair.

Mori's staring straight ahead, her face calm, her eyes blank. I shake her once, twice—then I slap her hard. Her face jerks to the side with the impact of my blow, but her expression doesn't change. I fumble for the flashlight on my belt and shine it at her face. Her pupils are dilated so far her eyes look black, unchanging when I shine the light directly into her eyes.

No. There were no signs—there wasn't any warning. Where were her dreams?

Alexi abandons the body in the mud and lurches to his feet. "Lee," he gasps, "we've gotta get out of here. It's going to get ugly, we need to be gone."

Then Mori wakes up. I'm the first thing she sees, and she blinks at me once before she speaks. "Hey, Captain. What's up?"

I'm frozen for half a breath before instinct takes over, and I'm jerking her away. I half march, half drag her back down the street while Alexi brings up the rear, Gleidel in hand, making sure no one's out for immediate revenge.

Mori's baffled questions halt abruptly. When I look down, I see her eyes fixed somewhere behind us. And I know she's seen the slumped, motionless form lying in the mud.

The shop's bell chimes, and the girl lifts her head from her reader. *Don't*, she thinks. *Wait. This one's different.*

"Welcome," her mother calls. The girl, under the counter, watches her mother's legs as she turns toward the customers. "Can I . . ." But her mother doesn't finish.

"Hello, Mrs. C." The voice is light, but the moment she hears it, the girl's heart freezes. "Had some time to think about our offer?"

The girl puts her eye to the crack in the plastene. She sees her father coming down the stairs, watches as he pauses.

"We told you we weren't interested," the girl's father says, slowly moving the rest of the way down the stairs, putting himself between the customers and the girl's mother.

"Noah," the girl hears her mother whisper. "They're on something— look at their eyes."

Through the crack in the counter, the girl shifts her eyes toward the men in the doorway. Their eyes look like dolls' eyes, like black marbles with no pupils.

TEN

FLYNN

THE WIRE AT THE BASE PERIMETER WHERE I GOT IN LAST time has been repaired, but the same weak spot repeats a hundred feet along, and this time I take care to wind the ends of the fencing back together more carefully and hide my tracks. It looks like they've increased their security since the shooting in town, but a few extra guard patrols won't be enough to stop McBride—especially when they don't know he's coming.

I hate that I'm here. My ill-fitting uniform, stolen off the back of a resupply shuttle a few months ago, feels itchy and coarse on my skin. No matter how many times I remind myself that this isn't a betrayal, that I have to warn the base if I'm going to avoid shattering the ceasefire and dooming my people, it *feels* like I'm a traitor. It was horrifying enough to discover the munitions cabinet was ripped open and McBride and his followers are armed. With this new killing they have the excuse they've been waiting for, and that means I'll be whatever I have to be, tonight.

I duck my head as I pass one of the patrols and hurry down a make-shift alleyway. For once I'm glad for the rain, which started back up as I poled my way here; it means no one's looking too closely at anyone's faces.

I shouldn't know where Captain Chase sleeps at night, but our intel on the base is better than the trodairí realize. They don't have the personnel to staff the base entirely with soldiers, so some of the people living in town get work here as cooks and stockers and janitors. Nothing high-security, nothing anyone could use against the base—except that janitors are invisible and they're allowed to go anywhere. We've got a pretty good map of this place.

Most of the officers' quarters are makeshift arrangements. Jubilee is stuck out in one of the temporary sheds, and I'm pretty sure her bedroom used to be a storage area. There's no real window, only an air vent they've enlarged a little and covered with clear plastene to let in some light.

The fear is sitting deep in my gut that if McBride has his way, this could be the day we've been dreading. The day the body count gets so high that TerraDyn and the military launch an all-out assault. That this could be the day we lose too many of our people, they lose too many of theirs, and Avon descends into the chaos that's been waiting for her for years.

I don't know how to stop it, so now I'm about to crawl through a window in the middle of a base full of soldiers, looking for the one ally who might have enough sway to help me hold our people apart.

It only takes half a minute to yank the covering off. I grasp at the sill, swinging myself up and ignoring the complaints of shoulder muscles sore from poling through the swamps. The room inside is sparsely furnished, exactly what I'd expect of a trodaire's quarters. My eyes go first to the pale gray combat suit hung neatly on the wall, standing like a ghostly sentry over the sleeping soldier nearby. If she'd been wearing it outside the bar, it's unlikely my bullet would've even scratched her unless I got lucky. I try to swallow the anger that wells up, a well-conditioned response to the sight of those suits. They get state-of-the-art armor as thin as cloth; we get nothing but smuggled munitions and heirloom pistols.

Jubilee sleeps on her side, one long brown leg curled up on top of the covers, one hand in a loose fist under her chin, the other tucked up underneath her pillow. I can see her dog tags against the sheets, hanging on the chain around her neck. She even sleeps in military khaki, though it's just a pair of shorts and a T-shirt. At rest, she looks gentler. I grip the sill and whisper her name. "Jubilee."

She comes to life, making it clear why she sleeps that way—her hand comes out from under her pillow gripping her gun, her legs kicking free of the covers as she sits bolt upright, lifting the weapon as she blinks away sleep. A second later she spots me, her mouth opening in shock. I actually see her finger tighten convulsively on the trigger, though not quite enough to shoot. "Cormac." She gasps my name. "What the hell are you doing here?"

"I'm alone," I tell her. "And unarmed. Don't shoot me, you'll have a hell of a time explaining what I'm doing in your bedroom."

The seconds drag out as she stares at me. Then she grunts assent, lowering the gun—though she doesn't let go of it. She keeps a wary eye on me as I slither through and drop to the floor. If she has a comment for my stolen uniform, she doesn't make it.

It's a small room, furnished only with a narrow bed, a clothes press, and a rickety bedside table holding a framed photograph. It's the only personal touch I can see in the entire sparse room. In the faint light through the window, I can make out a man, a woman, and a child I suddenly realize is a tiny Jubilee Chase. The man who must be her father is tall and lean, his skin much darker than Jubilee's, and her mother looks Chinese—I can see her features reflected in the face of the daughter who stands arm in arm with her in the photo. In the face of the girl watching me from across the blankets. I wonder what her parents are like and what they'd make of the two of us, tense and silent.

I break the quiet first. "What the hell happened last night?" I don't mean the words to sound like a jab, but I can't take them back, and they hang there in the silence between us.

"It was the Fury."

Always hiding behind their so-called Fury. I can't hide the doubt in my expression. She sees it, her lips tightening. Her gaze slides away from my face to fix on the wall. A guilty reaction. "I didn't move fast enough."

That hits me like a lead weight. "You were there? That was an innocent civilian who died, he didn't have anything to do with—"

"I *know* that," she snaps. "I don't need one of your speeches, Cormac. It shouldn't have happened. I should've stopped it." There's strain in her voice.

Our truce is shaky at best; I shouldn't be provoking her. Slowly, reluctantly, I mutter, "You didn't pull the trigger." *No, you just stood there and watched it happen.*

"It doesn't matter. It's my fault when it's my man blowing someone's brains out." She shakes her head. "She'd only been here a few weeks, she wasn't reporting any of the dreams yet."

"What do dreams have to do with anything?"

"They're the only warning the Fury gives us that someone's about to snap. If we get them off-world in time, they're fine. But every soldier posted to Avon gets them eventually, except—" She stops, but I know what the end of the sentence is. *Except me.* Even the Fianna know her reputation for being the only unbreakable trodaire on Avon.

Jubilee closes her eyes. "This time there was no warning, it was over in seconds. She didn't remember what happened, afterward."

How could she not remember? I sink down onto the edge of the bed and notice how tired Jubilee looks; there are circles under her closed eyes that weren't there that first night I pulled her out of the bar. Her eyelids are puffy, face drawn. With *grief.* She's telling the truth. Or what she sees as the truth

"What'll happen to her?" I ask finally.

Jubilee's jaw clenches as she opens her eyes again. "She's already on her way to Paradisa. Desk duty, most likely, until she retires."

How convenient. No trial for that soldier, no punishment for outright murdering a teenager. They hide her away somewhere quiet, and no one will ever know what she did. I want to scream at Jubilee that her side has it wrong.

But what if she's right? She seems so sure. What if the Fury does exist, and it isn't just an excuse for the military to persecute and murder civilians? I'm reminded abruptly of what she said when locked in a cell in the bowels of our hideout: *There are never just two sides to anything.*

"Cormac," she sighs, breaking into my thoughts. "Why are you here? Felt like a little chat with your favorite *hired gun?*" Her voice is bitter as she echoes the words I used.

"I'm sorry I said that." And I find I am. There's more to her than that. "I came to warn you."

"We know the ceasefire's on shaky ground," she replies, her voice shifting to that slow, dry lilt that conveys absolutely nothing. "Don't need you telling us this makes things worse."

"It's not about the shooting." I lean forward, reaching down the collar of my stolen uniform for my sister's key. I draw it out for her to see. "This is the key to our munitions cabinet. The bulk of our weaponry was locked up there. Keeping it that way was our way of ensuring nobody took action without agreement."

Jubilee's expression shifts a little. "Was?"

She could turn me in, she could demand I tell her base commander. She could pull her gun on me again. I swallow. "Someone destroyed the lock and broke in. The guns, the explosives, the ammunition—it's all gone."

Her expression freezes; only her lips twitch, revealing the same wash of icy fear that swept over me when I discovered the door half blown away. It takes Jubilee only moments to come to the same conclusion I did. "McBride?"

I nod, trying not to look down at her gun, which is still in her hand. "It has to be."

"How many supporters does he have?" Her voice is tight and cold, quick as gunfire.

"At least a third of us," I reply. *You're doing the right thing,* my brain reminds me, even as the rest of me recoils from sharing this information. "More, now. After your escape and the boy in town."

"I need names," she replies, voice swift and decisive.

"No names." I clench my jaw.

"If we know who we're looking for, we could start grabbing them before they've got a chance to—"

"No names," I repeat more sharply. "You find McBride out there, you can have him with my blessing. I'm not ready to give up on the rest of them yet."

Jubilee lets her breath out slowly. "God, Cormac. This is—why are you telling me? If we're ready for them, your people are only going to end up dead."

My stomach twists, guilt stabbing through it. "He'll come at you from the town side of the base, but not tonight. It'll take him some time to get organized, which gives you time to increase security there, put out some more patrols, bulk up armaments on the perimeter in a visible way . . . If he sees you're anticipating an attack, he won't risk it. He wants a fight, but he's not suicidal."

Jubilee doesn't respond immediately, pinning me in place with a long, even stare. Then her chin drops a little and she closes her eyes. "Smart," she admits, lifting her empty hand to rub at her forehead. "Does anyone know you're here?"

"Hell no." I try for lighthearted, but in the quiet, in the dark, I just sound small. Every inch as small as McBride claims I am. "I'm not suicidal either."

Against all odds, I spot the tiniest lift at the corner of Jubilee's mouth—the tiniest hint of a grin. It's gone immediately, though, as she sucks in a quick breath and exhales it briskly. "I'll speak to the commander about security, but you should get back."

I hesitate, my chest heavy. "I didn't just come to warn you. Jubilee—"

"It's Lee," she replies, her voice sharpening.

"Only when you're a soldier," I mutter. "I'm hoping today you'll be something else." When I look up, she's frowning at me. But I have little choice, and I push on. "Look," I start slowly, "you need to talk to your people. Figure out some *small* thing that you can give us. Something I can point to and say, 'See, they'll talk to us.' Otherwise McBride's supporters will only continue to grow."

"Cormac," she begins, exasperated, "even if I had the power to do anything about your situation, I wouldn't, not now. There are reasons behind everything we do. Real, honest security risks we're trying to avoid. The regulations are there to protect you as much as they are to protect us."

"Closing the schools? Limiting medical access? Shutting down the HV broadcasts?"

"We didn't do that," replies Jubilee quickly. "Avon's atmosphere interferes with the signals."

"But you're the ones who changed all the access codes to TerraDyn's retransmission satellites. We can't send or receive a signal at all now—we're totally cut off. If you could just give us that—not even newscasts. But movies, documentaries, any window beyond this life to show our children."

Her hand tightens around the grip of her gun. "Do you know how they organized on Verona ten years ago, Cormac? It was clever. They used a kids' HV show, broadcast across the galaxy. Coded messages out of the mouths of animated mythological creatures."

"I don't even know where Verona *is*," I retort. "And we're paying for it here, a decade later, light-years away. We have no sun, no stars, no food or medicine, no power or entertainment for relief, and no one will tell us if it's ever getting any better. They've swatted a fly with a sledgehammer."

"A fly?" She's fierce, every line of her tense, holding herself in check with an effort. "That's what you call the largest rebellion in the last century? They chose the slums of Verona, where people were most crowded. Where there'd be maximum damage. They smuggled guns, dirty bombs, you name it. When the uprising came, whole cities from November through Sierra were up in flames before anybody knew what had happened. Those the rebels didn't kill, the looters and raiders did. Thousands. Tens of thousands of people—they can't sing or tell stories at all now."

I feel like something's pressing down on my chest and preventing me from taking a proper breath. I can't imagine a single city that size, let alone half a dozen of them on fire.

She waits for me to respond, and when I don't, she gives a quick, tight shake of her head. "There are reasons behind every rule, whether you see them or not. Perhaps some of them are too harsh—that's not my call to make. But if you could spare one child the loss of her parents by swearing an oath, by upholding the law no matter what it took . . ." She swallows. "Wouldn't you?"

To hear a trodaire speaking of justice, of protecting people—it makes my head ache. McBride would say she was lying. Sean would say she was blind. Watching her in the meager light from the window, I don't know what I would say, except that there's a pain in her words as deep as ours. She's silent, and as I watch, her features are returning to that neutral composure everyone else is so used to seeing. But an awful certainty is starting to solidify in my thoughts. "Where are you from, Jubilee? Your homeworld?"

She takes a while to answer, and when she does, her voice is oddly detached. "I'm from Verona. I grew up in a city called November."

For a long while, the only sounds are the background noises of the base: shuttles taking off and landing in the distance, people moving to and fro, the faint strains of music coming from one of the barracks.

I'm beginning to understand this soldier a little, the fierceness there, the rage underneath that stony exterior. My sister would have loved her.

Well, no, I correct myself. *Orla would've wanted her strung up as an example to the other trodairí.*

But if Jubilee had been born one of us, Orla would've been her best friend.

I glance once more at the photograph on her nightstand. I don't even have a picture of my sister—I have only the blurry-edged memory of her laugh, her dark braid over her shoulder. Little things, like the way she tied her boots; and big, horrible things, like the look on her face when she said good-bye to me the day before her execution. It's not enough. It won't ever be enough.

Jubilee's watching me as the silence stretches out between us, until finally she breaks it. "I didn't tell them anything about you." She sounds halfway queasy about it, irritated and confused, but I believe her.

I'm trying to cling to the anger and desperation that brought me here, but it's growing harder to believe that Jubilee's the enemy, even one held at bay by a grudging truce. "Why didn't you?"

Her eyes dart toward mine, a brief glimmer of the lamp outside reflected there before she looks away sharply. "I don't know." Her fingers twist around the sheets, betraying the conflict behind her calm voice. "Because if your people listened to you, there might not be insurgents laying booby traps on our patrol routes. Because if you were arrested, maybe more of them would start."

I want to put my hand over hers and ease that white-knuckled grip. My eloquence fails me; there aren't words for the impossible strangeness of this, sitting on a soldier's bed in the middle of the night, wishing I could touch her. But I just look at her hand, fixing my eyes there, not trusting myself to look at her face.

Strangely enough, my voice is steady when I speak. "That's what scares me about dying. Knowing what will happen here afterward." Her hand tightens, and I breathe out. The words come from somewhere deep and hidden—not even Sean has heard them before. "And I think I will die, sooner than I want to."

She's quiet so long, I begin to think she didn't hear me. When she does speak, it's a murmur. "So will I."

I lift my head to find her watching me, her brown eyes intent on my face. The half-hidden empathy in her gaze ought to feel strange, coming from my enemy; the only strangeness is that it doesn't. "Why doesn't this Fury touch you?" I find myself asking. "Where are your dreams?"

Her eyes fall, tension seeping back in along her shoulders. A muscle in her jaw twitches before she speaks. "I don't dream."

"But you said everyone gets the Fury dreams sooner or later."

"I don't *dream*, Cormac. At all. Not once since—since my parents were killed on Verona. The doctors on the training base ran all kinds of tests on me, certain I just didn't remember my dreams, but their machines proved I simply don't."

"Everybody dreams, Jubilee. You'd go mad if you didn't."

"Some of the soldiers have a theory." Her voice is too light, and the smile she tugs into place doesn't reach her eyes. "They think the reason I don't dream is the same as the reason the Fury can't take me. They mean it as a joke, but it's as good a theory as any. They say I have no soul. That this place can't break me because I have no heart to break."

She's only lit by the outside lamp that shines in through her broken window, but I can make out the shape of her face, her high cheekbones and the way her lips press together as she works to keep her composure. "Well now," I murmur. "You know that's not true. And I know that's not true."

She doesn't answer right away, and she drops her eyes to the blanket, where our hands are inches apart. In the silence, I can hear the rain on the roof above us finally starting to die out. "You can't know it's not true," she whispers, refusing to look at me. "What do you know of souls and hearts and how they break here? You don't know me at all."

"Oh, Jubilee." My resolve shatters, and my hand slides toward hers. She doesn't pull away, but she doesn't look up either, watching my fingers curling through hers. "Hearts and souls and how they break? That's all Avon teaches anyone."

But words won't do.

It's wrong, and stupid, and a million other things that flicker through my thoughts. My hand moves anyway, drawing her closer so I can trace my fingertips down her temple and along her cheekbone. A weight carried deep in my heart shifts when my fingers register the softness of her skin, still flushed warm with sleep; it's a truth I couldn't dare admit to myself, not when I first saw her at Molly's, not when I treated her wounds, not when we spoke in the quiet of the Fianna's caves. But if it's all headed for an end anyway—if tomorrow is to bring war, and death, and chaos—then this truth, right here, is all I have. All either of us has.

She doesn't move until my fingers reach her jawline; abruptly she lifts a hand, fingertips connecting with my wrist as though to pull it away. But she doesn't. Her touch on my wrist is so warm, her heart beating so quickly that I can feel the flutter of her pulse in the contact of her thumb on my skin. She freezes there, watching me with those eyes. I can see her struggle despite the dim light; I feel it like my own. Because it *is* my own. Trodaire. Fianna. Fighters, both of us—tired of fighting.

"I do know you," I whisper, and hear her breath catch in the darkness.

I lean forward, tilting my face toward hers, the warmth of her pulling me closer. She shifts too, chin lifting—tiny movements, little invitations and questions, each of us hesitant. But then my lips graze hers, and for an instant, everything else fades away into the rain and the quiet.

Then her hand at my wrist tightens and she's shoving me back. "Get out," she murmurs, those eyes suddenly shuttered. Only the flush remains, shifting toward anger, away from . . . away from me.

"What?" I resist her for a beat too long, trying to pull my scattered thoughts back into place.

"Cormac, go. Now."

"Jubilee—"

Her other hand comes up, and it turns out she's still gripping the gun, pushing the barrel into my chest and cutting off my words. Her hair's mussed, and in her T-shirt she looks nothing like Stone-faced Chase, but her grip on the Gleidel doesn't waver. "I said get *out*."

I ease away slowly, keeping my hands where she can see them, and rise to my feet. "Please, Jubilee. We have to talk about what to do, for the ceasefire, for Avon." I know what else I should say: *I'm sorry.* But I'm not. I'm confused as hell, but I can't apologize; this is the first thing I've felt sure about in months.

"We?" She keeps the gun up, a barrier between us. "*We* don't do anything. You go home, Cormac, and I stay here. There's nothing more for you to do here. Go, and let me do my job." Her voice is utterly cold, making it hard to imagine there was ever a spark of heat in her response to my touch.

I back up a step toward the window. "Don't do this. I need your help. Together we have a chance to stop this."

She's in control now, a soldier from head to toe. "If you wanted a collaborator from my side, you should have picked someone else to kidnap. I don't work with rebels. Just go, Cormac." She swallows hard. "Please."

That last word is an appeal, not an order, and that's what defeats me. "Clear skies," I whisper. A refusal to surrender hope. A wish for the impossible.

She watches as I turn for the window, and when I glance back before climbing out through it, she's still holding the gun steady.

The girl is dreaming about the first time she flew. There are dozens of other orphans from the war on the shuttle with her, but most of them are from Oscar and Sierra, and she doesn't know them. Some are crying with fear, others are talking to combat it, and a few of them are laughing.

The launch silences most of the children, the shuttle engines roaring. It isn't until they break through Verona's atmosphere and the engines quiet a little that the girl hears the other children again, all gasping now, exclaiming at the way their arms and legs are floating up, with nothing but their harnesses to hold them in their seats.

The girl looks out the window, watching the gentle, familiar blue sky fade into darkness. The stars come out, slowly at first and then all together, diamond-bright, each one a new world to discover.

But no matter how long the girl looks, she feels nothing. Puzzled, she looks for the girl who wanted to be an explorer, the girl who wanted to learn deep-sea diving and mountain-climbing, the girl who wanted to travel the stars. But she can't find her. That girl died when her parents did, in a little shop in the slums of November. And now she has no soul left to shatter.

She closes the shade over the window.

ELEVEN

JUBILEE

I KEEP THE GLEIDEL TRAINED ON THE WINDOW FOR A FULL minute after he's gone. I don't know why—I'm not going to shoot him, and we both know it. Maybe it's just a reminder. Of what I am, of what he is. Of how things are supposed to be between us. We were only ever supposed to see each other across the barrel of a gun.

My heart is racing like I'm in the middle of a scramble drill, its beat wild and thumping painfully in my chest. How dare he—how could he be *so* stupid as to come back, and so soon after the incident in town? I may not have given a description to the commander, but there was a whole bar full of soldiers that night who would stand a good chance of recognizing him if they saw him again.

I force my arm to relax, letting the gun drop to my blanket, flexing my cramped fingers. I was gripping the gun far too tightly. An emotional response. I grimace, getting to my feet and reaching for the canteen slung over the room's desk chair.

I don't have the luxury of dealing with his hormones—or mine, for that matter. What, did he think I was just going to melt into his arms? Start a tragic and dramatic tale of star-crossed lovers on a war-torn planet?

I should have told him about the ident chip I found. It's proof he's not crazy, that there was something out there in no-man's-land. That while it might not be the full-blown conspiracy he claims, he's not entirely wrong either. But the moment I tell him he's right, we'll be bound together even more than we are now. He'd have reason to keep endangering both of us with this ridiculous notion that we're on the same side, that we could ever be allies.

I take a long pull from the canteen. But suddenly, that's not enough. So I splash some of the water on my face, scrubbing my hands over my cheeks, my eyes, my mouth. Trying to rid myself of the smell of him close to me, the feel of his fingers against my cheek, the soft feather touch of his breath.

But no amount of scrubbing will get rid of that tired longing in his voice, the memory of how he looked at me.

I throw the canteen down onto the bed and cross to the window. There's nothing to be seen there, only darkness. No stars, no moons— never on Avon. Only thick blackness stretching from here through the rest of the base and out into the swamp. In my mind's eye I can see the bioluminescent wispfire from the cave, blooming against the night, tricking my eyes. No wonder the men believe in will-o'-the-wisps.

And then, abruptly, there is a light. Gentle, orange, blossoming somewhere out of sight but reflecting against the buildings nearest me and catching in the rain so that for an instant, I can see individual drops as they fall.

Then the whole building shakes with a deafening boom that knocks me against the window frame, sending shards of pain shooting up through my ribs. Ears ringing, blinded against the darkness, I stagger to my feet. It's an explosion.

My first thought, as I try to get my feet working: Flynn. My mind goes blank, unwilling to imagine him caught in the blast.

I'm moving before I have time for anything else, jerking my combat suit on over my clothes. I grab my gun and my boots, and lurch for the door. It isn't until I'm sprinting toward the flames rising on the other side of the base that it occurs to me.

Maybe Cormac doesn't know his people as well as he thought he did. Maybe this is the beginning of the war.

Chaos unfolds before me as I reach the site. It's one of the barracks, but I can't stop to think about the implications of a bomb going off in a building full of sleeping soldiers. My eyes are used to chaos, and I shove aside a sobbing civilian in order to push closer.

Half the building is gone, collapsed into rubble, and the rest is burning fiercely. The stench of burned plastene and wood composite scorches the inside of my nose as I try to catch my breath. I unzip my combat suit and tear a hand-width strip of material from the T-shirt underneath, then wind it around my nose and mouth. There are a few bodies outside, people who were near the barracks at the time of the explosion. My stomach drops painfully, but I don't have time to see who's there. In the aggressive glow of the flames, it's impossible to see any details that will tell me if Cormac is among the dead.

Not many others have gotten here yet. I've served on a first response team, and it's drilled into me—but not everyone sprints *toward* the sound of an explosion. No other officers I can see, except for a dazed lieutenant standing a few feet away, one sleeve soaked with blood. No time for him right now.

The men and women in the barracks next door are starting to pour out, confused and wide-eyed. No purpose, no order. *Damn it. Fresh meat.* They think they're sending us trained fighters, but spending a few months on nice, safe obstacle courses and drills doesn't prepare a soul for life on Avon.

"Over here, soldiers," I scream at them over the sound of the flames, and hopefully over the ringing in their ears. Only a few hear me, and I go jogging toward them until I've got the attention of the rest.

"Six groups." I shove through the slack-jawed crowd, dividing soldiers up as I go. "You and you—yes, you, you can put your pants on later. Get the retardant canisters. You've *drilled for this.* Listen to me, look at me. Run back into your barracks and grab the canisters and get back here. *Now.*"

In their shock, the newbies are more afraid of me than of what's happening behind me. They go sprinting back toward their bunks as if a pack of wild dogs is on their heels.

I'm busy dividing the rest of the survivors into rescue parties, and as the rain and the fire extinguishers start opening a path, we head into the parts of the building farthest from the explosion site and not burning quite so hotly.

The moments that follow are lost in a sea of smoke and heat. We pull bodies from the building, some stirring and coughing, others silent and slick with blood. Every ten minutes or so a few of us duck outside for a few lungfuls of less contaminated air, but every time it's harder to catch our breaths. Firefighting teams have assembled, working with high-pressure hoses and chemicals that burn our eyes almost as much as the smoke.

After the fourth or fifth time I emerge, a hand grabs my arm and jerks me back when I turn to go back inside.

"Enough, Captain!" It's Major Jameson, shouting in my ear. "You're done."

I nod, unable to speak through the smoke in my lungs. I'm too relieved to have an officer outranking me, an actual leader, taking charge. Give me a few minutes to recover my balance and I can rejoin simply as one of the rescue squad.

But when I get back to my feet, Jameson drags me back through the churned up mud and bodily pushes me into the hands of a waiting medic before vanishing back into the haze of smoke. "You're benched," the medic shouts at me. I hear the words, but they don't process. The medic frowns and shoves an oxygen mask into my hands, then disappears to attend to patients in more dire straits. It's only then that I realize the soldiers from the neighboring barracks, the crews I organized, have all been replaced by fresher rescue workers. I catch sight of a few of the original crews huddled with oxygen masks and blankets on the edge of the chaos.

I tear the dirty strip of T-shirt from my face and suck a lungful of clean air from the mask. It's a while before I can stand again, dizzy with the rush of oxygen and with my sudden stillness. But I force myself to my feet, taking one last long breath through the mask before I make my way out of the medic's area.

There are stretchers everywhere. Some with survivors, being moved to intensive care at the hospital, others with casualties being transferred to a temporary morgue, which right now is no more than bodies laid side by side in the mud with sheets draped over them. I step back to let a team pass carrying a badly wounded man. He's burned so badly that it's impossible to tell where his clothes stop and scorched flesh begins. He's silent, though, when I would've expected him to be screaming. His eyes are open, staring at the empty night sky. As they pass, his eyes meet mine for a moment. I don't know him. My sudden relief at that makes me sick to my stomach. Someone, somewhere, knows him. It shouldn't matter that he's not one of mine.

I pick my way through the hordes of the wounded, examining faces. A few are mine. So far, none are wounded badly enough to be placed in critical condition. Sweat pours down my temples and my back, and the ash in the air sticks to my face. The flames are dying down, but someone's put up big floodlights around the site, so even as the flames subside, the night is held at bay. My feet itch to turn back for the building, which is starting to creak with the added weight of the water and the fire suppression chemicals. It won't be standing much longer, and they need all the help they can get evacuating the wounded before it collapses.

The medic who removed me from duty is nowhere in sight. But before I can head back toward the flames, I'm forced to step aside for another stretcher. I glance down—and the world stops for an infinite second.

"Captain, we need to get—"

"Where'd you find him?" I bark, gazing down at Cormac's face, what can be seen of it behind the oxygen mask strapped there.

"On the other side of the blast site."

"Your best guess?"

"Concussion, minor smoke inhalation. He'll live."

And then they're gone, and Cormac with them, headed for the hospital.

He was here. He was at the blast site. Could he have known what was about to happen?

But I don't have time to take the thought any further, because something else catches my eye. The floodlights are erasing the monochromatic orange glow turning everything to ember-red. I can see colors now.

And at the edge of the field of bodies underneath the sheets, I catch a glimpse of neon pink.

I'm moving before conscious thought has time to prompt me. I ignore the burning in my abused lungs, the shaking of my legs. I'm sprinting, the world narrowing to that tiny flash of color. It's a mistake. He's alive.

They've put him with the bodies by accident in the chaos. It happens all the time, they're sitting there identifying a field of dead men and some of them just get up and walk away.

I need to get to him so he can get treatment.

I throw myself down, sliding in the mud, and rip the sheet away. Alexi's eyes stare skyward, one cloudy and pale where it's set in a sea of ruined, scorched flesh. The other half of his face is untouched, almost serene, as beautiful as it was when we first met during training.

My hands hover, trying to find some way to smooth away the damage to his face, to his neck and shoulder. His hot pink hair is muddy and stained with ash, and I run my fingers through it to try to dislodge some of the grime. His voice comes abruptly, painfully into my mind. *I wouldn't be caught dead looking like this.*

I'm still trying to clean him up when hands close around my shoulders and try to pull me away. I scream at whoever's got me, fighting to be released. Voices are shouting in my ear, but I can't hear them. Then a fist catches me across the jaw, sending me sprawling into the mud, head spinning.

I gasp for air, spitting saliva and blood and then descending into a fit of coughing as my abused lungs catch up with me.

This time the hands that reach for me are gentler. I lift my head. It's Commander Towers, her blond hair straggly and tied roughly at the nape of her neck, her uniform rumpled and sweat-stained. Her hand is raw and bleeding where she hit me.

"Get yourself together, Chase," she shouts at me, taking me by the shoulders. Her face is only a few inches from mine. "Get out of here."

"Sir, I have to—"

"That's an order!" Her voice is nearly as rough and hoarse and raw as mine. "You don't get out of here *now*, I'll court-martial your ass, you hear me? You've done your work and you'll probably get another slew of medals out of it, for all the good that does any of us, but right now you have to *go*. You're done."

I gape at her, my head swimming. I nod, and we struggle to our feet together, slipping and sliding in the mud. I stagger away, leaving her to return to whatever she was doing before someone came to tell her Captain Chase had gone insane.

Alexi's ruined face threatens to blind me again, but I push it aside. Because I know where I'm going now. *Concussion, minor smoke inhalation. He'll live.*

He'll be in the makeshift sick bay, not the hospital, with minor injuries like those. I spit out another mouthful of mud and bile and blood, scrubbing my sleeve across my face. I reek of sweat and soot and death, but it doesn't matter.

Because if Cormac knew about this, if he sat there and smiled at me and touched my cheek so I wouldn't notice the rebels infiltrating the base—then I'm going to kill him myself.

This dream is about the ghosts on Verona. The girl remembers them, but only when she's asleep, because there's no such things as ghosts when you grow up.

She's at school. The teacher, a tall willowy woman with blond hair in a bun, fights for the students' attention against sirens and drone engines and, once, the crackling, powdery echo of a distant explosion. Eventually, the teacher gives up and puts down her reader, shutting off the display on the front wall.

"I think that's enough for today," she says, her lips pinched tight, her eyes darting toward the clock and back. "Do you want to talk about what's happening instead?"

The girl looks out the window. For a moment she thinks she's seeing the reflection of her face—but then it moves, becoming a tiny ball of light, visible only because the window lies in shade. It darts away, then comes back, then darts away again, waiting for the girl.

The green-eyed boy in the desk behind hers leans forward. "Don't follow it," he whispers. "It'll lead you into the swamp."

The ghost shivers and then zips away. A few minutes later a fire breaks out on the next block, and the girl is herded with the other children to safety.

TWELVE

FLYNN

MY EYELIDS FEEL LIKE SOMEBODY'S GLUED THEM SHUT, AND there's a sharp pain as I force them open. Light jabs at me like a knife, and I squeeze my eyes shut again, waiting until the pulsing dulls a little.

When I try again, it works a little better. A dirty gray ceiling swims into focus overhead, and I know immediately I'm not at home, where all the ceilings are carved from rock. My ears register a high, mechanical beeping, and I struggle for a few moments before I can place it. It's a medical monitor.

I turn my head a fraction, but the haze of light starts to blur and sparkle, and I'm forced to close my eyes. There's something over my nose and mouth, making it hard to breathe. I reach up and feel with my fingertips, encountering soft plastic, and start to tug it away. There's a sharp catch in my throat, but before I can start coughing the mask is back over my face, someone else's hand over mine.

When I risk opening my eyes again, I find Jubilee looming over me, holding the thing over my mouth. She's filthy, hair mussed, black smudges all over her face, eyes flashing. She's in combat gear, the dull, semi-metallic gleam of her armor-suit marred by grime and soot.

"Did you know?" she hisses. "I swear to God, I'll kill you right here."

I stare at her, trying desperately to swim toward understanding, but it feels like wading through waist-high mud. "What happened?" I ask, and she eases the mask away so I can speak. My voice is a wheeze, my throat raw, and it catches and constricts as coughing takes over my body. My vision starts to darken at the edges, and the black creeps in as I struggle for air, my pulse pounding through my temples.

She shoves the mask back in place, holding it there until the panic starts to recede. I blink back the tears, waiting for her answer.

Her voice is flat, furious. "A rebel managed to sneak onto the base. Planted a bomb at Bravo Barracks, killed over thirty soldiers while they slept." She leans in, eyes locked on mine. "While I was talking to you."

The shock that goes through me is a physical thing, the adrenaline surge rushing down my arms until my hands tingle. "No." The plastic of the oxygen mask swallows my voice. "Oh God, no. I didn't know. You *know* I wouldn't—"

She's gazing down at me, Stone-faced Chase, absolutely unforgiving, soot and ashes streaking her face like war paint. For a moment I half expect her to pull out her gun and shoot me on the spot, the anguish in her face is so clear. Then she breathes out slowly, dropping her head, and I realize she does know.

"You have smoke inhalation and a concussion, but they won't have had time to check beyond that," she says, softer, duller. "Does anything else hurt?" She reaches out to run her hands down my arms, watching for a wince.

"I don't think so." I ache all over, and I just want to close my eyes and let the pain carry me away. It has to have been McBride, or one of his lackeys. Everything's spinning out of control, and I don't know how to move, let alone steady Avon's course.

I manage to turn my head, scanning my surroundings. "I don't think I should be in a room full of soldiers when these guys wake up," I rasp. My shirt's been cut away, and there are electrodes stuck to my chest. I can hear my heartbeat on the monitor beside my bed.

She shakes her head in a sharp movement, running her hand up my leg and patting along my side to check my ribs. Only a few days ago I was doing the same for her. Maybe we'll never meet without one of us ending up in the hospital.

"Nobody here knows who you are," she replies. "You were still in *uniform*." Her jaw squares, and I know this is another tiny cut, another betrayal that's scored a line across her heart.

"I have to get out of here." I shove the mask aside so she can hear me better. "I have to try to stop this from getting worse."

She reaches for a bottle beside my bed, angling the built-in straw so I can take a sip. My throat burns as I swallow. "Keep drinking this, it will heal your throat. As soon as you can move, I'll help you get out, for whatever you can do out there." She sets aside the bottle and reaches for an adhesive bandage from a rack above my head. As I watch, she starts wrapping it around my forearm, covering my genetag. My heart skips. What would I have said if someone tried to scan it?

She finishes smoothing the bandage down, expression grim and locked away, then straightens. "I have to go. Anybody wakes up, say you're from Patron. A new boatload came in yesterday, nobody knows their faces yet."

She turns to walk away, her purposeful stride reduced to a weary shuffle. Even locked in a cell, beaten and bloody and tied to a post in the ground, she never let the steel go from her spine; now her shoulders are bowed, her hands trembling before she eases them into her pockets. And I know what's sweeping through her, stripping away her strength, because it's sweeping through me, too.

We've lost. The ceasefire is over.

She's there again when I wake, after a night spent choking down mouth-fuls of the sweet, cloying gel that starts to heal my burned throat, and pretending to be asleep to avoid questions I can't answer. Trying not to imagine Sean back home, making up some story about why I'm gone, covering for me and pacing, panicking about where I really am. I hope that's the worst that's happening. If this bombing was McBride's opening salvo, then all-out war could be breaking loose out there in the swamps.

In her combat gear it's impossible to think of her as anything other than a soldier, especially after staring down the barrel of her gun. But she's pulled a hard plastic chair up to my bedside, and now she's got her head pillowed on her arms, crossed on the edge of the bed. My eyes don't sting anymore, and one of the meds they gave me has dimmed the pounding headache enough that she's surrounded by only a faint aura of light.

From what little I can see, she's washed her face, but the soot stains are still there around her hairline, and she hasn't taken off the filthy combat suit yet. Which means the base is still worried that the bombing was the first stage of an assault. I push down the oxygen mask, taking an experimental breath. I can manage, if I don't inhale too deeply. So close, she smells of sweat and ash and grief, and I want to lift my hand and reach out to her, ignoring the ache in my arm. I don't, and a few moments later she seems to sense I'm awake, lifting her head.

She blinks at me once, and then comes alert faster than seems possible. She clears her throat. "He's dead. The bomber. Died in the blast."

I force myself to breathe in slowly. The air reeks of disinfectant, sharp on my tongue. My mind seizes on that fact, putting off learning what I don't want to know. It could be anyone from our camp. I don't want it to be anyone I know, not even the worst of them. "Was it—" My voice is still a rusty whisper.

"McBride?" Jubilee interrupts, saving me from speaking further. "No. There weren't any usable fingerprints left, but the dental records say it's a man called Davin Quinn. There aren't any arrests on his record, not so much as a fine. He lived in town."

She pauses to let me absorb the significance of that. In town. Not a rebel, not a soldier with the Fury. And I knew Davin Quinn, I know his daughter. He's not even a sympathizer. He's nothing to do with us.

She continues, frustrated and bewildered. "He was only in the system because he got a tooth pulled a couple of years ago. How did your people drag a man like him into this?"

It's a ridiculous reaction, but I want to laugh, disbelief still crashing over me. "We didn't. Quinn was about as likely to blow up this place as you. He must have had other business on the base. It wasn't him."

"It was." She leans in closer, keeping her voice down so the others in the ward won't overhear us. "He had the detonator on him. We've got security footage showing him talking to a girl as if nothing was wrong, then turning around and walking into the barracks a minute or two before the blast."

"Then somebody made him do it," I tell her. "He has a daughter my age." Sofia Quinn's face as it was when we were children swims up in my mind too, smiling in my memory. I wonder if she's the girl he was talking to on the security footage. "He wouldn't do this to her, Jubilee. He had no reason."

"Mori had no reason to fire on a civilian in the town," she says quietly.

"But that was the Fury," I press. "This is completely different. Your soldier was an off-worlder; Davin was born here. No native's ever snapped from the Fury." But something icy stirs inside me at the thought. I never doubted our belief that the Fury was a trodairí excuse until Jubilee looked me in the eye and swore it was real. But Davin Quinn was a man of peace, a man with no battle to fight and a daughter to live for.

"You're right about one thing. This wasn't the Fury. When our people snap, they grab the nearest knife and stab their friends and anyone else near them, Cormac. They don't build bombs." Her voice comes quick and sharp, and it's only after glancing over her shoulder at my unconscious roommates that she takes a breath and quiets again. "Building a bomb takes time, planning, deliberation. The Fury is . . . savage. Brutal. As quick to strike as it is to pass again."

I shake my head, gritting my teeth. "It wasn't *him*. I'll swear it on my life. Something, or someone, must have made him do it."

Jubilee gives a frustrated sigh, scrubbing her hand across her face. I can see she's troubled; it gives me hope that perhaps she believes me, perhaps there is something more to what happened on the base tonight. But then I realize she's watching me, her expression tight. I'm coming to see her better, to understand the nuances of her closed-off face—and I know this isn't the only news she came here to share.

"Just tell me." My voice won't come out right. The smoke I inhaled has turned it to a raspy parody of itself.

Her brown eyes fix on mine for a brief moment before flitting up to focus on the wall beyond my head, expression registering a fleeting but intense struggle. I'm afraid speaking will cause her to shut down again, so I wait, and let her fight her battle alone.

"You have to understand, Cormac. You're my enemy. I don't share information with rebels." She unzips her combat suit enough to reach into her pocket, hand emerging with her fingers curled tightly around something. "I was focused on escaping back to base—" Her voice breaks off abruptly, and instead she just holds her hand out to me.

I reach out automatically, and she drops the object into my palm.

"I found it when you brought me to the facility out to the east." She won't look at me. "The one that wasn't there."

I ought to be furious—I ought to want to punish her somehow for deceiving me. But I'm holding proof I'm not insane, and I can't find the anger anywhere. It's an ident chip, a little like the kind the soldiers carry embedded in their gear. Proof, surely, that *something* was there at one point. One side is covered with foil circuitry, and I turn it over in my hands, taking in the bar code on the other side. I wish I had a scanner. "Is this military?"

She shakes her head. "Ours are newer. This one's old, maybe twenty years out of date."

"You're telling me I somehow stumbled across a twenty-year-old facility that vanished a few hours later?"

"I don't know." She shrugs, watching me. "But I will say that while the older models don't carry as much information, they're more easily encrypted. This one would require a very specific scanner, one we don't even carry anymore. There's no way to scan this and figure out whose it is."

"Why are you telling me this now?"

"Because this is what you've been looking for. Proof. And I've been hiding it from you."

I try to read her face, but she's watching the wall now and I can't meet her eyes to decipher her expression. "Jubilee—"

She interrupts me with a shake of her head. "I saw something there; a flash, a vision, like the memory of the facility that used to be there. I don't know how, if it's gone now, but I did."

Hardly able to believe what I'm hearing, I drop my eyes to the chip, turning it over and over in my hands like I might be able to divine a new clue from it, some explanation for what's going on or where to look next.

"Wait—stop!" Jubilee lurches from her chair, her fingers closing around my wrist. I freeze, but her eyes are on the chip. "Turn it over."

I do as she says, and her fingers guide me, turning my hand just so. I see a flash as the foil catches the light. She makes a small noise of shock and then leans down so she can bring her line of sight alongside mine.

For a moment I'm utterly distracted by her closeness, despite the soot and the smell of burned chemicals. Then she's angling the chip so I can see what she saw, and all thoughts of her face next to mine vanish.

There's a letter hidden in the circuitry, visible only when the light hits the reflective surfaces the right way. It's a *V*, and we both stare at it, trying to figure out what it means.

"VeriCorp?" I whisper. But the logo for VeriCorp is both a *V* and a *C*, and they're not a big enough corporation to have their own ident chip manufacturers.

Jubilee's breath catches, and she reaches out to take the chip from me. Before I can protest, she's twisting it in her fingers—turning it upside down. Abruptly, it stops being a *V*. There's not a soul in the galaxy who doesn't know that symbol. A lambda.

"LaRoux Industries."

I want to ask her what it means and whether the military knows something we don't about why LaRoux Industries, which has no terraforming stake here on Avon, would have constructed a secret base out in the middle of the swamps. But I can tell from her expression she's as confused as I am.

Before I can speak, the com-patch on the sleeve of her combat suit buzzes to life. "Security to Captain Chase," it hisses, Avon's interference rendering the voice unidentifiable.

Jubilee looks at me for a split second and then turns away, but not before I see the alarm in her gaze. She lifts a hand to the patch, activating it from her end. "Chase here," she replies, ducking her head a little to bring her voice closer to the receiver.

"Can you report to the security office, sir?" It's not an order, but a request; I can see her shoulders relax a little.

"I'm a little busy," she replies, tweaking the blinds over the window with two fingers so she can peer out at the base outside. "Is it more info on the bomber?"

"No rush, but we could use your eyes, since you were there. We've got the guy who abducted you from Molly's."

The words wash over me like fire, and I start coughing, my abused lungs refusing to cooperate. Jubilee whirls, her gaze landing on mine as though she half expects me to have vanished into military custody. She waits until I've got my cough under control before thumbing the com-patch again.

"Say again?" she says, her voice as cool as stone. "Some interference on my end."

"The kidnapper from the bar," comes the voice. "It took a lot of combing through security footage, but we've got some now that'll help us identify him."

Jubilee's confusion is draining away into dread. "And? Who is he?"

"Well, the footage is pretty grainy, there's a lot of static interference. We're trying to clean it up now."

"You stay on the bombing," Jubilee snaps. She swallows, and when she speaks again, her voice is calmer. "Whoever the guy in Molly's was, he's long gone by now. We need to know more about the attack on the base, and whether Davin Quinn was acting alone."

"Well, sir," the voice on the com-patch replies slowly, "I've got most of my people on the bombing, but for base security we'll need to know this guy's face so we can identify him if he tries again."

Jubilee's gaze sweeps across the room's other few occupants, uncon-scious, unresponsive. "Okay," she replies. "I'll come by later and see if I can help." She lets her arm fall back down to her side, eyes returning to meet mine as the com-patch goes silent.

All I can do is stare at her, the bottom falling out of my stomach. The only sounds are the gentle beeping of the monitors and the muffled sounds of the base outside—vehicle engines, snatches of conversa-tion, the whine of a shuttle landing in a launch bay on the other side of the base. It's impossible to forget where I am: in the middle of enemy territory.

With an effort, I wrench myself out of my exhausted stupor and shove the blankets aside. Then I'm trying to sit up, pushing through the dizzi-ness and the nausea. I've got to run.

"Hey—stop that!" Jubilee reaches out, grasping my shoulders and pushing me back down. Right now, she's a lot stronger than I am, and I've got no choice but to let her. "If they were on their way here to grab you, do you think I'd be sitting here looking at you? I'd be dragging your ass out the back door by now."

I can't answer, my throat catching and drawing up a racking cough.

Jubilee waits it out with her hands still on my shoulders, bracing me. When I'm finished, she pulls them back slowly. "We've got a little time. Your lungs won't take a long trek through the swamp."

I swallow, making sure my throat's clear before I try speaking this time. "How long do I have?"

"I don't know." Jubilee paces a few steps to the foot of the bed. "Yesterday it would've been top priority, but now they're a little distracted. You can thank your man Quinn for that. I need to think." She closes her eyes, lips pressed tightly together.

"They're going to figure out that you haven't told them everything."

Jubilee's jaw tightens, and she makes a slicing motion with her hand. "For now they believe Commander Towers that it was trauma, and that's why I couldn't remember your face despite talking to you for a good ten minutes before you dragged me out of there."

"Tell them you got hit in the head—tell them it's amnesia or something. Be careful. If I lose you—"

"I know." Her voice is clipped, bitter. She hates herself for being here. For helping me. "You lose me, you lose your direct line into the military's plans."

My brain can't get past the *if I lose you*. I want to correct her, but I haven't worked out yet what the real end of that sentence is.

She sucks in a bracing breath. "Listen. I'm going to get back out there, but if I'm not back by morning, you need to find a way out of here on your own. Steal a boat if you have to."

I can't read what's going on behind her calm expression. But an edge in her voice is ringing an alarm. "What do you mean, if you're not back?"

She frowns, but doesn't skip a beat. "They're probably going to put me on duty soon. If it's the dawn patrol, I won't make it back, and you'll have to get out on your own. What is it your people say? Clear skies."

Those words, coming from her, slice at my heart. She doesn't give me a chance to reply and stalks toward the door. She pauses, bracing one arm against the door frame.

"Why couldn't you have just stayed away?"

"We told you," says the girl's father, "we weren't interested."

"Noah," whispers the girl's mother, "look at their eyes."

"Last chance," says the man with the marble eyes. The girl is watching through the crack in the counter and sees him lift his tunic to reveal a gun tucked into his pants. "Hate to go back and tell everyone you're a Lambda family."

"We don't support either side," says her mother. "We want no part of this."

The girl moves until she can see her parents instead, standing together in the front hall of the shop. "Please," says her father. "We have a daughter."

The world slows to a crawl. The girl hears the telltale click of the pistol being cocked, and her training kicks in. She dashes from the space under the counter; she pulls out her Gleidel; she throws herself between the gunman and her parents; she takes out two of them before the lead gunman can aim her way. It only takes a few seconds before she's got them all on the floor, disarmed, harmless.

Except it didn't happen like that.

THIRTEEN

JUBILEE

THE BASE IS STILL IN CHAOS. THE AIR SMELLS OF SMOKE and acrid chemicals, and though all the civilian staff have been removed, it's busier than I've ever seen it. Everyone has a job—or if they don't, they're hurrying in search of one.

I only stop long enough to change my clothes. With Cormac's assurance that Davin Quinn has no connection to McBride, it's unlikely the bombing was a declaration of war. I don't need armor for what I'm about to do. I peel the suit off with difficulty; it's stiff and sour-smelling with smoke, and I kick it into a corner of my room to deal with later. Even after I've put on fresh fatigues and my faux leather flak jacket, I still smell like fire. I should take a shower—hell, I should take a nap. But Cormac probably doesn't have that kind of time.

Maybe I shouldn't have lied to him. Maybe I should've told him what I was planning. But I'm starting to know Romeo, and how he thinks, and I know enough to see he'd never let me go through with it. Maybe he's the smart one.

The security office isn't far from my quarters, but my legs are so tired that starting the walk there feels impossible. So I break into a jog, trying to inject a little life into my muscles through sheer force of habit. My lungs start burning almost immediately, and I can't help but think what Cormac's must feel like, having inhaled so much more smoke.

When I reach the security office, it's crawling with staff coming and going. Even though the bomber's been identified and confirmed dead in the blast, our people are busy finding out everything about him, about the bomb itself, about how he did it. My heart pounding with unfamiliar uncertainty, I nod to the private stationed outside and then slip in through the door.

Security was one of the first permanent buildings erected on the base. No flimsy composite walls, no prefab rooms. All thick, solid plastene and concrete. The main room is the surveillance room, and my eyes flick to the banks of screens connected to the various cameras around the base. The footage itself is stored and accessed on a server down the hallway, but I can see the feed for the camera monitoring Molly Malone's.

I half expected the bar to be a ghost town, but Molly's is doing a stiff business right now. Another form of treatment, for the soldiers whose wounds can't be healed at the hospital. I scan the picture, eyes narrowing. No wonder they felt confident they'd be able to clean up the footage enough to identify my abductor. The image is low res, but there's a clear view of the spot where I usually sit, the spot where Cormac first pulled his gun on me.

I swallow, pushing thoughts of him back down. I take a step backward, intending to head for the room where the footage is accessed, but I collide heavily with someone behind me.

"Captain."

My stomach drops. "Commander." I step away from her, stiffening to attention automatically.

"I thought I told you to take the next couple days off." For once, Commander Towers isn't perfectly put together. Her blond hair is still tied hastily at the nape of her neck, her uniform still disheveled. Her face reveals none of her exhaustion, though, a quality I envy. I must look like I haven't slept in a week.

"Can't do it, sir. Too much at stake." That, at least, is no lie.

She nods almost absently, as if she'd expected that response. She seems distracted, anyway, her eyes going to the screens I'd been studying. They oversee every inch of the base, from the barracks to the bar to the very room we're standing in now. I can see myself at an angle, standing a few feet from the commander.

"Will you come with me, Captain?" Her voice is oddly formal under the circumstances, making my heart skip a little.

Stop acting like a guilty child, I tell myself sternly. *They can't read your mind.* "Of course, sir."

Commander Towers leads the way down the hall, scanning the rooms as we pass for an empty one. Eventually, she just sticks her head through a doorway and barks, "You—out."

A pair of startled privates come spilling out, eyes flicking from the commander to me. I follow Towers inside, only to have my muscles seize up as I realize where we are.

The security footage repository.

Commander Towers heads for one of the desks, pulling out a chair and sliding it across the floor toward me. Then she retrieves one of her own and drops into it heavily. I sink down more gingerly, keeping an eye on the commander while trying not to be too obviously nervous. If they've finished cleaning up the footage, then I'm too late. They'll have a clear view of Cormac's face. They'll know he's right there in our infirmary, and I've been to visit him more than once. And Commander Towers will know I lied to her.

But she isn't looking at the screens or the servers. "Captain, I wanted to see how you were." Her eyes meet mine, and though there's sympathy in them, I can see something else behind it. A keen interest, sharp and perceptive. "You've had a lot to deal with over the past few days."

"I'm okay." *Another lie.* A few weeks ago I would've been comforted by my commander taking a personal interest in me. Now it feels like she can see through my treachery, straight to the truths I'm hiding.

Towers nods, watching me a moment longer before letting her eyes fall to the floor between us. "I'm sorry about Lieutenant Alexi. I know you two had a history."

I fight to keep my throat from closing. Giving my head a brisk shake to clear it of the image of Alexi's ruined face, I say shortly, "Thank you, sir."

"We're still trying to figure out how it happened. Why it happened. The bomber—this Quinn man—came out of nowhere. We've got footage of him walking toward the barracks, right up until the explosion happened, and there's nothing. Our best behavioral researchers are analyzing it and there's just nothing there—no hidden aggression, no signs of guilt, nothing to suggest he was about to murder dozens of people."

I grit my teeth. It matches what Cormac said, that Quinn couldn't have been the bomber, that he wasn't the type. And yet, he was found with the detonator in what was left of his hand. Could it be he didn't know what he was doing?

"This place," murmurs Commander Towers, her eyes shifting to gaze past me. "It's eating away at us, bit by bit."

"Someone has to be here, sir." But it's a pale comfort when even in the depths of the security office we can both still smell the burning plastene. It clings to our hair, our clothes, ingrained in the pores of our skin.

Towers's eyes snap back to mine, and she nods shortly. "Of course. Sometimes I just wonder how long it'll take for Avon to consume us all."

It's unlike her to be so pensive. It's one of the things I like about the commander, that she and I are both outward people, preferring action to introspection, momentum to idle consideration. And yet here she is, her shoulders sagging a little, her eyes seeking mine as though I have answers for her.

But I've got nothing. For a wild instant, the truth bubbles up inside me, begging to be let out. I press my lips together tightly.

Commander Towers sighs, straightening. "Chase, I wanted to ask you about what you said during your debriefing after your capture and subsequent escape."

I try not to stiffen noticeably. "Sir?"

"You mentioned that the rebel thought we had some kind of base or facility out to the east."

I lean forward a little, unable to conceal the sudden spark of excitement leaping inside my rib cage. She knows something. "Yes, sir."

She leans forward a little too, mirroring my body language, picking up on all my cues. She's far more skilled than I am at interrogation and manipulation. I have to watch my step. I let my hands dangle where my elbows are resting on my knees. Casual. Easy.

"I've been wondering why he'd think that," she continues. "It seems an odd thing to believe. The locals know the terrain here so well."

I hesitate. She'll see it, know it's uncharacteristic of me, know I'm hiding the truth. But there's too much to consider. On the one hand, Towers could be an ally. I'm only a captain—but she's the commander of an entire outpost here on Avon, and if she's alerted to the possibility of a LaRoux Industries facility out there below the radar, she could be the key to finding out more.

But what if she's in on whatever strange conspiracy is unfolding out in the fens? Surely the person in charge of the base would have to be a part of the con?

I clear my throat. "That's what he said." I have to tread carefully, watching her face for any reaction, however small, that might tell of what she knows. "Sounded crazy to me too, but I went along with it while I waited for my chance."

Commander Towers doesn't react, listening to me with what seems to be polite interest and no more. Still, there's the faintest of twitches along her jaw, and my eyes seize on it.

"I'm sure there was nothing in it," I say dismissively, leaning back in my chair again. "Not unlike the fairy tales they tell to keep themselves company in the evenings. Stories about how they keep moving it and it's never in the same place twice, that sort of thing."

Towers nods. "Anything else?"

I shake my head. "Only rumors."

The commander straightens, running a hand over her hair and then getting to her feet. "Thank you, Captain."

I scan her face, looking for something, anything, that will explain her sudden interest and her just as sudden dismissal. There's little to read there—the men call me Stone-faced Chase, but I've got nothing on Towers when it comes to playing our cards close to our chests. But her gaze moves too quickly, lips thin, shoulders rounded more than usual. She's on alert, edgy. And I don't think it's solely from the bombing.

"Of course, sir. I don't think it's anything to worry about, though. Just stories."

She nods, lips curving in the barest hint of a smile. "Understood, Captain. Carry on—I'll be in touch."

I can't explain why, but I have the strongest sense she's not involved. That she's every bit as driven as I am to find out what's happening out there. Her movements are quick, jerky, anxious. She wants to be out of here as badly as I want her to go. I haven't forgotten why I'm really here.

For half an instant, I want to blurt the truth. But to do so would reveal my part in all of this; that I could have captured a key player from the Fianna and didn't, that I'd let him escape from me not once now, but twice. It would reveal that I'd betrayed my purpose here.

Most of all, it would betray Cormac.

And so I bite down hard on my lip and get to my feet, flashing a salute at Commander Towers as she turns and strides from the room. I stand there, gathering my wits, and then close the door lightly behind her.

By clearing the room of the techs, she's unwittingly given me my opportunity.

With one foot I nudge a desk chair over so that the door, should any-one open it, will hit the chair with a clatter. A locked door would scream guilt, but the chair might distract anyone entering long enough for me to distance myself from the consoles and hide what I'm doing.

Drawing in a deep breath, I drop into another chair and start hunting for the files I need.

It takes me several long moments to navigate to the places where the surveillance footage is stored, but that's not the hard part. Deleting those files is the work of a few seconds. The real challenge is locating the places where the various files are backed up.

My fingers know the way, my brain only half-focused on what I'm doing. One of the men I trained with taught me how to do this, and he learned it from a kid who did this for a living. My old captain, when I was a corporal, let us learn on the sly. You never pass up anything that can be used as a weapon, he said, any way of fighting that doesn't involve blood-shed. I chafed at the instruction at the time—why would I ever need to learn how to hack into secure files?—but now, I mouth silent gratitude for my old captain and his foresight.

I try to focus. I can't stop to think about what I'm doing, because it betrays every oath I've ever taken, every order I've ever received. It betrays everything I believe in. It's a violation deep enough to make my soul, whatever shreds of it are left, ache. I'm helping a rebel. A criminal. A person whose friend just killed over thirty people, including someone I loved like a brother.

My eyes blur with exhaustion, and I have to pause to wipe my sleeve across my face. It leaves behind a darker patch of sweat and grime on the fabric. Now and then footsteps approach the door, but they always continue on past, striding away in time to the pounding of my heart. Still, at any moment someone might pop their head in.

There—finally. The fourth and final backup. The military always does things in fours—three being the natural number, four to be safe. The system spends a long breath-stealing instant thinking about my deletion command—and then the file vanishes. No fanfare, no sign it was ever there. No trace of the treason I've just committed.

I quickly close down the computer, taking care to erase any record I was ever poking around in there. The monitor closed, the chair shoved back where it belongs, I slip out into the corridor and let the room close behind me.

Mind blank, ears roaring, I float down the hallway toward the exit, limbs starting to shake. I swallow hard, fighting nausea. I need to get back to my quarters. Have a shower, lie down for a few minutes. Let myself think, breathe. Find a way to get Cormac out, now that we have some time to work with.

The corridor opens up into the main room, where the techs from the surveillance repository have joined the officers currently on duty. They're all crowded around one of the monitors, which is no longer split to show the live feeds from the base. Instead it's playing the same three or four seconds of footage over and over in a loop.

I take a few steps closer, peering silently past their heads—and my heart stops. It's the footage I just painstakingly erased. One of the techs must have had it on a local drive so they could keep working while evicted from the repository.

Because not only is it the footage—they've finished cleaning it up and enhancing it. The clip playing over and over again shows him clearly: the handsome chin, the thick brows, the arrogant smile.

I back up silently, pushing down the impulse to panic. None of the techs notice I'm there, and I slip out into the night. I keep my head down, forcing myself to walk normally, return the occasional nod or salute aimed in my direction as I pass other, equally exhausted officers going about their duties.

The image is limited to the security office. It'll take them time— hours, probably—to run it through all the necessary levels before it's made public. My mind turns over and over, searching for a way to get

Cormac out before that happens. No time to think of the implications now. I have to get him out first, and think later about what that means for me.

And then, abruptly, the PA monitors crackle to life all over the base. White screens pop up on every building corner, shedding an additional layer of light across the paths and intersections. A voice booms into the night, deafening me. I look up—and there's Cormac's face, plastered across every screen on the base. There's one in Molly's, one in every barracks. There's one in every office and docking bay.

There's one in the hospital.

I abandon pretense and break into a jog. Who's going to stop me and ask where I'm going? I'm Captain Chase. I belong here.

I force open the back entrance to the hospital, startling an orderly into dropping a tray of food all over the floor. I mumble an apology and sweep up the hall, aiming for Cormac's room. I pause on the way by the laundry, picking up a set of scrubs that looks about his size. It's the oldest deception in the book, but I've got nothing else, and no time to work out a better plan.

When I burst into Cormac's room, my eyes fall first on the HV mounted in the corner. There's Cormac's face, smiling out at me, hair tumbling just so into his eyes. The second thing I see is Cormac's bed, the sheets rumpled and half tugged away, a few pinpricks of blood marring the sheets where the IV needle rests, as though it was torn from his skin. The oxygen mask is on the floor, and the monitors are all flatlining, electrodes scattered across the bed.

I brace myself against the door frame, dizziness sweeping over me with all the force of a tidal wave, my ears ringing as my knees threaten to give.

The bed is empty.

Most of the other soldiers are unconscious, but one lifts her head, groggy with pain medication and mumbling something at me that I can't hear through my panic. She must have seen him run; she's trying, through her haze, to tell me which way the fugitive went.

I stumble out of the room and break into a run toward the back exit. Cormac's injured, and he won't make it off the base before somebody spots him, now that they know what they're looking for. And even if he does, he'll never get back to the rebel hideout without a boat. It would take him hours, and in his condition he's as likely to drown as he is to reach his people. Though an exhausted corner of my mind shrinks from the idea of heading back out into that swamp, the rest of me doesn't hesitate.

I only get a few steps outside the hospital when my mouth abruptly floods with the taste of copper, the dizziness intensifying. My legs quiver the way they did on that marshy island, before I saw the ghost of Cormac's hidden facility. I blink, hard, as the sibilant sound of whispering surges over the background noises of the base. Separate voices—two, maybe three—but I can't tell what they're saying.

Have to make it to a boat. I grit my teeth, pointing my boots toward the docks. All I know, all I can think of, is that I have to find Cormac.

They're always together, the ghost and the green-eyed boy. They're in her mother's shop, they're at her father's garage. They're on Paradisa. They're in the outpost on Patron. He's one of the soldiers who died in the first few weeks after she transferred to Avon. His face is on every wanted poster on the base.

The ghost leads her down the deserted streets of November, and at the end of the swath of destruction is the green-eyed boy, with a box of matches and a charming smile.

"Don't follow me," says the boy, reaching out to touch her cheek. "Don't follow me this time."

FOURTEEN

FLYNN

THE MUD GRABS AT ME TO DRAG ME DOWN. MY LUNGS BURN,
pain knifing down my side with every breath as I force myself to scramble through the swamp. This trek is bad enough on foot at full strength, but I feel like I've been hit by a transport. One hour stretches into two, into three, and then I stop counting.

If I could've waited, I would have. But I can still see the footage from the bar, the loop playing over and over on the insides of my eyelids whenever I let them close: I see myself turn in toward Jubilee, smiling, starting to speak, and then it jumps back to the beginning. If I could've stolen a boat, I would have done that too. But the docks were crawling with patrols, and while my stolen uniform might have gotten me by, the bar footage was playing on the side of the docking shed.

I tried to make this journey before, on my own, just once. Then, I didn't have smoke in my lungs; but I was also only eight years old, fleeing the transports waiting to take me to an off-world orphanage. And I was found only a few kilometers outside of town by Fianna patrols looking for me.

This time I have no one to help me get home. I shove past a bank of reeds, my breath rasping, ears straining for any sound behind me. I can't afford to rest for more than a few seconds. My head spins, and for once I can't tell if the lights sparking in front of my eyes are wisps or my own hazy eyesight.

I push on through waist-high muck and sluggish black water. I wade and swim and when I can't stand I crawl, until I'm covered with mud then washed clean again.

My numb body knows where home is, and I drag myself toward it. The trodairí have footage of my face. If they catch me—if they recognize my face and scan my genetag—they'll use me to find the Fianna, and blame them for the bombing and for every other ill that ever graced Avon. And they won't rest until my people are dead.

It's another hour and a half of struggling through the swamp before the black silhouette of the cave complex looms up in the distance. It takes me a long time to register what I'm seeing. *Home.*

By now each movement is taking careful effort. I think to myself, *I'm going to reach out and take those reeds and pull myself forward,* and then, *I'm going to push with my foot.* My hands are a clammy white, and I'm soaked to the skin, hair plastered against my forehead.

I've never tried to climb up the side of the harbor from the water, only from a currach, and it takes long, gasping, shaking minutes before I manage the scramble. Uneasiness tickles at the back of my mind, and it takes me a moment to realize what's bothering me: there's a military launch vessel floating abandoned a few meters from the dock. A flak jacket rests on the bench; this wasn't stolen and brought here by one of the Fianna.

I stumble down the hallway, ricocheting off the uneven stone walls and trailing mud and water in my wake. No one has changed the lanterns, and the dark, silent hallways are streaked with something wet. There's a basket lying in the middle of the hallway, hard bread rolls scattered everywhere.

The main cavern is silent. The lights are high here, and suddenly the stains on the floor are a garish red; my gaze follows a smear to a bundle of rags dumped on the floor.

The rags have hands, a head, eyes staring at me—it's a body.

The world snaps into focus. The floor's slick with blood, and there are bodies—four, six, eight—sprawled near the walls. Some seem to have been moved, leaving bright trails of blood on the floor. Their wounds and clothes are scorched, and the air smells of burning flesh; our guns couldn't do this. This was the work of military weaponry.

I stagger backward and hit the wall, grabbing at it to steady myself as the world whirls. I can't drag my gaze away from them, the wounds, the streams of blood. The body closest to me—it's Mike Doyle, who helped me pull McBride off Jubilee, who had the best singing voice in the Fianna, and the loudest laugh. Then I see it, the way he's curled around the tiny body beneath him. I see a little hand under his, and as I blink, a small face comes into focus. It's Sean's nephew, Fergal.

I stagger toward them and drop to my knees, the pain of the impact shooting up through my hips to my back. "Fergal, please." My voice is hoarse and trembling as I reach for his small hand. "Talk to me. Please."

But I know as I touch his face, painting his pale skin with my bloody fingertips, that Mike, still curled over him, couldn't save him. Fergal's eyes are blank, unblinking.

"No." The moan tears out of my throat, horror sweeping through me as my stomach convulses. I push myself away from Mike and Fergal before I throw up, hands pressed white-knuckled against the stone floor. Gulping for air, I lift my head.

And that's when I see Jubilee.

She's on her knees toward the back of the room, as still as the dead bodies around her. She's staring straight ahead, one hand resting against the floor, the other holding her gun, dangling loosely at her side. The grip's sticky with blood, hers or theirs. Her gaze is vacant. If she wasn't upright, I'd think she was one of the dead.

Please. Please. The word beats at my consciousness in time with my heart, but I don't even know what I'm asking for. To wake up from this nightmare. To look again and see it isn't her. To turn around and see Fergal stand up and run into my arms.

I drag myself away from Fergal, my eyes blurring as I fix them on the trodaire, her bloody clothes, the gun in her hand. My gaze wants to slide away, refusing to see any of it, and I fall to my hands and knees in front of her.

"What have you done?" Grief wrenches the words from somewhere deep inside me, somewhere guttural and raw. "I trusted you. *I trusted you.*"

Her eyes are blank, the pupils dilated so far they look black. This is their madness, their Fury. She stares at me, frozen like a hunted creature; the soul is gone from her eyes, and I don't think she sees me.

"Say something!" My bloodied hand grabs her unresisting shoulder, shaking her until she moans, her dilated pupils unseeing and uncaring. My eyes sweep the cavern once more, still pleading for things to be different, searching for a way out—and they fall on the gun. In this moment, all I want is revenge. Grief and fury warring inside me, I grab it from her unresisting hand, my skin recoiling from its sticky grip, and swing the weapon around to point at the unresponsive soldier.

Then her eyes meet mine, and finally, through the shock, through the Fury, she recognizes me. Her eyes scan the cavern, falling on the bodies and the trails of blood. Horror sweeps across her features, as raw and real as pain, before she slumps, catching herself on her palms. Only then does she look down and see the blood coating her hands, gluing them to the cavern floor. Lifting her eyes to mine, she sees the gun pointed at her, its barrel shaking and wavering in my hand. I see it in her eyes, the understanding creeping through her, shattering us both.

The trodaire lifts a trembling hand toward the gun; my mind screams at my unresponsive muscles to pull away before she can disarm me and add my body to those littering the room. But her fingers curl around the barrel, not the grip. She pulls the weapon closer, until the barrel presses against her forehead.

She closes her eyes, holding the gun steady for me—but not before I see her in there, as broken and shattered as I am, begging for a way out. For *any* way out.

I can't pull the trigger.

Then pounding footsteps break the silence, and I spin around to face the tunnel. Turlough Doyle is the first into the cavern, and he stops two steps in, so the next man through—Sean—collides with him. McBride's the last one to appear.

For an instant the five of us are frozen in place. Turlough shatters the stillness with a shout, stumbling forward to drop to his knees beside Mike's body, grabbing his husband's shoulder and turning him over. He gives a broken moan, curling over Mike to bury his face against his shirt.

Then Sean sees Fergal. My cousin goes perfectly still, suddenly carved from stone. Even in the dim light of the cavern, I can see it when the blood drains from his face.

When McBride sees Jubilee, he tenses. Turlough's sobs almost cover the noise of McBride pulling his Gleidel out of its holster. "Move away, Cormac," he says, his voice low and level, absolutely calm. His face is empty and cold, as though the emotions that ought to be there have fled from the sight in front of him.

If I can't pull the trigger, McBride certainly can. I want to drop Jubilee's gun and push past McBride to get to Sean, but my body's shaking, won't listen to my orders.

McBride moves forward and shoves me aside as though I weigh nothing at all. I hit the floor hard, the jolt of pain coursing through the same path as my grief, eclipsing it for a fraction of a second. McBride stops in front of Jubilee, lifting his Gleidel, mouth curving to a slow, faint smile that only I can see. "Captain Chase," he murmurs, very soft. Just for us. Angling his gun, ready to put a shot straight between her eyes; she doesn't move. "Here's to peace on Avon."

His finger shifts on the trigger, and I surge to my feet, lunging at McBride and colliding with him; his shot goes wide, the scream of the Gleidel shattering my ears.

"Lower your weapon," I gasp before he can try again. My voice sounds different, my throat burning for each word. "There's something happening that's bigger than this—we need her."

Recovering his balance, McBride's starting to lose his veneer of calm. "Get away from her before I go right through you." He keeps the barrel of his Gleidel pointing square at my chest, his other hand coming up to steady it.

Behind me, Jubilee stirs, her skin scraping against the stone. "Just let him have me," she whispers, the sound sharp as shattered glass.

"No." It's like someone else is speaking. Someone above this hatred, this grief; someone who doesn't care that the sound of Jubilee's voice makes me sick, that her betrayal has broken something beyond repair. Someone who cares only that I need her to save my planet.

Sean gropes for his own gun, hands shaking violently as he holds it at his side, uncertain. "Flynn," he calls, hoarse. Straight from his lips to my heart. "Don't do this."

"What did she offer you?" McBride demands, voice thick with disdain. "You've always been weak, Cormac, but even I thought you were better than this. To give up your family for a taste of a trodaire."

I still can't take my eyes off of Sean. His chest is heaving, the gun trembling wildly now.

Hands shaking, I lift Jubilee's gun, flicking off the safety. The soft whine of the battery powering up fills the cave. For a moment, everything is still. Turlough, hunched over Mike's body. Sean, standing still, his eyes on my face. Jubilee, eyes closed, waiting for an end. For an endless instant, there's only the choice I've just made.

Then it's over. "Traitor," McBride whispers as I aim it at him, and the word goes through me like a knife.

I look past McBride, my eyes falling instead on Sean, still standing with his gun at his side. "This won't bring Fergal back. This wasn't her, it was the Fury. It's real. You've trusted me all our lives. Trust me now."

The world narrows, and all I can see is my cousin's face, and all the years behind it, the cocky smiles, the shared grief, the quiet moments without any words. He'll see. He'll recognize the truth, that the Fury's real; that our planet is diseased and the madness could come for any of us now, that Jubilee is our only hope to find answers. He knows me. He *knows* me.

Then Sean lifts his gun—and aims it at me. His red-rimmed eyes meet mine for half a second before my cousin pulls the trigger.

The shot goes wide, screaming through the cavern and breaking the spell.

McBride roars and steps forward, Gleidel trained on Jubilee once more. I dive for her, grabbing her arm and dragging her to her feet, my body between her and McBride. The laser shrieks. I keep my iron grip on Jubilee's hand and lunge for the passageway behind us.

My feet know the way, taking over from eyes blinded by images. Fergal's behind me, so unfamiliar in his stillness, and Turlough's still back there with Mike, and Sean, my Sean, is pointing a gun at my face. If I let go of Jubilee she'll fall. I wrap my arm around her, ignore her cry of pain when my hand squeezes the wound where my bullet grazed her side, and pull her on into the dark.

It comes in fragments. Her mother's scream. The smell of something burning. The counter vibrating as something hits the floor, hard. The sharp, shattering crack of gunshots. Someone's voice, saying, "That'll be a bitch to clean up." A little girl screaming from far away. The taste of metal.

She was supposed to be brave. But the girl was only eight years old, and she wasn't brave, and when the operatives from the orphanage came to get her, no one had bothered yet to clean the blood from her hands.

FIFTEEN

JUBILEE

FLYNN'S GRIP ON MY WRIST IS ICE−COLD AND UNYIELDING. I try to focus, to understand where we are, what's happening—my mind automatically tries to run through the checklist that's been drilled into me since basic training. Taking stock of the situation, location, hostiles, injuries, obstacles . . . It all blurs together, my eyes streaming and my breath gasping in and out of my lungs. He breaks off from the corridor and pulls me through a narrow fissure in the rock, the stone scraping my chin, my arms.

My thoughts keep reaching for images where there are none; I see the hospital bed where I left Flynn, I see myself deciding to take a patrol boat to look for him. But the only thing beyond that is blood; blood burning in my pores, metallic on my tongue, singing through my own veins. When I close my eyes I see the cavern, painted with blood, more than I've seen in a lifetime of fighting. Blood like art, declaring victory over the Fianna, the hardened, monstrous rebels too young or too crippled to fight back. Blood glues our hands together, Flynn's and mine.

All I can see is that child, half curled under another rebel who must have been trying to shield it. I don't know if it was a boy or a girl. I don't know—I don't know.

My body sags with the weight of the empty holster at my hip, the weight of what I've done. My knees give way and I go down, dragging at Flynn's hand. He's forced to halt, nearly jerking my arm out of its socket trying to get me back on my feet.

"Stop," I gasp, choking on the smell of blood on my skin. Now I understand that metallic taste, the shaking in my limbs; now I know what the Fury tastes like. *Blood.* "Stop—Flynn, please. Let them take me."

"Like hell," he says through gritted teeth. His face is unreadable.

He won't listen to me. Right now I don't have the strength to argue with him. He's made his choice, and if I keep slowing him down he's going to die for it.

I drag myself to my feet, leaning on him heavily. He grunts with effort, or pain, or acknowledgment, and we set off down the corridor once more.

The shakes hit me like a mag-lev train, ten times worse than on the island Flynn showed me to the east. Worse than after my first combat mission. Because this is nothing like that. No part of my training told me how to comprehend the massacre of unarmed innocents. Of children. My mind is tight and cold, like Flynn's hand around my wrist, and I can't break out through the narrow bands of panic and horror. Everywhere I look I see blood, smell blood. On my skin, my clothes, in my hair. I fight down my nausea, simply because I can't stop, not while we're running for Flynn's life from people who think he's turned on them.

Abruptly I see the end looming, the point at which I can't function—exhaustion, shock, guilt, and grief tangled together. It's like a rapidly approaching cliff, and I know that if Flynn pulls me off the edge I might never find my feet again.

I wish he'd just let them have me, and go. Anything would be easier than this.

And then he does pull me forward, wrapping his arm around my waist and leaping from a ledge. For a wild, confused moment we're falling—and then we hit frigid water. It closes over my head, and my mind goes numb.

In her dream she's choking, gasping for air where there is none, the vacuum of space closing around her. There are no stars, because there are never any stars here, only a thick darkness that rushes down her throat and into her heart. She dreams of drowning.

SIXTEEN

FLYNN

I KEEP AN ARM AROUND HER, STRUGGLING THROUGH MUD AND water as I drag her forward. Dimly, I hear McBride shouting some distance back, trying to find someone who can fit through the same crack I pulled Jubilee into. Silent but for soft splashes, we disappear into the dark.

I can almost feel Orla with me as I find my way to our rock. She had me rehearse the route so many times when I was a child, so I could get here with my eyes closed if there was ever a raid. The rock is about six feet long and only a couple of feet above the water. Not even Sean knows this secret.

I pull Jubilee closer in the water, inspecting her face. There's still more shock than sense there; bracing myself, trying not to recoil, I cup a hand under Jubilee's chin to turn her face toward me. I keep my other arm wrapped tightly around her, afraid she'll sink beneath the water if I let go. Her eyes open when I squeeze her.

"Jubilee, are you listening to me?"

She doesn't answer, her eyes darting around in the darkness, panic making her tremble in my arms.

"Soldier!" I bark, keeping my voice as quiet but tense as I can.

Her eyes widen, and I watch as the soldier takes over, her chin lifting a little.

"This rock here is hollow inside. I can pull you, but when we go under you have to hold your breath. Understand?"

She nods again, lifting one hand to rest it against the rock for balance and leaving a red smear behind it. The water hasn't been enough to wash the blood away.

I suck in a lungful of air, my throat threatening to close or catch in a coughing fit again. The water closes over my head, and I keep hold of Jubilee's wrist as I guide her in with me. The water carries the distant shouts of my people directly to my ears until we surface, choking, inside my tiny shelter. There's only a small space that's water; the rest is the natural rock and the ledge Orla built for me when I was Fergal's age.

I push Jubilee's arms against the rock until she instinctively grabs at it, leaving me free to reach up and fumble in the dark. The netting with emergency supplies is still there, and my heart slows a little in relief. I grab the tiny cylinder of the flashlight dangling from it and turn it on; the beam bounces around the two of us as I help her scramble up onto the little ledge and then crawl up after her. We huddle there in a space meant for a child, her breath coming in sobs.

I grit my teeth hard. I have to think of a plan, but my misery keeps tugging me back toward Sean. I need to be there for him as he grieves. I want to tell him I'm sorry I didn't get there in time, that I couldn't save Fergal. Instead, I cower here as Jubilee's tension starts to ease a fraction, and I angle the flashlight to see part of her face. Her lips are parted, eyes staring, water dripping unheeded from her nose and her chin. I have to get her moving. I have to put enough life back into her to get us both out of here. Swallowing my grief and my revulsion, I lift my hand to brush her wet hair back from her face.

She jerks away from my touch. "Please, Flynn, don't." She looks half her age, except for the bloodstains on her face. If any of my heart was left untouched, it would break right now—that this is the time she chooses to finally use my name. When I can barely stand to look at her.

The soldier I've come to know never would have done this, and yet her hands are smearing my family's blood on the stone. "Don't check out," I tell her. "You have to stay with me. I can't drag you to safety or they'll find us both."

"You should have let him have me." Her voice is empty and aching.

"It wasn't you." I have to force the words out. "It was the Fury." *It wasn't her.* My own thoughts repeat it, over and over, unwilling to face what I've seen. Wanting it to somehow reduce my pain.

"I don't remember anything." Her voice breaks, and as she curls in on herself she's still shaking, but this is different. It's not the trembling that came with the dilated eyes or the jerky movements. This is shock, and my arms move haltingly to wrap around her and keep her from sliding back into the water. Suddenly I'm not holding Captain Lee Chase, but a terrified girl who wants to press her way into the stone around us and stay there forever. "I killed your people. You should—you should kill me yourself, why aren't you?"

"Because it wasn't you." I'm repeating the words in her ear, desperately trying to make it true for both of us.

"You can't know that!" Her whisper is fierce. "Stop it, Flynn, you can't—just stop it." Her fingers wind into my shirt, at first to push me away, but her resistance crumbles, and she lets me pull her in close until she's clinging to me, shoulders shaking as she weeps against my chest.

Hot tears track down my cheeks too, and my throat closes as I swallow hard, fighting for composure. I wish that for one moment I could forget what's happened and hold her and let the contact between us heal us both. But I can't. Even her scent has changed; her hair smells like gunmetal.

My heart wants me to wrap my arms around her. My heart wants her to suffer for what she's done.

Her shivering worsens, and as if in answer, my body starts to shake as well. I reach up and feel around in the netting until my fingers close over a warming pouch; I activate the seal, then press it between our bodies to slowly heat up.

Now and then the murmur of a distant voice carries through the water and stone to our ears. It's not until there's been silence for some time that Jubilee speaks.

"What do we do now?" It's barely a whisper.

I want to have an answer. My heart slams against my ribs, tempting me to panic, to give in to grief and fear and exhaustion. Now that I'm still, my abused lungs ache. "I don't know."

"The LaRoux Industries chip," she says, eyes staring in the dark.

"When I picked it up on that island, it was the same feeling—the same taste in my mouth—"

The same unseeing, dilated pupils I saw in the cavern. I squeeze her before she can start shaking again, trying to keep fear from joining my grief in overwhelming me. I cannot think, now, about the possibility that a corporation is responsible for the madness plaguing my home.

"I have to get to the base," Jubilee says with a sudden, hollow urgency, as though reciting steps in a manual. "I have to report. . . . I have to tell them."

My head jerks up. "Jubilee, you can't. They ship soldiers off Avon when—" *When they turn into murderers.* My lips refuse to make the words real.

She blinks at me, haunted. "It's protocol. It's all I know."

"Listen to me." I grab at her shoulder, gripping it tight, until her eyes focus once more on mine. "You're all I have now. You're the only one who can help me stop whatever's happening to my home. I can't be on the base, looking for answers, but *you can.*"

"I can't—oh, God." Her eyes glaze, and I know she's not seeing me anymore. She sees blood, and bodies, and the barrel of a gun pointed between her eyes. "I can't."

"You can," I snap, my voice quiet and fierce.

"How can you know that?"

"Because you're Jubilee Chase," I murmur. "Not whatever the darkness makes you."

The gentle swaying of the dangling flashlight makes the hollows of her features shift and change, making it impossible to read her face until she looks up at me again. She gives a shudder, then nods. My breath comes a little easier, seeing finally a flicker of the girl I know in there, a flicker of the soldier I've put all my hopes on.

"Take me back," she whispers.

We switch off the flashlight and slip into the frigid water once more, leaving my sister's hiding place cold and empty behind us.

The boy who's not supposed to be in her dreams is lying next to her on the hood of a hovercar on the outskirts of town, a blanket binding them together. The boy has pink hair this time, though when she runs her fingers through it, it changes in response to her touch, growing longer, falling in gentle curls over his temples.

They're looking up at the sky.

"That one we'll call the huntress," says the boy, laughter behind his voice. "See, there's her gun, and that nebula is her hair, and this cluster is that line she gets between her eyes when she's yelling at me."

"Shut up, I do not."

"Your turn."

The girl watches the sky, but it's empty. The only constellations on Avon are the ones they imagine.

"I can't," she whispers, shutting her eyes. "I'm bad at this game." She knows what happens next in this dream. He'll kiss her and they'll lie there together, and when they sneak back onto the base she'll go back to work, and be unchanged, except perhaps a little colder without the blanket.

But this time the green-eyed boy takes her hand, and when she opens her eyes, the sky is full of stars.

SEVENTEEN

JUBILEE

THE UNDERGROUND HARBOR IS TEEMING WITH REBELS. They're like ants swarming around a nest, like repair drones clustering around a damaged Firebird. Some of them are marked with red and rusty brown, but they don't move like they're injured. There are too many people wearing their loved ones' blood.

"McBride doesn't have them organized yet." Flynn speaks in my ear, grounding me before images of the massacre can cripple me again. "We might be able to use that confusion."

Even through a whisper, I can hear his heartbreak. He should be with his people. He should be helping them figure out what to do. And he can't, because he's the one they're after. Because of me.

I search the dark waters of the harbor until I spot what I'm looking for, floating a few yards from the near bank.

"The boat I came in," I whisper back, pointing to where it sits, out of reach of the lights in the harbor.

A muscle stands out along his jaw. He doesn't look at me, or at the boats. His eyes are on his people, aching for them. But then he nods, gaze snapping back toward the clusters of little boats moored along the docks.

We wade through the water with painstaking slowness to avoid making telltale ripples, slower still as the water level rises to our knees, our hips, our waists. My training takes over, forcing exhausted muscles to function long enough for me to keep each movement careful and controlled.

Stealth, I can do. It's a task to focus on, something to keep my mind away from—from everything else.

We'd be spotted if we climbed in now, so when we reach the boat, we each take one side of it and start walking it toward the gaping mouth of the harbor. I'm about to let my breath out in relief when a light swings across the surface of the water and blinds me.

Flynn gasps a warning in Irish at the same time my muscles tense, reacting to the threat before my mind has time to process it. A shout echoes through the cavern, and the swarms of people head our way.

For an instant, we move as one. I grab on to the gunwale, steadying the boat as Flynn hauls himself up into it—then, leaning his weight to the side, he reaches for my hand and drags me up after him. He's fumbling with the motor. With the searchlight blinding me, our pursuers are little more than blurry shapes in my streaming eyes. Flynn jerks the ignition cable once, twice. The motor sputters to life, and he guns it too fast, briefly sending the nose of the boat skyward. A bullet punches through the gunwale, and shouts echo in the cavern. We both throw ourselves down into the bottom of the boat. Instinct takes over, and I lunge for him—for the gun he took from me.

I look up and see a fleeting ribbon of fear cross Flynn's features. Fear—of *me*. He says nothing, not even silently, not even a mute appeal. But with that same flash of connection that got us working together to climb into the boat, I know what he's seeing as he looks at me, still bloody, holding the weapon that killed half a dozen of his people. I feel sick, violated down to my bones by what I've done; I'd give anything, in this moment, for him to not look at me like that.

We speed toward the exit, but the rebels have found boats themselves, and they're in pursuit. Too close for us to lose them in the swamp beyond the harbor. Close enough to shoot us—and close enough to be shot at.

Flynn jerks his eyes away from me as I lift my head, looking for a clear shot. I'm not killing any more people today, not when I'm me, myself. Not even if they're shooting at me first. But they've got the searchlights pointed at us, and I can't see.

My eyes lift, seeking a break from the blinding white light in front of me, and I see the ceiling of the harbor. Rough stone, naturally striated and dripping with condensation. The Gleidel won't touch the stone, but it'll vaporize the water seeping through the cracks. I lift my gun and brace myself against the bench so I can shoot over Flynn's head, placing myself in clear view of those firing at us. Flynn shouts at me, but I can't hear him as my world narrows, focusing on my target.

The Gleidel leaps in my hands and I throw myself down again before the rebels can get me in their sights. Its scream echoes back at me from the cavern, followed by the crack of stone split by steam, and then the roar of boulders striking the water. Then the frantic revving of motors thrown into reverse, as the rebels zigzag wildly in an effort to avoid the stones now jutting out of the shallow water at the mouth of the harbor.

I lever myself up again in time to see the mouth of the harbor retreating away from us, half lost in the spray of our wake, and the cluster of boats attempting to navigate through the new maze of boulders trapping them.

I glance down, and Flynn's eyes flick up from mapping our route to meet mine for a split second. We're out.

We don't speak. There's nothing to say anymore, even if we had the strength to shout over the roar of the motor. I look back at him once and see a jumble of white face, red-rimmed eyes, tears mingling with the spray from our bow wave—and look away with a jerk. I don't try to look at him again.

The sky's just beginning to shift from ink to charcoal by the time the distant lights of the base rise, mirage-like, from the horizon. Flynn shifts the motor down, its roar muted to a purr. We weave our way through the corridors of water until the bow of the boat slides up onto mud with a sickening lurch. The motor cuts out.

The silence rings in my ears, like afterimages hovering after being dropped into sudden darkness. There are no frogs, no insects on Avon, nothing to color the quiet. I stare at the lights of the far-off base until my vision blurs.

"Where will you go?" I ask in a whisper that splits the silence.

"I don't know." His voice is rough. From disuse. From cold. From grief. I can't tell which. "I'll find somewhere."

I reach for my jacket, abandoned in the bottom of the boat, and press it into his hands. He'll need it more than me, out here with no shelter and no heat. "Molly, the barman. He can get a message to me if you—" My voice tangles and sticks in my throat. *If you need me.*

He nods, but I'm not sure he really heard me. I can feel shock trying to grab hold of me again, cold fingers sliding up my spine and seizing my muscles. My training didn't prepare me for this. Nothing prepared me for this.

If it were only me, I could just lie here until the boat rotted through and sank and the muck claimed my bones. But I can't. I swallow hard, pushing it away with every ounce of strength I have left. Flynn was right—I'm the only one who can get onto our base and try to find out more about what's happening to Avon.

I force my stiff muscles to move and carry me over the edge of the boat, to land in hip-deep water. I grab the gunwale to steady myself as my knees threaten to buckle in the cold.

"Flynn." It ought to feel strange to say his name. I avoided it for so long, striving to keep a distance between us. But instead I find I'm absorbed by the way it affects him. He's less guarded, though the sadness in his eyes doesn't recede; he looks back at me again, jaw tight.

"Flynn—I want you to know I never would have done that. To your people." I keep my voice low, too afraid to say these things loudly. It comes out tight, fierce. "I would never. I'd die myself first."

He watches me in silence while my heart pounds in my chest, painful, too large. When he does speak, his voice is low to match mine. "I know that, Jubilee." He levers himself up onto his knees so we're eye to eye. "I know who you are."

He knows. He *knows*, I believe that. But he can't even bring himself to look at me for more than a few seconds.

And I can't look away. "Don't give up." The words are as much for me as for him. "All you need is one true thing to hold on to. Something real in all of this."

He's looking at my hands on the gunwale—hands still sticky with blood, too congealed for the water to have rinsed clean. I start to pull back and hide them in the shadows, but he reaches out first, taking one of them gently in his. He scoops water over my skin and starts wiping the crusted, vile mess away.

My arms feel limp and heavy, like a doll's limbs, like they don't belong to me anymore. My eyes burn, vision clouding and blurring. All I can feel is Flynn's touch, rubbing at first one hand, then the other, slowly working the life back into them. Washing away every last trace of the blood claiming me for the Fury.

When he's done, he halts, looking down at my hand resting in his. The moment stretches long and thin, until it snaps and he lets go, pulling back, his grief-stained face turning away from mine.

My breath catches, responding to an unfamiliar pull in my chest, an ache in my soul. I shouldn't miss him, but I do; this boy who had every right to pull that trigger, and instead threw himself between me and death. This boy, the only one who believes I'm not what they say I am, what I believed I was: a soldier without a soul, a girl with no heart to break. He's the only one who's proved me wrong.

There's a desperate want somewhere inside me, a longing for his touch, for the quiet he finds in the midst of this chaos, for healing. For him.

But instead I just stand there, the meter of space between us as vast as any canyon. I wish the dawn had come, bringing light enough to see his features as more than shadow. Despite my words, I know he won't send for me through Molly. I know he won't come back. In my heart I know I'll never see him again.

"Good-bye, Flynn Cormac."

She's playing with the boy, no longer puzzled by the way her mind has stitched him into her dreams as though he's always been there. She's stalking him in the alleyway, her heart jumping gleefully at every noise. When she reaches the garbage incinerator, he jumps out from behind it, shouting, "Pshew, pshew! You're dead!"

The girl shrieks and obediently falls to the ground.

The green-eyed boy laughs and crouches down to lean over her. "Okay, you be the bad guy this time."

But when the girl sits up, the boy is gone. She's alone in the alley, and all around her, November has been destroyed.

EIGHTEEN

FLYNN

I CLOSE MY EYES. I CAN'T BRING MYSELF TO WATCH HER GO because she's destroyed me. And because I'll never see her again. And because the fire in my chest is for vengeance, and it's for her, and I can't tell which desire will win.

When I can see again, dawn is too close. Jubilee is gone, and with her all my hopes that she can stop this chaos. It was an impossible enough battle to face before, but the idea that LaRoux Industries' presence on Avon is connected to the Fury has left me shaken and struggling for my next step. What does it mean, that the Fury felt the same to Jubilee— the shakes, the taste of blood—as whatever took her when she found that LaRoux ident chip? We're the only ones who know about LaRoux Industries' involvement, the only ones who have any idea the Fury could be something not done by Avon, but something done *to* it.

There's only one other person I can think of who might hear me. Who's had to watch someone trusted, someone safe, turn into a monster. Maybe Davin Quinn's daughter hasn't heard of my betrayal of the Fianna. Maybe she'd wait to hear my side before turning me in. In a few days, when things are calmer, I might be able to risk showing my face in town to look for her.

Straightening from where I'm slumped on my bench, I shrug into her jacket, a little too tight on me, but warm. I try not to imagine Jubilee, her commanders, the relief of the other soldiers to have her returned to them. I try not to see her back at the bar, surrounded by her platoon, safe in a world where what she's done doesn't exist. But I see it all anyway. I watch her, in my mind, being reabsorbed into her world once more, the way I'll never be with mine again.

I reach slowly for the boat's oars and point the bow back out into the swamp. Away from the base, away from my home. Away from everything except the empty expanse of Avon's wilderness.

The girl is on Patron with her old captain, running patrols, when they get the call that shots have been fired in the next sector over. The rebellion on Patron has been over for a decade, but pockets of insurgents still hide here and there, simmering with hatred and boiling over at random intervals.

They're not geared for full-on combat, but her captain doesn't hesitate. It's a quick march back to the skimmer, and then he gives orders to head for the next sector, to back up the platoon pinned down at the edge of the forest.

The girl has never been in combat before, not front-line combat. She glances at her captain, and her fear is all over her face. Her captain looks back at her and winks, and she takes a breath. He has warm eyes, and she holds on to that detail.

"It won't be like your drills," he says, and though his voice is pitched for the whole platoon, he watches her while he speaks. "Anyone says it is, they're lying."

The girl swallows hard, shifting her grip on her Gleidel and wishing she had a rifle instead. When she looks back again at her captain, they're the only two soldiers in the skimmer.

"You're quick on your feet, Lee, and you learn fast. All you have to do is pay attention. Keep your eyes open. You'll see what no one else does."

NINETEEN

JUBILEE

THE SPOTLIGHTS ILLUMINATING THE BASE PERIMETER ARE blinding, and as I make for a weak spot in the fence that Flynn told me about, the adrenaline's starting to recede. In its wake I'm left numb, stumbling; my fingers struggle to unwind the parts of the fence enough to slip through. Entering through the checkpoints will raise more questions than I can answer. If they discover what I've done, I'll be transferred off-world and there'll be no one left to piece together what's happening to Avon.

I should try to sleep, or eat something to stop shaking, but I can barely remember which direction my bunk is. I find myself retracing the path Flynn took when he abducted me, ending up in the alley next to Molly's. It's full of graffiti, some half scrubbed away, some fresher. One is written half in Spanish, half in Irish—I can only recognize the word *trodaire*. The bright red paint was sprayed on so thickly that it dripped in long skinny rivulets before drying, and my eyes fix on them.

I can't escape the images burned into my mind of blood and scorched flesh and crimson-stained stone and . . . I wrench my gaze away from the red graffiti, shivering. *He didn't save you so you could fall apart.*

Before I can gather my strength to move again, the back door of the bar bursts open and out stumble three soldiers. Molly's close on their heels. "Go home," he's saying. Though his voice is firm, he doesn't sound angry. It's easy to see that the three rookies have had more to drink than they should, but they're all upright. None of them are from my platoon.

Molly spots me standing in the shadows and straightens. "Lee?" He flips on the light over the door, flooding the alleyway with a blast of illumination. Dimly I hear the soldiers speaking, calling to me, saying words I can't process. I take a step back, head spinning as my heart starts pounding so hard I can barely breathe. I reach out in the same instant I realize there's nothing nearby to grab on to, and I'm about to fall.

A strong hand grabs my shoulder, grounding me, supporting me. I blink to see Molly's face not far from mine, his eyes worried. "Think I've got that special order somewhere in the back, babe," he rumbles in that gentle, booming voice of his. The words are for the benefit of the trio now making their way back toward the barracks.

"Great," I say weakly as he starts marching me toward the back door.

As soon as he's gotten me inside the dimly lit, dusty storeroom, Molly guides me to an old packing crate and sits me down on top, so my quivering legs can relax. When I finally lift my head, he's waiting for me with concern and apprehension.

Even Molly can't see Captain Chase half ready to faint without wondering if the world's about to end.

"You look awful," he says in a low voice. "Something happen on patrol?"

I look down, noticing with surprise that my clothes are stained with mud, still wet in places. A few of the stains are different. Reddish brown. I open my mouth, but instead of a reply comes a half-hysterical gulp.

"I'll make you a drink," he says, fretting and starting to turn for the door.

I put a hand on his arm to stop him. "I don't need a drink right now. Molly—I need your help."

He rubs one hand over his shaven scalp, the tattoos winding around his fingers seeming to shift in the low light of the back room. Not for the first time I wish I could read the characters tattooed up and down both arms—but while I remember how to speak a little of the Mandarin my mother made me learn as a kid, the written characters have long since slipped away. Molly told me once that on one arm he'd gotten passages from *The Art of War* and *The Prince*, and on the other, quotes from wise men from every corner of ancient Earth, like Confucius, Dr. King, and

Gandhi. *War and peace,* he'd explained, when I told him he was a lunatic. *Light and dark. Yin and yang.*

Rebel and soldier.

Molly was big into trying to find himself in his cultural past and bought into every stereotype he could find in ancient movies and books. Probably why he liked me right away—I'm one of the few people on the base who can even pronounce his real name. He was a terra-trash orphan when he was a baby—parents brought him to a new world, died in the rough conditions, and he ended up adopted by a family on Babel. I've got no idea how he ended up here, in a colony largely dominated by Irish folks. He's got no link to our shared Chinese heritage except by blood, but it never ceases to fascinate him. Whereas I couldn't get far enough away from my mother's teachings.

But that was before she died, and I lost that connection forever.

Molly's still hesitating, as though he suspects a drink will fix my problems despite my protests. "What's goin' on?" he asks finally.

"I need you to watch for a message." Some part of me knows it's pointless, that there's no message Flynn Cormac could possibly need to send me now—but the rest of me refuses to sever this last thread between us. "It's important. I don't know who will bring it or when, but you have to bring it to me—don't tell anyone else."

Molly's brows draw in, concern deepening into a frown. "Babe, what'd you get into?"

I take a deep breath, feeling shaky now in the wake of the panic that greeted me when I first walked into the bar. "I can't tell you, Baojia."

There are only a few people on the base who know Molly's real name, much less use it. It makes him pause, then nod. He gives my shoulder a squeeze. "I'll watch for it. Get some rest, kid. Y'look like death on ice."

I try to do as Molly suggests when I get back to my bunk. Even after showering the last of the blood and muck from my skin and putting on dry, warm clothes, I still feel covered in grime. I'm trained to sleep wherever and whenever I can get it, but despite my exhaustion, my desperate need to close my eyes against the memory of this night, I find myself staring up at the ceiling.

Maybe it's because when I close my eyes, I see that child from the rebel base lying there, the side of its head blown away, the skin and hair around the area scorched in a way that only a military-issue Gleidel could have done. The child I killed while not inhabiting my own skin.

I roll over, desperately seeking some relief from the incessant tangle of my thoughts. If I had anyone I could call, even to have the most inane conversation imaginable, I'd do it. Towers might be a stickler for using the retransmission satellites for watching the HV, but we've got good, clear lines for getting messages off Avon. But we're not designed to have friends—we're not given the chance for it. Two years ago I would've called my fellow rookies, but we're spread out across the galaxy now. I've got no one. Alexi was the closest thing I had. Everyone else I've served with is gone. Dead, or else stationed so far away, they might as well be.

Sometimes I think they isolate us on purpose. It makes me wonder what my life would've been like if I'd stayed at that orphanage, if I'd never gone into the military. Or if I'd managed to put aside my need for vengeance. My old captain always told me I had to find something to fight *for*, not just a reason to fight. If I'd listened to him, would I have had friends that lasted beyond their next reposting?

I'm not sure what brought my old captain to mind, but now I find myself wishing he were here. He had a way of making impossible things seem okay, like climbing this mountain or traversing that plain wouldn't be so hard.

I sit up abruptly as an idea hits me hard. *My captain.* Flynn and I have been searching for a way to understand LaRoux Industries' involvement. For the reason there was a LaRoux ident chip on the site of the vanished facility. How could I have been so stupid? My old captain hasn't been on Avon for over a year, and there's a risk—but even brainwashed by fame and fortune, I can't believe he'd refuse to help me if I asked.

I shove my blanket away and slide into the chair. Sweeping the clutter aside with one hand, I press the palm of the other to the top of the screen. It swings open out of the desk obligingly, adjusting itself automatically to my height. The keyboard rises after it, out of the hollow below the screen. No eye-trackers here—strictly low-tech, nothing that would provide much benefit to the rebels if they got hold of it.

I start with the lines of code I need to get to a call screen. Just because my screen's low-tech doesn't mean you can't do a lot with it if you know how. And the man I'm about to call is the one who made sure I learned lessons others didn't.

I run a simple sweep for keytrackers, and once I'm sure I'm working unrecorded, I start. I key in the network address, adding in another line of code to ensure my request will route through a secure proxy, hiding my call's point of origin. I add in privacy tags to signal an approved personal call and take myself off the base's register—it's not perfect, but unless someone really digs, there'll be no trace I called at all.

But my finger hesitates over the ENTER button. The distraction of setting up a secure line can only last so long. What if he *has* changed, and he's not the same man I served with? What if someone's monitoring my computer activity, despite my best efforts to cover my tracks? What if . . .

I close my eyes. I could list a thousand reasons not to call. And only one reason I should: I trust him. My finger stabs downward, and I lean back, closing my eyes, waiting for the call to route through the retransmission satellite above me and connect through the hyperspace network.

After an interminable silence, the speakers give a tiny crackle, and light blossoms against my closed lids.

"What?" The voice is surly, annoyed, sleepy.

I open my eyes, and there he is. It's dark on his end, like it is in my room now, but I can see him lit by the glow of his computer screen. The gloom makes him seem pale, ghostly.

Despite the low light, he looks good. Better than I remember. He's not wearing a shirt, and his dog tags are gone. He's let his hair grow out, and there's an ease about the set of his mouth I don't remember being there before. Like he's found whatever he was looking for—whatever any of us is looking for, in the trenches and the bunkers and the swamps.

"Sir," I manage, my throat suddenly going dry.

His eyes open a little more, blinking in the light. "Lee?" He sits up a little straighter.

A muffled, sleepy voice comes over my speakers—not his voice. "Tarver," it says, petulant. "Come back to bed." Someone else is in the room with him. Someone female.

Merendsen glances over his shoulder, but his camera shows me only darkness beyond him. "Go back to sleep, Lilac." Despite the brusque words, there's a tenderness in his voice that, strangely, makes my heart constrict. I feel my face warming—I never would've expected to hear that tone from him. Suddenly, I wonder what I'm interrupting. He could be naked on the other side of the computer for all I know; the camera only shows him from the chest up.

Then he turns back to me, frowning, and the tenderness is gone in favor of sleepy exasperation. "Lee, do you have any goddamn clue what time it is here?"

I hadn't thought to check the time differences. I hadn't thought at all, beyond the desperate need to see a face I knew I could trust. "Sorry, sir." He's not military anymore, but I could never call him anything else.

Now that he's more awake, I can see confusion starting to blossom across his features. I can't blame him. We haven't served together in a year, haven't spoken to each other in nine months.

"What's going on, Lee?"

I hesitate, listening for sounds of life in the room behind him. I can hear none, but I'm all too aware of Roderick LaRoux's daughter lying in Merendsen's bed, hearing every word I say. "Is there another room you can pick up in?"

Merendsen pauses. "She's asleep. It's okay."

I shake my head, swallowing, not daring to speak.

Merendsen's eyes are slightly downcast, staring at my face in his screen and not at his camera. I lift my own gaze to the pinhole above my screen so he can see my eyes.

He doesn't speak, but pushes away from the desk and gets to his feet. It turns out he is dressed, wearing drawstring pants that hang low on his hips, but I can tell I hauled him up out of bed. He leaves the immediate circle of the monitor light, and as the camera auto-adjusts, all I can see is a shadowy form crossing to the bed and leaning over it. I hear Lilac LaRoux make a whiny sound of protest, see a pair of arms reach up in an attempt to pull him down with her.

Quiet conversation. Merendsen's soft chuckle. A sigh of capitulation. Silence. Then the soft, unmistakable sound of their lips parting.

He returns to the computer. "One sec." There's a jumble of noise and light, and I realize his computer's a mobile unit, that he doesn't have more than one, that he's not somewhere with screens in every room.

The jumble calms after a minute, and I see his face again. His camera blurs and refocuses, adjusting for a different level of light, and it turns out he's outside. It's night, the landscape beyond him silver and blue with moonlight. All I can see is a field of flowers.

"Okay, Lee." Merendsen takes one of those deep breaths I know is a bid for calm. "Tell me what's going on."

My throat's closed so tightly I can't speak. He's all at once so different and exactly the same that I feel an odd shyness creep over me that hasn't touched me since before I left Verona.

He leans forward. "Did you really call me in the middle of the night to stare at my bedhead?"

That particular streak of humor is so familiar that my heart hurts. I shake my head again. "Sir—can I still trust you? What you told me when you were reassigned, does that still hold true?"

Merendsen sobers. "Always, Lee." His voice is firm, the voice I remember. The voice of a *real* leader. "Always, you hear me?"

My vision swims as though I'm drowning, struggling to get enough air. "Your fiancée. How much do you know about her?"

"I know more about her than anyone else does, Jubilee," he responds, though his tone is cautious. His use of my full name is deliberate. He knows only my family called me that, knows the pain it causes—he's testing me. Testing my resolve, testing how badly I need his help. "Why are you asking me about Lilac?"

I lift my chin and gaze into the pinhole lens of my camera. "I need information about her father's corporation."

"You want me to spy on my future father-in-law?"

I try not to cringe; hearing the words now, I regret ever having called my old captain at all. "No, sir. I meant—"

"Because Lilac and I have gotten very good at that."

My eyes snap to the screen, surprise robbing me of speech.

"You don't want to get involved with LaRoux Industries, Lee. Whatever you're into, just . . . let it go. Fight your instincts and walk away."

"I can't. People are dying, and I think it's because of LRI. I had someone—but he's gone now. It's just me, sir. There's no one else to chase this."

"Lee," he says slowly, voice softening to match my own. "Where are you?"

"Avon."

He doesn't answer right away, but his expression shifts. Though I can't understand why, there's fear in his gaze. Concern. Somehow, across the millions of light-years between us, he's seen the echo of what's happened here in my face.

"Avon?" he echoes finally, his voice rough. "You're still on Avon?"

I nod, not trusting myself to speak. I feel like crying with relief. Until Flynn came into my life, I hadn't cried since Verona. Now it feels as though I'd just been storing up the flood for this moment. But Merendsen's the last man in the world I want to see me cry.

He's shaking his head. "Nobody lasts there more than a month or so—I barely lasted two."

"I'm okay," I lie. "But their planetary review with the Council isn't far off, and things are heating up here. And LaRoux Industries might be involved."

"What's happening?"

I want to tell him about the impossible disappearing base I saw with Flynn in the swamp, but the words refuse to form. "The Fury." I start there instead. "It's getting worse. Stronger."

"Get out of there," he says instantly. "Leave. Request a transfer. Go AWOL if you have to."

"AWOL," I echo, my voice halting. It feels as though the floor below me is heaving. "Sir, I don't—"

"You're not wrong, Lee. About LaRoux." Merendsen's voice is grim, his eyes shadowed. "I saw documents that mentioned Avon, back on— around the time I met Lilac. I assumed his experiments there were long over, though. I thought we'd ended them."

"What experiments?"

He hesitates, watching me in his screen, brows drawn. "You wouldn't believe me if I told you," he says finally. "Lee, just hang on. I'm going to figure out a way to get there."

"No," I reply, leaning closer to my screen as though he'll hear me better. "Sir, I wasn't asking you to come. The situation with the Fianna is too dangerous, and you're a civilian now. I'm only looking for information we can bring to the higher-ups to get answers."

"I'm not going to sit here and wait to find out you've been quietly erased for asking the wrong questions." Merendsen's voice quickens, a rare display of intensity. He leans in too—we're inches apart, if worlds away. "Some things I can't say over a comm line, not even a secure one."

The relief at his response to my suspicions about LaRoux Industries is rapidly draining away, leaving a tight, cold dread in its place. What could be so secret—so much worse than the Fury, than spying on his father-in-law and admitting to having seen long-buried documents—that he'll fly halfway across the galaxy to a war-torn planet to tell me?

"I'll be there," he continues. "Transports don't come here often, but I'll figure something out. I'll have to leave Lilac here—I can't bring her into this again. There's no telling what might happen."

I resist the urge to tell him that the last thing I want is for him to bring Lilac LaRoux here.

He's still talking. "Wait for me, will you? I'm serious, Captain. Don't run off and do something Lee-ish until I get there."

I nod. "Yes, sir."

"You swear?"

Bizarrely, Flynn's face flashes in front of my eyes. It could be weeks before Merendsen hops a ship to get here— What if, against all odds, Flynn sends for me through Molly because he needs me? How can I promise to sit here and do nothing when the idiot's life could be in danger?

But then it strikes me: it's not like me at all to think this way. In what universe would Captain Lee Chase risk life, limb, and the safety of her people for one exiled rebel and the planet he's willing to die for?

There's nothing Lee-ish about any of this.

I nod slowly, ignoring the sick feeling in my gut as I speak. "I swear not to do anything Lee-ish."

Merendsen eyes me, not trusting my hesitation. But then he nods and leans back. "I'll be there as soon as I can."

The monitor goes black, flashing the white text SESSION TERMINATED.

I press against the keyboard, and the whole thing folds back up into my desk, noiselessly hiding itself away. As if nothing ever happened.

I try not to think about what Flynn would say if he knew what I'd just done. In the morning I'll leave him a message at Molly's. I don't have much to tell him, except that I might have a way forward soon. It won't be enough. It could never be enough, and I keep imagining his grief, his frustration, his loathing of me and my world.

I know he won't get my message; I know he's on the run and this base is the last place he'd return. But leaving word is solace, somehow. Hope. A sign I haven't given up. That if he comes back . . .

But he's gone now. I'm alone.

"Xiao jie, mei kan jian ni lai guo zher."

The voice stops her short—it's been years since somebody spoke to her in her mother's language. She turns to see an enormous, intimidating mountain of a man covered with tattoos standing behind the bar. It's her first night off duty since she was transferred, and now she's wishing she'd gone straight back to the barracks.

"Sorry," the girl shoots back automatically. "I don't speak Mandarin." It's not a lie. She hasn't spoken it since her parents' deaths.

"Right," the bartender replies, his grin friendly, but knowing, like he can read her thoughts. "Well, I'm Molly. Welcome to Avon."

The girl can't stop staring, too confused by how strange his friendly voice feels against the backdrop of tattoos and muscle.

He laughs, as though he's used to people misjudging him. For a moment he looks a little like her father, though they've nothing in common. "We've all got pasts," he says, lifting an arm and indicating the tattoos, which seem to shift and change as she looks at them. "But here you get to choose what you hold onto."

TWENTY

FLYNN

THE PATROLS HAVE TRIPLED IN THE LAST FEW DAYS I'VE been hiding out in no-man's-land, and I suspect every one of them has been issued a picture of the rebel who abducted Lee Chase from Molly Malone's.

What they don't know is that sooner or later McBride and the Fianna will strike back in retaliation for Jubilee's massacre—an act of war the military don't even know took place—and when that happens, hunting for me will be the least of their priorities.

I've been careful to keep on the move, never too close to the perimeter, never too far away. The military base is like a squat, sharp monster crouched on Avon's horizon—Avon, a world of gently curved waterways and slow-moving clumps of algae. Against its foggy backdrop the prefab buildings are unnatural, made of right angles and rusted metal and plastene. I've always imagined the base like a scab needing picking away, full of booted feet treading the ground into bruise-colored slush. When I was little I always half imagined the scab would fall away one day and there'd be Avon again underneath, shiny and new and healed.

I give it a wide berth before finding a place near solid ground to hide my boat. A half hour later, I'm slipping between two buildings on the outskirts of town, avoiding the searching eyes of the soldiers on guard duty.

In the security footage from the bombing, there was a girl with Davin Quinn right before he used the detonator. I need to know if it was his daughter, Sofia. We played together as kids, and I think maybe, just maybe, she'll trust me still. I have to find out if she knows anything about what turned a peaceful man like her father into a killer. What turned Jubilee into a killer. That question—and the image of Jubilee's face, her eyes black like they were on the island, her features blank—has been my constant companion the last three days.

The town is a grid of worn prefab buildings divided by dirt roads, street signs showing only numbers. Normally there'd be people about, but this place is mostly locked down. A combination of curfew and caution. I wish I could say they were only afraid of the military's heavy hand, but more townspeople have been caught in the crossfire than anyone on my side would care to admit. I hurry past shuttered homes, head down, the collar of my borrowed jacket up to hide my profile. Clad in gray, I'm just one more shadow.

A dog comes skittering past me, hurrying for home or some bolt-hole. I turn my head automatically to check the way it came from, and freeze. Something's moving back there, something too large to be a dog. My heart kicks up a notch, and I force myself to move slow and smooth as I melt back toward the street beside me and the shelter of the buildings. That's the key—no quick, jerky movements to draw the eye.

There are three figures making their way up the street, and they're not trodairí. They don't step in time, beating Avon down beneath their feet. But they do move carefully, stealthily, and I recognize that movement an instant later: they're Fianna. McBride leads the way, flanked by two others; one of them I don't recognize, but I know at a glance who's walking on his left. It's Sean.

I ease back against the wall of a house as they approach the crossroads, bowing my head so my gray coat blends with the walls—in the dark, holding still is my best chance.

McBride stalks along like he owns the town, the other two close on his heels. He's headed away from the base, toward the edge of town; whatever his business was here, he's concluded it. Sean's hood is drawn, but I can see his always laughing, smiling mouth—now a grim line, jaw squared. Without Fergal, without me, he has no one.

I ache to reach out for him—I can imagine myself stepping forward, calling out—and I hold still, curling my hands to tight fists as the three of them disappear into the gloom. My heart tugs me after Sean, but I force myself to turn away. I came here for a reason, and if I want to help him—help all of them—I have to keep moving.

I nearly step straight into the path of a trodairí squad. They're still a block up, but with my mind squarely on my cousin, I spot them only seconds before crossing the street. Mentally cursing, I sink back into the shadows, watching as they approach. They move differently than the rebels, purposefully, and in that instant I understand they're moving *after* the rebels. They're following Sean and McBride.

I stoop, groping around in the mud until my fingers close over a stone, small and slippery. In a quick movement I send it flying up the side street, withdrawing into the shadows as the trodairí change their course, abandoning the receding figures of the rebels to go after this newer, closer sound. It's all the head start I can give them, and I hope it's enough.

I slip away, ducking up the third street along and counting the houses until I reach Davin's house. Sofia's, now, though not for long. She's not sixteen yet, not technically an adult. Odds are they'll have her on the next transport leaving the spaceport. I square my shoulders and knock quietly, keeping an eye out for more soldiers on curfew patrol.

It takes her a long time to answer—long enough that I know she must have been listening for the sound of my footsteps retreating. Then the door opens a crack to reveal a sliver of the girl I knew, slender and strawberry-blond. She sports a bandage that peeps out of the collar of her dress, and another encircling her wrist, and I'm reminded that the girl in the bombing footage was not far away when the explosion occurred. The pale skin of Avon's sunless skies is ghostly on her, black shadows standing out beneath her eyes in exhausted half circles. Grief has hollowed her out.

She barely looks at me, her eyes sliding away to rest on the muddy street. "Thank you," she says wearily, her voice hoarse, "but I really don't need any more food." The door starts to shut.

"Good," I say, pulling my hands out of my pockets to show they're empty. "Because I don't have any. Sof, it's me, Flynn. Let me in before someone sees."

Her gaze snaps into focus, lips parting in surprise, and for a heartbeat the grief is gone. There's a code between the people like her family—the townies—and the Fianna. They might not be with us, but they turn the other way when we pass by, and tell the soldiers they didn't see a thing. Not so secretly, plenty of them would like us to win, and though Davin was a cautious man, I'm desperately hoping the girl who used to steal books from the classroom and then spin fantastic lies to wriggle out of trouble has more fire in her. And that she has any of that fire left at all now.

After a moment that stretches into forever, she leans out to look up and down the empty lane, then steps back to invite me in. The house is small, exactly like all the others in town. You can see Sofia's little touches here and there—the bright red kettle on the stovetop, a strip of imported silk hanging on the wall. Otherwise the walls are painted the usual calming pale yellow, and the bland furniture is standard-issue. Her father's waders still hang by the door, along with his testing kit. Before his new job in the base warehouse, Davin scooped samples for a living, bringing them back to the labs so the technicians could confirm that, as ever, Avon is missing most of the bacterial life she needs to become a proper world. The small table in the center of the room is piled high with dishes and pots, offerings left by neighbors and friends with no other way of showing their sympathy for Sofia's loss.

She closes the door behind me, then turns to face me. Last time we spoke we were almost the same size, and she was trying to wrestle me to the ground in the muddy school yard. Now I've got a good three or four inches on her. I'm searching for words, some way to show her I'm sharing her pain, but she speaks first.

"What the hell happened to you?"

To my surprise, I laugh. And though it's a soft, sad sound, my chest loosens. I haven't spoken to another human in three days. "The swamp happened to me," I say, and her mouth quirks a little. "I'm so sorry, Sof. I wish there was something I could say that would make a difference. I know there's not."

Her mouth tightens to a thin line as her eyes slide away. She looks so tired. "You shouldn't have come here, Flynn. Your face is on every holoboard in town. Kidnapping an officer? What's going on?"

"It's an incredibly long story. Listen, Sof, I've got nowhere to go. I came here because . . . because I thought you might understand."

"Nowhere?" Her brow furrows, and I realize no one's told her about the massacre, about my choice to save Jubilee. "But the caves . . ."

I swallow hard. Three days, and I still can't speak about it. "McBride and the others want me even more than the soldiers do. I made a choice, and they don't understand why."

Sofia's eyes widen a little, but she's too good at concealing her feelings to show me anything else. "What did you do?"

"I saved a soldier's life. After she—" I clench my jaw, trying to keep control of myself. "It was the Fury."

Her gaze shifts, falling on the oversize waders by the door before coming to rest on me, her own grief welling up in response to mine.

"I just need a place to sleep for a night," I whisper. "And some answers. I know it's dangerous. I'll be gone by morning."

"Come," she says softly. "I'll draw some water, and you can get clean. You can borrow some of my father's clothes." She speaks without a hitch in her voice, but despite the long years we've been separated by this fight we've inherited, I still know her well. I can see the pain drawn clear on her face. "You'll stay here with me as long as you need to."

My heart thuds hard, fear and relief warring with each other. "I can't accept that, Sof. They find me here and they'll arrest you too. How can you—"

"Because you tried to save her from this Fury," she interrupts, voice quickening with the same fire I remember from when we were children. "Because if someone had tried to save my father, I would've kept them hidden until the soldiers came to drag me from this house."

It takes four basins of frigid water before the dirty washcloth wrings out clear, but Sofia keeps bringing new buckets from the pump anyway. Though the shirt and trousers she finds for me are far too large, the feel of clean, dry fabric without a trace of blood or grime is bliss. But once I'm sitting on the floor in front of the tiny stove, my thoughts return; my eyes are on the cuffs of my trousers, which have been carefully mended over and over again. The stitches are neat and orderly; the thread is a faded butter-yellow.

When Sofia sits down, handing me a thick, doughy slice of what we locals call *arán*, I notice the thread mending her father's cuffs matches the color of her tunic, which is a few inches shorter than it ought to be.

I close my eyes, the *arán* suddenly tasting like ash in my mouth. This isn't her fight—and yet it is. It's all of ours. I just wish it weren't coming to this violent end.

"Don't you need to eat too?" I ask once I've managed to swallow.

She shrugs, eyes on the glowing red coils of the stove. "Seems like all I do now is eat and sleep. People keep bringing me food. But I can't eat it all—there's only me now, after all."

It's always been just Sofia and her father, since we were children. Her mother left when the first rebellion started heating up, and as far as I know, Sofia hasn't heard from her since. I glance at the table piled high with offerings from the town. "It was you, wasn't it?" I lower my voice, though we're alone. "The girl in the security footage, right before . . . right before."

Her face tightens, eyes closing as she swallows hard, cheeks flushed. I want to take her hand, show her I feel this agony too, but the tension singing through her body keeps me still. "You know," she whispers, "you'd think the worst part about this would be the looks I get. It wasn't all soldiers who died in the explosion. People here lost family too. They all look at me like I should have known it was about to happen, or stopped it. But I don't care." Her voice thins and catches roughly. "I just miss my dad."

Her grief catches at mine, resonating hollow in my chest. Loneliness shouldn't be the worst of this; the thing that makes my heart hurt shouldn't be how much I miss the trodaire I've only known for a few weeks. Because the Fury took her from me too. "There was nothing for you to know," I murmur. "This never should have happened."

She inhales sharply, drawing her knees up and wrapping her arms around them. "It wasn't him, Flynn. I know they've got footage, I know they're saying he had the detonator. But he wasn't planning anything. He didn't want any part in the fight. He'd been vague, tired, but I thought it was just the stress of his new job on the base. He'd never have done anything to risk my life, and even if somehow he was forced, I'd have seen it in him." Her gaze is distant, replaying those last minutes. "I would have known."

"I believe you, Sof." My eyes fall on the bandages again.

"Well, if you believe me, you're the only one who does." She meets my eyes, the sharp edge of bitterness showing through. "The trodairí say the families always deny their loved ones are capable of violence."

"This Fury—this thing we thought was a trodairí excuse—it's real. I've seen it." I force myself to take another bite of the *arán*. I'm ravenous, and yet each mouthful is a hard lump in my throat. "And if it touched your father too, then it's getting worse."

"I was the one who got him the job on the base." She's still, betraying nothing with her body language. "Taking samples, being in that cold water all day, it was making his arthritis so bad he could barely walk in the mornings. I talked the military supply officers into hiring him as a stocker."

Even as a child, Sofia's silver tongue could get us out of any scrape.

"If it weren't for me," she whispers, her hollow eyes fixed on the waders still standing by the door, "he wouldn't have even been there."

In the morning, I'm ripped from sleep by the clatter of hail on the roof, and I lurch up with a rush of adrenaline. Shabby prefab walls surround me, and for a wild moment I'm completely disoriented. Then it comes to me: I'm at Sofia's, sleeping in her father's old room.

And that sound isn't hail. It's distant gunfire.

I clamber from under the thin blanket, dazed, stumbling to my feet and hauling open the back door. The muddy, makeshift streets of the town are full of people rushing this way and that as civilians try to find cover. The gunfire's echoing from beyond, out in the swamp. The military's increased patrols must have found McBride and his men—or else McBride has drawn them into a trap. Tactics my sister invented. Tactics I helped hand down.

Whole platoons of soldiers run double-time toward the sounds of fighting. There's no sign of Jubilee, but I'm not sure I'd be able to tell if she was among them. When they're all wearing their helmets and their body armor and power packs for ammo, it's impossible to even tell the men from the women. They all look alike.

A hand wraps around my arm and jerks me back. "They'll see you," hisses Sofia, face flushed with sleep and fear. She throws her father's shirt at me, making me realize I'm still half naked, sleep dazed, then shoves me away from the back exit.

The door slams, but I can still hear the smattering of shots fired, far away.

The fighting continues throughout the day, echoing from different spots; the shifts mean McBride's still out there, if not winning, then at least holding his own. The military have advanced weapons, greater numbers—but McBride and the Fianna know this land far better than soldiers who can't last more than a month or two before being reassigned.

Sofia ventures out a couple of times, bringing back bits and fragments of information with her. Through her I learn that open hostilities have broken out despite the base's added security, that the rebels in the swamps are attacking guerrilla-style—drawing out the soldiers with hit-and-run tactics, getting them out where they're vulnerable. It forces the military to play their game, to fight them on the ground, taking away the technological edge the organized troops have over us.

It's agony not running out there to stop it, or to help. Is Sean out there? Would he shoot if he saw me? I'd give anything for a chance to talk to him, to make him hear me and understand why I stood between him and Jubilee. His anguish is with me every moment—the instant he lifted his gun, all our years together not enough to bridge the gap between us. The crack of his gun still echoes in my ears. Did his shot miss me because he jerked his hand aside at the last second? Or was he simply shaking too hard to aim true?

Sofia tries to put me to work to distract me, pointing out furniture that needs fixing and leaks in the ceiling her father always meant to get to. My hands do the work, but my mind is frantic, leaping back into panic every time I hear a shot from a new direction.

"Do you think she's out there?" Sofia asks finally, watching me drop the screwdriver for the third time as I try to fix a wobbly chair. "The trodaire you saved?"

"I don't know," I reply tightly. "Probably."

"I can't believe she just left you, after that, with nowhere to go." Despite what she's said, I can hear the disgust and fear in Sofia's voice every time she speaks of the soldiers, of Jubilee.

"I left *her*," I whisper. The screwdriver feels like lead, and I let my hand fall to rest on my thigh. "I saved her because I need her alive. I can't find out what's happening alone, but I can't—" My voice cuts out as abruptly as if I'd been punched in the gut.

Sofia doesn't respond right away. "I'm sorry," she says after a drawn-out silence, her voice much softer now. "I know the pain of sitting, and waiting, and knowing answers may never come." I lift my head to find her watching me, her gray eyes thoughtful, concerned. "What can I do?" she asks finally.

"You've done too much already," I reply. "I'll be gone soon. I can't let you take this risk." *I just wish I knew where I was going to go next.*

"You're not the only one who's lost someone," she replies, voice sharpening. "I'll choose my own risks, Flynn."

When I look back she's staring at me, hard, her hands tightening into fists. I remember her as a child always being so careful not to reveal anything through her body language, through her voice; a natural at reading others, she never wanted to be read. Now, I wonder if she's choosing to let me see this. Choosing to show me this need.

"There's a place," I say slowly, "where she'll leave a message if she learns something. But I can't risk going there."

"Where is it?" she asks immediately.

"Molly Malone's, on the base."

"Keep the doors locked and the lights off until I get back."

The girl is waiting, listening to the heavily synthesized tech-rock ballad playing on the jukebox. The green-eyed boy was supposed to meet her at Molly's, but every time the door opens, it's someone else. A tall woman with blond hair takes the stool on the opposite end of the bar; a soldier with warm eyes and a laughing redhead on his arm occupy the corner in the back; a guy with pink hair tries to buy the girl a drink, but she doesn't want a drink, and he eventually gives up.

Her mother sits down on the stool next to hers, trying to get the girl's attention.

But the girl won't listen. "I'm supposed to meet someone," she insists. "I'm not supposed to have to do this alone."

Even the ghost from Verona has gone.

TWENTY-ONE

JUBILEE

FOUR DAYS AND THERE'S BEEN NO WORD FROM FLYNN; HE hasn't even gotten the message I left for him at Molly's telling him to sit tight. I shouldn't be surprised. I've found nothing since, despite my efforts to comb through the records in the security office, despite examining the security feed of Davin Quinn before the bombing. I find a few frames of myself the night of the massacre, passing through the cameras on the north end of the base, heading for a boat. I don't remember doing it, but there I am. I can't see my own face, but I act like me, I *move* like me. I've heard nothing more from Merendsen either—my one lead, my one hope.

I check the bar again and get only a sympathetic head shake from Molly. I try to contain my frustration as I stalk away from the bar, headed for my bunk. Luckily, I'm not known for being all sunshine and light, so if I'm looking a little pissed off, no one's going to think it's strange. I can't remember how I'd act if everything was normal.

Luckily for me, nothing is normal anymore. Our base is now a war zone, and we're under siege. For now we can still get people and supplies in and out by air, but munitions has reported a number of surface-to-air launchers missing, and there's speculation that the rebels have them. And that it's only a matter of time before they start using them on military vessels coming and going.

I punch open the door to my quarters, making the rickety prefab walls quiver. It's only after pulling off my boots and throwing my jacket over my chair that I see the monitor in my desk is up and its light is blinking at me. A priority message. It can't be good if it's from the brass. *Maybe it's from Merendsen.*

I throw myself down into the chair, pressing my palm to the screen to turn it on and register my identity. It takes the machine a few seconds to boot up, my heart pounding in the silence. Oh, what I wouldn't give for one of the machines they've got at HQ that goes from dormant to fully functional faster than your eye can follow the monitor. It's been four days; perhaps that's long enough that he's found out when the next transport is swinging through whatever isolated planet he's on.

Finally the monitor flashes to life, and I navigate through until I see the message that tripped my alert—it's from Commander Towers. Not Merendsen. My chest tightens with disappointment and apprehension. Though I know it's impossible, some part of me panics that she's discovered what I did at the Fianna hideout, or my distress call to LaRoux's soon-to-be son-in-law, or that I've begun systematically betraying every oath I've ever taken in order to help a rebel save his people—and mine.

I expect a video message, but when I open it up it's only a few lines of text.

TerraDyn's sending a field expert to evaluate the base's security effort after the recent attacks. He left to come here before the current situation erupted, but has decided to land despite the risks. I'm putting you in charge of his detail. Given your recent experiences, you've got the most insight into what's going on out there. Be dressed and at my office by 1900.—AT

My heart sinks even lower. How am I supposed to find answers, conceal my connection to Flynn, keep the rebels from overrunning the base, and meet with Merendsen when he arrives, if I've got some polished-up "expert" from a shiny city planet following me around the base?

I glance at the clock and groan. I've got ten minutes to figure out where the hell my dress uniform is and get to Central Command.

The girl is standing in the background, running a hand through her hair, leaning back against the lush wallpaper as though it might swallow her if she presses close enough.

A young woman with red hair and piercing blue eyes is applying makeup in a mirror to a face familiar from screens and billboards. She's blotting her flawless lipstick when she spots the girl and turns with a gasp of dismay.

"You poor thing," she exclaims. "You need a dress, or the boys will never dance with you."

The girl tries to protest, but the young woman with red hair can't hear her, and wraps her up in a long, gently shimmering dress the color of sunrise on Avon. When the girl looks in the mirror, she doesn't recognize herself—she's been transformed, changed for-ever. For the first time, she takes a breath and sees the reflection smile back. She turns, admiring the dress, which is the color of hope.

But then the girl notices a spot on the fabric. She rubs at it, but her fingers make it worse, smearing the stain. With both hands, she tries to wipe the stain away, desperate to keep anyone from seeing. She scrubs harder, but it's her hands that are staining it, and every effort leaves behind red streaks, until the whole dress is the color of blood, and she's sobbing with horror and shame and guilt, but the blood never washes clean, it never washes clean.

TWENTY-TWO

FLYNN

I CAN'T STOP REREADING THE WORDS. *I MAY HAVE FOUND* *something. Just sit tight.* There's no name attached, but the existence of the note itself tells me who it's from. "Are you sure this is all there was?"

Sofia, shedding her jacket and stomping the mud from her boots, raises an eyebrow at me. "You think there was another half and I decided to leave it behind?" The jacket goes on its peg, the boots lined up next to her father's. Everything in its place. It's been years since I lived in a house like this.

I turn the scrap of paper over. The other side is part of a receipt for a shipment to Molly Malone's, and though I try to see a hidden meaning, some code I could've missed, there's nothing there.

"You told me the bartender said it had been there for a few days— what, does she think I'll just wait here when she might know something?" I crumple the paper up, throwing it into the basin so the water will dissolve the ink.

"Maybe she doesn't want your head getting chopped off." Sofia's tone is light, though the humor doesn't touch her expression.

I stalk across to the window, peering through the gap between the shades and the frame. The sliver of outside shows me mud and not much else, except for the occasional flash of someone passing by too quickly for me to identify them. My legs are restless, unused to such inaction. Hiding out in the swamp, all I could think of was having a real bed to sleep in. Now I'm just aching to be free to go where I want.

And where I want to go is Jubilee.

"What is it she thinks she might have?" Sofia's voice interrupts my thoughts, and I look over to see her watching me, leaning against the laden table.

"You read my note."

"Please." She lifts an eyebrow. "Tell me what's so important."

"We're trying to figure out what's happening to Avon. Why this planet never changes, why it drives people mad, why corporations are hiding secret facilities in no-man's-land."

Sofia's quiet, not reacting to the revelations in my little outburst. "Well," she says slowly, "sounds like she's making progress. And you're safe here a while longer before they ship me out."

Some of my frustration drains away, sympathy rising in its place. Sofia's only a few months shy of sixteen, but according to the law she's a war orphan. She'll be bound for one of the orphanages on Patron or Babel. There's less of a chance rebel orphans will grow up into rebel fighters if you take them away from their homes. It's where I was going to be sent after Orla died, before I fled to live with the Fianna. "When?"

"Don't know." She lifts a shoulder, flashing me a wan smile. "They're trying to find my mother, but they won't. She's never wanted to be found. It'll be next supply run, or the one after—they don't tell you when they're coming for you so you can't run away."

My fault. Again. "I won't be here when they come, Sofia. I'm going onto the base. I have to find a way to get to Jubilee if she's found a lead."

"You're mad, right?" Sofia straightens, staring at me. "Yes, their attention's on the fighting, but your face still cycles through the security feed every fifteen minutes or so."

"Then I'll go tonight, when it's dark."

Sofia doesn't answer, chewing at her bottom lip, brows drawn together. She watches me, fighting some internal battle she doesn't voice—and then she breaks, muttering under her breath and turning for her room. "Wait here."

She vanishes into the next room for a moment before returning with the water bucket and a small canvas bag. She sets the bucket down and drops to her knees, upending the satchel and sending clothes and a few keepsakes tumbling. When a tiny framed drawing—most of the townsfolk don't have access to cameras—of her father clatters onto the floor, I realize what this is. It's her grab bag, for when the officials come to take her away.

But she's ignoring her things, emptying the bag and then grabbing a knife off the counter. She starts sawing through the lining, cutting away a false bottom. Before I can voice my surprise, she's pulling out a few unlabeled packets and looking down at them, expression unreadable. Then she looks up, half her mouth lifting in a smile. "Sit," she orders, jabbing a finger at the rug.

I sink down warily as she rips open one of the packets, giving its contents a curious sniff. Then she shuffles around behind me, out of sight.

Then something freezing cold dribbles onto my scalp, and I yelp. "What are you doing back there?"

"Trying to keep them from shooting you on sight," she replies blandly. She's working her fingers through my hair, quick and thorough, if gentle enough. A little of the gel smears across my forehead, and she brushes it away with her wrist. "I know I can't imagine you as a platinum blond, so I don't think anyone else will either."

"Are you serious?" I try to pull away, and she simply grabs a handful of my hair, holding me in place like a mother cat holds a kitten. "Where the hell did you get blond hair dye?"

"I asked for it," she replies simply. As though that's all it takes—and for silver-tongued Sofia, perhaps that's true, though I know she didn't come by her skills easily. She finishes working the dye through my hair and turns back for the remaining two packets.

She fetches a plate and a rag from the kitchen and returns. She empties the packets, which contain a brown powder, onto the plate and then dribbles some water over it until it forms a paste.

"Okay," she says, exhaling briskly. "Now, strip."

I lift my brows at her. "No need to order me, Sof. Most guys will pretty much get undressed any time a girl asks." She snorts, and as I'm unbuttoning my shirt, I find I can breathe a little easier for the pleasure of making her smile, even for a moment. "Now, since I know the answer isn't the one I'm hoping for, why am I taking my clothes off?"

"This will tint your skin." She dips the rag into the paste and reaches for my arm, scrubbing it in circles and leaving dark brown smears behind, like shoe polish. "You won't find a white guy from Avon with a tan. Everyone will assume you're an off-worlder."

"I'm going to look like an idiot," I mourn, looking down at the unnatural brown of my arm.

"What else is new?" she retorts. "Idiotic is good. Nobody pays attention to idiots—they dismiss them. No one suspects they're hiding anything."

I watch as she works her way up my arm. It's clever. It's beyond clever—it's *brilliant*. It's what a lifetime of living on a planet torn by war teaches you: How to read people. How to blend in. How to disappear. But this—this never would've occurred to me.

"Sofia—why do you have this stuff?"

She doesn't answer, her lips pressing more tightly together. Instead she concentrates on working the paste into my shoulders, my neck, my ears, my face. I watch her as she dabs carefully around my eyes, noting how different she is from Jubilee. Fair, gentle, her features soft, her mouth made for smiling. She looks innocent, even happy, but for the grief in her eyes.

"You were going to run," I say softly. "When they came for you."

"Where would I have run to?" She spreads the mixture down my chest a ways, stopping when she's sure the line won't be visible under a shirt. "There's nothing for me on Avon anymore. Unless you think the Fianna would take me."

I watch as she shifts, leaning over so she can work at my hands, staining carefully around the nails. Someone like her would've been a major asset for us—quick thinking and a silver tongue. Maybe she could have helped me fend off McBride.

Or maybe she'd have been dead alongside Mike and Fergal, and I'd have lost one more person that day.

"Don't go into the swamps, Sofia."

Her eyes search mine. "No," she agrees, letting her breath out. "Let that soak in for a while," she commands, getting to her feet and dipping a glass full of water with which to scrub at her stained hands over the basin.

"Whatever you were going to use this stuff for . . . can you get more?"

Sofia shrugs. "It's fine, I can take care of myself." She rinses her hands and tilts her head so she can peer at me. "But can you?"

"I don't think Sean would even recognize me now." There's a cut at my heart for that, but I shove it aside.

"That's not what I mean." Sofia's eyes are on mine, raking across my features, trying to read me the way she reads the trodairí when determining which one to try to swindle out of his extra rations. "Flynn . . . is she worth it?"

That brings me up short, and I stop picking at the paste drying to a crusty mess on my arm so I can gaze back at her. "She's not why I chose what I did."

The corner of Sofia's mouth quirks. "You can hide from the Fianna, Flynn, but you can't hide from me. Your eyes dilate when you think about her; you speak more quickly, less carefully. I'm used to watching for the signs—how do you think I get things out of the trodairí?"

I shake my head, knowing Sofia will read guilt clearly across my face. That the girl who killed my people, who I found covered in their blood, whose hands I had to wash clean—that the thought of her still does this to me is detestable. "It doesn't matter. What she's done, Sof—it doesn't *matter* what I think or feel."

"You were never a very good liar, Flynn."

She gives the dyes time to set and then helps me wash my hair and scrub the paste from my skin. To my relief, when the dark brown gunk is swept away, the skin underneath is a much more natural shade of golden brown. Still ridiculous on me, but it'll pass all but the closest of inspections.

I brought nothing with me, so once the mess is cleared away, I'm left standing by the door, bracing myself to step outside. It's begun to rain, its patter on the roof muffled by the moss that grows there for insulation from the cold.

When I look back at Sofia, she's biting her lip, her tired eyes finally lighting a little in amusement. Seeing my glance, she quips, "You *do* look like an idiot."

"Good, I guess."

"You can get into the bar via the back door. It's in the alley behind the building, it leads into the storeroom." The amusement flees her expression. "I'm probably not going to see you again after they take me away."

Her matter-of-fact tone cracks my heart. "Maybe not," I concede. "You never know." She's my last hint of home—the last person truly of Avon to look at me without hatred in her gaze. I'm forced to swallow, clear my throat as it threatens to close. "I'll think of you."

She shakes her head, lips curving a little. "I'll think of you too. I'll remember you looking absolutely ridiculous."

"At least I'm memorable." It's gallows humor, but it helps. A little. I step toward her, lifting an arm to reach for a hug.

Her half smile vanishes, and she pulls away as her gaze slides from mine. "It'll be easier for me if you don't," she says softly. "I have to stop thinking of this place as home. It has to just be a place I lived for a while."

My throat does close then, and we're both silent, with only the rain on the roof to break up the quiet. I study the girl I knew, another casualty of this fight, wondering how the wounds of it will mark her. "Clear skies, Sof." It's all I have left to say.

"Clear skies," she whispers. "I hope you find what you're looking for."

The girl grips her brush, tongue poking out the corner of her mouth as she focuses on the page in front of her. The trick with calligraphy is to commit to the stroke. Her hand can't waver or the ink will blot. The beauty will be lost.

She needs to write a note to the green-eyed boy, and it cannot wait.

But her fingers tighten around the brush's handle until her knuckles whiten, and she's pressing too hard. The characters writhe on the paper and weep fat tears of ink so they blur into one another. The girl can't read them, and she can't remember what she meant to write.

She stares down at the paper, the urgency beating through her in time with her heart, the memory hovering just out of reach. What did she need to tell the boy?

The blurred letters fade out as the girl watches, and soon the paper is blank.

TWENTY-THREE

JUBILEE

"CAPTAIN CHASE, YOU'RE LATE." COMMANDER TOWERS IS glaring at me. But I don't care. I can't find my apology—I can't even find a salute. I'm too busy staring at the man standing on the other side of her desk. He still sports a holstered Gleidel at one hip, too long a soldier to come to a place like Avon unarmed despite having resigned from the military. He's wearing clean and tidy civvies, practical and suited to Avon's muddy surface: boots, trousers, a fitted T-shirt, like the most casual version of our uniform. With my hair hastily pinned up under my hat and my buttons in severe need of polishing, I feel like an idiot.

But mostly, I feel relieved. Because of all the people I expected to be escorting around the base, Tarver Merendsen was the absolute last on the list.

"I was just telling the commander that you and I have served together in the past," he says, turning to face me. His mouth twitches, the barest hint of a familiar smile visible there. "It's good to see you again, Captain."

"Sir." I'm struggling to speak—struggling to breathe. It wasn't so long ago I was calling *him* Captain.

Commander Towers turns off the e-filer in her hand and tosses it down on the desk with a clatter. She seems agitated, her typically frosty exterior cracking as if under some unseen pressure. "Merendsen's here to evaluate base security in light of recent events," she says, her gaze snapping between me and the man by her desk. "Someone raised a concern with TerraDyn that the military isn't holding up its end of the bargain, and because of his experience, they've taken him on as an independent contractor to review our arrangements."

I can read the annoyance in Towers's voice. She doesn't like the implication that she can't do her job.

"I have some experience with life on Avon," says Merendsen easily, turning to nod politely at Commander Towers. "I certainly understand the challenges you face, Commander. I'm sure a lot has changed since I was posted here, though. Perhaps Captain Chase could give me a brief tour?"

Commander Towers is no more immune to Merendsen's charm than anyone else. A bit of the tension leaves her shoulders and she gives a flick of her hand, dismissing us both. "Go right ahead. If you need anything while you're here, Captain Chase is your man, understand?"

It's an unspoken order to me to play nicely. Towers's eyes shift toward me, stern and piercing. So I straighten as if suitably chastised and toss off a stiff salute. Merendsen simply nods, and then we're both headed for the door.

"One moment, Captain. Mr. Merendsen, do you mind waiting outside?"

Her referring to Merendsen as a civilian makes my muscles twitch, but he doesn't seem fazed. His gaze flicks from Commander Towers to me, and I realize he's wondering if it's safe to leave me with her. He still doesn't know why I called him here or who he can trust.

I don't even know who to trust.

I give the tiniest of nods, and Merendsen reaches for the door. "Of course, Commander. I'll have a look around out there."

Commander Towers waits until the door closes behind him. I can't look away from her—there are circles under her eyes more pronounced than the ones I see in the mirror each day, and I can see minuscule lines around her mouth, like the past week has aged her.

"Captain." The intensity in her eyes frightens me more than anything else, like she's exhausted but too wired to switch off. She's unraveled since her strange debriefing, when she shut everything down as soon as I asked about the sector to the east, where I saw the ghost of Flynn's secret facility.

I wait, but she doesn't speak. "Sir?"

Her lips press together, a struggle taking place behind her expression. Finally, she says softly, "Don't tell him what's been going on here."

My heartbeat quickens. "Sir—sir, he knows what's been happening, that's why he was sent. The attacks—"

"Not that," Towers interrupts, giving a dismissive jerk of her head. "Don't tell him everything. Let him do his job and then get out of here."

I'm fighting to stay casual, to play dumb. "Sir, I don't understand."

"Just—use your best judgment," Towers snaps. She pauses, getting control of herself with a visible effort. She draws herself up, straightening her shoulders. "Don't tell him what you've heard about there being a secret facility east of here." Her eyes meet mine.

"I'll do my best, sir." The lie comes so easily to me now—how quickly I've grown accustomed to deceiving my superior officers. The thought makes my stomach twist, sick.

Commander Towers relaxes a fraction, and I take a beat to consider my words before I add, "But you know I trust Merendsen, right?"

"He's not the one I'm worried about," she replies. With a jerk, she retrieves the e-filer from her desk and flicks it on again before shoving it my way. It's the front page of one of the entertainment magazines—and it's got a loop of Merendsen and Lilac LaRoux posing for the cameras. As I watch, Merendsen ducks his head to press his lips to Lilac LaRoux's temple.

I swallow hard, ignoring the impulse to blurt out the truth to Commander Towers. She's got to be holding more pieces than I am. If she knows about LRI's presence here, and the facility, then she could know how it's connected to the massacres involving Mori and Davin Quinn—and me.

I need to find out what Merendsen can tell me first. He clearly knows some secret about his fiancée's family business, and if it helps me find answers, I may not need to involve Commander Towers at all. Because right now, I don't know whose side she's on.

Shaken, I slip out of her office to find Merendsen some ten paces away, arms folded behind his back. Commander Towers is so sure I can't trust him—what makes me so sure I can? People change, after all. There's every possibility he could be in this as deep as anyone.

When the door closes behind me, he turns and regards me with that same half smile he always used to give when he was waiting for me to figure out I was in trouble. Only this time, he's waiting to help me get out of it.

No, I decide. *I have to trust someone, and I trust him.*

"It's good to see you, sir."

"It's just Tarver, now."

"If you say so, sir."

He grins at me. "It's good to see you too, Lee." His smile twitches as he looks over my dress whites, and he adds, "Nice hat."

His smile eases my tension for a few breaths, and I'm able to grin back at him as I lead the way. The base is busy, as it always is in the evenings. The patrols are changing, one watch giving way to another.

I turn to face Merendsen, wanting nothing more than to let the events of the past two weeks come pouring out of me. But instead I say quietly, "Are you hungry, sir? I thought I'd bring you to Molly's for something to eat."

He lifts an eyebrow. "I was thinking we ought to take a look around the base, see what's going on. Things got a little hairy on the descent, it looks like you've got a bit of a stalemate happening outside the perimeter."

There's nowhere else quiet enough, unexpected enough, to have the conversation we need to have. For all I know, if I've aroused anyone's suspicions, my room could be bugged. So instead I say, "Molly's got some good stuff hidden away in his back room, sir. Sure you're not hungry?"

Merendsen lifts a hand to rub it over the back of his head. I recognize the gesture from when he used to keep his hair cropped close. Now his hair is longer—not quite standard, but he's not subject to regulations these days. He's watching me closely. "On second thought, I am feeling a bit peckish. Lead the way, Captain."

I pick my way through the crowds, avoiding the worst of the mud puddles and quagmires along the way. One of many reasons we rarely ever get up in our dress whites on the base. They never stay white for longer than five minutes, unless you stand perfectly still, indoors, and don't think too hard about the swamp. We have to take the muddier, more crowded route through the middle of the base, making sure to keep rows of buildings between us and the swamps beyond the fences. I didn't bring Merendsen all the way here only to have him picked off by an errant bullet from a trigger-happy rebel. As we walk it starts to rain, first only a few drops that patter off the prefab roofs, and then more. I quicken my steps.

The back door to Molly's storeroom is locked, but I know where he keeps the key. I reach in under the bottom step, feeling for the indentation in the wood and then prying the key out with my fingernails. I fumble awkwardly with the lock, aware of Merendsen's eyes on me. It'd be so much easier if the buildings here were fitted with standard thumbprint scanners, but with the constant power surges from storms and the length of time it takes for replacement electronic parts to get here when something breaks down, low-tech is better. And at least this way, Molly doesn't have to explain to anyone why he added me to the list of stockers and deliverymen who'd have reason to have access to the bar.

Finally the lock gives way. I stow the key again and lead Merendsen up the wooden steps, shutting the door firmly behind him. The light's on, but the room's empty, no sign of Molly or any stock workers. *Good.*

I turn to face Merendsen again, but my explanations die on my lips. He doesn't look at me the way Flynn did—he doesn't see me covered in blood. He doesn't look at me and see a murderer. He's grinning at me, in that same way he used to when I screwed up in the field, when he was my captain a year ago—and suddenly it's like no time has passed and nothing has changed. My mouth goes dry.

"All right, Lee." His voice is soft, but firm. He has a way about him I've never managed to emulate, an ability to be confident, even stern, while still being pleasant and encouraging. "I've only got two days here—the military kicked up a fuss over a private auditor coming in with no warning, so that's the limit. We have to work fast. Start at the beginning."

I want to answer, but my throat is too tight, my mouth refusing to open. How can I begin to tell him how lost I am?

"Everything's messed up, sir. Everything . . ." I drop my head, shutting my eyes and hating that he's seeing me this undone. But then his hands come to rest on my shoulders, squeezing tight, and when I look up he's gazing down at me, unwavering.

"Nothing we can't fix," he murmurs, words I've heard from him a thousand times.

I nod, not trusting my voice, and the lines of his face soften as he breaks every protocol we've ever known and draws me into a hug. He's warm and solid, and smells a good sight better than anyone else on Avon, having not showered yet in badly filtered swamp water. I cling to him, trying to banish the thought of green eyes and pain, and the realization that his arms aren't the ones I want around me.

I'm holding on so tightly that I don't properly register the sound of the back door easing open. Merendsen does, though, and he lifts his head. An instant later he squeezes me, but this time it's a warning. I pull back so I can look at the door.

It's Flynn.

I freeze, going rigid in Merendsen's arms, unable to speak.

"Can I help you, friend?" Merendsen's voice is cheerful as he eases back from me, slowly enough not to arouse suspicion. *Nothing to see here,* his actions say.

Flynn doesn't even look at him. His eyes are on me, his face devoid of emotion. He's breathing hard, like he's been running, but now his muscles are rigid and tense. He's soaking wet, his hair dripping—his *hair.* I stare at him, suddenly noticing that in the days we've been apart he's acquired a tan and that his dark curls are now bleached platinum and plastered to his head by water. He looks so different. He looks exactly the same.

My throat closes, my mouth going dry. I can see nothing in his face. No sign of forgiveness. No sign of revulsion. No sign of anything, except that he can't seem to look away either.

A tiny sound breaks through to my brain—it's no more than a scrape of fabric, but I'd know it anywhere. Merendsen's pulled his gun out of its holster, slowly. When I jerk aside to look at him, his gaze is flickering between me and Flynn, his friendly smile gone.

"Stop," I gasp, as though I'm the one who's been running. "Don't."

Merendsen holds, though the gun doesn't drop back into the holster. "What's going on, Lee?" he asks, his voice low, demanding an answer.

But Flynn's still ignoring him, as if he hasn't even noticed we're not alone. "Your note," he manages. His voice is rough and broken, bearing the signs of whatever he's faced since we parted. "I came."

"I told you to wait," I reply, my voice coming out sharp. Tense, like a taut wire.

The muscles stand out visibly along his jaw before he speaks. "Would *you* have waited?"

For that, I have no answer. Or rather, I do—but it's not an answer that would help my argument.

Finally, Flynn's eyes shift, and I realize he hadn't missed Merendsen's presence at all. His gaze is chilly at best as he looks over my former captain. "Sorry, friend," he says, echoing the word Merendsen chose. "I was startled. Just shipped in. Looking for work."

He can't lie convincingly—not here, not now. "It's okay," I tell him. "Merendsen and I go way back. We can trust him."

Flynn doesn't answer, glancing from Merendsen to me, and it strikes me that Merendsen still *looks* like a soldier, despite the civvies. He stands like one, reacts like one. It's impossible not to know he's military.

Merendsen looks no more convinced than Flynn, eyeing him and taking in the bleached hair, the faux tan. The disguise works, and the fact that he looks ridiculous enough to brush aside is a good thing, but the desire to defend him from Merendsen's unspoken judgment surges up anyway. I push it back down.

"Merendsen, this is Flynn. Flynn Cormac. Orla Cormac's little brother."

Flynn's breath catches as I betray his true identity. But his reaction is nothing to Merendsen's, whose dubious half smile vanishes as his expression goes cold. There's not a soldier on Avon, past or present, who doesn't know that name.

The air is thick with tension. Merendsen doesn't lift his gun, but I can tell by the way he steps back on the balls of his feet that he's poised to fight if necessary. I can't help but wonder what happened to him while he was marooned, that his instincts are as finely honed as when he was on active duty.

"Okay, Lee. Tell me what's going on. I assume we're not all here to kill each other."

Flynn's watching me too, his eyes narrowed, his own muscles tense.

You're not handling this awesomely, Lee.

I brace myself. "Flynn, this is Tarver Merendsen, my former captain when he was posted here. I called him to come help us." I can tell from the blank look on Flynn's face that he doesn't recognize the name. And how could he? They don't have HV news coverage out in the swamps. They aren't going to know about the crash of the spaceliner *Icarus*. So I add, "Lilac LaRoux's fiancé."

Flynn's gaze swings from Merendsen's face to mine, accusing, horrified. Underneath his fake tan, his face has gone pale. "What the—" He jerks back, smacking into the stacks and making the bottles rattle. The noise makes Merendsen tense further, ready to act, his eyes not leaving Flynn's face.

"Both of you, *stop*." I snap the words, my voice cutting. "The last thing I need is you two trying to ice each other. Just—just listen to me, okay? Flynn, I trust him. I'd trust him with my life. We served together here, he knows Avon. He's a good man, and even if he's marrying Lilac LaRoux, that doesn't change who he is. He's our way in—he can help us."

God, I hope I'm right about that.

"And sir." I turn to face Merendsen. "He's—Flynn isn't . . ." I struggle, searching for some way to explain my connection to Flynn in a way that makes sense. That doesn't sound like I've completely lost my mind.

Who says you haven't?

"He's not what you would think," I say lamely. Next to my testimonial to Merendsen's worth as an ally, it's a sad, sorry statement. But how can I begin to describe what Flynn's come to mean to me? My mind shies away from that thought, that truth it's been avoiding for days. For once, I'm glad I don't dream, for fear of what my dreams would say of Flynn. I shiver. "Will you guys promise not to kill each other long enough for me to explain what's been happening here?"

Merendsen's the first to answer, straightening a little and leaning back against the wall. The pose looks nonchalant, but my trained eye can still pick out signs that he's alert, still ready for action. "Of course," he says.

Flynn's attention jerks back from Merendesen to me. I can see the hurt in his gaze, the anger there at being left out of my plans. Even though both of us know we were supposed to never see each other again.

"Fine," he mutters.

I take a deep breath. "Okay. Sir, you might want to sit down. I'm pretty sure you're going to think I've lost my mind, but I promise you I haven't. Well. Not in the last day or so, anyway."

I start with the night I met Flynn, and I stabbed him in the leg with a cocktail skewer, and we went in search of a secret facility that doesn't exist.

The girl stands in front of the classroom, and all eyes are on her. The students sit in rows, and the walls are decorated with posters colored by hand. This week it's the girl's turn to talk about her family. Her mother gave her a silk jacket, but she hid it in the bottom of her bag and has a holo-picture instead. It shows the three of them, the girl standing between her mother and father, smiling and waving as the picture loops over and over.

"But who is that?" the teacher asks, pointing at the photo, and when the girl looks at it again, there are four figures. A boy has appeared, dark-haired and handsome, with dog tags gleaming around his neck.

"Who is that?" the teacher repeats, and the girl stares at him, willing the answer to come, wanting to be sure she gets a good mark. It's not the green-eyed boy. This boy has brown eyes.

The boy stands between the girl's mother and father, and suddenly she remembers.

"He's my big brother," she tells the class.

"I'm not her brother."

She looks up, and the boy is sitting in the front row of the class.

He shakes his head. "I'm not her brother. Don't you know what she did?"

She casts her gaze down, burning with embarrassment, and finds the photo in her hands is bleeding, the red trickling down her fingers to her knuckles.

TWENTY-FOUR

FLYNN

I CAN'T STOP WATCHING HER BODY LANGUAGE AS SHE TALKS to him, leaning in to drink in his every reaction, eyes locked on his. I don't want to see it, but I can't look away. Watching them, watching her, is a torture as unbearable as listening to my people fighting without me. She's not alone anymore, surrounded by her platoon, her commander, her old captain. She's found her way out.

But I still need her, and I hate myself for it.

She starts with the night we met and talks him through our attempt to find the vanished base, her escape, then Davin Quinn's suicide. She's quiet, objective—she gives me more credit than I expected, and she holds it together to give a military-style report. That is, until she catches up to the night I left the hospital and she ended up out in the swamps. Then her voice gives out, and I see an echo of her shell-shocked horror when she woke to find herself surrounded by death.

I can barely stand to hear her tell it, and I turn away, gripping the shelf I'm leaning against until my fingertips ache. The grief in her voice should help, should remind me she hasn't forgotten; but all it does is make me long to touch her, to find stillness and quiet in the way our wounds mirror each other's. She hasn't been out of my mind the last few days. Hiding out in the swamps, holed up in town with Sofia, Jubilee's been my constant companion.

I thought it would be better once I saw her, but it's still here, this tug-of-war between wanting her, and just wanting her gone.

She stops trying to explain the massacre of my people and finishes abruptly. "And then Flynn helped me get back here. He's been in hiding since then, because his own people will kill him for protecting me, and I've been here, trying to find some trace of what's happening. That's why I called you. Because you're close to LaRoux Industries, and you're the only one I know who won't think I've simply cracked. You're the only one I know who won't kill him on sight." She nods at me for that.

"He's thinking about it." I can hear the edge in my voice, sounding like everything I try not to be. Combative. *Like McBride.*

He shrugs. "If you needed killing, Lee would have taken care of that." He finds a crate to haul up and sit on. "All right, so the Fury is getting worse. Taking people like Lee, who used to be immune, and civilians, who were always safe before."

"And we think it has something to do with LaRoux Industries." Jubilee's focused on Merendsen. "They shouldn't have any interest in Avon, but they have a presence here for some reason. Or had, anyway. The ident chip I found won't be enough proof for the higher-ups, but it's enough for me."

"You think the facility that Cormac saw was LRI? I wouldn't put it past Monsieur LaRoux, he's arrogant enough to think he's untouchable. Mostly because he is." Merendsen rakes his fingers through his hair. "God, what a mess. LaRoux is dangerous, Lee. You can't go up against him alone."

"That's where I'm hoping you can help," Jubilee admits. "Given your new connection." I can tell by the way her jaw squares there's more coming, and it looks like Tarver Merendsen knows her as well as I do, because he waits too. It shows up in one quick, short burst: "Why in God's name are you marrying *Lilac LaRoux*?" She's chagrined a moment later, but lifts her chin, defying him anyway.

Merendsen dissolves into laughter, holding up one hand to bid her wait as he recovers enough to talk. "Oh, I knew that was coming," he mutters. "Because I like the cushy lifestyle, Lee. You know me, I like my luxuries. Why the hell do you *think* I'm marrying her?"

"I honestly don't know, sir. I keep trying to . . . But it's Lilac *LaRoux*, for God's sake." She spits the name, as though it's an argument all on its own, like he'll see his mistake if he hears it one more time. "She's one of *them.*"

Merendsen just grins. "Because I'm in love with her, Captain. Because she's stubborn, and kind and strong and smart, and I don't want to go a day of my life without her, not ever again."

Jubilee crosses over to where he's seated on the crate, dropping to a crouch in front of him like a supplicant. "Tell me I haven't lost you to them, Tarver."

The first time Jubilee used my first name, I was betraying everyone I care for and realizing I was falling in love with the girl who killed my family. But now, his name rolls off her tongue with ease. I clench my jaw and avert my eyes, unable to watch her gazing up at him any longer.

Merendsen lets out a soft, slow breath. "Lee, I left what precious little time I have alone with Lilac and volunteered to get myself dropped on this ball of mud—no offense, Cormac—and here I am. Remember me?"

"Sorry, sir." But she doesn't sound sorry. I hear grief in her voice instead. "I've missed you."

"I get that a lot," he replies easily. "Now, my girl's exactly who we need if we're going to do a little digging. Where's the most private com-screen we can access?"

"My quarters." She pushes to her feet and seems to remember me, tilting her head to beckon me along behind them. "I'll show you."

Her former captain simply nods, and we both follow her out the door, me trailing behind the two of them. I can hear the sound of distant gunfire as we walk—the sound of my people fighting for their lives, without me.

The girl and the green-eyed boy are racing each other, sprinting through the alleys and byways of November. The girl slows just enough that the green-eyed boy will think he's catching up, and then she darts up a side street. He slips while trying to follow her and goes crashing to the ground.

The girl hears him cry out and runs back to his side as fast as she can. He's skinned both his knees, and blood is dripping onto the cracked pavement below. She tries to bandage the scrapes, but they won't stop bleeding, no matter what she does; when she looks up, the boy's face is draining of color.

"You did this to me," he whispers, reaching toward her face. But before he can touch her, his fingertips crumble away into dust.

"No," cries the girl. "I'm sorry. Please, don't go."

But the green-eyed boy has turned to ash, and she can't touch him for fear he'll shatter, and even the shape of who he was will be lost.

"Flynn—come back to me."

TWENTY-FIVE

JUBILEE

MERENDSEN PRODUCES A HANDHELD DEVICE FROM HIS pocket and presses a couple of switches, moving slowly around the confines of my room to check for bugs. He never had tech like that when I knew him. It's only once we're certain we won't be overheard that he gestures for me to start up my computer. I'm acutely aware of both guys watching me as I type away at the console sunk into my desk.

I know Merendsen's monitoring my efforts to secure this end of the channel—making sure there aren't any keytrackers or recorders running and that the military call log software gets bypassed properly—but I can't figure out why Flynn's so intent. Though I can't see him standing behind me, I feel his stare like a red-hot laser, burning into the back of my neck. Flynn won't know anything about computers. He's probably never used one; there certainly aren't any comscreens with hypernet connections handed out to the rebels in the swamps. But his eyes stay on me anyway.

I shift uncomfortably, fingers fumbling and forcing me to backspace before I can summon Merendsen with a jerk of my chin. He inspects the screen, then bends down over my shoulder to key in Lilac LaRoux's address. We've got the lights low in the hopes anyone passing by will think I'm grabbing some much-needed rest. Merendsen straightens and I get to my feet as the call starts connecting, letting him take the chair instead. Lilac LaRoux has no reason to talk to me—best let her fiancé handle this. I drift backward, clasping my hands behind me.

"Let's hope she's awake," Merendsen murmurs, voice quickening. *Anticipation,* I think. He's eager to see her, his whole body angling toward the screen. I glance over at Flynn, but his eyes are fixed on the monitor, his jaw clenched and his shoulders tense.

I sigh. "I just hope she's not at one of her famous parties with a dozen of her chattiest friends."

Merendsen exhales a laugh, speaking with a smile in his voice. "I don't think that's going to be a problem."

Before I can ask him to elaborate, the call connects and the picture pops up. There's a woman in the image—a girl my age, maybe younger. For a moment I don't recognize her without the hair, the makeup, the glitzy dresses and jewelry. I find myself staring, trying to connect this sleepy-eyed, fuzzy-haired girl with the heiress to the LaRoux fortune. She's pretty—beautiful, even—but nothing like the creature I think of when I think "Lilac LaRoux."

"Tarver," she mumbles, stifling a yawn and rubbing a bit of sleep out of the corner of her eye. She's clearly been woken up; she's wearing a silk robe over whatever she was sleeping in.

"Hi, beautiful." His voice is soft in a way I've never heard from him before. "Am I off the hook for running out yet?"

She wakes up a little more, a smile lighting her features as she leans a little closer to the screen's camera. "Tarver!" she repeats, more alert now. Her smile grows wry, amusement coloring her face. "Have any of the nasty swamp people shot at you yet?"

I have to stifle a protest, swallowing it down. It's clear Lilac LaRoux can't see me or Flynn standing in the background.

But Merendsen just snickers, as if she was joking. "No, but it's still early days. How are things at home?"

"Good. I haven't had a chance to try the bathtub yet." Lilac's leaning closer still, one hand appearing as she lifts it to trace the neckline of her robe. Coy, flirtatious, her movements graceful enough to make me strangely envious of that skill. I look at Flynn again, but this time he's staring at the floor, keeping his eyes averted from the girl on the screen.

"Someone's got to test out the new plumbing, make sure it all works." Merendsen's amused, his voice low and private.

"Do you have a little time? I could bring the comscreen with me. Show you how much I wish you were here." Her finger pulls the neckline of her robe open a little.

I see just enough skin to realize she's not wearing anything under it before I jerk my eyes away and stare intently at the ceiling. Too late, I get why Flynn's watching the floor with such dedication.

"Oh, come on." Tarver groans. "I said I was sorry for leaving, do you have to torture me? And, uh"—his voice turns a bit sheepish—"Lee's here, so you might want to . . ." He trails off and glances over his shoulder at me.

Dammit, Merendsen. I clear my throat and step forward, into the light cast by the screen.

Lilac gives a startled squawk, grabbing her robe closed up under her chin. "Tarver!" she gasps. "Why didn't you say someone was there? Who the hell is this?" Her face is burning with embarrassment.

"This is Lee." I can tell Merendsen's aiming for bland, but he's not hiding his amusement very well. "Don't worry, I'm sure she was staring at the wall. She's very discreet and she doesn't believe in romance."

I pull my eyes away from the girl on the screen, trying to offer her a little of her dignity to cling to. "The ceiling, sir," I correct him.

There's silence from the computer while Lilac stares at the picture on her own screen. Then, in a low, careful voice, she asks, "Lee is a *woman?*"

I have to choke back a sound of surprise. Merendsen didn't tell his fiancée he was flying to the next system for a girl? I know it's because he doesn't see me like that—to him, he flew for a day and a half for one of his soldiers. I'd do the same for mine. But to Lilac LaRoux . . .

"I've never really noticed," Merendsen replies, carefully not looking in my direction. "Lee's friend is here too. Lilac, can you get us a secure line?"

She sobers, and all traces of the wounded, sulky bride-to-be vanish. She nods curtly. "Give me two seconds."

And then she's busy, typing away—doing as I did, not trusting the eye-tracker interface. She gets up, reaching for something behind the screen that we can't see. It sounds like she's flipping switches. I can't understand what she's doing. Whatever it is, it's far more advanced than anything I did at my end. Merendsen couldn't have taught her that.

Finally, Lilac settles back in her chair with a small device that, when she turns it on, sends a wave of static through the picture. It evens out after she starts making tiny adjustments to a dial on the device. Some kind of dampening field. I find my gaze creeping over toward Merendsen, wondering why they have such a need for secrecy.

"Okay, go." It's a completely different girl than the coy, flirty creature there a moment before. This Lilac is all business.

"This is Flynn Cormac," Merendsen says, prompting Flynn to step forward into the light. "One of the rebels here."

I half expect a dramatic exclamation from flighty Lilac LaRoux, some shallow declaration about how ridiculous he looks with his bleached hair. Instead she leans forward, inspecting him in her screen. "Goodness," she says mildly. "This is one of the infamous Fianna? He isn't exactly what I might have expected."

Flynn speaks up, deadpan. "That's why it works so well. It's better if you don't actually *look* infamous." It's an imitation of his usual humor, but there's something different about it. A note that's missing I didn't know I'd learned to recognize until it was gone.

Lilac grins, an expression I never would've expected from her. "Well said," she says approvingly. "I see we're all experts here at seeming to be what we're not."

Except me, says a tiny, seething thread inside my mind. *I'm only exactly what I ever was.*

I expect Merendsen to go into a detailed explanation, relaying what I told him. Instead, he cuts straight to the point.

"From everything Lee's told me," he tells the girl on the screen, "I think you were right."

"Whispers?" Her face in the glow of her monitor is ghost-pale.

Merendsen nods. "And they're getting stronger. People here are going mad, like the researchers in the station did, but much quicker."

Lilac's eyes close, the features so suited to laughter and frivolity now bearing signs of a deep, biting grief. "I knew it," she murmurs. "I told you I could feel—"

"I believe you," Tarver interrupts her, and though he doesn't look back at us, I know he's unwilling to share the whole story behind their cryptic conversation. "I'm not about to make that mistake again."

Lilac's eyes fly open then, refocusing on her screen. "Are your friends okay? Have they . . . Are you okay?" She's addressing me and Flynn directly now. There's such a shift in her voice, her compassion so clear, her expression transformed. Somehow she knows what we're going through. But how? It's her own father's company; what could it have possibly done to her?

My voice tangles with uncertainty. "I—I'm not sure."

Merendsen speaks up again. "We'll figure it out. We'll help them."

"Tarver, you know you can't stay there for long. I'll try to find out what I can, but if what's happening there is connected to the whispers, then your poking around will only draw the wrong kind of attention. They're watching us constantly as it is; it'll only get worse."

Who's watching? Her father? But their conversation is moving lightning quick, and I don't have time to analyze that before they're moving on.

"I know. I've only got two days here before I'm due off-world with the report. But Lee and Cormac are looking for a facility LRI might have here, somewhere out in no-man's-land. It's not the first time they've used another corporation's territory in secret, so they've had practice burying the records."

"Patron." Lilac's face is grim, her eyes glued to her monitor as though trying to read the minute details of Merendsen's face.

He nods. "But this one would have been moved recently from one location to another, and that's got to leave a paper trail somewhere. Can you look into that?"

"I'll try to get into my father's files. He's changed his passwords, but I can . . ." She hesitates. "I'll talk to the Knave."

Merendsen grimaces. "Are you sure? We keep feeding him more information, trusting him with more of our secrets."

Lilac shakes her head. "Come on, Tarver. He taught us how to protect ourselves, keep our lives private. Without him we wouldn't be having this conversation. We have to trust him."

Merendsen grumbles wordlessly, the sound approaching a growl, but he nods.

I clear my throat. "The Knave?" I can hear the dubiousness in my voice. It's one thing to bring in Merendsen and to let him bring in his fiancée. But this is rapidly spiraling out of my control.

"The Knave of Hearts," says Lilac. "A hacker based somewhere on Corinth. Don't worry, Captain. He can be trusted."

Merendsen's eyes are still on the screen, and when he speaks his voice is soft. He misses her. "I'm sorry to bring you into it, Lilac. We may not be able to call again. It's hard enough setting up a completely secure line under the best of circumstances, and these aren't those."

"I'll get word through somehow," she says confidently.

Hackers, socialites with hidden tech skills—it's all too much. "This is ridiculous," I burst out, earning stares from everyone. "Sir." I shift my gaze to Merendsen. "I expected you to help me bring this up the chain of command. It's what I should've done in the first place." I can feel Flynn's eyes on me.

"You can't." Lilac's voice cracks whip-like from the speakers, stopping me cold.

"I appreciate you wanting to help, Miss LaRoux." Speaking to her, this creature from a world entirely separate from mine, feels strange. "But if I take this to General Macintosh, he'll have the power to actually do something."

Lilac LaRoux doesn't answer immediately. I half expect Merendsen to take over and fight this battle for her, but instead he waits, watching the girl on the screen. Finally, she tilts her head to one side and speaks. "The planet we crashed on, Captain, was not what the reports later said it was. By the time Tarver and I were rescued, we had discovered a mountain of evidence implicating my father's company in a conspiracy that would have ruined him."

My mouth goes dry, and I find myself looking for Flynn, who has finally pulled his gaze up off the floor. "So why not go public with it?"

"Because he destroyed it."

"No one can destroy *all* the evidence of a conspiracy like that," Flynn argues, and I know he's thinking of the LaRoux Industries ident chip I found in the swamp.

"No, not the evidence—Mr. Cormac, he destroyed the *planet*."

The silence pours in to follow her words. I can feel Flynn's panic matching my own, a thickening of the air that makes it hard to breathe. My gaze pulls toward him, and I find him staring hollow-eyed at the screen. My heart squeezes, a low painful wrench.

"We let him bury it," Lilac murmurs, closing her eyes. "We thought that . . . well, we thought the story ended there. We knew he'd taken whispers from the rift, but we didn't think any were still alive until a few months ago."

"Whispers?" I interject.

Merendsen shifts, clearing his throat in such a way that forestalls any answer to my question, and I realize he's afraid to discuss it over the computer, despite their security measures. "It's not your fault, Lilac," he says quietly. "Now we know."

"He can't destroy Avon." Flynn's voice is hoarse, torn from his throat with an effort that makes his shoulders quiver. "There are people here. Not just colonists—soldiers, civilian personnel, corporation representatives. It'd be mass murder."

But Lilac LaRoux is listening with a weary grief in the slope of her lips, the drawn brows. "You don't know my father."

I'm still struggling to digest what Lilac LaRoux has just told us. It means there's nowhere to go. If we tip our hand, even if we start to win this secret struggle behind the war, the moment LaRoux begins to suspect he's losing control of Avon, he could destroy it, and all the lives it harbors. Me. Commander Towers. Molly. Flynn.

We're all alone.

"Your only hope is to find proof." Lilac LaRoux is all business again, that grief tucked away where no one can see it. She's far better than I ever was, Stone-faced Chase or no. "You find proof of what's going on there, and you find a way to go public with it, tell everyone who will listen about what my father is doing—that's your protection. He can't destroy anything if the galaxy is watching."

Then, eyes drifting away, no doubt searching for me in her picture, she raises her voice again. "Mr. Cormac, Captain, you're not alone. You hear me? I'm going to help. Just hang in there." Neither of us expected the daughter of Roderick LaRoux to care that people were dying on Avon, much less offer us help or compassion.

"And Captain—" Lilac's still talking, pulling my attention back. "If my father's experiments are involved, then you can't trust anything. Trust Flynn, trust yourself, but trust what you feel, not what you see. They can do things—put pictures in your head, make you see things, hear things, that aren't there. Trust what you feel."

I take a step back, not knowing how to respond. *Trust what you feel.* I manage not to look at Flynn again, but I can feel his eyes on me.

Merendsen saves me having to reply. "We should get off the line, just in case."

Lilac nods. "Of course." No pleas to stay or coy demands that he spend more time talking to her. She's calm, quiet, competent. For a wild moment I think she'd make a good soldier—and then I have to dismiss the thought for sheer ridiculousness. "I'll see what I can get by tomorrow and send it your way."

Merendsen exhales audibly, the sense of urgency fading. I can't see his face, but I can tell he's gazing at his fiancée on the screen, having run out of words.

Her eyes soften. "Be careful, Tarver," she says simply. "Come back to me."

"I promise." He lifts a hand, fingertips brushing the screen—and after half a second, hers lifts as well. As though they're reaching across the intervening light-years, palm to palm. I look away, not wanting to intrude on this intimacy. There's silence for a few heartbeats, and then the light cuts out abruptly as the picture vanishes. I look up to see the words SESSION TERMINATED flashing along the bottom of the screen.

Merendsen leans back, inhaling briskly. It's a few seconds before he turns, swiveling in the chair to look at me. "Well," he says heavily. "That's my girl. Still don't understand why I want to marry her?"

I have to swallow to find my voice. "I was wrong, sir. I'm sorry."

He grins at me. "She's used to it. And so am I, now. Or at least I'm getting more used to it. It's not easy listening to people dismiss her as a fashion-obsessed idiot, but it's what's best, and it keeps anyone from thinking she's hiding anything."

"What *is* she hiding?" Flynn speaks up, making me jump. For a moment I'd almost forgotten there was anyone else in the room besides Merendsen and the image of his fiancée on the screen.

Merendsen shakes his head. "It's all a bit—I can't tell you everything.

You're going to have to trust me on that. There are some things we can't tell anyone. But I can tell you a little. Enough."

We settle in, Merendsen in the computer chair, me on the top of my clothes trunk, Flynn on the end of the bed. Merendsen's struggling, searching for a place to start. His fingers fumble with each other, a nervous gesture I've never seen from him before—not out in the field, not even when he got called up for his first medals and had to accept them in front of the entire company.

It hits me that we're the first people he's *ever* considered telling whatever it is he and Lilac LaRoux are hiding. Whatever was worth destroying an entire planet to conceal.

"Do you remember the crash of the *Icarus* eight months ago?"

Merendsen launches into the strangest story I've ever heard—a shipwreck with two survivors, a planet terraformed but with flora and fauna twisted, voices on the wind, visions everywhere. He tells it briefly, matter-of-fact and confident, but even so it's difficult to believe. A planet terraformed in secret, no settlers, no record of it in the government's permits. But he's not done.

"We found creatures there. Beings. Different from anything we have here."

"Here . . . on Avon?" Flynn's sounding as dubious as I feel.

"Here in this universe." Merendsen hesitates, then plows ahead. "LaRoux Industries opened a rift on that planet, a gateway between this dimension and another. Like the ones ships use to travel through hyperspace, but this one was permanently jammed open, and there were sentient creatures living there. LaRoux's scientists pulled these beings through and trapped them."

"Beings?" I can't conceal my skepticism. He sounds like the rookies we get here on Avon, all too willing to believe the locals' wild tales of wisps in the swamp.

Merendsen flashes me a grim smile. "You don't know the half of it. I don't know what they were, not really. Lilac and I called them the whispers."

"Why do you think this has anything to do with Avon?" Flynn's voice is taut. "There are too many people here—someone would have noticed if there were creatures on this planet."

"Not if LaRoux were concealing them in a secret, moving facility," Merendsen replies, raising an eyebrow at Flynn. "The whispers could do things we couldn't begin to understand. They changed the planet we crashed on in the years they spent there. They sped up its plant growth, altered the animals originally seeded there."

My eyes snap to Flynn, who stands suddenly stricken as he stares at my former captain. He and I only met because he was there that night in Molly's, pumping soldiers for information about how the facility in the swamp might be connected with Avon's stunted terraforming progress. The arguments that had sounded so insane to me at the time—his conspiracy theories that Avon's owning corporations were slowing down its development on *purpose*—come rushing back in a flood that sends a chill down my spine.

The tang of sudden anger prompts me to lurch to my feet. "If you're right, how can we hope to fight these things?"

Merendsen's eyebrows shoot up. "Fight them? Lee, they're not the enemy. They're LaRoux's victims as much as Avon's citizens are. The whispers were never hostile toward us—in fact, they helped us. But they're not like us, they don't see us the way we see each other, as individuals, unique. They don't really understand death. They're all connected." His eyes flick toward the window, avoiding mine.

I can sense him avoiding the truth, picking up on a dozen tiny clues: the way he won't meet my gaze; the twitch of his hand as he stops himself from running it through his hair; the short, casual sentences that belie the importance of what he's saying.

"Sir, what aren't you telling us?"

He glances up, eyes falling first on me, then on Flynn. He's silent for a time, then sits up straighter. "Something happened there that . . . changed us. Changed me, specifically."

"An experience like that would change anyone." Flynn's voice is dry.

"I mean really changed," says Merendsen quietly. "I can sense them sometimes—they're a part of me still. Distant, and quiet, but there. And they've been getting louder."

My body wants to shiver, to scan Merendsen's features and try to find some evidence of what he's telling us. I'm slow to sit back down, my anger on Avon's behalf—on Flynn's behalf—draining away. "What are you saying? That you're not . . . you anymore?"

"I'm me," he replies instantly, an uncharacteristic hint of defensiveness in his tone. "I'm me, the same person I've always been. You know me."

He's right. I *do* know my captain, and he's never been overly concerned with protecting himself by hiding the truth. The shiver is spreading, sending a creeping, cold certainty through my body. "What would happen if LaRoux Industries found out about you?"

Merendsen meets my gaze finally, and in his face I see the confirmation of my suspicion: fear. And I don't think I ever saw him afraid in all the time we served together. "They'd take me away, Lee."

I think of the girl in the monitor, the times Merendsen stopped her from speaking, how quick he was to come when he realized these so-called whispers were involved. All the little clues, the fragments in their conversation, the pieces Merendsen's left for me to assemble. *It keeps anyone from thinking she's hiding anything. They're watching us. Trust what you feel. That's my girl.*

"I understand, sir." My voice comes out fierce.

Merendsen nods. "Thank you, Captain."

Flynn's watching us with a wooden expression. I know he doesn't understand what I've just promised my friend; you'd have to know Tarver Merendsen the way I do to begin untangling these clues. But Flynn knows *me*. He recognizes the intensity in my voice, the feeling in my expression. And when he sees me looking at him, he jerks his eyes away.

"Sir." My voice shakes, and I can't stop it. "When you were talking to Lilac, you said these whispers had caused a bunch of researchers to go mad before." If it was one of these creatures controlling me, and not my own mind cracking and my insanity massacring those people, would it be any better? Would it matter to Flynn? The questions die on my lips as quickly as they come to me.

Because what if the answer is no?

Merendsen's watching me. "You want to know if they could be the cause of the Fury?"

I don't answer—I can't, my throat so tight I can barely breathe. I want to look at Flynn, to see if there's any chance this would change things between us. But I know it won't. It was still my hand. My gun.

Merendsen sighs. "They didn't do that to us. But we did find a . . . a record of sorts, of what happened to the original research station near where we crashed. And yes, Lee. It looked very much like the Fury." His tone is quiet, even gentle, but I know him too well to believe it. There's a steady anger hidden deep in his voice that makes me wonder what happened to him on that planet that he's still not telling us. "Whatever LaRoux is using them for, perhaps the Fury is a side effect. Either way, LaRoux's experiments didn't end on that planet."

I turn away, eyes sliding past Flynn until I can fix on the door instead, hands curled tightly against the lid of the trunk. I can still feel him there, the weight of guilt strung between us like a cord; bound together, held apart.

"Lee, give me your gun." Merendsen's on his feet, one hand extended to me. Soldier or not, it's an order, and I comply, pulling it holster and all off my belt and handing it to him. He pulls the Gleidel out, as familiar with it as I am, and turns it over so he can reach the access panel. Flipping the cover up, he hands it back to me. "Take a look at the readout. When was this last discharged?"

I let my eyes fall to the display. "Four days ago. I shot at the ceiling to cause a rock fall to give Flynn and me time to escape."

"And before that? How many times was it fired?"

My heart shrinks. "Please—sir, I can't look, you don't understand—"

"That's an order, Captain."

I force myself to drop my eyes and scroll the button backward, expecting to see twenty, thirty shots registering on its record. Instead there's nothing. Not for days and days, and after a while I stop scrolling, and my hand falls into my lap, numb.

He leans over to rest his hand on mine. "A whisper may have brought you there, but it wasn't to kill anyone. You never fired your weapon."

My mind is reeling. "I didn't kill those people." I can't think, can't process. I'm struggling to breathe. All I know, all I can think of, is Flynn. I lift my head with an effort to find him looking straight at me, his face pale. I'm caught by that gaze, my blood thundering in my ears, frozen where I sit.

He tears his eyes away and stumbles to his feet. I want to speak, but I can't, and he turns swiftly for the door, fumbling for the latch. He's gone before I can speak, and I'm left sitting there staring after him, still trying to find my equilibrium.

Merendsen drops down into a crouch on the floor in front of me, reaching over to gently guide my face back toward his. He's treating me the way we're taught to treat disaster victims reacting in shock. Some detached part of my mind recognizes the training.

"I can't believe you didn't think to check its memory," Merendsen says quietly, a smile in his voice. "You haven't changed. Always looking forward, never back."

"You weren't there." My voice breaks despite my attempts to find calm. "You didn't wake up with no memory of how you got there, covered in blood. You didn't see the—"

"Hey, shh." Merendsen gives my shoulder a squeeze. "Now you know. And so does he."

I glance toward the door, though Flynn's long gone. "He left."

"He needs time to understand."

I shake my head. "Him and me both."

Merendsen sighs. "You know he's falling in love with you, right?"

My head snaps up, my eyes finding him again. If he wanted to cut through my shock, he certainly managed it. "Don't be ridic—"

"Come on," he interrupts.

I swallow, thinking of the night Flynn told me he could prove I had a soul, that I wasn't heartless; the night he kissed me. I think of the way he washed the blood from my hands even when he knew he'd likely never see me again. I think of his face, standing in the back doorway of Molly's, watching me with Merendsen.

"They all think they're in love with me at some point or another," I say finally, uncomfortably. There's a difference between the way Flynn acts and the way the new recruits act when they first start taking orders from me, but I'm not ready to analyze that. "He'll get over it."

"And he's like all your rookies?"

My heart pounds in the silence, stomach twisting. I feel sick, a hollow grief welling up inside me. "It doesn't matter if he's different," I whisper. "We're on opposite sides. We're enemies, he and I."

Merendsen's mouth shifts to a faint smile. "You're talking to the guy marrying Lilac LaRoux," he points out. "Nothing's insurmountable."

That, at least, makes me smile a little in return. "I hardly think class differences are quite the same as 'my people try to kill his people and vice versa.'"

His smile fades. "I said I couldn't tell you everything that happened to us on that planet. Believe me when I tell you it wasn't just that she was rich and I was poor."

I swallow, dropping my eyes. "You didn't have to wash the blood of your people off her hands. Some things you just can't live with."

Merendsen reaches up and takes my hands, wrapping them briefly in both of his. "Some things you can't live with*out*."

The girl wakes from a dream within her dream, safe in her bed above her mother's shop.

The ghost is there, casting its soft, greenish light around her bedroom.

She sits up, but for some reason she isn't afraid. Hovering half-way between sleep and dreams, she remembers that she's seen it before, not only at school, not only in the alley, but everywhere.

"I know you," she whispers, not wanting to wake her parents.

The little wisp of light sways gently, and the girl feels a shiver wrack her body, the taste of metal flooding her mouth; but this, too, is familiar, and she's not afraid.

In between one breath and the next, the world around her changes; her wallpaper is water, her curtains seaweed, the glow-in-the-dark stars on her ceiling now jellyfish of all shapes and sizes. She's sitting on a bed of coral, and she can breathe the water like air. All around her is the world she dreams of, as real and vivid as life, and she laughs, delighted.

In front of her blooms a vivid purple sea anemone, and then another, and another, until there's a road of violet leading away, into unexplored territory full of submarines and sea monsters, waiting only for her to discover it.

TWENTY-SIX

FLYNN

I HAVE NOWHERE TO GO, NO TIME TO PROCESS. I STUMBLE as I make my way down the muddy main drag of the base, my mind churning. My clothes are still soaking, and abruptly I'm freezing, my teeth chattering. I should be trying to comprehend what Merendsen just told us, his talk of creatures from another universe—but right or wrong, the only place my mind wants to go is Jubilee. The grief starts to well up, like it's safe to let it happen now that I know it wasn't her hand, her gun.

But there's so much to think through—*if it wasn't Jubilee, who was it?*—and I'm surrounded by trodairí. With my thoughts flapping around like loose ends in the wind, I only stop when a soldier nearly runs into me. Our eyes meet, and I ease my weight back, lifting my hands to claim the blame. His mouth's opening to ask a question when I turn on my heel, striding away. I shouldn't have run out of there, the one place I was safe. I need to find somewhere to hole up and think. The soldiers who see me here, out in the open, are all going to assume I'm supposed to be here—but if any of them talk to me, what will I say?

I slip into the alleyway behind Molly's, wishing I could look over my shoulder and see if I've been followed. Looking furtive is always a mistake—one of Sofia's tips. I force my shoulders down, make myself lift my chin instead.

Easing the door open, I step inside, thinking of the stacks of crates. I can hunker down there, probably find something to eat or drink, buy myself a little time to *think*.

And that's when I come face-to-face with the bartender. He's a wall of a man, looming over me, and as I stare at him, he reaches for a bottle, hefting it meaningfully in one hand.

"Wait." I spit the word out before I have time to think about what to say next, and stop that bottle from connecting with my temple. "Wait, I'm with Jubilee."

That's enough to buy me a stay of execution, but his gaze bores through me like he can see all the way to the back of my skull. See the tangled confusion inside me, the mess of questions and hurt and need. "And why'm I believing that?"

I scrabble for an explanation that will reassure him. "She left a message with you—that was for me. Jubilee will vouch for me."

The silence draws out, and I force myself to hold still and bite down on the inside of my cheek to stop myself from speaking. Finally, he rumbles, "You can stay here, an' I'll check with Lee. But if you do cause trouble, and anyone ends up dead 'cause of you, I won't pause 'fore I call in the troops." With a sickening lurch of my stomach, I realize he *recognizes* me. Either from the night I took Jubilee, or from the footage of my face being circulated around the base. But he's waiting—because of Jubilee. His voice drops as he folds his arms across his chest. "And if you hurt *her*, even a little, I won't bother calling the proper authorities."

"Yes, sir," I say quietly. I wish I could promise Jubilee would be safe with me. But we'd both know I was making promises I can't keep.

He studies me for a long moment, and I study him back: shaven head, tattoos all the way up his arms in foreign characters that look like art, twangy backwater accent just like some of the other off-worlders. He's a mystery. I wonder what brought him here.

"Come on out front," he says.

"Out *front*?"

"You think I'm leaving you here unsupervised?" He claps me on the shoulder, and my knees nearly give out. "You can come an' polish some glasses right where I can see you."

I need to stop, to think. I need time, I need quiet. Because if Jubilee wasn't the one who shot my people, I need to know who did. But the bartender's posture makes it clear that in this, I have absolutely no choice. I swallow. "Yes, sir."

Heart pounding, I follow him out into the bar full of trodairí. He jabs a thumb at the bin of clean glasses under the bar, so I get to work—and keep my head down, praying my tan and my hair are enough to hide me behind the scuffed bar top. But no matter how I try to clear my head, to stay focused, all I can see is Jubilee's stunned face, her heart in her eyes as she looked at me. My world has been torn apart and stitched back together too many times, and now I exist only as a tattered patchwork of myself—unable to think, unable to feel anything other than numbness.

It's about an hour later when the door swings open, and I look up to find Jubilee there with Merendsen. She looks ragged in a way she hasn't since the massacre, and my hands fall still on the glass I'm polishing. Merendsen barely glances my way before heading for a table full of trodairí, but Jubilee freezes for the tiniest instant when she sees me. There's relief there—the raggedness was for *me*—and then it's gone, replaced by anger. She starts to head for the bar, but Molly casually steps in between us and she stops, looking up at him. He shakes his head a fraction—*not now*—and after a long, burning moment of hesitation, she nods. She turns her back on me and slides in to sit beside Tarver Merendsen.

The trodairí vie to buy him drinks, and he plays them like he was born doing it. Despite the heavy dread in the air since the Fianna attacked and hostilities resumed, Merendsen eases them back into the world and has them laughing at his stories. Mostly at his own expense, though a couple are about a younger Jubilee. He spends a good twenty minutes on the time she hit her head hard enough that all she could taste for weeks was dead rat, making the table erupt into easy laughter. He's good at this. You'd never know he was in her quarters an hour before, whispering the darkest of secrets.

Jubilee is different, though. Her laughter comes a second after theirs, never quite reaching her eyes. She lets Merendsen take over, take the lead, relieving her of any need for a response. She nurses her drink longer than they do. Her eyes fade in and out of focus, gaze growing distant, though it never shifts to seek me. How long is she going to leave me here, polishing glasses in a room full of people who want to kill me? *Damn it.*

But I can see the way her muscles are still coiled with that graceful readiness that's hers alone, her body still tense. She's reeling like I am, so shaken she can't react. I want to go to her. I want to . . . I have no idea what I want to do.

As the night wears on, the other soldiers drift away until the only ones left at the table are Jubilee and her old captain. A few late drinkers line up along the bar, and Molly tallies the till as I clear up. Jubilee's tracing a design into the spilled beer on their table, knotwork. It's Irish. I wonder if she knows.

I can't slow down my head. Regret and relief crowd my thoughts, which won't stop turning, won't stop reaching for Jubilee. Then I look up, and she's standing a few yards away, speaking to Molly. I drop the glass I'm polishing, and it shatters on the floor. Molly frowns at me and tilts his head at the door that leads out the back. I go.

Jubilee slips through the door not long after me. My heart jumps as I recognize her silhouette in the half darkness, and I make myself stay where I am, leaning against a stack of crates. My head's swimming with tiredness, and just having her in the room hitches my pulse up a notch, though I don't know if it's wanting or anger or something else completely. My heart is so tangled I can't think.

"Molly says you can stay here in the back room." She sounds tired, at least as tired as I am. "If anyone asks, you'll say you're his cousin."

Posing as the cousin of a three-hundred-pound Chinese man would be beyond even Sofia's talents. "I don't—"

"Molly's an orphan, like me. He was adopted. Off-world, families who aren't blood-related happen all the time. You're just not used to it here."

Lapsing into silence, she leans against the stack of beer crates opposite me and folds her arms across her ribs, tight and uncertain. She just stares at me, for so long I feel I might shout to break the quiet, until finally she blurts, "Are you trying to get yourself arrested out there, breaking glasses and drawing attention?"

Frustration takes the lead among my competing emotions, and I come to my feet. "You're the one who left me working behind the bar for hours, under the same damn camera that's broadcasting my face to the whole—"

"Because you stormed out! If you'd stayed, I would've been able to plan our next move, someplace to hide you while I figure this out."

"Hide me? While *you* figure it out?" The frustration coursing through me is real, but right behind it, the knowledge that she wasn't the killer. I could touch her now and not hate myself. But she's still a trodaire—I can't let myself think this way.

I search for words that will push her away, put some distance between us so I can't reach for her. "So you think I'm going to hide somewhere safe and trust you to fix this while I'm sidelined? You and your old captain have it under control?"

"Sidelined?" she snaps, incredulous, though there's relief in her gaze too. Her eyes rake over me, unable to look away. Neither of us can talk about how everything is different now that Jubilee's innocent. Anger is easier. "Damn it, Flynn, I'm betraying everything I'm sworn to, hiding you here. I'm a traitor now. I'm the bad guy."

"You're doing it for the right reasons," I offer, but I know for Jubilee, the words ring hollow.

"I know," she replies tightly. "I know that. And I'd do it again. I just—I never thought I could ever in a thousand years be here, in this spot." She turns away, twisting the heel of her hand against her eyes for a moment. "I told you my parents died in the uprising on Verona. But I didn't tell you that it wasn't even rebels who killed them. The men who killed them were sympathizers. Supporting the rebels. People like me."

I stay silent. This isn't a conversation—she's not expecting me to argue or tell her it's not her fault. I just listen.

"They wanted to use my mom's store as a staging area. My parents wanted no part of the rebellion, so they refused. And the sympathizers killed them for it." She swallows, hard, and steadies her voice. "They were people we knew, Flynn. Neighbors. Coworkers. People you'd say hello to in the park. And because they picked a side in a war that wasn't even theirs, they shot two people while their eight-year-old daughter hid under a counter."

Slowly, I ease in closer to her. "That's why you hate it when I call you Jubilee. Because that's what your parents called you."

"I don't hate it anymore." She swallows again. Her voice, when she can continue, is wrenching. "You've ruined my life, you know."

I can't speak, my breath coming as quickly as hers, frustration and longing twisting together, like a quick-burning fuse.

"I was fine before you turned up here and dragged me into the swamps." Her voice rises, halfway between tears and violence. "I was supposed to have no soul—I was supposed to be dead. Jubilee was supposed to have died with her parents, in their shop in November; Lee was no more than a dream."

In the bar, the jukebox comes on. Molly must be trying to drown out the sounds of raised voices. I move toward her, unable to resist; her eyes are wet, her face flushed, and I can finally look at her, want her, let myself touch her without grief turning everything to ashes in my mouth.

"You've ruined me," she repeats, her voice quieting a little as it catches. "You've ruined me—you made me wake up. And now I can't get rid of you." Her voice surges again as I reach out, curling my hand around her arm, her skin flushed hot under my fingers. "You won't leave me alone."

I scan her features, my eyes trying to make up for too much time spent trying not to look at her. I can't look away. "You think I want to be here with you?" I reply, my voice hoarse. "You think if you walked out right now, I'd chase you?"

She gazes back at me, her eyes a challenge. "Wouldn't you?"

"You know I would," I snap, surrendering. "And I have no idea why that's such a problem."

She jerks her arm free and backs up a step until she hits the door. "It's a problem because I'd *let* you!" she blurts. Then, after a harsh breath, she murmurs, "It's a problem because I'd want you to."

I move after her and duck my head to find her lips with mine. It's all I want to do. She surges up against me like she's been waiting for this, lips parting, arms curling around my neck. Everything crowds together— grief, desire, anger, and beneath it all, a desperate hint of hope, and I can feel the sharing of it in the energy that wells up between us. I drag my hand up from her waist, my fingertips finding bare skin and the dip of her spine as hers tighten in my hair. She gasps against my mouth, a split second pause, and then we're together again as if we'd been parted for an eternity.

With a strained noise she breaks away and turns her head to stop me from picking up the kiss where we left off. Her breath comes quick and heavy, and I lean in closer to pin her against the door, my hips finding hers. This is what I want.

"God, Flynn, we can't." She's panting the words. "We can't."

I bend my head to kiss her beneath the line of her jaw, and I feel her body shift against mine. "One true thing," I breathe into her hair, remembering what she said the night I brought her back to the base. The night I washed the blood from her hands. "Something real in all of this. This is real."

"We're enemies. That's what's real." Despite her protests, her arms are tight around me, unwilling to let go. I press a kiss to her temple and rest my forehead against her dark hair.

"I'm not your enemy, Jubilee Chase," I whisper. "And I don't think you're mine." I lean after her until I can capture her mouth again. My hands burn where I touch her, everything else fading away into the background, drowned out by this, by her, by *us*.

The music coming from the bar changes, and as if the shift broke the moment, Jubilee gasps and mumbles, "It's too dangerous."

"Don't care." And I don't, finding bare skin at her neck beside the chain of her dog tags, hearing her lose her words as I nip, push her collar aside to find the juncture between her neck and shoulder, kiss her soft skin.

Her body arches against mine, responding to my touch. A split second later, though, she goes still, and I lift my head to find her biting her lip, grief in her eyes.

"Flynn, we *can't*." Her lips are flushed, eyes dark, but as she swallows and tries to collect herself, I can see the determination bleeding back into her gaze. "It's not that it's too dangerous for *us*, Flynn. It's too dangerous for *them*. If you had to choose, if it came down to it, who would you save? Your people, or me?"

She lets me brush her hair back from her face, trail my rough fingertips down the smooth skin of her cheek, waiting as I try to gather my scattered thoughts. I picked my side in the cavern when we ran from McBride, but I don't know which side I chose. Was I trying to save this girl, or was I trying to stop a war? I can't let myself think ahead to the day when I'll have to choose one or the other.

It all threatens to well back up, the tangle of things I'm too exhausted to face. There's only one thing I know with absolute certainty, and as I whisper her name and lean in to her again, she lets me. Her hand leaves my chest and invites me in—she cups my cheek as our lips meet, drawing me away from the frantic heat and toward something slower, something quiet. Something real.

We both pause to breathe after a time, and she ducks her head. I kiss her temple and wait for her to speak.

"Sooner or later one of us will have to make a choice, and if we do this we'll make the wrong one. We're the only ones who can see what's happening. They need us." She turns to slip out of my arms, putting herself out of my reach—or me out of hers.

"Don't you ever get tired of being needed?" Suddenly that's all I am—tired, heartsick for my sister, my cousin, my friends. Worn down by McBride's anger, Sofia's grief, by my own helplessness. I want refuge. I want Jubilee.

"Not until this moment." She's stricken, but she stands there by the door, and she doesn't reach out to me. Everything in me aches, but I don't reach out to her either. Because she's right.

"Go." It takes everything in me to let her leave. For the sake of people who'd shoot me on sight. Who think she's a murderer and I'm a traitor.

She doesn't speak, standing and staring at me for two long, slow breaths. Then her hand fumbles for the door handle, wrenching it open so she can stumble out into the night. The door bangs shut behind her so hard it misses the latch, shuddering open again with its momentum.

I slam my palm against the wall, feeling the sting of it, the pain shooting up all the way to my shoulder. As the door eases back open, I can see her walking away. I watch her as she passes under the floodlights.

Just before the door swings closed, I think I see her catch her step, start to slow. Then the gap I'm watching through is gone, and with a click, we're both alone.

The girl is waiting. She's at a spaceport she's never seen before, orbiting a planet she doesn't recognize. All she has are the clothes she's wearing, but she's glued to the viewport, heart jumping with each new ship that eases into the docking bays. She's certain she'll recognize hers when she sees it.

A man comes to find her, to tell her that the exploration vessel she's been hired on is ready to depart. He escorts her to the right docking bay, where a small but sleek ship waits for her. The viewports are glimmering gold-and-green, and through them she catches glimpses of people—a child with dark hair, a sullen teenager with a fake ident, an older woman she doesn't recognize.

Her escort, who is also somehow the captain too, gestures toward the gangplank.

"Well?"

Somewhere, deep, deep in her thoughts, something stirs—the certainty that this never happened, that it couldn't be happening now. This isn't how her life will go. It'll be dark, and cold, and likely very short; and the glittering lights of the spaceliner were never for her.

"I can't," she whispers, the words wrenching at her soul. The captain turns toward her, and she can see her own heartache reflected in his green, green eyes. "I'm sorry. I can't."

TWENTY–SEVEN

JUBILEE

I DON'T REMEMBER THE WALK BACK TO MY QUARTERS. BUT abruptly I'm there, my head still spinning, skin tingling. It's easy enough to run myself through the motions as I get ready for bed, my routine ground into me through years of being too tired at the end of the day to do anything else. I can't let myself think, can't let myself dwell on the fiery adrenaline surging through me. I can't let myself replay what happened with Flynn.

I can't let myself continue to fall for a boy who represents everything I've been fighting against since I was eight years old.

But since I can't actually stop myself from doing any of those things, at least I can stop myself from touching him ever again.

I'm not on duty the next day until mid-morning, but I wake at sunrise anyway, the habit too well ingrained to set aside. There's no word from Merendsen about our next move, giving me no outlet for the need to act, to keep my thoughts away from dangerous territory. I should be giving my body as much time to recover as I can before I'm out on the fences again. It's cold, wet, hard work out there; the rebels are invisible in the swamp, the bullets coming from nowhere. They keep too close to the base for us to call in an airstrike, but too far for us to pick them off from behind our fortifications. We're forced down low, and the mud oozes inside my combat suit, itching like mad once it dries, and I smell like a swamp no matter how hard I scrub afterward. When we follow them farther into the swamps they vanish into nowhere, drawing us onto unsafe ground like will-o'-the-wisps.

It's hours before I'm on duty, but my skin's crawling for action, and every time I sit still—every time I close my eyes—Flynn's there.

One true thing, he said, his lips finding a hidden spot behind my jaw. *This is real.*

I throw on the fatigues I was wearing yesterday, wrinkled and untidy—but laundry is the last priority on the base right now, and no one's about to judge me for looking disheveled while going for a run. Hesitating only briefly, I buckle on my holster and my Gleidel. Awkward to jog with, but this is the wrong time to go anywhere on Avon unarmed. I choose my running shoes over my regulation boots and duck out into the misty, cold dawn. With Avon's overcast skies sunrise is slow to take, as though the light itself is slowed down, oozing over the landscape gradually. It's still dark, but I can see the fog lit overhead as the diffuse sunlight peeks through.

It's too dangerous to do the usual training run, the eight-klick perimeter of the base that culminates in the obstacle course by the gym. There are rebels beyond the fences who know the land better than we do, and I don't relish the idea of running ten feet away from someone with a gun pointed at me that I can't see.

So instead I weave through the buildings, ignoring the way the mud splashes up at my pants legs. It's a struggle not to push myself harder, to get to the point where I don't have the focus to think about anything but one foot in front of the other, but I can't waste all my energy while off duty.

I head past security, my breath steaming in the clammy air, and aim for the road that heads toward Central Command. It's less torn up than the other paths, not as muddy. Easier to run on.

My path takes me straight up past Central Command in time to see Commander Towers disappear into her office. I stop short in a spray of mud. We need proof of what's happening—Lilac LaRoux said as much. And while she and Merendsen might be content to put our fates in the hands of some hacker on the other side of the galaxy, I'm not used to waiting for someone else to save me.

I know Commander Towers knows more than she's telling me. And

I can't believe she's dirty. If she was in LaRoux's pocket, why would she have warned me about telling Lilac's fiancé what was going on here?

I wish Flynn were here. I hate the idea of leaving him in the dark, especially after seeing his anguish last night at having to continue hiding instead of finding justice for the massacre. But I'm not ready to face him yet; just the thought of him makes my cheeks burn. I shove his image away and turn toward Commander Towers's office. My feet thud in time with my heart against the wooden stairs up to the prefab trailer.

"What?" Her voice shouts from inside; she's not happy about being interrupted.

"It's Chase, sir. Can I speak with you?"

The silence from the other side of the door stretches a fraction too long. "Of course. Come in."

I shove the rickety door open and slip through. "Commander."

"Shut the door!" she hisses, standing by her desk.

I blink, taken aback, but instinctively slam the door behind me.

"Sorry about that, Captain Chase. But you can't be too careful. You don't know who's watching us."

I suppress a shiver and take the seat she gestures at, expecting her to take a seat behind her desk. Instead she starts to pace, her eyes on the door instead of on me. I wait for her to gather herself, to speak to me, to let me explain why I've come—but it's like she's completely forgotten I'm in the room.

"Uh—sir?"

She stops pacing mid-stride, turning toward me. Her blue eyes are glittering, too bright. I don't think she's slept since I last spoke to her. "I'm sorry, Captain. You wanted to speak with me?"

"Yes, sir." I swallow, my mouth suddenly gone dry. *Trust what you feel,* Lilac LaRoux told me. I believe in Commander Towers. "Sir, I know what's going on. I know about LaRoux Industries, I know there was a hidden facility to the east, and I know it all has something to do with the Fury. And I know you know something about it."

The silence is broken only by the frantic pounding of my heart, echoed briefly in the distance by a patter of gunfire. Commander Towers watches me, her breath coming rapidly, the circles under her eyes more pronounced than ever. I find it hard to meet her gaze; there's fear burning behind her blue eyes, the desperation of a woman on the edge.

Then she closes her eyes. "God, Lee, you don't know what a relief it is to hear you say that. This can't leave my office, but . . ." She trails off, shoulders drooping as if with the weight of her secret.

My own relief is like a gust of fresh air, letting me breathe again for the first time since I stepped through her door.

She turns away, leaning on her desk. "I know you went out to that facility; I know that's why you were asking about it. I was afraid of what you might have seen there. You don't know what they do to people who know too much. They know everything—they can see inside your mind."

Lilac LaRoux's warnings echo in my mind, and I try not to let my own fear rise in response to my commander's. "Sir," I begin, "LaRoux Industries is—"

"LRI?" Towers stares at me. "I'm not talking about them. I'm talking about the—the things that are out there. In the swamp."

My skin wants to crawl, remembering what Merendsen said about his whispers, things we could never hope to understand. "If there ever was anything out there, sir, it's gone now. There's nothing to see but empty swampland."

"That doesn't mean they're gone," she mutters, raking her fingers through her hair and disheveling her normally neat bun. She takes a few more pacing steps, then whirls abruptly and crouches in front of me.

All her blinds are drawn, making her office seem even more cave-like than most of the buildings on Avon. Now that I've had a chance to look around, I can see empty ration packets strewn about, dirty coffee mugs littering the drinks station and her desk. It looks like she's been holed up here for a week.

Her voice is ragged when she answers. "Everyone goes mad, everyone. Except for you. Why don't you? Why *don't* you?" She leans forward, bracing her hands against the armrests of my chair, her face only a few inches away.

I did, I want to scream. *I killed over half a dozen people.* Except I didn't. Tarver Merendsen proved that.

"I don't know," I whisper instead.

"The facility you saw wasn't military," she says finally. "It belonged to LaRoux Industries."

My pulse quickens—I have to tread carefully to get the answers I need. "Why? What interest do they have in Avon?"

"They approached me when I was first assigned here, said they were working on a way to stop the Fury. They said all the base commanders for the past ten years had been allowing them to do their research here."

But why? To what end? I open my mouth, but Towers is still talking, her head down, mumbling in a low, droning voice that frightens me.

"We find them out there sometimes," she mumbles. "Soldiers taken by the Fury. Drowned or buried in quicksand or dead with guns in their hands and bullets in their brains. They go east, into no-man's-land, if there's no one nearby to kill when they snap. They're looking for it. They're looking for the place. But it's moving, always moving. It's never in the same place twice. I tried to find it, but . . ."

If I didn't have reason to believe in at least some of what she was saying, I would tell her she'd lost *her* mind. Her gaze is wild, her eyes sunken, lips chapped. She hasn't been taking care of herself. She clearly hasn't been sleeping. She looks like I did, drowning in guilt the morning after the massacre at the rebel base, when I believed I'd killed all those—

I freeze. "Sir, what have you done?"

Commander Towers shakes her head. "It seemed like nothing at the time. An extra bonus finds its way into my account every month, and I provide copies of our medical records. Sometimes the bodies disappear, the ones we find in the swamp. You have to understand, LaRoux Industries conducts such revolutionary medical research, and no one else is helping us, helping my soldiers. I thought they might have an answer to the Fury. You understand that, you know what it is to live and die with your platoon."

"Yes, sir," I say cautiously, keeping my voice free of judgment. I'm not sure I would have done differently in her position, and I want her to keep talking.

But it's like she doesn't even hear me.

"I can't do it anymore," she's whispering. "That place, the things they study—the Fury's only getting worse. Taking civilians now, like that man Quinn with no history of violence. I've told them I won't cover for them anymore, Lee. And I'm telling you, in case . . ." She swallows, taking a deep breath that restores a little of the sanity to her expression. "In case something happens to me."

My palms are sweaty, pressed against the seat of the chair. "Why me?"

"Why you," she repeats. "That's what they want to know. I've figured it out. LRI wants to know why you don't snap, why you never get the dreams. That's why you're still here. Lee, they didn't just pay me to look the other way. They paid me to watch *you*."

Dread grips my throat, chokes my voice away. "Who? Who's doing this?"

She gazes back at me, still standing close. Her mouth opens, then closes. I watch as her eyes focus past me, then snap back, then blur again. "Lee," she whispers—and then again, this time with an odd urgency. "*Lee.*"

"Sir?" I force myself to move, to break out of the fear holding me down so I can reach for her. "Sir, what's happening?"

As I watch, her pupils dilate, her muscles beginning to tremble. It's what happened to Mori, how she looked as she blew away that teenager in the town. I reach for my gun, but my fingers seize when they touch the familiar grip; I know I can't shoot my commander.

The first time I watched a fellow soldier die was a few weeks after I went on active duty. We were on a patrol, and he stepped into a poorly constructed—but effective—booby trap leftover from the long-ago rebellion there, and it blew him half to pieces. But there was a moment, after his foot tripped the wire and before the explosives ignited, when we both knew what had happened. His eyes met mine, and that instant unspooled into an eternity stretching between us, the knowledge unfurling on his face that he was about to die, the helplessness on mine, unable to stop it. It was only a split second, but it lasted forever.

That moment comes back to me now as Commander Towers meets my eyes. For an instant, she knows she's falling.

I brace myself, waiting for the violence to erupt.

Instead, the moment passes, and she straightens. I'm left tense, watching her, waiting for her to snap like Mori did. She gazes through me, her pupils still dilated—and then, giving herself an odd little shake, she turns away and reaches for a stack of files on her desk, walking sedately around to her chair.

I stare as she goes back to work, waiting for the other shoe to drop. But it never does. Though her pupils still seem unusually large, the rest of her body language and movements are utterly normal. More normal, in fact, than she was acting when I first stepped into her office.

"S-sir?"

She looks up, blinking in surprise. "Captain," she says mildly. "I didn't notice you come in. How can I help you?"

It's like a blow to the gut, and I'm left searching for words, floundering for understanding. "Sir, I came in here to speak with you. You were telling me about the medical records. About LaRoux Industries."

"I was?" She frowns at me, reaching up to neatly tuck a lock of hair into place. A habitual, familiar gesture I recognize, but a tad too jerky. Just a little bit wrong. "That doesn't sound right."

"Sir, the records—the facility to the east—"

"I have a lot of paperwork here, Captain," she says gently. "Can it wait?"

If I hadn't just seen her ten minutes ago, I'm not sure I'd be able to tell anything was wrong. But looking at her now, I can see it—little signs, here and there. All her gestures are right, the inflection in her voice, her turn of phrase. But it's all muted. Muffled. It's like she's herself, but somehow . . . *less*.

"Yes, sir," I stammer, backing toward the doorway. "I'll—thank you, sir."

She doesn't look up as I salute and hurry through the door.

It's all I can do to walk back toward the other side of the base and not run; it's all I can do not to find the nearest shuttle and get as far away as I can from this place.

I don't know why LaRoux Industries is here on Avon. I don't know why my commander was being paid to watch me. But whoever she really was behind the bribes and the guilt, that person is gone now. Because the thing that just politely showed me the door—that *wasn't* Commander Towers.

I intended to go look for Merendsen and tell him what I heard so we can try to put the pieces together. Instead I find myself heading for Molly's. With personnel on duty around the clock, it's always open. I try telling myself it's because I want the comfort of a crowd, but I know that's not why I'm going there. I try telling myself it's because I want Flynn's input on what's going on, hoping he has some rational explanation for what I saw.

But I know the real reason my feet are taking me his way, and I'm not proud. I'm terrified, and for the first time since I was eight years old, I just want someone to tell me it's going to be okay.

I'm halfway there, my thoughts whirling, my eyes blurring with exhaustion and fear, when my nose starts burning; I recognize the choking, acrid smell of smoke. Something, somewhere, is on fire.

My head snaps up. I can see thick black smoke billowing up in the distance, and automatically I break into a sprint. It could be any number of buildings over on that side of the base; there are a couple barracks there, a few supply sheds, even the munitions depot. But disastrous as that would be, somehow I know it's not.

God, no. Please no.

I'm barely aware of the distance elapsing between me and Molly's— it's not even a shock when I burst out from between two barracks to see the bar in flames. I keep running, stopped only when someone grabs my jacket and hauls me back, my momentum knocking me to the ground.

Scrambling in the mud to find my feet again, I'm lurching toward the burning bar when those same arms grab hold of me again.

"Chase!" shouts a dim voice in my ear. "You can't go in there!"

"There could be people in there!" I scream, my voice breaking as I struggle to get free.

"If they are, they're dead, and you can't help them!" It's Captain Biltmore, and he's not letting me go. "Get ahold of yourself, Captain!" he snaps.

When he lets go of me I fall again, and this time it's enough to jar me free of my desperate need to get inside. I stare at the flames, my thoughts grinding to a halt. There's no sign of Flynn anywhere. I can't think, can't feel. There's no room for grief—I don't understand it yet, can't accept it. Not like this.

My heart empties.

I can hear the shouts of the emergency crews, the coordinated efforts of the firefighters, getting the blaze under control before it can spread to any other buildings. A beam crashes down, sending a torrent of flames and sparks shooting skyward. The windows have all shattered from the inferno, and through an empty frame I can see the outline of the bar, red-hot against my eyes. Every breath scorches the inside of my nose with the smell of burning chemicals. Absurdly I think of Molly's antique jukebox, its red and gold plastic melting in the heat, its memory banks full of old Earth music reduced to nothing more than melted circuitry and noxious fumes.

Someone knocks into me, making me stumble and driving the image out of my mind. Catching my balance, I see a couple of medics hauling a stretcher out of the smoke, laden with a body wrapped in a sheet.

It's a large person—too large to be Flynn. In an instant I understand who it is and shove past Biltmore.

"What happened?" I snap to the medics, reaching for the sheet. "If it's just smoke inhalation, maybe he's not—"

"No, Captain, he's dead. Please, don't—" One of the medics tries to intercept me, but I'm stronger than he is, and I shove him aside so I can get at the sheet and haul it down.

There's Molly's face, calm and lax. It looks like he's sleeping, or like he's faking somehow. But then I see the blood, the scorch marks against his shaven scalp. I lean down and realize part of his skull's been blown away in the back.

Everything around me slows. Dimly, I hear the medics saying things. He was dead before the fire started. Shot, and with one of our own weapons. The bolt came from a high angle, suggesting he was made to kneel before he was killed. Executed.

When I lift my eyes from Molly's face, they fall on a pair of soldiers dragging someone away, a middle-aged man struggling and shouting curses.

"Who's that?" My voice comes out quiet, cold. Very calm. Good.

The closest medic glances at me, then at the man being dragged away. "One of the bastards responsible," he answers. "They think it was a whole crew that snuck in somehow, but he's the only one they caught. Gonna interrogate him."

My heart fills again, rage taking over as the whole world narrows down to the man being dragged away. The man responsible. They won't need to interrogate him officially—I intend to find out everything myself, no matter the cost. I pull my gun from its holster and slip quietly after him and his escort, steps quickening.

I'll find whoever did this, and I'll tear them apart.

The girl is drowsing, up past her bedtime, listening to the click of imitation ivory as her mother stirs the mah jong tiles. She's curled up with her blanket under the felted table, surrounded by her mother's friends on all sides.

A tile etched with the picture of a chrysanthemum falls to the floor, and a rumbling voice says, "I'll get it." An arm descends over the edge of the table, and the girl stares—it's covered in tattoos, more than she's ever seen in one place.

The adults chat as the girl's mother deals, and the low hum of voices nearly lulls the girl to sleep.

"Who will watch the store while I'm gone?" her mother is asking.

"I can do that," says the man with the tattoos.

"And when you're gone? Who will watch her then?"

TWENTY-EIGHT

FLYNN

I'M WATCHING FROM AN ALLEYWAY BETWEEN A BARRACKS and the munitions shed, leaning against the hard wall and forcing myself to breathe. I can't make out who it is they're hauling away, and I can't see Molly's huge silhouette anywhere, and I can't do anything but stand here, hands curled into fists, and wait. If my people did this, and they see me, all hell will break loose. More people will die.

When Jubilee stalks past, I'm so fixed on the flames I nearly miss her. I reach out to grab her arm and swing her in toward me, reflecting in the same split second that she'll probably break my nose for this. I'm sure if she were any less shocked, she would. Instead, I catch a glimpse of something wild in her eyes, of a soot-stained hand lifting to reach for me, and I duck. "Jubilee, it's me."

With a wordless sound, her face stricken, she jerks back from me and stumbles to crash into the barracks wall. The jolt makes her look up, her gaze focusing with an effort—and then she sees me, her heart in her eyes. The gun she's gripping goes clattering into the mud. Her hands grab for my arms, grasping at my sleeves and pulling me closer, as though she has to convince herself I'm real. "Flynn?" she whispers.

The mix of anguish and relief on her face has me moving before I can think to stop myself, and I pull her in against me so I can wrap my arms around her. She holds me just as tightly, and for a moment we stand there together, unmoving, as the chaos beyond the mouth of the alley unspools.

"I thought you—" she rasps, easing a half an inch away, shaken by the intensity of her own reaction.

I'm a little shaky myself, and I have to clear my throat before I can speak. "I was on my way to the supply shed when I heard the shouts. Where's Molly? He was in there when I left, I should—"

My words die in my throat as the look on her face delivers the news. Our hands fall apart, and I have to brace against the munitions shed to stop my knees from giving out.

"They caught one of the rebels who did it." She turns toward the mouth of the alley. "The others escaped. I was heading to interrogation, they're taking him—"

"Get me in there," I interrupt, urgency making my voice stumble. "Maybe I can convince him to talk. Offer him a deal."

"He's a murderer, Flynn," she snaps, her grief over her friend turning white-hot. She retrieves her gun from the ground, her face grim. "He doesn't get a deal, he gets justice."

"And if he's one of McBride's men? What if he knows what they're planning next?" I can't imagine any of my people starting the fire. It has to have been a mistake. "Please."

She knows I'm right, but the desire for vengeance runs almost as deep. I watch her struggle, feeling it echo deep within my own heart; whoever killed my people is still out there too. Finally, shoving her Gleidel back into its holster, she murmurs, "Don't promise him anything."

When we reach the holding cells, she sends away the guard with a couple of snapped orders. The nervous corporal looks at me but doesn't stop me from following before he vanishes. Perhaps he hopes I'll stop her from killing the prisoner.

My heart sinks when I see who's huddled on the bench in the corner of the room. It's Turlough Doyle, his mop of blond hair turned gray with ash, his eyes red with smoke and grief. He was only ever in the swamps because his sister sabotaged one of the algae farms, and the trodairí wouldn't stop coming by to ask him where she was, more forcefully every time. Then he met Mike, and he had reason to stay. But he's no blood-soaked rebel. He used to be a biology assistant.

His head's down, exhaustion and fear taking their toll. Jubilee doesn't hesitate, slamming the cell door behind us. "Who did this?" she snarls, stalking over to meet him eye to eye.

She was too blinded by shock and the Fury in the caves to recognize the man widowed by the massacre. But Turlough remembers her. When he lifts his head, his eyes fix on her face with a single-minded hatred that makes my heart freeze. "You're going to kill me anyway, trodaire." He spits the word. "I won't help you kill anyone else."

"You tell me," she spits right back, "or you're goddamn right I'm going to kill you, and I'll make it last. Which one of you killed Molly?"

Turlough sucks in a shaky breath, his round face losing all color— from fear or rage, I can't tell. "Me. I acted alone."

"You didn't," she shouts, voice cracking. "Those burn marks on his skull, only a Gleidel does that. You're carrying an antique."

"*You* carry a Gleidel," he shoots back. "You killed our people, our children." His gaze pins her now, eyes boring into hers. "You killed my *husband*. I hope you rot in hell."

My brain's still stuttering, and I'm pinned against the wall by the door, unnoticed by either of them. Molly was *shot*? I find my own stomach twisting with grief.

Jubilee stares back at him, and I know by her silence that she's recognized him. Then she squares her shoulders. She doesn't bother to deny his accusation, and I ache for her, but I know why. What could she possibly say that he'd believe? "I'm giving you one more chance, rebel. Names. Now."

Turlough just glares, terrified but determined. Only grief could give such a gentle man this kind of strength. Another time, I'd almost be proud of him for showing so much spine. Now, Jubilee's going to rip it out if I don't do something. I step away from the door and into the light. Turlough's gaze slides past Jubilee, and his mouth falls open as he recognizes me. "What are you doing here?" His whisper is like a bullet straight through me. "She *killed Mike*," he goes on, voice rising to a ragged shout, "and you're standing next to her."

"It wasn't her. I give you my word. She was there, but she didn't do it."

He watches me in silence, making me wonder if my word holds any value for him now. Beside me, I can hear Jubilee's harsh breathing, keeping time with the pounding of my own heart. If Turlough can trust me, then I can believe Sean might. I can believe the gulf between us might close, that we might be able to grieve together.

My voice is soft. "Where's McBride, Turlough?"

His expression flickers, the grief and anger giving way to a quick, icy flash of fear. "I don't know," he says tightly. But his loyalty is brittle, that terror more real than anything he's shown Jubilee.

"You're afraid of him," I say softly. "Tell me."

He hesitates, gaze flicking from me to Jubilee and back again. "He shot him," Turlough gasps finally. "The bartender, the big one. We went in looking for Captain Chase—we were only going to scare people until someone told us where to find her."

"Go on." Jubilee's expression is unreadable, her anger draining away to something else, something cold.

"McBride kept screaming at the guy, over and over. The guy wouldn't tell us where to find you, trodaire. So McBride shot him and set fire to—" His voice catches, fear making it difficult for him to speak. But when Jubilee turns away, her shoulders tense, Turlough's grief surges again. "She was *there*, Flynn. Everybody knows it. She has to pay."

I feel like there's a weight on my chest. "I know she was there, but her weapon was never fired."

"Well, those people—Mike, the others—they weren't killed by ordinary gunfire. It had to be a Gleidel. Who else has a weapon like that, except a soldier?"

Suddenly the room's silent. Jubilee's looking up, and the same realization hits all three of us. The bottom drops out of the world, and my skin's all pins and needles as a wave of dizziness sweeps over me. We all know who has that kind of weapon, because he just used it to shoot Molly in the back of the head.

Gunfire roars in the distance as Jubilee and I cross the base. The air splits with the crack of the old-fashioned ballistics weapons the Fianna use and the shriek of the deadly Gleidels. The stench of singed plastene and burned chemicals hangs in the air. I want to put as much distance as I can between us and the holding cells. Away from Turlough Doyle, away from Molly's, which will never be Molly's again. As my feet drag and I start to stumble, Jubilee grabs at my arm to keep me moving.

McBride. For all our differences, for all his thirst for war, I always believed we wanted the same thing—prosperity for Avon, peace and justice for our people.

But he murdered Fergal. He murdered Mike. He murdered every person who lay dead in our sanctuary, just to light the fuse behind this war. And now Molly, because he wouldn't betray Jubilee.

And he's still out there somewhere, with Sean. *Oh God.*

I'm jerked back to the present as the com-patch on Jubilee's sleeve buzzes, and she ducks into the shelter of a building to hear it better. The voice is tinny with interference, but familiar. "Lee, this is Merendsen, report."

She lifts her wrist to speak into the patch. "Go ahead, sir."

Merendsen's voice is muffled, but clearly identifiable. "Lee, Commander Towers has raised your threat level and ordered all nonessentials off the base and off Avon. That includes me."

"Because of Molly's?" She closes her eyes as she speaks his name.

"Because they've confirmed the Fianna have anti-aircraft weaponry. The next shuttle out of here could be the last, and I'm on it. I'm willing to accept the risk if I stay, but the commander said if I don't board myself, she'll have me escorted. I'm heading for the orbital spaceport. You're my security detail, but if you aren't here to pilot it, someone else will." He pauses, the static hissing. "I wouldn't mind a chance to say good-bye." Though the words are casual, I can tell what he's trying to say. *I tried to stay, they won't let me. I have to talk to you before I go.* But their comm system is not private.

"On my way," she replies, pushing her shoulders back, voice crisp. Back on duty, Captain Chase once again. Whatever Merendsen has to tell her, we need to hear it more than ever.

"There's one more thing, Captain."

"Sir?"

"They're rounding up all the civilians over in the mess hall for a security check, scanning their genetags." He pauses, the silence hanging heavily. "If you see any, you should send them that way."

She looks across at me, her gaze worried. "Got it, sir. Thanks for the heads-up," she replies, voice even.

My mind's still thick with fog—McBride's name beats against my skull like a drum. But then Jubilee's yanking my sleeve down more, better hiding the spiraled code of my genetag tattoo. Then she plants a hand between my shoulder blades, and with a shove, she gets me moving.

We break into a jog toward the launch bays. An explosion echoes in from the swamps, a shuddering reminder of McBride's madness. And we're about to lose our only connection to LaRoux Industries, our only chance to find out what's killing Avon.

The girl is searching for her November ghost. She is so certain that it's here, somewhere, in the endless halls and chambers. It's never left her before, and a ghost shouldn't care what planet she's on. She's been searching for hours. The orphanage is emptier on the inside than it is on the outside, and she'll never search all the rooms.

In one of the dormitories is a miniscreen, smuggled in by one of the other children, old-fashioned but durable. The room is empty, but someone has left the screen on to crackle and jar the silence. On it, a woman is talking about a war ending on some planet far away, as hovercopter footage of destruction and refugees scrolls by.

The girl looks at the screen, and the city is November.

But when she moves closer, she realizes it can't be her November. The city on the screen is healing, buildings being rebuilt, children there in the street lighting firecrackers. It looks like a toy, a model, a copy of where she used to live; images on a screen will never be real for her.

The November inside her was torn apart, and it always will be.

And the November ghost is gone.

TWENTY-NINE

JUBILEE

MY BODY'S PROTESTING THIS ABUSE. THE CONSTANT FIGHT-ing, running, hiding. Not enough sleep, and too much grief. I can feel it burning through my blood as I run harder, aiming for the launch bays. If I'm not there to pilot Merendsen's shuttle, I'll lose my chance to find out whether he heard back from Lilac—and judging by the urgency in his tone, I'm sure he did. We have to have that information. I haven't even told him or Flynn about Commander Towers yet. What could I possibly say?

I focus on my aching muscles as I run. I'm trying not to think about Molly; I'm trying not to imagine him at gunpoint, still refusing to tell McBride where I am.

My eyes water from some mix of grief and cold air, and I lift a hand to dash the sparks of moisture away. I can hear Flynn half a step behind me—when I speed up, he speeds up with me. A couple of weeks ago I would've been surprised he could keep up. Not anymore. I never thought life in the swamps was a picnic, but I didn't know how closely his training—because it was training, even if he wasn't in uniform—resembled mine.

Our route takes us past the mess hall. What looks like half the civilian population of the base is in there, the long line snaking around between tables and benches. A couple of uniforms make their way along the line, and in anticipation the civilians are rolling up their sleeves to offer up their 'tags for scanning. Security only caught one of the perpetrators at Molly's. Everyone else who's not military has to prove they're supposed to be here.

The launch bay is a series of long, low, massive hangars that only stretch to two stories aboveground but drop underground to hold all the vehicles, military and civilian alike, associated with the base and the town. One of the curved roofs is open, a sign that a craft's about to take off—or just did.

We skid to a halt outside the door, and I turn to Flynn. "Okay. Remember your cover story as Molly's cousin. You've got every right to be here. Act like you're thinking of leaving Avon now that Molly's—" My voice cracks, and over the tangle of emotions rising in me, I choose anger. It's easier to deal with. "Now that Molly's gone. That should delay them scanning you awhile."

He nods. "Got it. Where do I go once you're shuttling Merendsen away?"

I'm still catching my breath. "You hide. Maybe in my quarters, if they don't search the base. I don't know where you go after that—back out into the swamp again. I don't know."

I don't know. Some of my least favorite words in the galaxy, and I've been saying them a lot lately.

The launch bay's always busy, but today it's absolute chaos. Flynn joins a group of civilians milling about in the passenger area, blending in like he was born to, and I resist the urge to look back at him as I head toward one of the traffic controllers, a short middle-aged man I recognize. There's an engine warming up nearby and I'm forced to shout.

"Merendsen?" I holler, leaning close. "The guy from TerraDyn here to evaluate security?"

The controller peers past me, then throws a gesture in the direction of a shuttle four or five down from me. "Better hurry—everyone's taking off soon."

I catch Flynn's eye back in the crowd, signal my destination, and then head toward a group of uniformed officers near the shuttle. Merendsen's there—I breathe a sigh of relief when I see his familiar features.

He spots me and pulls away from the officer shaking his hand in order to come toward me. "Captain," he calls, tension in his voice. I catch sight of Flynn, who's headed up to us at a jog.

"Hey," he calls loudly, offering his hand to shake. "Sorry you're headed out."

Merendsen claps his palm to Flynn's. But when he speaks, his voice is pitched lower, barely audible to me over the engines all around us. "I've heard from Lilac. It's a message. She couldn't risk a verbal transmission, but she got some text through. We have a code, whenever we can't speak face-to-face. I've decoded it for you, here." He shoves a crumpled piece of paper into my palm. "Read it when you're alone."

"Sir," I manage, trying to look casual while keeping an eye on the military personnel swarming around the various shuttles. At the far end of the hangar, one takes off upward with a roar, the noise providing perfect cover for our voices. "Thank you."

His gaze fixes on mine, his voice low. "Lee, listen to me. These creatures LaRoux is using, they aren't bad themselves. But if he's found a way to compel them, then I don't know what he might be capable of. Just—be careful. Please."

I know what he's trying to say. *Don't be rash, don't rush in. Don't be Lee-ish.* I manage to nod. "I will. I promise."

"Lilac was right," he continues, this time glancing at Flynn as well. "You need proof, and you need to create a whole galaxy of witnesses. You need so many eyes on Avon that LaRoux wouldn't dare touch it. Maybe when you get back, you can search for whatever happened to that facility to the east."

Before anyone can reply, an air traffic controller jogs up to me. "Time to go, sir, not much time left. Last shuttle out."

I can see the line of civilians and soldiers alike boarding the shuttle. Most of the soldiers sport visible wounds, but some have the reddened, haunted eyes of those who've had their first unnatural dream and are afraid to go back to sleep, for fear of the Fury. There are only a handful of civilians, the lucky few who have family waiting somewhere in the galaxy to take them in. They walk quietly, heads down, as though they don't want to draw attention to themselves.

Behind them all are half a dozen soldiers forcibly preventing a desperate throng of townspeople, all wanting to get out before they lose their chance. The launch bay officials are herding them back toward the base, for all I know to have their genetags scanned. There's no way out of this building for Flynn—except on the ship I'm flying.

The control officer's still issuing me warnings in a tight, quick voice. "Rebels have got surface-to-air missiles now, they got to a supply craft on its way in. Ain't safe to fly anymore, sir. We've got a brief window now, but then that's it. If you take off now, there's a good chance you'll be fine—but you probably won't be able to come back."

"For how long?" I ask him.

"Don't know, sir. Maybe an hour, if the ground teams can recapture the anti-aircraft guns. Maybe not until the war's over."

My head jerks up. *If I leave now, I might never be able to come back.* "What's happening over there?" I ask, tilting my head at the civilians they're herding away. I can't send Flynn off to join them until I know where they're being taken.

"If they're not getting on a shuttle, they're being scanned and having their identities verified, sir."

Flynn's eyes meet mine. I see it hit him, his eyes widening on impact.

The tech is still talking. "We did your preflight checks for you, sir— but you're on the roster to fly this thing because you're Mr. Merendsen's security detail, and you've got to do it *now*, commander's orders."

I'm being manhandled back toward the nose of the shuttle to carry out my orders, but my eyes are on Flynn's, and for a moment there's no sound, nothing but my heartbeat as the chasm between us widens. Time slows, the milliseconds trickling by, whispering like dust.

Then everything rushes back and Flynn darts forward. "Me too," he blurts with a gasp. "I'm going too."

The officer glances at him, and at the crowd fighting to board. Flynn's on this side of the soldiers holding the others back, and the man assumes he's already been through the security check. That he's meant to be on the shuttle. "Okay, but you know you might not be coming back? Heck, you might get blown out of the sky if they get those missiles up and running ahead of schedule."

"I know." Flynn's breathing hard, his eyes on my face. "I know."

And then he's gone, time speeding up as if to make up for its hiccup a few seconds before. Merendsen's hauling him toward the passenger door, and I'm forced to turn and race for the cockpit, climbing up into the pilot's seat. No copilot on this one; we've got no one to spare.

My hands are shaking. Though I've been flying a few times a month since basic training when I was sixteen, I'm no pilot—but routine transport missions are half automated anyway. *Except dodging surface-to-air missiles was never part of the routine.*

Muscle memory takes over, and I get myself buckled down and the engines humming. The check lights all along the ceiling flash green one by one to tell me that the passengers are all strapped down, that the doors are closed, that we're pressurized. That we're ready to go. I pull on the comms unit headset and hear the control tower squawking at me to move, move now.

I punch the engine, feeling the whole shuttle shudder briefly as the VTOL jets lift us up off our supports. I take a long, steadying breath, then let the shuttle dart up into the sky.

The girl is cowering behind a hummock, her hand over the mouth of the soldier next to her to stop his groans of pain from carrying. She needs to go back, to rejoin the fight, but she can't—her legs won't move. She's found out how easy it is to run away; she's letting her platoon, her captain, fight without her. It isn't until the rest of the platoon falls back that her captain finds her, still frozen, the soldier she dragged out of the fight unconscious now.

"You okay, Corporal?" Her captain crouches, inspecting her for signs of shock.

"I ran away," the girl whispers. "I ran away."

"Don't think Jessop would see it that way." Her captain is taking the other soldier's pulse. "Come on, we're holed up on the other side of the ridge."

She sits there as her captain hauls the wounded man up onto his shoulder and begins the trek back to the rest of her platoon. She tries to stand, but she can't, and she watches him grow smaller and smaller until she's alone again, the only soldier left on the plain.

The girl was supposed to be brave, and she ran away.

THIRTY

FLYNN

MY STOMACH TRIES TO FIGHT ITS WAY UP THROUGH MY THROAT as the jets push us away from Avon, and I catch myself grabbing at the armrests of my chair. The shutters around us are closed tight, denying me a glimpse of the blue sky above Avon's constant cloud cover, or the stars. I don't know if the dizziness is motion sickness or my mind's inability to process the last few hours.

With a jerk, the engines slow. It's only once the thrusters aren't slamming me back against the seat that I realize gravity's fading out, and the nervous tapping of my foot takes no effort at all. My weight falls away just as my connection to my home did—in a long, drawn-out silence, my mind spinning, my chest hurting. I have no direction now. I'm not even sure which way to point to find home.

If I crane my neck I can see Merendsen's profile up ahead of me, and once he turns his head to meet my eyes, but neither of us can unclip without setting off alarms. I haven't known him long, but I can tell it's killing him to walk away.

The view shields all stay in place, giving us no warning we're about to dock, no view of the spaceport as we ease in. Every person who comes or goes from any colony on Avon passes through here, transferring from massive spaceliners to shuttles like this one, built to withstand gravity and atmospheric pressure. I can't imagine what the spaceport would look like, such a vast thing suspended against the stars, if the viewports were unshielded. Instead the ship clangs loudly as it settles into its cradle, and then Jubilee's throwing off her harness and striding toward the back of the shuttle to see her passengers out the exit. As she passes me, she murmurs in a low voice, "Don't get off the ship. Hang back, stay out of sight."

The passengers begin filing out of the shuttle. I see Merendsen's head turn toward Jubilee, but there are soldiers and passengers everywhere, and they can't speak. Merendsen nods, his eyes meeting Jubilee's; their look is weighted with their history together, the moment stretching long and thin. Jubilee's jaw clenches, and she nods back at him before he's carried off in the current of travelers, vanishing into the crowd.

It's not until I'm casually letting the others in my row of seats leave before me that I realize Sofia Quinn's on board too, her strawberry-blond hair standing out among the other passengers. On her way to that off-world orphanage—or to whatever escape plan she'd been devising. Around me harnesses clink as the passengers unclip, and I hang back as they file down the aisles to the back of the shuttle, clutching armfuls of their belongings. Sofia glances over her shoulder to make sure she hasn't left anything and goes perfectly still as she spots me. I lift my hand to press it over my heart, and she nods. Then the man behind her jostles her with his bag, and she steps forward.

Sofia pauses at the bottom of the ramp, speaking to one of the soldiers manning the spaceport and letting him scan her genetag. They're scanning *all* the passengers for genetags. My protesting gut suddenly stills in horror. They're going to know who I am the instant they look at that code on my arm. The soldier scanning her lifts his head—and looks straight at me.

Sofia twists suddenly, leaning against the guardrails and clutching her middle. Silver-tongued Sofia. Always ready.

She groans, letting her knees start to give. "I'm gonna throw up, I can't do this. It's the gravity. You gotta find me somewhere, I'm gonna—" Her lips clamp together. As the soldiers fuss over her, and one unlucky volunteer gets lumped with taking her off somewhere she can lose her lunch, I sink down behind a row of seats to crouch, out of sight. *Thank you, Sofia.*

Jubilee brushes by me without another glance, and I watch through a crack in the seats as she hands a thin e-filer to one of the soldiers. "The manifest's a little off," she says apologetically. "Things are crazy down there."

"You're telling me," says one of the soldiers. "It's a madhouse up here too, Captain. Everyone wants off that planet."

I can see a little line of tension in Jubilee's jaw, her eyes narrowing as she watches the soldier, and I know what she's thinking. Down there, it's people shooting at each other and people being torn from their families. Up here, it's a lot of paperwork. But she simply nods at him. "I want to get this shuttle back down before the rebels get their anti-aircraft up and running. Can we make this quick?"

"Sure, Captain." The soldier tucks the e-filer under one arm. "We've just got to search the shuttle."

I freeze, heart stopping for a split second.

"Search the shuttle?" Jubilee echoes, her voice sharpening. "Why? There's no point; if anyone had stowed away, they're going right back to the surface."

The soldier on duty shrugs. "It's commander's orders. Came through right before you landed."

"Before—before *I* landed?" Her head half turns, but she catches herself before she can look at me. They know. Somehow, they suspect I'm here. Or that Jubilee has been sheltering a fugitive. Maybe someone at the spaceport recognized my face before I got on board.

"Yes, sir." The soldier regards her with respect, but shows no signs of wavering.

She hesitates. "Fine, fine, search it. But make it quick." She stalks back up the aisle, footsteps tense and quick. She comes to a halt right beside the row I'm hiding behind, her body further concealing me.

I sink down, no longer able to risk watching through the seat cracks. Instead I can hear their booted feet clanking up the grid floor, the dull click and slam of lockers opening and hatches being inspected. Getting closer.

Jubilee's grip is white-knuckled on the armrest beside my head. The soldiers—I can make out three distinct sets of footsteps—are nearly on us.

"Satisfied?" she says, interrupting them. "They need me on the ground, I can't afford to get stuck up here on the wrong side of a blockade."

The footsteps halt. "Yeah, yeah, okay," says the one who insisted on the search. "You're good. Move out, guys."

I let out a slow, silent breath as the footsteps start to retreat. I can see Jubilee's shoulders relax a fraction, and with the soldiers in retreat, she spares a glance at me; her eyes are wide, but there's relief on her features. She turns to make her way up the aisle and head for the cockpit.

"Wait—Captain, your paperwork!"

The moment freezes, then unspools with slow, heavy finality. The booted feet come running back up the aisle. Jubilee whirls back around. A voice breaks the fuzzy roar in my ears. "There's someone here," it says. I look up, and there's a soldier staring at me. His hand moves toward the gun holstered at his hip. The other two soldiers are coming up behind him. I look up for Jubilee and find her eyes on me in an instant of horrified indecision.

Then she flows into action. Lunging forward, she grabs at the man near me and hauls him down so she can knee his shoulder. The gun drops from his nerveless hand. Jubilee's boot catches the man's jaw, then she steps forward to get an elbow under the chin of the second soldier, this one a woman, sending her reeling backward to hit the wall with a crack. Jubilee's perfect, deadly, a predator.

All this has happened in the space of a heartbeat. Jubilee whirls to face the third soldier, a man who has kept his distance just enough to escape the initial blows. "Captain," he gasps, clearly afraid. "I am placing you under arrest for assault and—and treason—"

Jubilee's breathing hard, her muscles tense. "Back away, Private. This isn't your fight. Take your friends to the sick bay, and report me there."

The third soldier hesitates, his eyes swiveling from Jubilee to the two motionless bodies slumped on the floor. Then his fingers twitch, barely noticeable, but it's enough; Jubilee sees him reach for his gun and gets there a moment before he does, the two of them grappling for the Gleidel. A bolt screams in the confined space of the shuttle, but dissipates harmlessly off the metal interior.

Jubilee wrenches the gun from his grip and then lashes out with it, slamming it into the soldier's temple. It's over before I can blink.

Jubilee stands above the three unconscious soldiers, chest heaving as though she's run for hours. Gun in hand, she has her feet planted firmly, like she's ready to start all over again. Nothing I've heard about her is true. She's even faster than they say. She could have killed me a dozen times each day we've been together.

Though we're only standing there a few seconds, it's longer than it took her to drop the three soldiers. Finally she moves, looking at me over her shoulder and then tossing me the gun she took from the soldier. "Know how to use one of these?"

I swallow as I catch it, my stomach uneasy. "You sure about this?"

"Just point that end at the bad guys if we make it back to Avon."

"And who *are* the bad guys?"

She doesn't have an answer for me, and for a moment I can see the weight of what she's done in her eyes. She's crossed the line. When these trodairí wake, they'll report her for treason. Like me, she can never go home.

Jubilee clears her throat, and then the two of us drag the unconscious soldiers out onto the platform, concealing them behind some cargo containers. It won't last long; someone will find them, or else they'll wake and sound the alarm. But it'll buy us a little time. Time to figure out our next move. We clamber back aboard, and this time Jubilee has me sit in the copilot's chair. She starts flipping switches, so quick and so sure that I almost can't see the way her hands are shaking. But I can tell by the set of her jaw she doesn't want to talk about it, doesn't want to process what she's done. She just wants to keep moving, and that much I understand.

The shuttle shudders as the autolaunch takes hold of us, and there's a faint sense of movement as we're lined up on a launching pad. Jubilee's silent as she programs in the holding pattern. The computers take over. There's another shudder, and a hum, and then I'm pressed back against my seat as we're shot out into space once more. Neither of us speaks as Jubilee guides us forward. She's monitoring our course on a readout, the viewshields still in place; finally she stops, toggling another series of switches until the engine noise cuts back to a tiny hum and the cabin lights dim.

"Okay." She leans back in her seat, palms braced against her thighs. "We're far enough out, and small enough that hopefully scans will think we're another satellite if we stay dark."

"They'll find us eventually, though, won't they?"

She swallows. "Yes."

I want so badly to reach for her, to wrap her hands in mine and thank her for defying her people for me; but I know she wasn't only doing it for me. She believes in this fight now. She knows as well as I do that saving Avon is more important than her people, or mine. And I know she doesn't want to be comforted.

So I clear my throat. "Merendsen's note," I say, shattering the quiet. "Maybe it has something we can use."

Jubilee reaches into her pocket to pull out the coded message from Lilac. We lean together to study the folded sheet.

It's a printed message, with Merendsen's handwritten translation scrawled between the lines. Lilac is talking about all the things Jubilee seems to associate with her—parties, clothes, vacations—and though some of it's left alone, Merendsen has translated other parts in hurried handwriting.

Knave got access, it reads. *No records of a facility being moved on Avon. But Knave found hidden manifests from ten years ago, from unknown location in sector where* Icarus *crashed. Three shipments, three destinations. Corinth, Verona, Avon.*

The paper starts to tremble; Jubilee's hand is shaking. She grew up on Verona. And a rebellion happened there, too—ten years ago. I reach out and cup my hand under hers, steadying the page.

LRI using Avon as laboratory, soldiers as subjects. Whispers would never harm them; Fury must be side effect. Only way to stop everything is for J and F to find proof to show the galaxy. Don't let my father do this to anyone else.

The rest of Lilac LaRoux's message is talk of parties again, rambling on as though fashion is her only care in the world. Jubilee lets her hand drop, the page resting against her thigh.

"Why is he doing this?" I can't think, the background hum of the engines shattering my thoughts. "What does this man have against Avon?"

"It's not Avon itself," Jubilee says quietly, lifting her eyes to meet mine. "Avon's convenient. Far away from the galactic center, too young for anyone to be watching it. An endless war, providing an endless supply of test subjects."

"Test subjects for *what?*" Frustration makes my voice crack. "What good does it do him to make people snap with the Fury?"

"Lilac said it was a side effect of whatever he's doing. Maybe he just hasn't perfected it yet." She draws a shaky breath. "I didn't have time to tell you before, but something happened to Commander Towers, just before—just before everything with Molly."

The raw fear in Jubilee's eyes makes my mouth go dry, forcing me to clear my throat. "She snapped?"

She shakes her head. "No, it was something else. She was telling me that LaRoux Industries has been here for years, studying us. They told her and her predecessors that they were studying the Fury, but . . ." She looks down at her hands, and I know she's thinking of the bloodstains I washed clean. "She didn't snap, didn't attack me. She just *stopped*. Went back to work. Like something just . . . took over."

"Like something was controlling her?" I'm trying not to acknowledge the chill running through me, my conversation with Sofia coming back to me. "My friend in town, the one who helped hide me—Davin Quinn's daughter. She said her father was vague for a week before the bombing, distracted. You said the Fury is always quick and brutal, but that's not what happened to Davin, who would have needed time to make and plant a bomb. Or Commander Towers. Or—" My voice gives out.

Jubilee's nodding, her face ashen in the glow of the control panels. "Or me." The background hum of the engines and life support is thick and heavy. Jubilee's voice is quiet, as though to speak the words too loudly might make them true. "Maybe Davin was a test run. Maybe Towers too, to stop her from revealing his secrets. But what wouldn't a man like Roderick LaRoux do to wield the ability to control people's minds?"

Sometimes the girl dreams in colors. Her classes at school are the yellow of butter and flower petals, and her books are the rich blue of the deep oceans she reads about. Her mother is warm red-orange, and her father is a lighter peach that highlights it, mingles with it to turn them both the color of sunrise.

But her dreams always fade, and she can never tell what color the orphanage is, or the training base on Paradisa, or the bar where she goes when she's off duty. She exists there in a colorless world—not black and white, but a muted, faded gray. She doesn't even know to miss the colors, as though someone has reached into her thoughts and pulled out the memory of what color is.

The girl knows that the boy is looking for her. And when he finds her, his eyes will be green, and she'll remember.

THIRTY-ONE

JUBILEE

"NO SIGN OF EIGHT-ONE-NINE YET. SCANS CONTINUING. Traffic control on alert, orders to fire at will. Traitors on board." The comms chatter is all about us. I've set the comms headset floating a few inches from my face, which is buried in my hands. With a groan, I thumb the mute button, and we're left in abrupt silence. The heat shields are all still closed, and without the vastness of space around us, I can almost imagine us back in Flynn's hideout, trying to wait out our pursuers.

I don't know what to do next, and that's killing me. I lift my head to see Flynn watching me, his expression unreadable. "I'm so sorry, Flynn. I never meant to take you away from your home."

He shifts in his seat, running a finger underneath one of the straps of his harness. "It was my call," he says quietly. "I could have tried to run. I chose to come."

He's as tense as I am, maybe even more so, but it's so hard to reconcile that with the serenity of weightlessness. His faux-blond hair is floating out away from his head. He's wearing a worn, much-mended, and too-large shirt his friend in town must've found for him, to help him blend in. He looks nothing like the Romeo who dragged me off the base, nothing like the Cormac who threw himself between his own people and me. It's like that guy's gone, and I killed him.

"I'm sorry anyway," I mutter. "God, why is everything so fucked up?"

"Because we make one hell of a team," Flynn replies lightly, his voice a strained tease. I notice his hands are gripping his armrests, and as he shifts I can see the faint outlines of dampness beneath his palms against the plastic.

It's with a jolt I remember he's never been in space before—he's never even been off the ground before. And he's trying to relax *me*.

"Hey," I try, leaning out as far as my harness will allow me, my hair drifting after me in slow motion. "Do you want to see the stars?"

He blinks, his false bravado falling away as he stares wide-eyed back at me. "The—the what?"

"The stars." I gesture to the covered viewport in front of us. I could tell him that this might be his last chance to see them, but he already knows that. "They're right out there. Normally we keep the heat shields on, but there's no actual need for them out here, only when we're going through atmo. Want to take a peek?"

He swallows, fingers tightening around his armrests. I want to tell him he's got nothing to be afraid of—for now, we're safer up here than we ever were on Avon's surface. But I know telling him will do no good, because it's not a rational fear. Even I feel a surge of primal adrenaline when I get up here, every time.

It's like underwater diving, part of the training all soldiers get during basic. The moment the water closes over your head and you take your first breath through the respirator—your body tells you it can't breathe, that it's falling, that you're going to die. And no amount of logic can stop the feeling, you just have to let it course through you and sweep on past. You have to embrace it. I hold my own breath, watching Flynn.

Slowly, he nods.

I lean forward in my harness and reach for the shield controls, hitting the release button with a light thunk. There's the hum of the shield mechanism, and then the thick sheet of metal dilates outward—and the sky is full of stars.

The air leaves Flynn's lungs in an audible rush, and he presses himself back in his seat. I look over to see his eyes flicking this way and that, and I reach out to grab his hand. His fingers wrap around mine with the grip of a drowning man.

"Hey, I'm right here." I shift my hand so I can weave my fingers through his.

Just let the water close over your head and trust your respirator. Don't fight it.

Gradually his breathing slows and his painful grip eases. I watch his face as the fear fades and his eyes focus. There's nothing but stars as far as the eye can see, except for the sliver of Avon at the far left, little more than the gentle blue-gray glow of its constant cloud cover. It's enough to illuminate Flynn's features, though, as he leans forward against his harness.

He can't take his eyes off the stars, but I can't take mine off his face. I can see the stars reflected in his eyes, can see the wonder of it in the way his mouth opens but no sound comes out. His eyes, his face—they're beautiful.

My eyes start to burn, and abruptly I let go of his hand. Clearing my throat and ducking my head so I can fumble with my harness, I manage hoarsely, "You hungry? We might not get a chance to eat later, and there should be an emergency pack or two somewhere."

Flynn has to hunt for his voice too, but when he murmurs, "Sure," he gives no sign that he noticed my inexplicable surge of emotion. Maybe I'm just remembering the first time I saw the stars from space. That's what I fight to tell myself, anyway.

I shove the straps of my harness away and let myself rise out of my seat, using the handles to gradually walk myself back into the small cargo area. On the big passenger ships and space stations, they use rotating rings to generate gravity, but on the shuttles, we're stuck dealing with weightlessness.

I turn back to find Flynn watching me, studying the way I move in zero-g. I reach the lockers and hook my toes under the handles on the wall there. From his perspective it'll look like I'm standing on the wall, but from mine, the lockers are now sunk into the floor and much easier to access.

There's a full emergency pack in the first locker I try. Two of them, I discover as I pull the first out. "It'll be freeze-dried rations," I warn him. "You can come back, if you move slowly. Tiny movements go a long way. Don't overcompensate if you find yourself moving in an unexpected direction, just let your hand or foot graze something lightly to correct it."

Flynn unbuckles his harness and pulls himself along with exaggerated care, his face a study in concentration. "Just like poling a boat through the swamp." His grip slips a little, and I reach out with my free hand to grab a handful of his jacket to steady him. "Well, mostly."

He's doing what all the new trainees do, trying to keep the "floor" of the shuttle below his feet, though there's no gravity to hold him there. I want to laugh at him—but I'm forced to admit he's doing okay.

I toss him one of the ration bars and then take a few bites of one myself before shoving the rest into my back pocket for later. Flynn looks as worn down as I feel, exhausted and restless at the same time. I know we need to find a way back down to the surface, but now that I'm able to breathe, I'm realizing how tired I am.

I have to keep moving or I'll never get up again. "Wonder what else we've got up here," I muse aloud, reaching for the next locker over and finding more of the emergency packs, all with their seals unbroken. "Each of these is designed to keep a pair of soldiers alive for a fortnight, with the ship's H_2O recyc system."

"That's months' worth of food," Flynn replies, finishing his bar and popping open a few more lockers, all stuffed with the emergency packs. "Or even years."

"There are dozens of them." My mind is turning over slowly, inching around an idea, unwilling to look at it directly. "It must've been set up for a transport mission, so it could take a shuttle full of soldiers somewhere remote."

Flynn's turned to the other side of the shuttle to see if there are more of the packs in the rest of the lockers. But I can't stop looking at the one I opened. Months' worth of food for a platoon.

Years, for two people.

"We could just go." The words come out in a whisper, and as I say them, I find I can't look up, can't see Flynn's face. I can't bear to know his reaction.

Still, I can feel him turn toward me. I can feel the air move as he makes his way back. He ducks his head to try to see my face, but I still can't look at him. No matter what he's about to say, I don't want to hear it. Hearing it will make what I've just said real.

"Never mind," I say sharply. "I was just kidding."

But I wasn't.

"Jubilee." He's got one hand wrapped around a handle to steady himself, but the other reaches for me, his fingers tracing the outline of my face.

"Just drop it, Flynn. Forget it."

He's silent for a few seconds, speaking only with the weight of his eyes on me. I can feel my face flushing hot with shame, with guilt, under his gaze. "Where do you want to go?" he asks finally, a smile in his voice.

I glance at him and then away again. "What do you mean?"

"Where do we go? Anywhere in the galaxy. Where does Jubilee Chase want to live?"

This time I look at him longer, properly, scanning his face for some sign of what he's thinking—some judgment, some hint of blame or guilt that I'm standing there, talking about leaving his people and mine, about abandoning our whole lives. About running away. But he only smiles at me, his fingers sliding from my cheek to twine around a floating lock of hair, making it spiral slowly in midair.

"Not Corinth," I say finally, my voice emerging somewhat hoarsely. "Too busy, too many people. But not any place too new either. Maybe Patron, I liked it there. Haven't been any rebellions for quite a while now."

He grins, his smile easing away some of my horror at my own impulse. "As long as there's a sky there, like this one, I'm game."

"It's not quite like this, the air gets in the way. But we could find ourselves a mountaintop where the air's nice and thin, and it'd be awfully close."

Flynn shifts, sliding his foot more firmly under the handle bracing him. "And what does Jubilee Chase want to do with her life, if she's not hunting down rebel leaders and skinning them alive?"

"I don't know. Something extremely boring. I could go to night school and learn dentistry."

That makes him laugh, a quick burst of a chuckle that makes my own lips curve. "Oh, God no. No way could you be a dentist."

"I could! I'd be a damn good dentist."

"Lots of call for dentistry on deserted mountaintops, eh?" He's watching my face, eyes tracing over my features like he's trying to memorize them.

"Well, what about you? You could go be an accountant or a mechanic or something." I try to gesture at him, but I end up unbalancing myself.

Flynn leans forward, wrapping his arm around me to steady me and him both. "Definitely not an accountant." His voice is low, thoughtful. "Maybe a mechanic, though. I could be the one to keep the engine of our . . . What do you drive when you live on a mountain, anyway?"

I have absolutely no idea. The only time I was ever on a mountain was during basic, and I had to learn the bare essentials for snow combat. "Uh. Skis?"

"Well, I'd make sure the skis kept running smoothly, didn't break down."

His face is close to mine, his hand warm against my back through my shirt. Despite the smile on his lips, his gaze is so sad it feels like my heart is ripping in two, turning to ash as I look at him. He knows as well as I do that neither of us is leaving Avon alive if we touch down again. He'll never see snow, and I'll never teach him what skis are.

I want so badly to just turn off communications for good, to go dark, to let this shuttle drift until we get captured by the gravity of some distant star. I want to wrap my arms around him and let my feet come free from the handles and just let our bodies go. His eyes move to my lips, and I know he's thinking the same thing; I can feel it in the way the air charges between us. I can almost taste him half an inch away, can feel the way the tiny hairs on my skin lift and reach for him like plants seeking the sunlight.

It's the hardest thing I've ever done, fighting the impulse to just lean forward that fraction of an inch, to close the gap between us. All I can feel is the heat, the roaring in my ears, the tiny shifts of our bodies, the twitch of his fingers against my back, the way his breath catches and releases, catches and releases. I see his throat move as he swallows. His dark lashes sweep low, his eyes on my mouth. We hang there weightless, on the edge, each waiting for the other to pull us over. To succumb to the gravity between us and fall.

Then someone, one of us, moves just a little. I press my lips together and swallow. His eyes flick up, his jaw clenches. I let out a breath, and his arm loosens a fraction. Tiny shifts, imperceptible movements, as each of us steps back from the cliff, bit by bit, to a point where we can collapse, shaking, seeing in our minds' eyes the leap we nearly took.

"Oh, Flynn." I barely recognize my own voice—it's soft, broken-hearted, full of a grief I can't name. "I don't know how to be anything other than what I am."

His fingers curl around my shirt, crushing the fabric. He's unwilling to let me go even after we agreed, silently, to turn our backs on the path not taken.

"And I don't think you do either," I add.

"I have to believe there's a new way to be what we are." His voice is weary, all humor gone. He's sad, so sad—and I know it's not all for me, and it only breaks my heart all the more to know that. He turns his head, and I can see the glow of Avon through the viewport gilding his nose, his artist's mouth.

I pull in oxygen, reminding my lungs how to breathe. "We don't even know each other, Flynn. Not really. Not outside of this." My gesture indicates the shuttle, but he knows I mean all of it. "Maybe we wouldn't even like each other if we weren't fighting for our lives every second of every day."

"Maybe someday we'll get the chance to find out." He eases back away from me, his hand sliding around as though his body is reluctant to part from mine. His fingers trail along my rib cage, the last thing to pull away.

Someday. It's the same day his people will be free and mine won't be fighting anymore. The same day he'll grow old—the way he never will because he'll die young, the way I'll die young, and we'll both be gone before this never-ending war finally ends—and get to see the clouds clear, get to see the sunrise on Avon. It's always the same *someday.*

I listen to my heartbeat, pounding in anguish as the warmth of his arm around me begins to fade.

"Someday," I echo.

It's New Year's Eve, and the girl is on duty. On Verona, whose year is nearly the same length as Earth's, the holiday fell in the middle of spring throughout the girl's childhood; and to her, that felt right. Resolutions budding with the leaves, warmth banishing the chill of doubt. Here on Patron, the New Year comes at random; the holiday is timed to Earth's year, but the seasons here are tied to a calendar half again as long.

This year it falls at the end of autumn. She tries to imagine shedding the past the way the trees shed the shriveled leaves clinging to their branches, but the leaves are never truly gone. They fall to the ground and lay there in a shroud around the tree, to rot.

Someday, she thinks, *I will spend New Year's Eve in the sky.*

A wind picks up, robbing the trees of their last few leaves and making them dance sluggishly around her in a parody of the November ghost, like dead stars that have lost their shine, and as her breath steams the air, the girl thinks, *Close enough.*

THIRTY-TWO

FLYNN

I'M ALMOST TREMBLING WITH THE EFFORT OF KEEPING myself from reaching out for her again, my head aching as I clench my jaw, force my hands down to my sides where they curl into fists. I know what she wants from me, though, and what I have to do, so I reach for an expression that feels nothing like a real smile. In a slow movement, so I don't unbalance myself, I brace against a locker. "The things you don't know about me are terrible, Jubilee." A part of me marvels at how light my voice sounds. I hate this. I hate this. "I'm actually incredibly messy. Terrible with laundry." Sean's voice is in my head, another wound, with his stories of Oisín and Niamh. Their worlds couldn't combine either, no matter how hard they tried.

There's something in her eyes for an instant that's an acknowledgment of sorts—agreeing that together, we'll find a way to push off from where we are and strike out for safer ground. I turn my gaze out to the stars, letting myself become absorbed in the swirls of light, trying to comprehend the distances between them. I never imagined anything so vast as the stars suspended in space.

"We need our next move." Jubilee's voice breaks the quiet. "We're not running away, and we can't stay here forever. So that means . . ."

"We go back." My heart aches at the words. The idea of going home shouldn't be so terrifying. "We do what Lilac LaRoux said, and we try to find proof of what LaRoux is doing."

I shift around in my seat until I can scan Jubilee's expression for signs of the dread coursing through my own system. A week ago I wouldn't have been able to find it. But I can see now the sharp angle of her brows, the way she blinks a little too often, the way she moistens her lips. She's afraid too.

"What you did back there at the spaceport," I begin, hesitant. "For me—"

She shakes her head, cutting me short. "Don't." Her quick smile softens what would've been a sharp reprimand. "We're beyond thank-yous, Romeo. There's no point in keeping score anymore."

"Still."

This time her smile lingers, her gaze meeting mine. We watch each other, illuminated by the stars and the glow of Avon's atmosphere. I want to cling to this moment, a tiny shard of peace in the middle of the oncoming storm.

The communications console crackles to life, splitting the quiet. "Eight-one-nine, this is base. Come in, over."

I jump, staring at the dashboard. "I thought you turned off the comms."

Jubilee swallows, her eyes fixed on the headset still floating above the controls. "I did. This isn't background chatter—they're hailing us directly."

"What does that mean?"

The voice, female and sharp, repeats its hail while Jubilee abruptly starts flipping switches, turning on scanners monitoring readouts. "It means they found us."

I lean forward, looking down at the scanner as she jabs a finger at five blips on the screen, approaching the center. Though I've never seen this technology before, it doesn't take training to know what it means. There are ships coming at us on an intercept course.

Jubilee reaches for her headset and pulls it back on with shaking hands. "Base, this is eight-one-nine. We are unarmed—tell your fighters to stand down."

"Captain," says the voice on the radio, "is that you?"

"Commander," Jubilee replies. Her face has gone ashy in the planet's glow, and I recall what she told me about her last encounter with the base commander. That Jubilee watched something take over her mind, right there in her office. "Yes, this is Lee Chase."

"Captain, we don't want any further bloodshed." The commander's voice crackles and blurs with static, the interference from Avon's atmosphere wreaking havoc with the signal from the base. "I don't believe you have criminal intentions. Surrender now and be escorted back to base, and we can talk."

Jubilee's eyes are on mine, her face unreadable except for the depth of mixed emotions there.

I know what she's asking. If she goes back, I'll be arrested. *I trust you,* I mouth silently. I know what this second chance means to her. I know what it would mean to me, if my people offered me a way back.

"Surrender *now,*" the commander says again, "and give up the rebel you've been harboring. He will be taken into custody, but he will not be executed without a fair trial. We can still discuss this, Captain."

Jubilee doesn't hesitate any longer. She reaches up and pulls the headset off like it's burned her. She shakes her head, slamming her palm down on the communications kill switch. "That's not Commander Towers," she says, closing her eyes. "It's not real, what they're offering."

I look out, finding the stars again, knowing I might not get to see them again in this lifetime.

Jubilee's eyes are on the scanner, watching the five ships flying in formation, approaching us from behind. "Flynn?" she says, dragging my attention back away from the endless panorama outside the viewport.

"Yes?"

She curls her hands around the controls, taking a deep breath. "Put your harness back on."

She's having the drowning dream again. She gasps and gasps, but all she breathes is darkness, rushing into her lungs like water, hollowing her out, leaving her empty. She tries to scream, but the vacuum of space is quiet, and still, and black. . . .

Until a gentle, greenish light makes her open her eyes. The green-eyed boy is there, and he reaches out to take her hand and pull her close—and suddenly, she can breathe the darkness. Like the underwater dreams she had as a child, the girl can feel the darkness in her lungs, but it hurts her no more than air does.

He speaks, and though she can't hear him, the vibrations of his voice travel through their joined hands and she can understand him anyway. "Trust what you feel," he says.

THIRTY-THREE

JUBILEE

THE DASHBOARD LIGHTS UP WITH WARNINGS, ALARMS
screaming at me from overhead; I'm coming in too hot, my angle through
the atmosphere dangerously close to free fall. But that's what I'm counting on. The ships in pursuit are fighters, and there's no way for a simple
transport shuttle to outmaneuver them in open space. So I'm going to
have to out-dare them.

The viewport shields slam closed as we hit the mesosphere, shielding
us from the white-hot temperatures generated by our descent. The second we hit the denser air the whole shuttle starts shaking, its lockers and
seats not designed for this kind of stress. I can hear the empty harnesses
behind me clanging and slamming against each other.

The shaking of the shuttle threatens to wrench the controls from my
hands, and I clench my fists around them as tightly as I can. My harness is cutting into me as momentum crushes us down against our seats,
making my whole body ache. I wish I could check on Flynn; this would
be enough to make a seasoned veteran start praying to any gods who'd
listen, and it's Flynn's first time up. But I can't, because if I make one
wrong move, if I misjudge this maneuver, the shuttle will break apart and
we'll both be dead in an instant.

Without the viewport, I'm forced to rely on the digital imaging screen
on the dash. I'm looking for the lines to shift, indicating we've reached
the cloud layer; I've never been so glad to be on Avon, where there are
clouds everywhere. The clouds are where I'm going to lose our pursuers.

The second we're in, I jerk back on the stick. The shuttle screams a protest, and I'm slammed down into my seat so hard by the g-forces that my vision blurs, my peripheral sight going dark. I struggle for air, easing up on the stick enough that I can breathe. With any luck, the fighters, unable to track us in the clouds, have zoomed right on past toward Avon's surface. We level out, my vision returning and my temples pounding with light-headedness, and I immediately roll off to the right until I'm headed east. No rebels out there, no military patrols; only the island where Flynn's secret facility used to be. That's where I'm aiming.

My ears recover, and I can hear rapid, panicked breathing; when I try to speak, I realize *I'm* the one hyperventilating. I shoot a quick glance over at the copilot's seat.

"Flynn? You alive?"

He doesn't answer immediately, and when I take another look, he's got his head pressed back against the seat and both hands gripping the armrests, white-knuckled. "I hope not," he gasps, closing his eyes more tightly.

The laugh that escapes my lips is only a little hysterical. "We're not down yet," I warn him. "And we can't land at the base."

"Can you land this thing in the swamp?" he manages, voice choked.

"More or less," I reply through gritted teeth, trying not to let him hear my own fear. A trained pilot could do it. But I'm a combat specialist, and this . . . no one trained me for this.

We stay in the clouds for a while, the turbulence throwing us around nearly as badly as the descent did. I can't see any sign of the fighters on my screens, but that's because Avon's atmosphere makes the scans almost useless in the air. The same thing I'm counting on to hide us will keep me from knowing if we're still being pursued.

I keep my eyes on the topographic map scrolling by on the left side of the dash until I start to see familiar patterns. I shift our course to take us wide of the military base, making for the island to the east instead, the one place I know there's some solid ground to retreat to. I can't land on the island itself; without a paved landing pad I need soft ground to avoid a crash. But I can set the shuttle down in the swamp a few klicks away, and we can abandon the ship and make for the island before the military shows up at the crash site.

It's not my most graceful landing ever. The ship ends up at a slant, the landing pads half submerged on one side. I want to see if Flynn's okay, but I can't make myself let go of the controls. I can't take my eyes from the instruments. In the end, Flynn has to unbuckle and come get me, wrapping his hands around mine.

"Jubilee—we're down. We're here, we're fine. You can let go." He pulls my hands away, massaging life back into the whitened knuckles.

I wrench my eyes from the screens. "Are you okay?"

He nods, though I can see his face is bone-white in the gloom of the cabin. "Just don't make me leave the ground again any time soon."

Together we stumble toward the back of the shuttle, and I hit the door control. The gangway comes down at an angle sharp enough that its hydraulics can't compensate, making it rattle when it splashes into the water. The shuttle groans as it continues to settle into the swamp's thick muck, confirming that we're never taking off in this thing again. I close my eyes, letting the damp, swampy air caress my face. Night has barely fallen, only a tiny bit of light left on the horizon to mark the last remnants of day.

"That was incredible," Flynn says softly.

I shake my head. "If I were a pilot it would've been smooth as butter. It was stupid, is what it was. We're lucky we didn't break apart."

"How far are we from your base?"

"Three, four hours by boat. Quicker if they spotted our descent and send a chopper or a skimmer. The shuttle's too easy to spot—we can't stay here."

Flynn doesn't answer right away, gazing out into the darkness. His body's angled toward the distant hideout that shelters the Fianna, where he's lived for the last ten years. I want to touch him, show him somehow that he's not alone without them. But before I can, he gives a sharp exhale and a nod. "There's a dugout not far from here, totally invisible from the air. There's a few days' rations, a med supply kit; it's supposed to be a hideout if any of us get separated and can't make it back to the caves. We can hole up there until they stop looking for us."

I glance at him, even though his features are concealed by the gloom. "Seriously? God, Flynn, how many of these secrets do you have tucked away that the military doesn't know about?"

This time I can see his smile in the glow of the emergency lights, tired and grim. "At least one more, luckily for us."

It takes only a few seconds for the runabout to auto-inflate, but we take the time to stock up on the emergency ration bars from the shuttle and raid the first aid kit for anything useful. The footing is treacherous on the wobbly, unlit gangway, but we can't risk a light that could carry for klicks and betray our position. The only illumination is from the emergency exit lights on the shuttle. I'd shut those down if I could, but they're designed to stay lit no matter what.

It's only after we've got everything I can think to grab on board that I pause for a breath. I can see Flynn only as a silhouette in the dim, reddish glow of the emergency lighting. He comes closer, reaching for me—it's as much to be sure where I am as to take my hand.

"Ready to go?" His voice is quiet, though there's no one to hear him but me.

"I'm ready," I say, but I can hear how very tired I sound.

His fighters, my soldiers; there are enemies on every side, and none of them know what's really happening. They're all pawns in this sick experiment of LaRoux's, and these whispers, these tortured, vicious things, they're making it happen.

He lifts my hands in his, ducking his head to touch his lips to them. "We'll get through this. We'll disappear into the swamp if we have to, we'll search this place meter by meter until we find proof."

Even here, in the middle of the swamp with no hope, his voice carries a certainty he can't possibly feel, a fire that starts to banish the icy dread in my heart. This is the same passion his sister used to incite a war. I'm glad he's on my side.

"Let's get . . ." I start, but the words die in my throat. Over Flynn's shoulder, out in the darkness of the swamp, is a light.

It's so faint at first that I almost believe my eyes are playing tricks on me. Too small and pale to be running lights on a military launch, but too steady and green-white to be the lamps used by the rebels. It reminds me strangely of the phosphorescent algae in the rebel caves, as though it took wing and followed us out into the swamp.

Memory unfurls, no more than a single thread unraveling from my subconscious. It carries no image, no event, only the certainty that I've seen this before. The natives call them wisps, but I . . . I called it something else.

Flynn sees my expression and turns, his breath catching as he sees it too. He steps back, body tense with fear. I know I ought to react, ought to tense as well, let my training and caution win out. But the little ball of greenish light holds me transfixed, calling to a memory long, long forgotten.

Flynn's talking, shouting in my ear; when I can't answer, he draws his own gun, the one taken from the unconscious soldier at the spaceport, and aims it at the light. "Jubilee, snap out of it!"

"Wait." I gasp the word, shaking myself free of my memory's spell. "Flynn—stop. I've seen this before."

"Avon's wisps?" His voice is short, tense. The gun doesn't waver; he may not be prone to violence, but he handles the weapon with confidence, with ease.

"No." I reach out, laying my hand on his arm. "Not here on Avon. I've seen this on Verona."

Flynn's eyes finally snap to mine, away from the wisp bobbing gently in the air. "There were wisps on Verona?"

"In November," I reply. "I'd forgotten them, until now. But I . . . I know this thing. I called it my ghost. . . ."

But the wisp is answering me, dipping in time with my words, sweeping a glowing path through the night as though dancing with my memories as I try to piece them together.

"It could . . . create things," I murmur. "Paint pictures in my mind."

"Lilac told us the creatures—the whispers—can make you see things that aren't really there." Flynn glances from me to the wisp, the gun lowering, though he keeps both hands firmly in place. "And that LaRoux Industries had brought them to Verona."

My thoughts are spinning, trying to piece together fragments of memory, things I'd long dismissed as childish imagination. I take a step forward and the wisp leaps up, darting away, then pausing—then darting again. "It wants us to follow it," I gasp. But before I can move again, the wisp is gone, its glow flickering once, then vanishing. "Maybe Lilac was right, maybe they're trying to help."

"Unless LaRoux knows we know. If Avon's wisps have been Lilac's whispers all along . . . this could be a trap." Flynn slowly tucks his gun back into his waistband, and when he speaks again, his voice is shaky. "I've caught glimpses of the wisps, but I've never seen one so . . . My cousin Sean said he saw one once, that it tried to lead him away through the swamp, to the east."

"To the east?" My skin prickles; to the east lies the spot where Flynn's vanished facility stood. Commander Towers's words ring in my ears. *We find them out there sometimes. Soldiers taken by the Fury. Drowned or buried in quicksand or dead with guns in their hands and bullets in their brains. They go east, into no-man's-land, if there's no one nearby to kill when they snap. They're looking for it. They're looking for the place.*

My eyes are still searching the horizon, afterimages taunting my sight. I keep thinking I see the wisp, only to blink and find darkness. "Flynn," I say slowly. "You mentioned Lilac—she said not to trust what we see."

"Right."

"Well, if these whispers can make you see things that aren't there, what's to say they can't keep you from seeing things that really *are* there?" I turn away from the black swamp. "Flynn, we walked *around* that island. We never walked across it. Something kept us to its perimeter, and we never noticed."

"The facility was never *moving.*" Flynn's eyes lift, fixing on mine. "It was there all along, being hidden by the whispers." For the first time in what feels like centuries, I see a flicker of hope there. It's like surfacing after a long dive and tasting oxygen again. "Forget the hideout—*that's* where we need to go."

Before I can reply, a distant shout makes us both jerk our heads up. We freeze, listening hard.

There are voices out there in the fog—too far away to be clear, but there's an unmistakable note of urgency in them. Whoever's out in the swamp, whether military or rebel, they've seen us. And they'll be coming our way.

I hit the button to retract the gangway and follow Flynn down so we can jump off into the boat. The emergency lights cut off as the door closes, leaving us in utter blackness. Flynn grabs for the oars stashed along each side of the runabout. They won't work as well as the rebels' clever poles, but they'll get us moving without the noise of an engine.

Flynn settles in to row, leaving me free to cover our retreat if necessary. I touch his shoulder to get his attention, since he can't see my face. "The shuttle's pointed north, and we're about half an hour west of the island. Can you find it again in the dark?"

"I can navigate Avon with my eyes closed." I can hear the smile in his voice. The same arrogance that used to drive me up the wall is now making my own lips twitch. We have a plan, a destination; we've got hope.

"Good. Maybe we can lose them in the fog. But if not . . ."

Flynn reaches up to squeeze my hand. "If not, we just have to hope we find our proof before our people find us."

There are engines echoing through the swamp, and distant lights, and the splashing of poles and oars—in the dark, without any reference points, it feels like both armies have us surrounded. I let Flynn guide us, trusting his almost supernatural ability to navigate without stars, without compass, without anything except the bond he shares with Avon. His adjustments to our course are quick and sure.

We slip through the reeds in tense silence, waiting. Watching. I keep my hand on my gun, always. Now and then I think I see the wisp, a dim flicker of light out of the corner of my eye, always dancing out of reach, but I can never be sure. My mind is still surging, confused. Fragments of the little girl I was keep surfacing, pulling with them flashes of pain, of happiness, of despair, all the colors in my mind I've been ignoring since I was eight years old.

It's well into the night when the boat finally crunches up against solid ground. Flynn jumps out, landing knee-deep in water, and steadies the boat as I climb after him. We operate in total darkness, not able to risk a flashlight, moving by feel and keeping track of each other by the sounds of our breathing. I hear Flynn turn away to face the center of the island.

"Flynn, wait." I reach out and touch his shoulder. "LaRoux's been able to force these creatures to do terrible things. They're responsible for the Fury. They're what took over Commander Towers's mind right in front of me. They're what sent me to your caves when McBride massacred those people."

"I know."

I can't stop the fear coursing through me, no matter how I try to shove it down. I can handle getting shot, blown up, beaten to a pulp while tied to a stake, because through all of that, I'm still me. "We're walking into the center of it all, into a place that's already taken over my mind once. What's to say they won't do it again?" If I wake up someplace again, covered in blood, with no memory of what happened . . .

"I won't let it happen." Flynn's voice is hard.

"You can't stop a thing by willing it not to happen." I can't help the note of fondness that escapes alongside my exasperation. "Flynn—promise me something."

"What is it?" He sounds wary. I think he suspects what I'm about to ask.

"If—if it happens again, just know that it's not me. I'm not in there. That—that person who ordered us to turn ourselves in wasn't Commander Towers, and I had to disobey her. And if it happens to me, then it's not . . . It's okay."

"Okay?" Flynn's voice is stiff. "Okay to shoot you, you mean."

My heart tightens. "I don't know. Maybe." I can feel his anger and frustration radiating through the darkness, and part of me longs to reach out for him. If our positions were reversed, I don't think I'd be able to listen to this either. But it has to be said. "Yes," I whisper. "That's what I'm saying."

"Then I can't promise you that," he says tightly. "And don't ask me again, Jubilee."

"You can't afford not to! This isn't about us, this is everyone, all of my people and all of yours. This is *worth* dying for, Flynn, this chance to save Avon. We can't afford to let anyone stop us. Even if that someone ends up being me."

Flynn doesn't answer in words. Instead he reaches behind his back to pull his stolen Gleidel from his waistband. Then there's a loud thud as he tosses the gun into the bottom of the boat.

"Flynn, you can't—"

"I'm going in there," he says, as fierce as he's ever been. "But I'm not shooting you, no matter what happens."

I want to argue, I want to tell him he's being sentimental and foolish, that this is what I was trying to avoid when I stopped him that night in the back room of Molly's. That choosing me over everything else is weakness. A few weeks ago, that's exactly what Captain Lee Chase would've told him. But I can hear the strength in his voice, and in the choice he's making. Because it's not that he's choosing me, a girl he met less than a month ago—he's choosing a world in which no one has to die.

I want that world to be real. I want it so badly my pulse quickens, the air sharpens. Captain Lee Chase never goes anywhere unarmed; it's against her nature. My hand's gripping my Gleidel so tightly I'm half afraid my skin's going to fuse with the metal.

Lee doesn't leave her gun behind—but maybe Jubilee could.

I exhale slowly, easing my Gleidel out of its holster. It fits so easily in my hand, its cold weight so comforting, so familiar. I swallow, then toss it down with Flynn's.

When I lift my eyes again, Flynn is no more than a silhouette. He moves toward me, taking hold of my arm and pulling me in against him. He doesn't speak. Our brief time together, the extraordinary circumstances that made us allies—there aren't any words to give it shape. He could tell me he loves me, but he doesn't know me the way a lover would; he knows the shape of me, though, the curve of my heart, as I know his. He could tell me he doesn't want to lose me, but we're both already lost, and only the tether between us keeps us from drifting out into the black.

I hear him draw a quick, shaking breath, and then his mouth finds mine. His kiss is fierce, his fingers splaying across my back, pressing me close. His lips this time ask for nothing, no demand for fire or for possession, nothing like the way he tasted in the back room of Molly's, turning my bones to ash. He's just kissing me, holding me, searing me into his memory. I lean into him, making his arms tighten around me in response, and we stand there, the water quiet around our ankles, as though all of Avon is holding its breath.

When we let each other go, we don't speak. Instead Flynn braces his foot against the edge of the boat and shoves, sending it drifting back out so anyone who finds it won't know where we are. I watch it cut through the mist until the fog closes back up around it and it's gone.

She's had this dream before, too. This one starts with fire, but she's not afraid. It sweeps through the shop like it's alive, but when it reaches her, it feels like nothing more than a summer breeze, pleasant and warm. She can control the fire, she can make it go where she wants, and she can keep it from consuming a single mote of dust in her mother's shop.

She tells the flames to pull back, to return to being a merrily crackling fire on the hearth. But this time the fire doesn't listen.

The girl tries again, and again nothing changes; the fire flares instead, and this time it burns her hands. She feels no pain in the dream, but she's afraid. She knows she has to run, but the fire is all around her now, and there's nowhere to go.

Her only choice is to let the fire take her.

THIRTY-FOUR

FLYNN

THERE'S NO WAY BACK NOW. I KNOW THAT AS THE BOAT vanishes. For an instant my heart tugs me after it—a place to hide, to hold Jubilee and be held. I can still feel her against me, and I cling to that warmth, pushing from my mind the possibility that I've kissed her for the last time.

I turn toward the seemingly empty muddy island before us. "How do you find something you can't see?" I keep my voice low—out in the swamps I can still hear the subtle sounds that tell me there are Fianna hunting for us.

She squints toward the center of the island. "We know it's there. Now that we understand what we're looking for, maybe we can bypass whatever the whispers are doing to our heads to conceal it."

I scan the flat expanse of mud. "All right," I murmur. "Come on, let's see you." I pull up the memory of the facility I saw. I'm looking for straight lines on a landscape that's all curves. Walls, corners, a chain-link fence. There's a dizzying compulsion to look away, and I narrow my gaze and try again.

It's only when Jubilee grabs my chin and turns my face toward the center of the island that I realize I'd turned away after all. She has a sympathetic grimace, and we link hands to keep ourselves from moving apart. Our fingers wind tightly together as we edge forward, pausing every step to check we're still moving toward the center.

The air shimmers before me, and I let myself close my eyes for just a second, pain creeping in at my temples. My whole body's starting to protest, shoulders aching where the harness cut into them, gut still settling after our wild ride. I wait until the pain dims a couple of degrees.

Don't trust what you see, Lilac LaRoux said. I dredge up the memory of the facility again. Then I open my eyes and there's a chain-link fence a foot in front of me.

I jerk to a stop, and a second later Jubilee walks face-first into it. It clangs and rattles, shedding droplets of condensed fog in a glittering shower. We both freeze, waiting for a sound in the swamp behind us or a shout from within the compound. Seconds tick by, and as though we've turned a key, the rest of the fence slowly materializes, and a clump of prefab buildings behind it. The shimmering's gone, and the air in front of us is clear.

"Son of a—" Jubilee swallows down her protest, lifting a hand to swipe the water from her face. "Stopped just in time, but you couldn't warn me?" But her mouth's quirking, and despite everything, I want to snicker.

I take a step back, trying to follow the perimeter of the fence in the darkness. "That tower—is it a security checkpoint?" I point to a low, squat blackness some distance away.

Jubilee shakes her head, eyes lifted. "It's a communications tower—see the satellite dishes? But they'll have an alarm system there too, and there are floodlights on every fence post. We go near that tower and get spotted, they'll light this place up like a parade route and we'll have nowhere to run."

"I could try to make a hole up here, then, the way we do on your base to sneak in."

Jubilee just rolls her eyes at me. She drops my hand and takes three steps back, staring up at the fence, which has to be at least four meters high. Then she runs at it, using her momentum to clamber to the top in seconds, swinging a leg over and leaning down to wink. "Hurry up, then. Need a hand?" Faced with a task she knows, she's every inch the soldier, grinning and self-assured. I would have hated her for it such a short time ago, but now her smile's familiar.

My grin matches hers as I climb up after her, and for a moment it's like being with my friends when we were kids, seeing who could scale the highest spire of rock. We get only a few seconds to revel in our small victory. Then there's a sharp whistle out in the fog, and my heart leaps. "That's the alert," I say, translating the Fianna's signal for her. "They've found our boat."

Jubilee's smile vanishes, and once more we're fighting for our lives. "Let's go."

The facility seems to be almost empty, at least from the outside. Once we see a figure in night vision goggles disappearing around the corner of a building, but though we crouch and wait, the guard doesn't return.

Keeping to the shadows, we make for the nearest door to the main building, only to find it locked tight. If this were a normal facility it'd be print-coded with the latest security—but print-coding would leave a record of the people who've accessed the place. Instead the handles are the low-tech kind, requiring manual keys. I feel around the door frame, but we're not lucky enough for someone to have stashed a key some- where. Instead we're forced to make our way along the wall, testing the windows until we find one that Jubilee's able to pop open with a dull *thunk* of her elbow against the frame.

The small room we climb into is empty but for a few supply cabinets; we've entered through some kind of storeroom. When we slip out into the hallway, muddy footprints mark the floor, telling us people were here recently. Beyond the room is a series of hallways, but a faint trail of dirt shows which path is most traversed. Jubilee takes point down the cor- ridor, and I move silently after her, ears straining for any sign of life. My heart's beating too fast, and I can feel a corresponding pulse in my head. There's no sign of the wisp; our guide, for better or for worse, is gone.

Jubilee stops at the first corner, easing her head out to check that the way ahead is empty. Lifting her hand, she jerks two fingers to bid me fol- low and eases forward again.

The facility is laid out like a maze, but the paths and doors are labeled. We reach a branching corridor, and I tap my finger against a sign with an arrow that reads MAIN CONTROL ROOM. Jubilee nods; from there we might be able to get an idea as to the layout of this place and find some sort of records room or computer access.

A few doors feature glass panes, revealing unrecognizable equip- ment and fully stocked laboratories beyond them. Some are occupied by white-coated scientists, and we're quick to move past those. True, we could grab one or two of them to interrogate, but there's no guarantee that they even know who they're working for. We need hard evidence.

On one group of researchers, my eyes linger. They're gathered around a man's body laid out on a table. He still wears his camouflage trousers and military boots, and the scientists are gathered around his head. When one of them moves to retrieve a tool from a nearby tray, I can see that the whole top of his skull has been removed; the scientists are carefully removing pieces of his brain, laying them out in a neatly labeled row. A glance at Jubilee tells me she's as tense as I am, her shoulders drawn in tight. But we can't help him now, we both know that.

Our path leads to a door marked MAIN CONTROL ROOM, and Jubilee pauses to look back at me. I'm watching her eyes, checking her pupils, looking for that vacant hint that will tell me she's under the influence of the whispers, but I've never seen it happen like she has. I don't know what I'm looking for, and it's keeping me sick with tension.

Then abruptly the door opens, and we're face-to-face with a startled man in a white coat.

For a long moment, we all just stare at each other in surprise. He opens his mouth to shout an alarm, and Jubilee moves instantly. She punches him, and the way his head snaps back as he folds to the ground would be comical any other time. I can't help but wonder if that's what I looked like when she decked me before escaping the Fianna caves.

Now she and I move as one—I get my hands under his arms and she grabs his legs, and we haul him back into the room. A quick look over my shoulder shows it's empty, and we're alone save for a long bank of computer screens and an unconscious scientist.

I crouch to take a look at him, and as I peel back one of his eyelids, all I can see is the white of his eye. "You really had to hit him?"

Jubilee's standing by the door, listening for trouble. "What else could I do? I didn't hit him hard, he'll be fine."

"You really have to start thinking laterally." I roll the man onto his side so he doesn't choke on his own tongue while he's out.

"Not my forte." She shrugs, abandoning the door to prowl the room. "This is monitoring Avon's climate," she says after leaning down to study a screen. "It's got terraforming data displayed here for the last two decades. Far more detailed readings than what we get sent by TerraDyn." She falls silent, but I know we're both thinking about Merendsen's theory that Avon's progress, like the progress of the planet LaRoux destroyed, is being tampered with.

I stay by the scientist's side, and he doesn't stir as I check him for weapons, then push aside his white coat to make sure there's nothing clipped to his belt. All I see is an ID badge, and I'm about to drop the fabric when a glint flashes through the plastic cover of the pass. Sitting alongside a card showing a serial number—no name or photo—is a tiny ident chip. It's exactly the same as the one Jubilee found on our first visit here, right down to the tiny lambda. The room spins a little and I rub at my eyes, trying to remember when I last had more than a few hours of uninterrupted sleep. "LaRoux Industries," I say, pushing slowly to my feet.

"That won't be proof enough," says Jubilee with a grimace. "They try to stop it, but head down below street level in Corinth and you can get anything on the black market. A raider ship could outfit themselves with old LRI ident chips with enough credits; LaRoux could easily say these were stolen, especially since they're so antiquated."

The man at my feet gives a tiny groan, and I glance at him before saying, "What about the computers? There has to be something incriminating there."

"They'll be encrypted, for sure." Jubilee turns back to me, drawn by the signs that the scientist is coming to. "Unless we have someone with the password."

At my feet, the white-coated man moans again, rolling over onto his back and lifting one hand to claw at the air, as though he can grab something and pull himself closer to consciousness. Jubilee's at my side so fast I barely see her move, but I reach for her shoulder before she can grab him. "Let me," I murmur, and she scowls her acquiescence, muttering under her breath. The guy on the floor flinches at her tone and opens his eyes.

I look down at him. "Took a fall there, friend. What's your name?"

"Carmody." He's still confused. "Dr. Terrence Carmody. Who are you?"

"I'm the one who wants to talk to you," I say quietly. "She's the one who wants to break your legs. Let's start with the talking." I keep my eyes on his, gazes locked. Now that the adrenaline of breaking into the facility is starting to recede, my body feels leaden. I focus, reaching down inside to pull up a version of me I barely remember. Confident, imposing myself on others by sheer will. I can do this.

"We know what you're doing here," I start, and panic flickers across his face. "You're going to tell us everything about LaRoux Industries, and where you're hiding the creatures he's using."

"Please," the man gasps, stuttering. "I-I'm just a researcher. I don't know anything, I swear."

"Your password, then," Jubilee interrupts, her voice quick with tension. "For the computers."

The man swallows, his Adam's apple bobbing frantically. "I'm only cleared for this level—I'll give it to you, but it's just climate data, it's only what you see here. I don't know what you're talking about, with LaRoux Industries." He looks too terrified to be lying.

I meet Jubilee's eyes; I can tell from the tension in her gaze that she believes him too. But even if he doesn't know about the whispers, maybe he can still help us find proof of LaRoux Industries' involvement here.

I open my mouth to press him for more, but I'm cut off by a long, low blast of sound from speakers set up in the ceiling. The blood rushes in my ears, every ounce of adrenaline flooding back in and leaving a metallic taste in my mouth. The alarm is followed by a man's voice, quick and urgent.

"Attention all nonessential personnel: facility security has been compromised. Repeat: facility security has been compromised."

The girl is home again, in a shop, in a city called November, on a planet named Verona. Her mother is calling her and her father is washing his hands and his arms in the kitchen sink. The girl runs to her cave, the nest she's built under the shop's counter, and folds herself inside.

The green-eyed boy is there, somehow, though the space is only big enough for the girl. "You keep coming back here," he whispers, a terrible sadness in his voice. "After all these years."

"I was safe here," the girl whispers back.

"What's the real reason?" asks the boy, and when he looks at her, she knows she can't lie.

"Here," says the girl, "I'm not alone."

The boy takes her hand, and the girl notices the way their fingers interlock, as if they were meant to fit that way. "I thought you were supposed to be brave."

"I'm not brave enough to die alone."

THIRTY-FIVE

JUBILEE

I GESTURE AT THE RESEARCHER, WARNING HIM TO BE SILENT without a word, but he's too busy trying to cram himself in under one of the consoles, as though that might hide him from whatever punishment we have in mind for failing to help us. I inch toward the door and press my ear to it—I can't hear anything, no sounds of rushing security guards, nothing that sounds like a response to the alarm, which has gone silent again now. It's as though the place is abandoned.

A whispering rises all around me, as though I'm standing in a windstorm—but the air is utterly still. And I know what it is. Swallowing the metallic taste of blood in my mouth, I only have time for a glance down at my hands, searching for the palsied shakes that I know are coming. Except my hands are steady, but for the faint tremor of panic.

Before I can process what's happening, a groan from behind me shatters my heart. *Oh God, no.*

I whirl to find Flynn leaning with one hand braced against the console, his face white, gaze fixed on the floor. "Jubilee—" He gasps my name as though it's with his last breath.

I throw myself back, reaching for Flynn, as though his touch might banish the sudden razor-edge of fear slicing down my spine. "Talk to me!"

But he can't answer; he sags back against the wall, and for an instant his head lifts enough for me to see his gaze, his dilated eyes, the terror as he fights the thing that's happening to him.

"No—no, I can't—" My heart snaps, and with it the fear holding me hostage, and I stagger half a step toward him.

It was supposed to be me.

I swallow my fear. "We're getting out of here, now." Whispers be damned—Avon's fate be damned. I cannot watch Flynn's soul, his heart, vanish in front of me.

"Actually, you're not." I'd almost forgotten the researcher—Dr. Carmody—cowering on the floor. I turn to snap at him, and freeze.

He's got a weapon aimed at me; he must have had it hidden underneath the console. I should have been watching, I should have tied him up. I should have had Flynn . . . I choke, unable to focus on the man's gun. All I can see is Flynn, half-curled against the console, trying to fight the whispers.

"Fine!" I snap at Carmody, lifting my hands. "Arrest me, shoot me, I don't care. Just let me help him—" I take a step toward Flynn, but Carmody thumbs the switch on the side of the gun. Its whine as it charges rings in my ears, and I stop again.

"You can't help him," replies Carmody, sparing only a glance for Flynn before pinning his gaze back on me. "He's already gone."

I open my mouth, trying to find words to deny what he's said. But before I can, Flynn's moving. He's quick, so quick my eyes can barely follow him. He slips behind Carmody, grabbing his arm and jerking it up. The gun fires; not a Gleidel, this one leaves a smoking hole in the ceiling and sends plastene shards raining down onto the floor. Before I can take a step to help him, Flynn's other hand wraps around the back of Carmody's neck and slams his head down into the console with a sickening crack. He doesn't pause, but slams the researcher down again, and again, and again, until blood coats the controls and I cry out, still rooted to the spot.

Flynn, only his profile visible to me, releases the dead man and lets the body slump to the floor.

It's all happened in the space of a few heartbeats, so quickly I haven't drawn breath. Spots swimming in front of my eyes, I gasp for air. "F-Flynn?"

It takes an eternity for him to turn around, in which I imagine him a thousand times with his usual smile, his cocky air, the depth of his green eyes. He'll be standing there as though nothing has changed; he'll tell me he learned self-defense from me; he'll turn around and look at me and he'll be whole.

But instead he stands a few feet away, his face empty, the green eyes seared into my memory gone. In their place is nothing more than black glass, reflecting my own face back at me.

"No," he says in a calm, collected voice. There are flecks of Carmody's blood on his neck and chin. "Not anymore."

I stand there, unable to move, unable to breathe as he stoops, collecting the gun from Carmody's lax hand. He inspects it, not bothering to keep an eye on me. When he looks up, there's nothing in his face but blank serenity.

"It was supposed to be me," I whisper.

"We need you," says the thing in Flynn's mind. "We feel you are the better choice."

My legs tremble—with anger, with fear, with exhaustion—and I reach out for the wall for support. "What does LaRoux want with me?"

The Flynn-thing regards me flatly. "You are speaking of the one who binds us?" His head tilts slowly to one side, in a mockery of thoughtful interest, until it stops at an odd, unnatural angle. "We are not acting under his orders anymore."

My throat tangles with a brief, insane flicker of hope at those words— but then my heart plummets as the barrel of the gun swings over to point at me.

"We are not acting under *anyone's* orders anymore. We have seen what humanity is: beyond salvage." There's no violence, no hatred in his voice; the calm there is more terrifying than if he came at me screaming and spewing threats. He gestures with the gun toward the door, nudging Carmody's body aside with one foot to clear his path. "And you will be the one to set us free."

My hand closes on empty space as it reaches automatically for the gun that isn't there anymore. I take a step back toward the door, not taking my eyes off of Flynn. Off of what used to be Flynn.

Don't think, don't crumble. Just keep moving.

"You don't understand," I say as his eyes follow me. "We want to stop LaRoux too. We're not like him."

"You are all like him."

I grasp for the handle behind me, but don't turn it yet. The creature keeps his distance, too smart to come close enough for me to think about wresting the gun from him. Flynn, I could probably disarm and disable. But after seeing what he did to Carmody . . . No human can move that fast.

"Lilac said you helped them," I murmur, shooting a quick glance at the hallway through the window in the door. It's empty, as it was before.

Flynn's blank expression doesn't shift. "We know this one you speak of. She was with us in the darkness for a time."

With us? But I seize on that recognition, speaking quickly, trying to moderate my voice the way Flynn would. If only he were here, with his passion and his diplomacy; I'm only good for fighting. "Then you know her. You know she's not like her father. Neither am I—neither is Flynn." My voice chokes on his name.

"All patterns of data contain anomalies." Flynn halts, though the gun doesn't move. "Continue walking."

I ignore his order. "Why lead us here?" I think of the light in the swamp, the green glow that looked so much like the November ghost in my dimmest memories. "Why not just force the scientists, force LaRoux, to let you go?"

"Our keeper never comes near enough for us to take him. These others, he has operated upon and made it difficult for us to inhabit their minds with any precision." Flynn nudges Carmody's body again, this time to roll him over onto his stomach. Beneath the mess of blood and hair, just below his ear, is a tiny scar, too straight and precise to have been from an accident.

I swallow down my nausea, jerking my eyes away from the bits of skull protruding from Carmody's head.

He doesn't flinch. "Before we were brought here, we existed as pieces of a single entity, part of one mind. Our keeper has learned that to be sundered from each other is the worst kind of agony we can know. When we displease him, he puts us into the dark place." The whisper's face, Flynn's face, shows me nothing. No fear, no hatred, not even the flicker of remembered pain. "He will not do so again after we are free."

It's getting harder to breathe, my chest tightening with a kind of panic

I haven't felt in years, not since my first time in combat. No way out. No way through. I close my eyes for half a breath, focusing on the air moving through my lungs.

"Why should I help you?" I have to fight to speak my next words. "You've taken away the one thing I had left. You've taken him—"

"Because he is still in here. Because if you set us free, we will return him to you. And we will save you, and this planet, for last."

My heart starts again with a lurch that makes my eyes water. But the rest of the creature's words ring in my ears. "What do you mean, 'save us for last'?" I whisper. "What will you do when you're free?"

"We will start with our keeper," the whisper replies, dead-eyed and soft. "We will give him the same pain he has given us. We will take his family from him, and all he knows, and every soul who has ever touched him. And then we will spread this death, as your kind has spread, and we shall make him the last of your species. And then, once he has realized the thing he has done—then we will leave him, howling, in the dark."

My eyes blur, stinging with tears of horror and grief. "No," I whisper. My voice shakes, but behind the tremor there's iron, and I can feel its strength as I straighten. "No, I won't help you. Shoot me if you want, but I'm not setting you monsters free."

Flynn merely looks at me, mouth lax, eyes empty. He looks like a mannequin, like a doll of himself, and my heart tries to claw its way out of my chest. "All right," he says calmly.

And turns the gun on himself, pressing the barrel to the underside of his chin.

"No—!" My voice tears from my throat, stabbing the air as I jerk forward half an inch, hand raised. "No, stop!" I gasp for air, nausea sweeping through me to follow the path of my fear. "What are you doing?"

The Flynn-thing doesn't even flinch, watching my distress without reaction. "If you refuse to do as we ask, then we have no further use for this vessel." I can see the barrel pressing hard enough into Flynn's neck that the skin around the metal edge is turning white.

"Okay." The word comes like a sob, wrenching from my lungs so painfully I have to take a breath, and another, before I can speak again. "Okay. I'll do it."

It's been ten years, and every night the girl keeps searching for the November ghost. Sometimes she finds her mother or her father; sometimes the girl finds friends she recognizes, and enemies she doesn't. She finds the green-eyed boy everywhere, and sometimes he helps her look.

She's wandering the swamps of Avon now, alone, gliding on the water in an old, narrow boat. She's searched the entire world and found nothing—no green-eyed boy, no people at all—and no November ghost. She looks up at Avon's empty sky until the anguish is too much, and she drops back down into the bottom of the boat, resting her forehead against the wood.

Then something makes her lift her head.

In the water below she sees a million stars reflected, and the swamp becomes the sky, and her boat a ship. The stars are blinding, welcoming her, each one a tiny, dancing ball of light. All around her the swamp is illuminated.

THIRTY-SIX

JUBILEE

MY MIND IS TOO WELL TRAINED. IT KEEPS TRYING TO FIND A way out, some tactic with which to disarm the creature, to gain the upper hand. Move more quickly around this corner, surprise him when he follows; duck inside that doorway, then slip out behind him when he passes.

But even if I could do it, even if I could wrest the gun from the thing that killed Carmody with its bare hands—what then? I can't hold at gunpoint a creature willing to kill Flynn simply because he's no longer useful. Even if I could point a gun at Flynn. Even if I could . . .

But he's not Flynn anymore; the boy I knew is gone. There's no warmth in his gaze, no life in his voice. It's not *him*. Even if the creature was telling the truth, even if they could bring him back to me . . . could he forgive me for what I'm about to do? I clench my jaw. *Keep it together, Jubilee.*

I was never supposed to be the one on the outside of the mind control. That's Flynn's job. I hit things, I shoot things, I pass on the orders that are passed to me. He was supposed to be the one having to make this call, to kill me if I wasn't coming back, to decide if I was a lost cause.

I can't make this kind of choice alone. Flynn would never want me to sacrifice humanity to keep him alive for a few more years—or weeks, or days, I don't know. Not even for Avon. But I cannot watch that thing pull the trigger; I can't stand here and watch it blow Flynn away. I could more easily cut out my own heart. *Flynn, what do I do?*

The corridors ahead of us are empty. It isn't until the thing control-ling Flynn leads me to an elevator and I press the button that I glance back—and freeze.

Shuffling after us, filing out of the rooms and down the corridor, are the facility's staff. Dozens of them, filling the hallway; some in the white coats of the lab techs, others in combat gear like mine. They're silent, blank-faced, moving with a strange, disconnected gait, shoes dragging against the floor. Their slow, sluggish movements are so different from Flynn's, hampered by the surgical procedure LaRoux used to prevent the whispers from being able to fully control them. And every single one has eyes like marbles.

The thing controlling Flynn motions me into the elevator when its doors open, and for the first time I move quickly, my spine prickling and skin itching with horror. I press my shoulder blades against the far wall of the elevator, turning in time to see the half-controlled facility workers come to a stop just inches away from the lip of the door. They say nothing, only continue to gaze at me while the elevator doors close between us.

The elevator descends, and then the whisper leads me through a secu-rity check manned by a still, blank form seated at the desk, with the same black-eyed stare as the sentries up above. Then he leads me to a second elevator; we go down again, down farther, down staircases and ramps, down into what feels like the heart of Avon. The farther I walk into the belly of this secret facility, the heavier the air presses in all around me.

Flynn doesn't speak to me again.

We reach a door with another security pad, though this time there's no one there to wave us through. This door is different from the others—it's round, designed to dilate open. If it were a regular door I might be able to force it, but these are the kinds of doors they use on ships as fail-safes. Airtight, absolutely secure.

Flynn comes to a halt beside it and turns to me expectantly. Finally we've reached a place with no others, no witnesses. Nobody here but us. I wait, but Flynn does nothing, simply gazes evenly at me. I get the uneasy impression I could stand here forever waiting for him to speak and he would never crack. I clear my throat. "What am I supposed to do?"

"Open the door."

"It needs a key, and I don't have one." My terror is dimming to a kind of dull numbness, my whole body aching with tension and grief.

"You are incorrect," the Flynn-thing says coldly, the dilated pupils fixed on my face. "You have had a key all this time."

I swallow, my eyes blurring. Hearing his voice is like a constant searing fire—knowing it's not him in there, that he's not speaking to me. "What? How could I—" But then I stop short, heart pounding in the silence. Because I *do* have a key. I have the ident chip we found the first time Flynn brought me here—I reach into my pocket to fish it out.

Though my skin crawls, I force myself to go nearer to the Flynn-thing to examine the security pad. There are numbers for a password, but also a small rectangular indentation on the bottom right. I press the ident chip into the slot, and it fits perfectly. The keys all light up green with a cheery beep, and then the door whooshes open.

The inside is so bright that for an instant my eyes are too dazzled to see. A hand between my shoulder blades propels me forward, and the touch is so like Flynn's—and so unlike it at the same time—that I'm too dumbfounded to resist. I stumble over the lip and into the room, blinking.

Flynn follows, and the door whooshes closed again. I turn, heart seizing in alarm. I'm trapped. But before I can react, Flynn goes crumpling to the ground.

I give a wordless shout and throw myself down next to him, grabbing at him before his head can hit the solid plastene floor.

"What the—Flynn? Flynn, wake up. Please." I give him a shake, but his head lolls back. I bend my head close, putting my ear to his lips—he's breathing, but only barely. His pulse is slow.

Cradling him against me, I lift my head and look around. I'd expected machinery, transmitters, a central hub crawling with technicians. Instead, the room is empty. We're in a large white dome with no visible light source, despite the brightness reflected off the curved walls. The floor and ceiling are made of plastene panels that tingle to the touch, as if they're somehow conductive, except that plastene is an insulator by design.

As I draw in a ragged breath only to have the sound swallowed by the space, I remember another property of plastene: it muffles noise. No matter how loud I scream in here, no one's ever going to hear me.

My fingers run through Flynn's hair, desperate for his touch even if he's unconscious. Even if he's not him anymore. *Don't leave me here alone, Romeo.*

Then, as if in answer to the thought, a breeze traces along the back of my neck. I shiver in response, jerking to the side. There's nothing there, and when I lift a hand to rub at my neck I realize the collar of my shirt would prevent a breeze from reaching my skin. Nevertheless, the hairs are rising on my neck and my arms.

I know this sensation too well to ignore it.

We're not alone.

"I know you're there," I say, trying to sound harsh and competent. "Show yourself. *Now.*" But no one answers; all I can hear is my own breathing.

The light is too bright to be sure, but for an instant I think I see a faint green glow hovering only a few feet in front of my face.

Then Flynn stirs with a tiny groan, and my attention snaps back down. He lifts his head from my lap, pressing one hand against the floor.

"Flynn?" I duck my head to try to see his face. I can't afford to hope.

His eyes open, showing me only blackness, and my heart sinks. I swallow the sob that wants to escape, and scramble back from him, getting my feet under me and reaching for the gun he dropped when he collapsed. He finishes picking himself up slowly.

"We are sorry," Flynn whispers, almost to himself, his movements slow and measured.

"Sorry?" I stare at the creature, the gun clenched in my grip, though I can't make my arm lift it.

The Flynn-creature finally swings his gaze over toward me. "Yes. We—I—" The word is slow to leave his lips, as though it feels wrong. "*I* am sorry. You must listen, we don't have much time. The others will know I have interfered."

I press my back against the sealed door. "Others," I repeat, so confused I'm only able to echo his words. "You mean you're not the thing that took Flynn?"

Flynn shakes his head. There's nothing to suggest he's changed; his eyes are still black, his face still devoid of emotion. "Once, we were all the same. Part of each other. But that was when the rift still connected us. Now we're alone. And I do not wish for the kind of freedom the others want."

For the first time since Flynn turned those empty eyes on me, my heart flickers with hope—a tiny, guttering flame that makes my eyes burn. I want so badly to believe the creature. I want so badly not to be alone. But I tighten my grip on the gun as panic sweeps back through me. "It's a trick," I spit. "You're trying to—I don't know. If you really were different, you'd let Flynn go. You'd give him back to me."

"We can't."

"What do you mean, you can't? Upstairs you said you would let him go if I helped you."

"The others have learned deception. It is a human art, and we have had a very clever teacher." The thing makes Flynn shake his head. "When we take a mind this deeply, for this long, there is no going back. His mind is still here, but it would be damaged beyond repair if I tried to leave him now."

Despair surges in me. "You took me over for hours and I'm still here. You made me go to the rebel hideout, and I came back, and I was fine. My mind's intact."

"You're different." Flynn's eyes stay on mine, watching me. There's an odd, probing quality to his gaze. I can't shake the disturbing feeling that he can see my thoughts.

"Different. Soulless, like the men say?"

"The opposite." Flynn's mouth curves into something not very much like a smile, but far from being comforting, it's just a reminder that it isn't Flynn, not really. That smile should be his, for me. Not an echo summoned up by the creature infesting his mind. "You and I have met before."

"You've got me confused with someone—"

"We do not have time for me to be gentle," the whisper interrupts. "I cannot hold off the others forever. You *must* remember. You are Jubilee Chase, daughter of Mei-Hua and Noah Chase, and we have been together for a very long time."

It's like someone's punched me in the stomach. I can't breathe, I can't see—my vision blurs, my hands lose feeling. I gasp for air.

Flynn isn't done. He's watching me curiously, as though he's a scientist observing a particularly fascinating chemical reaction. "You've felt our touch before, when we were first learning to understand your kind. When you were young and malleable. This has made you different. This has made your mind stronger. Your soul stronger. We remember you." He pauses, hesitation briefly so human, so familiar, that I ache. "I remember you."

"I wasn't imagining it all." The fragments of memory refuse to coalesce, leaving me with pieces of truth, too fractured to help me now. "There were whispers on Verona; I thought they were ghosts. I remember. . . ." I swallow a sudden, dizzying sweep of grief. "Then it *was* the Fury that caused the riots there. You made those people kill my parents?"

"Death does not exist for us. How could we have understood, then, what our keeper was forcing us to do?" His jaw is squaring now, black gaze locked on me.

"Forced," I echo. "By LaRoux?"

"He told us that if we complied he would send us home. Only after he moved us here from the place you call Verona did we realize his deception, but by then he had learned how to cause us great pain."

"He's torturing you." My stomach roils, sickened, hatred surging for the man I've only ever seen in holovids and news feeds.

Flynn nods. "Each time he punishes us the others grow further apart, more and more different. They are lost, alone. And their agony infects your kind; it is what drives them mad."

"And you? Why are you different?"

"Because I remember *you*, Jubilee Chase."

"I'm not special," I snap. "I'm no more important than anyone else."

"You're the most important thing in this universe. You; this vessel; the people of this planet; lovers, warriors, artists, leaders, dreams more numerous than stars. Each mind unique, each thought created for an instant and then broken apart to form new ones. You don't understand the unbearable beauty of being *you*."

My eyes burn, and though I try to reach for detachment, the barrier of stone that saw me through the years since my parents' deaths, my voice shakes when I speak. "We can still feel alone."

The whisper gazes back at me through Flynn's eyes. I feel hollow, as hollow as that stare; and yet there's a knot of sympathy smoldering in the back of my mind. Perhaps I can't understand the agony of true isolation; but right now, looking at Flynn, inches from me but infinitely far away, I feel like I can imagine it.

"You wished to be an explorer," the creature says, still holding my gaze. "You wished to explore the seas and the stars. You dreamed of it so brightly." Behind him, the white room is changing. Blue and green unfurl from the walls, spilling across the floor, enveloping me. Seaweeds and corals sprout like flowers, and a million kinds of fish, each one a different color, dart here and there.

I gasp, but I can breathe this ocean like I breathe the air.

"You once called me friend," says the whisper.

"You—*you* were there." A thousand memories come flooding back to me. "In November—with me."

The vision of the ocean fades, the fish becoming ghosts of themselves, still swimming toward something in the moment they vanish. But the memory remains, and with it, the memory of a dream, long ago forgotten and buried beneath my grief. But no less real.

"I have wronged you," the whisper says quietly, and though his expression shows no shame, he speaks slowly, each word heavy with regret. "Mine are not the actions of a friend. I stole from you."

"My dreams." I'm still clinging to the ocean, the memory of the dream enveloping me, something I haven't experienced since before my parents were killed.

"I thought I was helping you, sparing you from reliving the pain of your parents' deaths in your dreams. I thought I was easing your pain. But even your painful dreams are beautiful, Jubilee Chase, and I had no right to take them from you. They changed, as you grew, and there was healing in them. You needed them, and I took them from you."

"All these years, you've been—intercepting my dreams? Taking them for your own? *Why?*"

"Because through them I could feel less alone." Flynn sighs, tilting his head back and looking up at the dome of the whisper's prison. "The others believe there is no hope for your kind, that the bursts of violence they cause, your Fury, it means nothing. But I've felt your grief, your loss.

And though your species is capable of horrors, it's capable of beauty, too. To end it now would be no better than taking your dreams away; to bring death robs your species of the chance to heal."

I reach up to dash my hand angrily over my cheeks, hating that I feel for this wretched creature wearing Flynn's face, hating that I can no longer fight without feeling. Hating that now I wonder if I ever did. "I want Flynn back," I say, voice cracking. "If you can see my heart, then you know I need him."

"Your bond with this vessel is why I chose him."

"Stop calling him a vessel," I burst out, anger sparking tears in my eyes all over again. "He's a person. He's smart, and kind, and braver than you could ever understand, and you've gone in and taken him away like it's nothing."

"Are you in love with this vess—this person?"

I gape at him, caught off guard. The absurdity of the question here, in the bowels of a secret research facility, conversing with a creature from another universe, is so striking that I have to fight the hysterical impulse to laugh. But his eyes are so grave, so serious, that the urge fades and I'm left looking at him, my heart tight and painful.

"I—I don't know," I whisper. I remember the shape of his heart and mine, and his kiss at the water's edge. "But I wanted the chance to find out."

Flynn's eyes flicker. *He's here now,* the creature had said. I swallow, wishing I could shout at him, wanting to beg him to come back to me.

"I do not know how to leave him without destroying his mind. But if you destroyed my connection, *our* connection, with him . . . perhaps then he would be left whole."

"Destroyed," I echo stupidly. "You mean—"

"I want you to kill us, Jubilee Chase."

The words knock the air from my lungs, leaving me unable to reply until I've gasped a few breaths.

The creature inside Flynn watches me, searching for a sign of my reaction. "I do not wish to become like the others, to fall into violence and despair, into pain. We aren't built for it. We can't stand it."

"And you think we can?" I choke back a sob. "Life is pain. We're all in pain, all the time."

"There are other things this universe has to offer," says the creature. "Light. Life. Touch. Sensation. The way you are all made of the same pieces, the same fragments of stardust, and yet you are all so different, all so alone."

"You think being alone is a good thing?"

"For us it's agony," he says simply. "For you, there is strength in individuality. We admire it. But we were not made to emulate it."

I gaze back at him, trying to see traces of the creature inside Flynn as he bows his head. But all I can see are Flynn's cheekbones, his mouth, his hair tumbling over his brow. There's nothing about him that speaks of the passenger inside him except for the emptiness in his eyes. I bite my lip, mind turning over. "Are you sure?" I say softly. "Maybe there's some way to set you free, to let you go so you can . . ." But my voice gives out. I can see the creature's answer in Flynn's features.

"Our keeper's mistake was in creating a prison powered by our own energy. We are a part of it." Flynn takes a step toward me. "Destroy the machinery holding this place together and you will destroy us with it. And without our interference, forced to keep this world secret, always hidden, you can broadcast your story to the stars. Begin your healing, perhaps. Prove your species deserves life."

"But all those things you said were good about this universe. The things you could experience. Light and—and touch . . ." My voice gives out.

Flynn's shaking his head slowly. "We have no desire to live without hope of returning home. I wish . . . to rest."

"All right," I whisper. "I'll help you."

Flynn beckons me closer and we kneel together on the blinding white floor. He shows me the nearly invisible seam in the floor and the faint outline of a human hand—a scanner, meant to unlock the control panel beneath.

"It merely requires a hand," he tells me. "Anyone's hand; a deft way of keeping us, we who cannot touch anything. We've tried to lead others here before, but our keeper seems to take pleasure in our failures."

"Lead others . . ." But before I can ask, realization courses through me. "The will-o'-the-wisps." The locals were right. The wisps *were* leading them somewhere.

"The others tried for years," the whisper continues. "But when I realized that what I wanted was different, I—I was afraid."

I search the lax features for some sign of that fear and find none, from this creature with no way to express itself. "Afraid of what?"

"Of dying alone." The whisper, behind Flynn's face, meets my eyes. "Of dying without meeting *you*."

I gaze back, my heart thumping with grief—for me, for Flynn, for this lost creature huddled inside him. Before I can speak, a ripple runs through Flynn's features, making me jump.

"You must hurry," the whisper gasps. "The others will not stay quiet for long; I cannot hold them."

I gulp back a sob and fit my hand to the indentation, trying not to flinch at the tingle of current that courses through me in response. The scanner beeps and flashes green, causing a section of the floor to rise upward, up and up, until there's an eight-foot column of circuitry and wires towering over me. Destroy this and the whispers die.

I can feel the whole thing humming with power, so strong it sets my teeth on edge, makes my hair lift as though a lightning bolt were about to strike. It won't be hard to overload it all, with that much power coursing through it.

Flynn staggers, but catches himself before he can fall. His voice is a rasp, but for now, he has control. "When it is done, you must go and stop what is happening outside."

"Outside?"

"Your people, his people; this prison has become a battlefield."

The bottom falls out of my stomach. We knew the Fianna were close behind us when we found the facility, but the military must have been tracking us too. Two armies, converging; there'll be a battle raging above, fueled by deaths that mean nothing, no chance of realizing they should all be on the same side against a sadistic madman worlds away. It'll be a bloodbath.

This creature, who claims it cannot understand death—its compassion has robbed me of breath. With that realization comes another, and I swallow hard. "It was you," I whisper. "*You* took me over the night of the massacre, not the others. You brought me there to the caves."

"This vessel—this person—his pain is yours; you share it the way my kind shares everything. You would grieve for those deaths as he would. But I brought you there too late to stop it."

I was there to save them. Even through its anger and its pain, this creature whose kindred sent my friends mad one by one had tried to save Flynn grief.

The whisper waits patiently until I look back up, then speaks. "I have answered your questions. Will you grant me something in return?"

"What is it?" My voice cracks.

"May I . . . touch you?"

I blink, eyes snapping up to meet his. "Uh—excuse me?"

"We cannot experience physical sensation in our world, and in this universe we have been always alone." Flynn's face looks so young.

I swallow. "Okay. Okay, sure."

Flynn's hand slides forward, reaching for mine. I let him take it, his fingertips grazing my skin as he turns my hand over. His knuckle brushes across my palm—his eyes are fixed on our hands, wonder transforming his features.

"In our world," he whispers, "we are always together, completely, utterly. We are all a part of each other." He exhales slowly, his breath puffing warm and gentle across our hands. "But it means we never know how precious it is to be able to do this, to be apart and then come together." He weaves his fingers through mine.

I half expected his hand to be clammy, or to tingle to the touch. But his skin is warm, and familiar, and our fingers interlock as though our hands were designed to do it.

A droplet splashes onto the back of my hand, and my gaze snaps up. Flynn's eyes are wet, and as I watch, another tear slips free and tracks halfway down his cheek before dropping away. "Thank you," he whispers. "Jubilee Chase, I wish—"

His voice cuts out abruptly as his fingers tighten convulsively around mine. His eyes snap back up. This time I can see the panic there, an almost-human desperation reaching out through those blank, black eyes.

I cannot hold off the others forever.

"Wait!" I cry, my heart pounding with sudden fear. "Just—just hold on. Please, there has to be a way to . . ."

To save you.

There's only a flicker of grief—of true despair—on his features before blankness sweeps across them. The change in Flynn, inhabited by my November ghost, had been so gradual that I almost hadn't noticed how unlike the other whispers he was. But this coldness, this blankness—it calls up an answering chill from the pit of my stomach. My November ghost is gone.

It takes the Flynn-thing only seconds to focus on my face, a jolt running through me. I left the gun on the floor; it rests between us, and he sees it too. The instant I move, he will too—I'll only have one shot.

One shot.

I wrench my hand from his and throw myself forward as both of us dive for the gun. My hand wraps around the grip as I hit the floor and roll, certain I'm going to feel the creature's inhuman grip crushing my ankle or my windpipe at any moment. The air grows thick with whispering voices calling to me, visions of loved ones long dead flickering in front of my eyes as my mouth floods with the taste of copper. I blink frantically as I come back up on my knees, dizzy and blinded by the false messages the creatures are sending my mind. I swing the gun around, drawing one breath, time slowing to a crawl. Then I let out the breath and fire.

A circuit board among the machinery explodes into fragments, sending a shock wave of electricity through the wiring. The entire room flickers wildly, the core of machinery flashing through the dark like a strobe. The whisper, inches away from grabbing me, suddenly drops to the floor with a scream. I can see Flynn's dilated eyes fixed on mine, lips parted in pain.

The power crackles and surges, building to a roar that sends me crashing to the ground. I crane my head, trying to see Flynn—trying to see the creature inside him, the creature that's dying—but I can see only his outline silhouetted by the sparks and surges. I shout, but I can't hear my own voice over the roar. I reach for Flynn, trying to drag myself upright, but just as I'm about to take his hand, the entire core blows with a force that sends us both flying, and the room goes black.

The girl reaches out her hand. The stars are so close she can graze them with her fingertips, but each time she touches one, it shatters into a thousand pieces. The girl hangs suspended, her hair floating in Avon's currents, water and darkness and space no harder to breathe than air, and searches for the November ghost. She knows it's here, hidden—and she must ask why it left, why it abandoned her in the moment she needed dreams most.

She pushes through the broken stars, which shatter and fall around her like curtains of rain, vanishing into the bottomless waters, down into the heart of Avon.

THIRTY-SEVEN

FLYNN

THIS FEELS LIKE THE TIME SEAN SHOVED ME OFF THE TOP of the lookout rock when we were eleven. Every bone in my body aches, pain lancing along my ribs as I inhale. I grope my way toward consciousness, white lights exploding against my closed eyelids.

Then there's something touching my fingers—it's another hand, squeezing mine. "Flynn?" Jubilee's voice is ragged. I open my eyes to find myself in a dimly lit room with a domed roof. What light there is comes from the hallway outside. I squeeze her hand in return and hear her gasp a sob as I concentrate on breathing, and wait to understand.

Between one blink and the next, I remember the passengers in my mind, and the conversations between myself and Jubilee that I watched through a gauzy veil, too slow and stupid to remember how to reach out and speak my own thoughts. I remember the wrench of separation, and what it was to die, and my breath catches in my throat.

I blink again, and as I manage to focus my gaze, our eyes meet. For an instant I see it all in her eyes as she looks back at me—the pain of bearing witness, the last vestiges of her fear. Her sadness. Her hand shakes as she reaches out to touch my face, to see the way her touch affects me; her relief swells, and when I try to smile at her, a weak fragment of a thing, she lets out a harsh, wrenching sound, head dropping.

She stays that way for a heartbeat, letting out a breath. When she lifts her head again, I see her soldier's mask slide back into place, despite the tears still wet on her cheeks. But there's something different about that shield now, a warmth I can't identify until she looks at me once more, and I realize her heart is still in her eyes. "Can you move?" She's speaking as she climbs to her feet, taking my hand to pull me with her. "There are monitors everywhere—LaRoux will know what we've done."

"The comms tower." I stagger upright, keeping hold of her hand. "Like Lilac said, a galaxy of witnesses, so he can't destroy Avon. So he can't silence us."

"The military and the Fianna are out there." She shakes her head, gasping the words as she shoves the gun she took from the whisper into her holster.

"A broadcast is the only way to keep Avon safe." I squeeze her hand, knowing what I'm asking. The odds that both of us will make it through the chaos of open war unscathed are almost impossible. "If I can make our people hear me too, maybe we can end this."

Jubilee gazes back at me for a long moment, then tightens her hand in mine. "Then let's go."

The facility is chaotic. Mercenaries freed from their trances stagger from room to corridor, trying to understand where they are and why. Scientists and researchers in white coats lie still where they fell, though I can't tell if they're dead or unconscious. Perhaps it's LaRoux's last failsafe, part of whatever he did to their brains, a way to make sure they couldn't talk.

We work our way up staircases and through hallways, climbing to the surface. We're just two more bodies in the chaos, and I keep my head down, hand wrapped tight around Jubilee's as we race down the hallway. With every step my energy's returning, hope surging through me. The fight's not over yet. My head's clear, my lungs are working more easily. By the time we reach the door to the compound, I feel better than I have since we climbed onto the shuttle to head for the spaceport. I feel alive. Now all we have to do is stay that way.

Outside it's still dark, dawn at least an hour away. There's a faint light to the east, enough to make out the silhouettes of people running everywhere. This facility, hidden until now, has become a battlefield. We stare out of the open doorway until, with a low cry of warning, Jubilee yanks at my arm to pull me down to the floor. Half an instant later, a laser ricochets off the metal door frame inches from where I'd been standing.

The muddy smell of swamp seeps in to overtake the filtered air of the facility, carrying with it the acrid stench of burning from laser and gunfire. Somewhere on the other side of our building I can hear McBride roaring like a man possessed, bellowing orders. Through the crack in the doorway, I see Pól and Liam O'Mara dash past, faces visible for an instant in a flash of light as half a dozen Gleidels go off at once. My heart clenches, but neither of them stumbles.

Jubilee's face lights in a flash of laser-fire. Her eyes are wide, gaze scanning the battlefield like she's trying to find openings or search for patterns. "This is suicide," she breathes.

I scan the chaos as her soldiers gain ground against my Fianna, breaching the fence here and there and pinning them against the building we're hiding in. I trace the line of the fence until I reach the comms tower, studying it through the muted light. There's a door at the base, but it's closed, and for all I know it's locked. There's a maintenance ladder running up the outside of the building, though; rusted, rickety, but it looks like I could climb it, maybe.

"We have to try." I flinch as one of the Fianna goes down with a scream. I don't recognize the voice, but my gut clenches at the sound. "Can you get me to the tower? If you can hold them off, I think I can still stop this." The guns are roaring outside, lasers screaming and lighting up the compound in quick flashes. More every second, louder every minute. I glance at Jubilee as her eyes sweep across the battle, taking stock of all that's happening. I can see her mind working, trying to figure out how fast we can run, whether we've got any chance of making it before someone shoots us. She draws in two long, slow breaths, easing her gun out of its holster. I hope her aim is good enough to avoid killing anybody—neither of these armies is our enemy anymore. Then she nods, saying nothing, but there's determination in her gaze.

Sheltering behind the cover of the doorway, I reach for her to tug her in closer, until we're a hand's breadth apart. Beyond, I can hear the shriek of Gleidels and the crack of the Fianna's ancient weaponry—then the ground beneath our feet shudders with the force of an explosion. Heart thumping, I look across at Jubilee, and despite the low light, I can see the lines of her face—her lips, her cheekbones, the swoop of her lashes. "Hey," I murmur. I don't know what I want to say, but I have to say it before we walk onto a battlefield, into the path of two armies that both want us dead.

"Hey," she whispers back, close enough that I can see the tiny shifts in her eyes as she studies me. She's tracing out the lines of my face, just as I'm drinking in hers, memorizing her features. "Flynn—I'm glad you ruined me."

Her voice stabs my heart, because I recognize that tone. I've heard it before. "Don't start with the good-byes," I say. Her lips twitch in a tiny smile, and I drink it in. My voice shrinks to a breath as I remember what she said when I was only a passenger in my own body, when the whisper asked if she loved me. "I want us to have the chance to find out, too."

She recognizes her own words echoing back to her, and her lips quiver, her eyes fixed on mine.

I brace my shaking hands against the floor. "Ready?"

She nods, gaze swinging away to lock on the comms tower. "Ready."

We burst from the doorway and run.

The girl pushes through the last of the stars, scattering them into glittering dust that settles on her skin and glimmers as it sinks through the water. All that's left is darkness, and there's no sign of the November ghost.

The green-eyed boy reaches out and touches her cheek, his movements slow and deliberate in weightlessness, in water. The light from above filters down through the water, dim and green, illuminating his face.

Then he looks up—and when the girl follows his gaze, she sees something shining, up above water, glimmering just out of reach. She gasps, and swims for the surface.

THIRTY-EIGHT

JUBILEE

WE SPRINT THROUGH THE PREDAWN GLOOM, MAKING straight for the comms tower, ducking low as bullets fly over our heads. We don't bother to dodge or weave; there's so much gunfire in the air, it'd be pointless. Trying desperately not to slip on the marshy ground, I strain my eyes in the darkness, but the world is full of shadowy silhouettes— soldiers repositioning themselves and trying to gain ground, the Fianna darting in and out of the battle to move wounded.

We reach the comms tower, and I smash into the door an instant before Flynn. We flatten ourselves into the shelter of the door frame, and he grabs at the handle, twisting and yanking it with white-knuckled urgency. It doesn't give.

Flynn lowers his head to shout in my ear. "We have to climb!" He grabs at the rusted maintenance ladder to the right of the door and ducks out of the doorway a beat ahead of me to start climbing. My muscles scream a protest as I follow, grabbing the rungs to pull myself up after him.

Four or five meters up, something invisible slams my shoulder against the tower. I try to force my hands to grip the ladder harder before I'm knocked free, but only my left hand tightens. There's a spatter of blood on the cement wall that wasn't there before, and I stare at it, uncomprehending. My right hand's letting go, fingers unpeeling from the bar in slow motion. I feel nothing, no pain, only confusion when I realize I'm falling.

I hit the ground, the impact driving the air from my lungs just before the pain explodes, screaming up my right arm to my shoulder, down my elbow, fire erupting inside my veins.

Her November ghost is waiting for her when she reaches the surface. It lights the way for her as she climbs back into the boat and stands there, dripping, strands of stardust in her hair. She can't wait any longer, words tumbling out of her.

Where have you been?

The November ghost is no more than a whisper, but when the girl closes her eyes, she can hear it:

Looking for you.

THIRTY-NINE

FLYNN

I'M SCRAMBLING, BULLETS PINGING OFF THE LADDER AROUND me, when suddenly Jubilee's not below me anymore. I nearly lose my grip, grabbing for a rung as I twist to see where she's gone, fear singing through me.

She's on the ground. *Oh God, she's on the ground.* And even in the dark, even in the mud, I can see she's been hit, blood flowering out across her arm.

"Jubilee!" My scream is hoarse, barely audible even to me over the gunfire. My muscles start moving, sending me sliding and stumbling back down the ladder; I can't see anything other than her body.

Then she lifts her head, and my heart nearly gives out with relief. She starts to move, getting her left elbow underneath her, then falling back into the mud once more. It takes me a long moment to even realize her mouth is moving, and I can't hear what she says as she stares up at me, but I can read the word on her lips. *Go.*

I hang from the framework, helpless—hope above me, my heart on the ground below. Then she screams at me again, and this time I can hear her shout. *"GO!"* I can see what the effort costs her.

So I do the only thing I can. I force my arms and legs to move against the frantic orders my heart wants to issue, and I scramble up, grabbing each handhold and hauling, muddy feet sliding off rungs and finding new purchase. There's a window at the top—it serves as a lookout tower too, perhaps—and I turn my face away and smash my fist against the pane. It shatters, and I smash out the pieces, making a hole I can scramble through, landing in a muddy heap on the floor of the empty tower.

I don't waste a second, pushing up to my knees, trying to keep my head below the line of the windows. I'm surrounded by a bewildering array of broadcast equipment, a thousand times more complex than the simple radio gear we use in the caves. And yet it's not completely alien. Something about the controls is familiar.

I close my eyes, trying to ignore the tug of my heart back down to where Jubilee lies, trying to tune out the sound below and send my focus back. Back before the last planetary review, the last rebellion, back to a time when home meant a roof, a bed of my own. I can't remember my mother's face, but I can see her hands still, curled around a transmitter. They took away hypernet communications technology during the rebellion, but now I watch the memory unfold, kneeling on the floor of the tower. I see her hand holding the transmitter, her fingers reaching across to depress a button so the display leaped to life. And I *remember.*

I grab the receiver, fingers running over the buttons until I find the sequence I need to transmit my broadcast to the galaxy. There's a row of switches labeled EXTERIOR LIGHTS, and I flip them, the courtyard suddenly dazzlingly bright—the figures below freeze, half blinded, stumbling and ducking for cover. The shooting starts to die away.

Next to the light switches are those for the loudspeakers, and I flip those too. The speakers above me awaken with a crackle. Now I'm transmitting to my people and Jubilee's in the compound below, as well as to every corner of the galaxy.

I hold down the button on the side of the transmitter and start to speak. "My name is Flynn Cormac."

Below, I see a couple of heads snap up at the sound of my voice, or maybe at my name—I can't tell whether the silhouettes are soldiers or Fianna. "This is a transmission for the people of Avon, and for all those beyond Avon who can hear me. I'm the third generation of my family from this planet. We've been locked in conflict for years now. Fighting for the right to be heard, fighting for the right to live, just because our planet hasn't passed review yet. And the soldiers here have been fighting too, for order, for peace. Terrible things have happened to all of us. Good men and women have died, and the people of Avon have been driven to turn on each other." I'm forced to stop, swallowing so hard the lump in my throat hurts, as I think of Fergal's tiny body and unseeing eyes, and of the madness and grief that drove McBride to kill him. "Desperation has led my own people to the murder of innocents because they can no longer imagine a future without war."

There are so many things I want to say—I want to talk about the whispers, the way LaRoux isolated them, tortured them, forced them to evolve into individuals they were never meant to be, so they could never go back. I wish I knew how to share their grief with the galaxy, but I don't know how much time I have. "I'm broadcasting from a secret facility LaRoux Industries has had here for years. LaRoux himself has been keeping beings on Avon, creatures completely different from us. Whispers from another universe with the power to control thoughts. He's used them to slow down our terraforming, to block our transmissions so no one could hear us calling for help. Until LaRoux is brought to justice, we're not safe. None of us are."

I see figures huddled wherever there's shelter, ready to resume fighting in an instant—but for now, they listen. I clear my throat, force my voice to sound strong.

"We need you to watch us. We need you to ask about us, and care about us, and remember your colonies were once young too. We need your protection, and we need you to know that if anything happens to Avon, it was LaRoux, not an accident. Don't let him hide the evidence of what he's done. We're asking you and trusting you to bear witness for us." I suck in a deep breath and let it out in a rush. "Thank you. Message ends."

I bow my head, and my hand's trembling, gripping the mic so tightly I can't seem to make my fingers unwind. Below me the silence echoes. But if just one person's finger slips on a trigger, a single gunshot will end all hope of peace.

I flick the switches that will end the transmission across the planet and the galaxy, but I leave the loudspeaker in place, lifting the transmitter one more time. "I'm going to come down now. It's time to talk."

And finally, I let the mic go. There are stairs leading down inside the tower, and my legs are shaking as I descend, my footsteps the only sound. Jubilee's at the bottom of these stairs. Badly injured, certainly.

Perhaps dead by now. My mind is numb, my heartbeat leaden. My fingers fumble with the lock from the inside until I can open the door and step out into the open.

"Mr. Cormac." The voice rings out from the swamp, and I know it—Commander Towers herself. I crane my neck until I see her, approaching the fence, which was torn to pieces in the battle. Some of the Fianna are melting out of the swamp as well, revealing their battle plan, clearly intending to flank the military in the darkness. It might even have worked.

Though they hang back in the shadows of the buildings, crouching low and keeping out of sight, I can see a hundred of the Fianna at least, the whites of their eyes showing against the mud camouflaging their faces. Plenty of guns still trained on me. "Stop," I call. "We need to tend to our wounded, and talk."

Our wounded. I can see Jubilee just a few meters away, slumped unmoving in the mud. Every muscle in my body wants to run to her, to throw myself down at her side. Suicide, she'd called it, the plan to run across the battle to reach the tower. She got me my chance to stop this war; I can't risk shattering this fragile balance and let that sacrifice be for nothing.

"Please," I whisper, and though it carries toward the soldiers in the silence, my eyes are on Jubilee.

"Flynn." My heart surges up into my throat. It's Sean. One side of his face is bloody where a laser clipped his ear, and my heart shrinks to see him looking so warlike. Our eyes lock, and despite the distance, I know what's in his gaze. Blood and betrayal, Fergal's ghost and Sean's cutting grief standing between us. "What did that mean? That we turned to the murder of innocents?"

There's no forgiveness in his tone, but the fact that he's talking to me at all—the fact that he *listened*—makes my heart race. It's the smallest glimmer of hope, like electricity running through me. But before I can respond, a flicker of horror runs through Sean's features and he takes a step back, turning to find McBride some distance behind him. Sean's eyes drop to the Gleidel in McBride's hand, and as their eyes meet, something cracks in my heart.

"You've been lied to, all of you." I harden my voice, make myself stand straighter, moving forward past Jubilee. It's torture not looking back at her, and I force myself to keep my gaze up, to finish this. I can still see the desperation on her face, the pain, as she stared up at me. *Go.* "You've been manipulated into breaking the ceasefire by a madman."

McBride's shaking, the gun at his side trembling with suppressed rage. "No one is going to take the word of a traitor like you." He's beyond reason now—I can see it in his jerky movements, hear it in his voice.

"Nobody needs to believe me. They can see it themselves. Hand over your gun, McBride. We'll check the readout and see how many shots it fired that night." Because I know, and he knows, that if he refuses to let us see the data on his Gleidel, he's announcing his own guilt.

A ripple of confusion runs through the crowd, and I cling to that—it means some of them do doubt him. Some of them want to believe me.

McBride's eyes bore into mine, all the hatred and disgust he's been trying to hide for years burning openly now. "Avon will rise from the ashes of this war, and you were always too weak to be the spark, Cormac. Doyle and the others couldn't fight, but they could still serve our cause. They were kindling for the flames, and that was an honor." His lips creep into a stiff rictus of a smile. "You can still serve, too."

In slow motion I see his arm start to lift, and a vision of the next thirty seconds plays out in my mind. I see him drop me to the ground, I see the gunfire start up on each side once again. I see bodies crumple.

Then Sean's beside him, grabbing at his arm, forcing the Gleidel down again with a grunt of effort. He knocks McBride off balance, but only for a moment; McBride is bigger, stronger, more experienced. He wrenches the Gleidel free of Sean's grip, twisting an arm around his neck and pulling him in close to act as a shield, gun at his temple.

"Someday," McBride hisses, "you'll understand why I—"

The shriek of a laser rips the air, and my heart stops; the whole world stops. But it's McBride, not Sean, who drops to his knees. He's dead before he hits the ground, a neat, round hole smoking in the center of his forehead.

Sean falls, dragged down by the arm around his neck, but he rolls free, coughing, to come up on all fours.

Hundreds of guns lift, and the world holds its breath. Then I realize where the shot came from. I turn to see Jubilee on her knees, holding her gun in her left hand, her right arm hanging uselessly. I run back to her, my world narrowing to this one moment, everything else falling away as

I drop to the mud at her side. She's alive. Bloodied, trembling, leaning into me as I wrap an arm around her, but alive.

And for all her reputation, all her ruthlessness, I realize I've never seen Jubilee kill anyone before.

I hear her draw a slow, steadying breath beside me. "Anyone else want to start a war today?"

Just the touch of her skin on mine sends warmth and strength flooding through me. It's all we can have, right now, but it's enough. I lift my head. "We need to talk. All of us, Fianna and soldiers. Let us show you the truth of what's been happening here."

I see the murmurs run up and down the group of my people, and I suddenly, painfully, want them to be that again, to call myself one of them. But I can't order them to take me back. They'll choose it, if they're willing to trust me one more time.

Sean climbs slowly to his feet, bowing his head as the muffled conference travels in from the edges of the group of fighters to reach him. He glances at the gun he dropped when McBride grabbed him, but he doesn't reach for it. Instead, our eyes meet as he walks toward me, out into the light.

"Flynn." Jubilee breathes my name, and I turn my head to follow her gaze.

Out in the swamp, the soldiers are still standing, and now they're lowering their weapons. Commander Towers is walking in to join us.

The girl is dreaming about the ocean. One day, she thinks, I'll take the green-eyed boy and go, and we'll buy a submarine, and live together at the bottom of the sea.

It's the last thought she has before the dream fragments into shards of places and memories, people she's fought and people she's loved, and the spaces between are filled with nonsense, a jumble of things seen and done and thought of, and forgotten.

And the rest of it, she doesn't remember.

FORTY

JUBILEE

"AND SO IT'S IN THE SPIRIT OF PEACE THAT WE WOULD LIKE to offer our assistance with the reconstruction efforts here on Avon. We may not have our money invested here, but we can't stand idly by when disaster strikes."

Listening, I grip the edges of my seat with my left hand, fingers shaking with the effort of keeping still. My right arm throbs in its sling as I keep my eyes on the man speaking at the head of the boardroom. I know his face—everyone knows his face. Roderick LaRoux looks almost kindly, with twinkling blue eyes and silver hair thinning at the crown of his head, but I find myself staring intently, trying to find signs of the monster I know resides behind that mask. I can imagine those blue eyes hard, the firm features turning to granite. I know why his daughter was so frightened of him.

My gaze flicks to Lilac, where she sits behind him next to Merendsen, looking like the perfect daughter. Hair just so, makeup flawless, dress worth more than a year's wages, but not too elaborate—a dress that says *I'm outrageously rich, but I chose something understated for today's colonial outing.* I'm trying to connect what I see with the quick intelligence and warmth she displayed over the hypernet connection, but there's nothing to hang that depth on. Her facade is as flawless as her appearance.

Her father is still speaking. "As most of you know by now, there have been claims my organization was involved in the inhumane and illegal experiments that led to this outbreak of violence." Roderick LaRoux gives a sad shake of his head, letting his eyes fall with all the grace and poise of a saint. "I can't explain these claims except to say that there will always be those who seek to blame others for their failings. Mine is, and always has been, a philanthropic corporation, concerned only with providing the best in cutting-edge technologies to the galaxy. There is nothing these . . . fringe conspiracy theorists can say to change that."

LaRoux's gaze lifts again and sweeps the chamber. For the briefest of instants, his eyes meet mine. He knows what we found there, in the bowels of that facility. Just as he knows his words are true; there is nothing we can say.

Not yet.

Watching him, I realize something. Though he's used Avon as his own private laboratory, practicing this art of ripping into people's minds, it won't end here. The thousands of soldiers affected on Avon mean nothing to him . . . but what of just a few minds in the right places? The President's closest advisers; the general in charge of troop deployment; the forty-two senators that make up the Galactic Council?

I tear my gaze away from Roderick LaRoux as he continues his flowery speech to announce the resources and new infrastructure being offered by LRI—a bribe, masquerading as charity, to shrug off any public suspicion about his involvement in these events. I find I'm not the only one gazing at him with dislike, or at least with suspicion. Though we sent multiple squads through the research facility after the ceasefire, there wasn't a single hint anywhere that LaRoux Industries was involved— even the ident chip I'd found and used to open the whispers' prison was gone. Though the staff remained, not one of them remembered where they were or what they'd been doing for the time they'd been posted there; and not a single one still had their ident badges.

There was no reason for anyone to believe us that Roderick LaRoux was behind the madness and the secret base. The official story was that some terrorist group had camped out in the swamps and was experimenting with psychotropic drugs, and that was what had led to the open hostilities two months ago between the Fianna and the soldiers.

Still, a few did believe. Commander Towers, for one. Several of Flynn's people. A few of my soldiers, those with more faith in me than sense. And there are rumors out there now, passed along in secret, gathering strength. Netsites claiming conspiracy theories, articles being written by anonymous authors about secret projects decades back in LaRoux Industries' history. It's enough that as I gaze around the room, I can see more than one stony glare among the nodding masses.

Monsieur LaRoux acts as though he's untouchable, but I see him now. I've seen the fallout from his ruthless experimentation, his obsession with controlling those around him down to their very thoughts. Alone, I'm no threat to him. One ex-soldier against a massive intergalactic corporation would be laughable odds. But Flynn sees him too, and so do others here. So do Merendsen and LaRoux's own daughter, the daughter who can feel the whispers in her thoughts, who can sense their pain. And though Merendsen and his fiancée pretend to want nothing more than to live quietly in their house on the edge of the galaxy, I imagine us all in the center of a web of secrets and lies, searching for a way to expose Roderick LaRoux to the galaxy. If he plans to use what he's learned from the creatures he enslaved, he'll have to find a way to do it while all of us are watching.

Flynn and I may not have proof, but the proof is out there somewhere, and someone is going to find it. I will Roderick LaRoux to hear me, to feel the force of my certainty, but he keeps speaking as though invincible to the stares around the room.

He thinks I'm finished here, that I'll slink off to some dark corner of the galaxy now that there's a spotlight on Avon. He thinks I don't still have ways to fight for this place that's become my home.

There's only one instance when LaRoux's gaze falters: when it reaches Tarver and Lilac, sitting with their fingers twined together. They look back at him, as blank and courteous as if he were a stranger. His eyes stay on her, searching for a connection—and in that moment I can see another reason why a man like him might want to control minds.

Or hearts.

LaRoux finishes speaking and sits down, and the Planetary Review Board summons the first in a long line of speakers for and against Avon's admittance to the Galactic Council. As the day wears on they call expert after expert: scientists from Terra Dynamics and the other contributing terraforming corporations; historians and sociologists specializing in colonial rebellions and reconstruction; politicians arguing about the wisdom of continuing to expand the Council to include representatives from more planets. The arguments fascinate me, the rhythm of the back-and-forth, like a dance—like a battle.

The board adjourns for lunch, and when we reconvene, Roderick LaRoux doesn't return, and the air in the room is easier, lighter.

Commander Towers speaks, proposing a system of pardons and work exchange to bring outlaws back in from the swamps, legally, without resorting to the executions that ended the rebellion ten years ago. Flynn himself was granted such a probationary pardon; in exchange for his service to Avon as a local representative, speaking for the natives—and, less officially, helping keep the peace—he's not being arrested for his crimes.

I won't be asked to speak. I have no official title or insight in the eyes of the Council. But at Flynn's insistence during the ceasefire negotiations, I was added to those present at the Planetary Review Board hearings, included in the official record. It prevents LaRoux from having me quietly erased. Flynn's turned the spotlight on us both, and for now, we're safe. Because everyone is watching.

Finally, the head of the board turns to Flynn. We aren't sitting together; he's across the room with his cousin. They're the only two Fianna present, and a trio of guards sits conspicuously behind them, weapons across their laps. No one is forgetting the violence. But at least they're here.

"Flynn Cormac, you are hereby asked to testify for or against Avon's viability as an independent member of the Galactic Council."

Flynn stands slowly. I can see no signs of hesitation or nervousness. I'd rather stare down a line of loaded weapons trained on my face than this council, but he gazes back at the row of men and women arrayed before him without fear. Without uncertainty.

"Thank you," he begins. Though he pauses before continuing, it's a pregnant pause, not so much a hesitation as an invitation. It makes me want to lean closer, to hang on what he's about to say. "My people and I are called a lot of things. Rebels and Fianna; terrorists and patriots; criminals and martyrs. And all of those things have been true at times over the last ten years. But if this long journey has shown us anything, it's proven that we are fighters."

His eyes sweep across the representatives from the Galactic Council, lighting on each of them in turn. "We fight for our home with whatever weapons we have. And if you let us, we will fight for it with hard work and passion, and devotion to this planet. You could not ask for a people more dedicated to making Avon what it was destined to be. If we're only given the chance, we'll prove to the galaxy we're worthy of it."

It's a struggle to tear my eyes from his face, but I glance over at the Council representatives as he continues to speak, laying out a vision for the Avon he's always dreamed of, the planet he believes in. They're well trained by galactic politics to maintain their granite-like expressions at all times, so it's impossible to tell whether Flynn's passion is reaching them at all. But while I watch, I see a tiny, nearly imperceptible shift—as though the man at the end is nodding to himself, just a little.

It'll take weeks of deliberation before the review board makes a final decision about Avon. And there's nothing to do until then except wait. Wait, and rebuild; because decision or not, it's a new Avon beginning here, and this is the chance we've been fighting for.

I find myself lingering when the board adjourns for the night, gathering up my papers slowly, watching as the soldiers and locals and government officials and reps from TerraDyn and the other corporations all mingle on their way out the doors. I keep my eyes on them, though I know they're not the reason I'm hanging back.

An arm snakes around my waist, a voice murmuring in my ear, "Are we still on for tomorrow morning?"

I don't fight the foolish smile that creeps across my features as I turn to face Flynn. "I had something else in mind. Can we do breakfast another day?" He's still careful to avoid brushing my arm in its sling, and I can see his eyes lingering on it. A few inches over and the bullet would've perforated my heart instead of passing through my shoulder. As it is, I'll be out of the sling in another week.

"Sure." Flynn's head tips to the side, his curiosity piqued. "What's the new idea?"

"You'll see."

I meet him just before dawn the next day—with every hour we're not at the hearing tied up in reconstruction meetings, this is the only time we can steal. We head out together, taking it slow as we move across the muddy base compound. I still have to remind myself that I don't need to watch for anyone who might recognize Flynn, blow his cover, realize I'm harboring a fugitive—because he's not anymore. And I'm not either. I thought it would be impossible to connect Jubilee with Captain Lee Chase, to merge the two into one life, but more and more it doesn't seem like they're different people after all. At least now I have time to figure it out.

I nod to the guard at the north gate, and we pick our way over the spongy ground beyond. It's not as wet here as it is elsewhere, but water still collects in the dips and wallows of the land, making the footing treacherous, especially in the dim light of the predawn.

Half a klick away I can see the new construction site, where the town hall and the school are coming together. Sean's taken us through the site twice already—Flynn jokes that he wants to supervise every nail that's hammered into *his* school, but we both understand. He's part of the group who will create our classrooms and teach our history. And for now, it's a place for him to pour in enough effort every day that he can sleep every night, while he waits for his own healing to begin.

It's about ten minutes of hiking after we leave town to reach the start of the hills and find more solid ground.

We trek up, and I pause to look around and get my bearings—then head for the one landmark I know, the one the soldiers on the base used to call Traitor's Bluff. I don't tell Flynn that, though. Instead, I come to a halt, and he comes up beside me.

"So why here?" he asks, looking around as if half expecting me to have prepared some kind of picnic or other surprise.

I take a deep breath, slowly turning until the breeze is at my back. There's a faint hint of orange to the east—anywhere else, the last stars would be disappearing overhead. Instead there's only the dim inky blackness of Avon's overcast skies.

"You told me that when your sister was executed, they didn't even return her ashes to you."

I can feel Flynn stiffen beside me, his grief still real, still present. I swallow, suddenly unsure. But it's too late now to go back, so I push through.

"This is it. This is where her ashes were scattered. This hill."

I risk a glance at him and see him gazing out across the lightening landscape, his lips parted, brows furrowed. I can't read him in this half-light, can't tell what's going on behind those artistic features.

"I—I wish I could have given you something real, something you could hold or see, but it's not policy for us to keep the remains. I researched it to make sure, and this is where—"

"No." Flynn's voice is hoarse, his eyes distant. "No, this is beautiful. Thank you."

I feel the bands of nervous tension easing a little. I step closer to him, reaching for his arm so I can slide my fingers through his. "We had no right to keep her from you." I press my lips to the fabric of his jacket, over his shoulder. "I know it's not much, but at least you know now."

"It's everything." He turns and wraps his arms around me, head dropping, cheek warm alongside mine. "Thank you, Jubilee."

We stand that way for a time, unmoving in the chill, letting the dawn gather itself to sweep across the landscape. Finally, Flynn pulls away enough to run a hand down my arm and take my hand again.

"So tell me about that dream you had." He gives my hand a gentle tug, summoning me down to sit on the grass beside him so we can watch the sunrise paint the clouds.

I lean back on my elbows. "Did you ever want to be an explorer when you were little?"

I go on to tell him my other dreams; small dreams and big dreams, realistic and nonsensical dreams. Snatches of Avon, of Verona, of different times and places. Of my parents, my fellow soldiers, of my November ghost, the shining light that I now know was the whisper.

I tell him how in every dream, he was there. He kisses my temple, and laughs softly when he hears my breath catch, and tells me he always will be there.

We talk about ten years of dreams stolen by that lonely creature, forgotten, coming back to me now a little each night. Flynn's laughter rings through the hills, carried on the night air, mingling with my own. Flynn told me once he thought his sister would have liked me; I like to think she'd be happy, hearing him laugh. Watching a former soldier and a former rebel sit together in the gathering dawn.

Our voices rise, and fall, and fall again. The silences are comfortable, warm despite the chill in the air. We gaze upward, and for a long moment, neither of us realizes what we're seeing: an odd spark of light, high above where the clouds are still indigo, like landing lights or my will-o'-the-wisp in the sky. Except this light's not moving.

Then the light vanishes with a swirl of cloud, and I gasp. "Flynn, did you see that?"

"I saw it," he says, puzzled, "but I don't—"

"It was a star," I whisper.

Flynn's reaction is electric, for all he only moves an inch, straightening, gaze fixed on the sky overhead. Though his eyes are on the clouds, I can't help but watch his silhouette in the darkness. The way his mouth is set, the hope and determination there—the strength in his shoulders, the energy in the way he gazes skyward. The breeze stirs his hair, and I find myself transfixed.

I think of my answer when the tortured soul in that prison underground asked me if I was in love with Flynn. I didn't know, then, but more than anything I wanted the chance to find out. A chance without wars and blood feuds and madness everywhere on this shattered world—a chance where we could just be us. *This* chance.

"What does it mean?" Flynn turns to gaze at me, eyes finally meeting mine.

I find myself smiling, because I know exactly what it means. "It means the clouds are clearing on Avon."

ACKNOWLEDGMENTS

THE JOURNEY FROM *THESE BROKEN STARS* TO *THIS SHATTERED World* has been wonderful, and we're so grateful to the many people who supported us as we brought Avon to life.

We owe a debt of gratitude to the experts who gave up their time to help us get the details right. Thank you to Ben Ellis for checking our physics and making sure things only went wrong in the ways they're supposed to. To Yulin Zhang, for generously sharing his Chinese upbringing and his culture—your thoughtful comments were invaluable. To Eamon Kenny, for guidance on radio transmissions and the blocking thereof. To Steve Tuck, for helping destroy things. To Josie Spooner, for early advice on ecosystems and the creation thereof. To Dr. Kate Irving, for medical advice, critique, and twenty years of the deepest friendship—here's to twenty more.

Many thanks to Niall O'Leary and Will O'Shea for getting us started with our Irish, and *go raibh maith agat Pól Ruiséal, Stiúrthóir, Ionad na Gaeilge Labhartha, Coláiste na hOllscoile Corcaigh* (many thanks to Pól Ruiséal, Director of the Centre for Spoken Irish, University College Cork) for very generous help with the Irish in this book. In relation to all the wonderful advice we received, any errors are, of course, our own.

Josh and Tracey, and all the Adams Literary Team—we couldn't do you justice with pages and pages. We couldn't do this crazy thing without you, and we wouldn't want to. You are our rocks. Thank you.

To the many wonderful people at Hyperion we've had the chance to meet, as well as those we haven't, who work so hard in every department, our heartfelt thanks. Emily Meehan and Laura Schreiber, thank you for all the time and effort you've put into making *This Shattered World* the best it can be. Jamie Baker, thank you for going above and beyond! To Kate Hurley, our copy editor, thank you for putting up with our irrational love of em-dashes and commas. Whitney Manger, thank you for another incredible cover.

To the wonderful Allen & Unwin team, as if one home wasn't enough, you gave us a second. Thank you so much for welcoming us into the family! We brought cake.

To the wonderful readers, booksellers, librarians, reviewers, and bloggers we've met since the launch of *These Broken Stars*, thank you for your support. It's been a privilege to meet and correspond with so many of you.

To our friends, who are always patient, always supportive, and often slightly amused—lots of love. To our wonderful support networks: the Chocolate Lounge girls, the Roti Boti ladies, the FOS crew, the Plot Bunnies, the Pub(lishing) Crawl gang, the League, the Luckies, the TJ/NoVA crew—we couldn't get by without you.

As much love as ever to Michelle Dennis, for reading, and reading again, and always being there. To Kim Nguyen, thank you for all your design magic, as well as your treasured friendship. Thank you to dear friends Kat Zhang, Olivia Davis, Marie Lu, Beth Revis, Marion Cole, and Jay Kristoff for critique, support, and too much awesome to be confined to one page.

As always, our families are at the heart of it all. Thank you for your love and support, which mean the world to us (and for telling everyone you know to read our books). Our storytelling began with the books you gave us, the stories you told us, and the games we played with you.

Brendan, whether you're reading one more time, listening to one more slightly disturbing video call about death and destruction, or doing any one of the thousand things you handle with such grace, calm, and good cheer—thank you doesn't cover it. You are the reason this book is out in the world.

And finally, reader, our heartfelt thanks to *you*, for joining us in the worlds we love to build. We hope you enjoyed Avon . . . and we'll see you on Corinth!

And now for a sneak peek at the
thrilling finale to the Starbound trilogy

A ripple.

The stillness quakes and splits and where once there was nothing, only us, there is something new. Bright and hard and cold and skimming the surface of the stillness, the new thing is there only an instant before it is gone again.

But we gather. And we watch. And we wait, because there has never been anything new before, and we want to see it again.

ONE

SOFIA

THE DAPPLED SUNLIGHT THROUGH THE GRASS IS BEAUTIFUL, though I know it's not real. The light casts no warmth on my skin; I'll suffer no burns, no freckles. The grass doesn't bend under my feet, though they sink through it to the marble floor beneath the holographic images. A year ago I would have gasped aloud at the sight of sun and blue skies, even holographic ones, but today I find they just make me miss home. What I'd give, now, to lift my head and see bruise-colored clouds sweeping down to meet the marsh, a vastness to the horizon that no holographic lobby in an office building could hope to replicate.

The holosuite is full of people, and while many of them seem to be employees here at LaRoux Industries Headquarters, others are harder to pinpoint. Some carry old-timey briefcases in a nod to ancient vintage fashion from 1920s Earth, the current fad among the upper crust. Others sport only their palm pads; the affectation of carrying purses and cases is absurd, when everything that would've gone inside—money, documents, telephones, identification cards—was digitized hundreds of years ago.

But the trend does make it easy to carry around everything I need without anyone asking questions. Only a couple years ago I would've been stuck in pseudo-Victorian garb if I wanted to be fashionable, hiding the tools of my trade under an unwieldy skirt. As it is, my tea dress is light, easy to run in if necessary, and—most importantly—an airy, innocent ivory lace that makes me look even younger than seventeen. I tuck my handbag close to my body, taking a deep breath and scanning the throngs of people.

There's a tension in the air that makes my pulse quicken. It's subtle—those hiding here in plain sight are doing so flawlessly. *Almost.* But I grew up on Avon, and I know how to read a crowd. I know how quickly a protest turns into a riot—I know how quickly a peaceful town becomes a battlefield.

I don't know if the vast security network at LaRoux Industries is aware of the underground protests scheduled to occur today. I only know about them because I was told by one of my contacts in Corinth Against Tyranny—a ridiculous name, but it's a romantic notion to fight the good fight against the oppressors. Looking around the holosuite outfitted with lemonade dispensers and sodas whizzing here and there on hover trays, the air littered with conversation and laughter, I can't help but think that these people don't know what oppression is. I tear my eyes away from a couple indulgently watching a child of five or six chasing a pair of holographic birds through the air. There's a reason LaRoux Industries tops the "best places to work in the galaxy" list every year, and if I'd been the one organizing today's protest, I certainly wouldn't have chosen the new twentieth-floor holosuite as the setting.

Free for employees, and available to the public for only a small charge, the holosuite is part of LaRoux's new outreach program. "See how generous I am?" he's saying. "I'm dedicating whole floors of my headquarters to providing safe, fun places for you and your children." His campaign to make the galaxy love him, to make people forget the accusations leveled at him in the Avon Broadcast, is enough to turn my stomach—not least because it's working.

The people here do seem happy. No one here cares that people were dying on Avon before Flynn Cormac's now-infamous speech a year ago. Nobody cares that Roderick LaRoux is a monster—mostly because only small pockets of people here and there actually believed a word of Flynn's broadcast. These people are here because it looks good on their media pages to say they were at a protest. Some of them are probably hoping to get arrested so they can later post their mug shots on the hypernet.

But it *does* make a great distraction for what I'm here to do.

I have only a name for the contact I'm meeting—Sanjana Rao—and though it speaks of family roots in old India, it's just as likely she could be blond-haired and blue-eyed, given the way all the races and blood-lines from Earth have been jumbled up over the centuries. She'll ping my palm pad when she's here, but I can't help but look for her anyway.

I find my gaze creeping toward the elevator doors, cleverly concealed in this park simulation as the entrance to a carousel. This is the closest I've been to LaRoux himself after a year of chasing him, and all I want to do is break into their secure elevators and climb to the penthouse floor. A year of burned identities and isolation; of painful tattoo removal surgeries that still haven't completely erased my genetag; of keeping all traces of myself, all remnants of my old life, with me at all times in case today, this moment, is the one where I'm going to have to pack up and run again.

But LaRoux himself is nearly impossible to reach. If he wasn't, some-one would've already killed him years ago—for all that the galaxy at large loves him, enough of the people he's trampled on his way to power see him for what he is. No, a head-on approach will never reach him. Taking out LaRoux requires subtlety.

I glance at my inner arm, a habit I still haven't broken. Someone clever could guess at what the look means—no one born on Corinth or any of the older planets is given a genetag at birth—and yet I do it anyway. The faint remnant of my genetag tattoo is safely hidden, though I have to take care not to rub against my dress and risk transferring a telltale smear of concealer to the fabric. I want to grab for my palm pad, to check it to see if I could have missed Dr. Rao's ping, but standing here repeatedly checking my messages would be a clear sign of nervousness, if anyone was watching me.

It's only when I lift my head that I realize I *do* have an audience. And that it isn't my contact.

A young man's seated on the floor, his back against a tree—a tree that isn't really there, of course. His back is against a marble pillar, but the holographic skin of the room makes it look like he's relaxing in a park. Except, of course, that he's got a lapscreen and it's plugged into the side of the tree. There's a wireless power field here, so I know he's not charg-ing his screen. It's a data port, which is odd enough, given that any info accessible in a public place like this would be on the hypernet. But that's not what makes me stop, makes my heart seize. It's that he's wearing the green and gray of LaRoux Industries, and that there's a lambda embroidered over his breast pocket. He works here—and he's watching me.

My mouth goes dry, and I force myself not to jerk my gaze away. Instead I tip my head as if puzzled, trying my absolute best to seem intrigued, even coy.

A grin flashes across his features when I catch him watching me. He makes no attempt to pretend he wasn't, just flicks his fingers to his brow and then away as though tipping an imaginary hat. He doesn't look like a typical office worker, with longer hair of a shade hovering somewhere between sandy blond and brown and a lazy, almost insolent cast to his body as he leans against the pillar.

I take a breath to settle, hiding any trace of fear that he knows I don't belong here. Instead I smile back, settling easily into the façade of shy and sweet; to my relief, his grin widens. Just flirting, then.

He winks, then presses a single button on his lapscreen. A holographic bird with brilliant red plumage swoops across my path and then freezes in midair. Abruptly, all the background sounds halt: birdsong and rustling leaves and even some of the laughter and conversation—all gone. Then, without warning, the entire holopark vanishes, leaving us in a vast white room.

The only thing in the room, besides the people, the projectors, and the pillars like the one the boy's leaning on, is a vast metal ring twice my height at its center. It stands upright, made of some strange alloy that shines dully in the bright white light, and is connected to the floor at its base by a pedestal covered with dials and instruments. LaRoux's particular holographic technologies are proprietary, but this looks like no projector I've ever seen—and while the other projectors are flickering and whirring and trying to overcome whatever glitch made them stop working, the metal ring is still and silent.

A murmur of confusion sweeps through the throngs of people, as groups abandon their conversations in favor of looking around, as though the room might hold some explanation. Its other features stand out now that there's no masking hologram in place—the drink dispensers are bare and stark, the various projectors and speakers littering the low ceiling like misshapen stars.

Whatever's going on, it wasn't planned by the protesters. Everyone, employees and public alike, is milling around in confusion. If it were planned, the protesters would be using the glitch to launch their protest, but instead even the security guards at the edges of the room look unnerved. I let my eyes widen, using a group of interns as cover to move as quietly and purposelessly as I can toward the emergency stairwell. If I'm caught, the worst they'll assume of me is that I was here to protest. But I'd rather not get in their books at all.

Before I can make it to the fire exit, a flicker of color grabs my eye and I turn in time to see the boy with the lapscreen pull a chip the size of his fingernail out of his screen and stow it in his pocket. Glancing up at the ceiling, he gets up and takes two slow, easy steps to the side, neatly placing himself in the security camera's blind spot.

Then he's shrugging out of his LaRoux Industries uniform until he's just wearing an undershirt, tattooed arms bare for half an instant. He turns the garment inside out, revealing a garishly striped shirt matching the high-fashion trend of the moment—and just like that, he melts into the crowd. No longer an employee of LaRoux Industries.

And far, far too clever to be one of the protesters now milling around, confused and annoyed that they never got their chance to get on the news.

"Ladies and gentlemen, your attention, please." A voice, smooth as cream and amplified over the noise of the crowd, emerges from the speakers. "We've detected a security breach and traced its source to this room. Please remain calm, and cooperate with all security officers to the fullest extent, and we will have this resolved as soon as possible."

The security guards, operating on some order given via the implants in their ears, have started funneling people off one by one, presumably to interrogate them individually. One of the guards is still standing by the door, blocking the exit to the stairwell—blocking my escape route. The concealer on my arm might fool a quick glance from someone at the front desk, but now I have no chance of passing myself off as a protester—a security breach will have them on high alert. The first thing those guards will do when they grab me is check for a genetag tattoo, certain that border planet insurgents are the most likely culprits. I close my eyes, calling up the floor plans I've been studying for a week and a half. They'll have shut down access to the elevators on this floor, but there's another fire exit and another set of stairs through one of the hallways leading off from here. I scan the crowds until I find that exit, and the guard ushering people in that direction.

What I need is a diversion.

My eyes fall on a loud, red-and-gold striped shirt. Whoever the boy is, he's not from LaRoux Industries, and he's not supposed to be here either. And while I can't be sure that keystroke of his is what took down the holo-projectors, I do know that if we get grabbed together, he's the one who's going to look far more suspicious than I am once they realize he's got an LRI uniform sewn into his clothes. I mutter a curse under my breath and rush forward to the guard's side.

Sorry, Handsome. I'm pretty sure you want to be center of attention just about as much as I do. But if there's one person here in more trouble than me, it's the guy with the fake LaRoux Industries uniform on under his shirt.

"That boy there," I say, keeping my voice low, forcing my eyes wide. "I think he needs help." With any luck, they'll go check on him and I can slip out once they discover he's not supposed to be here.

The guard's gaze swings around immediately to rest on the boy in the striped shirt, who's watching us with a slight edge to his nonchalant air. His smile dies away entirely as the guard takes two steps toward him, and I ease my weight back, the first step toward the door the man was guarding. *Slowly, slowly, don't draw attention.*

As if my thought was spoken aloud, the guard reaches out to wrap a hand around my arm. "Show me," he orders. I freeze, and, to make matters worse, he lifts his hand to signal to one of the other heavies over in our direction. Now I've got two guards watching me, and the door's about to be blocked again. *Damn it.* If they make me go with them, they may well assume I'm *with* him when they discover his fake LRI shirt. Now I have to get us both out of here.

Good work, Sofia.

My mind throws up a flurry of possibilities, and in a split second I sort through them, discarding the impossible, left with only one way to divert both of them to the boy.

"Please hurry," I gasp, focusing the muscles in my face until my eyes start to water with tears. "He's my fiancé—he has a condition, stress makes it worse." In the confusion, with so many people to process, I can only hope the guard doesn't want to ask too many questions.

The guard blinks at me and, when I turn to indicate the boy in the striped shirt, follows my gesture. The boy stares back, openly wary now, eyes flicking from the guard to my face. *Please,* I think. *Just don't say anything until I can get past them.*

"You were both fine a minute ago." He exchanges glances with his colleague, who's standing by me now. "I'm sure it can wait." His voice is even, giving not an inch, but his hand strays, shifting from the weapon at his waist to tug at his sleeve.

I double my efforts, forcing my voice to crack. "Please," I echo. "I'll stay, I'll answer any questions you want. Just go check him and you'll see, he needs a doctor or else he's going to have an episode." I just need both the guards to turn toward the boy long enough for me to slip through the exit, uncounted and unescorted.

The nearer guard's weight shifts, making my breath catch, but he doesn't move as they exchange glances again. "I'll call for the medtech on duty," he says finally. "But he looks fine."

My mind races, scanning the guard for anything I can use. He's in his forties—too savvy, probably, for me to flirt my way out, especially when I already used the fiancé cover. No signs on his clothes of pets or children, nothing I can use to establish any connection with him, any appeal to his humanity. I'm about to go for my last resort—the little-girl wail of hysterics—when, without warning, the boy with the lapscreen sways and drops to the ground with a moan.

Both guards gape, and for half a second, I'm as stunned as they are. The boy on the ground twitches, limbs quivering, looking like he's having exactly the kind of fit I'd been warning them about. For a quick, searing moment I wonder if somehow my lie stumbled upon something like the truth—but I can't afford to find out. I'm just about to bolt for the exit when the nearest guard sticks his hand between my shoulder blades and pushes me forward. "Do something!" His own eyes are looking a little wild.

Damn. Damn. DAMN. Still, if I end up in an ambulance with this guy, it'll be better than ending up in an interrogation room at LRI Headquarters. The EMTs will scan the ident chip in my palm pad, but the name they'll get from that is Alexis. And they won't be looking for genetags. I drop to my knees at the stranger's side, reaching for his twitching hand and curling my fingers through his as though I'm used to touching him. One guard's talking hurriedly into a patch on his vest, summoning backup, doctors, some kind of support.

The guy's fingers tighten around mine, making my eyes jerk toward his face—and abruptly, all my simulated tears and panic come to a screeching halt. He's actually starting to foam at the mouth, eyes rolled back into his head. He can't be that much older than I am, and there's something definitely, dangerously wrong with him.

One of the security guards is trying to ask me questions—has he eaten anything recently, when did he last take his medication, what's his condition called—in order to brief the EMTs on their way. But his voice trails off as another sound rises from the center of the room, quickly growing in volume and causing the other nervous conversations in the room to peter out. The metal ring, the one the holo-projectors had been concealing, is turning itself on.

A number of lights along the base come to life, indicating that there's data to be read now from the displays there, and the panels overhead lighting the room flicker as though the ring is drawing too much power. But neither of those things is what's made the entire roomful of people go silent.

Little flickers of blue light start to race around the edge of the ring, appearing and vanishing as though weaving directly through the metal. They move faster as the sound of the machine coming to life intensifies and smooths out, until the entire edge of the ring is crawling with blue fire.

A hand on my arm jerks my attention away, my heart pounding as I look down.

The boy is beside me, raising one eyebrow. "Care to tell me when the wedding is, darling?" His voice is barely audible, words spoken without moving his lips.

I blink. "What?" I'm so thrown I can't find my balance.

The boy glances at the security guard nearest us, whose attention is completely absorbed by the machinery in the center of the room, and then back at me. He wipes the remnants of foam from his mouth and then props himself up on his elbows. "Think maybe we should start the honeymoon a little early." This time his whisper carries an edge, and he jerks his chin meaningfully toward the emergency exit.

Whoever he is, whatever he was doing here, right now we want exactly the same thing: to get out of here. And that's enough for me. I can always lose him later.

I give him a hand up—the guard doesn't even look in our direction—and slip back toward the exit. We reach the door just as a flash of blue light illuminates the white walls before us. While the boy in the striped shirt fumbles with the door, I glance over my shoulder.

The flickers of light around the edges of the ring are now reaching toward the center, tongues of blue sparks snapping out and vanishing, like lightning-fast stellar flares. Every now and then they meet with a tremendous flash of light—until finally the entire center of the ring is filled with light, crackling like a curtain of energy.

While I watch, a man standing near the ring collapses, sinking to the floor without a sound. I'm waiting for the people nearest him to react, to rush to his side and break the spell of fascination, but they're all motionless, slack, like machines whose power's been cut. More and more people are going still and silent with every passing second, security guards and protesters alike, in an expanding circle around the device at the room's center. Every now and then another person drops to the floor, but most are standing still, upright, casting long shadows that flicker and reach toward us as the machine fires.

In between flashes of light, I can make out the faces of those on the other side—I can see their eyes.

And in that instant I'm standing on a military base on Avon, watching my father change in front of me. I'm seeing his eyes, multiplied a dozen times over in the faces around me, pupils so wide the eyes look like pools of ink, like the starless expanse of night over the swamps. I'm reliving the moment my father walked into a military barracks with an explosive strapped to his body. I'm remembering him as he was the last time I ever saw him, a shadow of himself, nothing more than a husk where his soul used to be.

There are hundreds of people still dotting the white expanse of the holosuite—and every single one of them has eyes like darkness.

Praise for *Light Is the New Black*

'*Light Is The New Black* is an inspiring book with a message that is so needed right now. Rebecca courageously guides us to turn our lights on and follow the daily calls of our soul so we can all light up the world with our authentic spirit.'
– SONIA CHOQUETTE, BESTSELLING AUTHOR OF *THE ANSWER IS SIMPLE*

'I'm a super-fan of Rebecca Campbell and her new book, *Light Is the New Black*. This book is relatable, real, soul-centered and empowering. Rebecca guides her reader to step into their authentic power so that they can live and lead at their highest potential. *Light Is the New Black* is a must read for all Spirit Junkies on their path to living a miraculous life.'
– GABRIELLE BERNSTEIN, *NEW YORK TIMES* BESTSELLING AUTHOR OF *MIRACLES NOW*

'Prepare to be lit from within, to remember the tremendous levity of the soul, and to return to the limitless home of love and light that is our birthright. *Light Is The New Black* contains the same mystical energy that compelled Rebecca Campbell to write it. It's pure transmission. It's pure memory of our truest purpose while here: be the light. And it's a pragmatic, spiritual guide for being the light right now – right in the midst of our messy, everyday lives.'
– MEGGAN WATTERSON, AUTHOR OF *REVEAL* AND *HOW TO LOVE YOURSELF (AND SOMETIMES OTHER PEOPLE)*

'Rebecca Campbell is a modern day High Priestess led by the Divine. I've never in my life met anyone who shines like she does. Rebecca is the real deal. Bringing clarity to the deepest of spiritual subjects, this book is a response to the call of the soul. Will you step up? It's your time to shine! We are born with light – it's within us right now, but the busy world can make us forget. Through *Light Is the New Black*, let Rebecca lead you back the source of light so you can share it with the world and live a life that's filled with soul and purpose.'
– KYLE GRAY, AUTHOR OF *WINGS OF FORGIVENESS*

'Each new generation needs a new inspirational voice. To me, Rebecca Campbell is that voice. I just love witnessing a new, young talent about to unleash a storm that will change the way we think about our personal empowerment and spirituality.'
– MEL CARLILE, MANAGING DIRECTOR, MIND BODY SPIRIT FESTIVAL

'Rebecca Campbell courageously illuminates the way for a new w~ rant visionaries to emerge and own their full-spectrum radiance nd part guidebook, *Light Is the New Black* invites the rea~ feed her spirit and allow her soul to shine and ser~
– NANCY LEVIN, BESTSELLING AUTHOR OF *JUMP... AND YOU~*

'Rebecca is authentic, empowered and beautifully honest in her writing and as a person. This book is soul treasure; drink in her wisdom and let it light your way to a deeper experience of your true self and your divine purpose.'
– HOLLIE HOLDEN

'In order to light up the world and throw our arms around our most authentic selves, we need to ask questions, and then, oh boy, do we need to listen. *Light Is the New Black* is for the real you. Raw, honest, and heart achingly bright, Rebecca's words hone directly in on the lost knowledge that you have deep inside. In one invigorating swoop, her gentle wisdom and straight-to-the-core practical tools guide you to reignite your inner pilot light. There is no going back now; this book is your golden wake-up call and the ultimate Q & A for your soul.'
– LOUISE ANDROLIA, ARTIST, INTUITIVE, EMPOWERMENT COACH, AND MAGIC MAKER

'In *Light Is the New Black*, Rebecca Campbell shares a great truth, a "secret" that most of us don't discover until much later in life, if ever. Our light comes from within, and when life conspires to turn out that light we must find it for ourselves, within ourselves. You'll love taking this inspiring journey with Rebecca to reconnect with your own light, turn it on, and illuminate the path to your soul's calling. Once you do, everything in your life reflects back that light as you express the truth of who you really are.'
– GAIL LARSEN, FOUNDER OF REAL SPEAKING® AND AUTHOR OF *TRANSFORMATIONAL SPEAKING: IF YOU WANT TO CHANGE THE WORLD, TELL A BETTER STORY*

'The Divine has found a beautiful voice in Rebecca's new book, *Light Is the New Black*. What lies between these pages cracked me open and reminded me that I'm no longer alone. Written with a big, open heart and a fierce commitment to sharing the truth, Rebecca's spiritual journey will inspire you to turn on your light and shine it bright.'
– LISA LISTER, AUTHOR OF *CODE RED: KNOW YOUR FLOW, UNLOCK YOUR MONTHLY SUPER POWERS & CREATE A BLOODY AMAZING LIFE. PERIOD.*

'Rebecca is a vibrant and authentic voice in the emerging self-empowerment landscape, and effortlessly marries the numinous call of the soul with real-life wisdom for women on the rise. *Light Is the New Black* is a call to arms for the next generation of spiritual seekers to get switched on to their true path, and make each minute of this life really count!'
– RUBY WARRINGTON, FOUNDER OF THENUMINOUS.NET

'Rebecca's new book is as soulful and light-filled as she is. If you have a burning desire to discover yourself, answer the callings of your soul, and live a marvelous life, look no further! *Light Is the New Black* is a must read for every Modern Mystic who wants to create magic, work their inner light, and burst its unique brightness onto the world.'
– BELINDA DAVIDSON, MEDICAL INTUITIVE, SPIRITUAL MENTOR, AND FOUNDER OF SCHOOL OF THE MODERN MYSTIC

LIGHT
IS THE NEW BLACK

A Guide to Answering your SOUL'S CALLINGS
and WORKING YOUR LIGHT

REBECCA CAMPBELL

HAY HOUSE, INC.
Carlsbad, California • New York City
London • Sydney • New Delhi

FOR BLAIR, WHO NEVER DIMMED HIS LIGHT.

LET NOTHING DIM THE LIGHT THAT SHINES WITHIN.

MAYA ANGELOU

Published in the United States by: Hay House, Inc.: www.hayhouse .com® • *Published in Australia by:* Hay House Australia Pty. Ltd.: www .hayhouse.com.au • *Published in the United Kingdom by:* Hay House UK, Ltd.: www.hayhouse.co.uk • *Published in India by:* Hay House Publishers India: www.hayhouse.co.in

Cover design: Michelle Polizzi
Interior design: Leanne Siu Anastasi

Song lyrics p.11 © Gurunam Singh, devotional singer/Naad yoga teacher (gurunamsingh.com)

Library of Congress Control Number: 2015935173

Tradepaper ISBN: 978-1-4019-4850-4

20 19 18 17 16 15 14 13 12 11
1st edition, July 2015

Printed in the United States of America

Certified Chain of Custody
SUSTAINABLE FORESTRY INITIATIVE — Promoting Sustainable Forestry
www.sfiprogram.org
SFI-01268

SFI label applies to text stock

△
CONTENTS

Part III – Work Your Light

Part V – Be the Light

△

FROM THE UNIVERSE TO ME TO YOU

Listening is one thing; acting on what you hear is another. When I first woke up to the callings of my soul, I lacked the courage, confidence, inner support, and practical tools not to hear the callings of my soul but to let them truly lead my life. There were pieces missing, a journey needed to be taken. I called upon the Universe and spiritual teachers to support me. This book is the result of that journey.

You can read it in one sitting, one chapter a day or pick a page at random for an instant hit of guidance. Throughout you will find 'Work Your Light' exercises, mantras, and affirmations. I created these with the intention of guiding you not only to *hear* the callings of your soul, but to *act* on them too.

While I was there for the writing of these pages, I cannot take credit for them all. They are a combination: one girl's journey (that'd be mine); channeled messages from the Universe and the Councils of Light; lessons learned from my teachers; and the poems, prayers, and words of encouragement that I needed most.

There is no one word that captures the magnificent, illuminating presence that connects us all. However, in an attempt to do so, I have used the terms Source, the Universe, Light, God, and Grace. If the particular word I have used doesn't resonate with you, just trade it for one that feels right.

Also mentioned is the term 'Lightworker,' by which I mean someone who consciously chooses to answer the call of spirit/soul/Source/the light over the call of the ego/fear/control/darkness. Just by reading this book, you are working your light. Thank you for working your light.

I pray that you experience a sense of remembering of the beautiful being that you already are and were always destined to be.

I pray that you never feel alone, that you always find the light nestled just behind the shadows, and the courage to act on the gentle, constant callings of your soul.

I pray that you find the inspiration, courage, confidence, inner support, and practical tools not only to act on the unique callings of your soul, but to let them lead your life.

I pray that you discover the authentic gift to the world that you already are and choose to serve the world by being You.

The world doesn't just need light; it needs your unique light.

So much love,

Rebecca x

THE WORLD WILL BE SAVED BY THE WESTERN WOMAN.

THE DALAI LAMA

△

INTRODUCTION

'Never doubt that a small group of thoughtful,
committed citizens can change the world;
indeed, it's the only thing that ever has.'
MARGARET MEAD

At the Peace Conference in Canada in 2009, the Dalai Lama said, 'The world will be saved by the Western woman,' and it was a call to action for women throughout the West. This book is a response to that call.

It's a book for a new breed of women and men who are here to be bright lights in the world: modern-day Lightworkers, who agreed at a soul level to be here at this time in history, to bring us into the Age of Light (led by spirit and Divine Feminine). I know because I'm one of them and I know I am not alone.

This time we are living in right now has been prophesied by the mystics and sages of all the ages. It is an era in history in which we are all being called to embrace our truest, brightest, most authentic selves and rise up.

In order to succeed in the Age of Light, everything in our lives must be an authentic expression of who we truly are. There is a global shift occurring where inauthenticity no longer stands a chance. Relationships, jobs, brands, or anything that is not in alignment with the flow of the Universe (and who we truly are) is becoming harder to hold on to. It's as though our inner and outer foundations are crumbling away, in an effort to reconnect us with the authentic light within, so we can get back in flow with the Universe. And the falling apart will not let up until our inner and outer worlds are aligned.

Seemingly overnight, my whole life came crumbling down. No matter how hard I tried to hold it all together, anything that was based on fear, neediness, force, control, or inauthenticity was unable to survive.

For too long we have been living in a patriarchal society, where the ego-driven powers of fear, unconsciousness, separateness, and control have been at the forefront. During this time there have been amazing advances in technology, standards of living, and education, yet we are more depressed and lonelier than ever.

Moving out of patriarchy is not about the feminine ruling over the masculine, rather a more balanced state of being where we embrace the authenticity of who we are and realize that we are all connected, part of a larger whole. The rising feminine can be found in both men and women. Therefore, when I mention 'she' or 'sister,' I am speaking to the compassionate, protective, intuitive, and conscious feminine that is rapidly awakening and inviting that part of us to rise up.

With the planet in the state that it is, we cannot continue the way we have been. Mother Earth is calling forth a new awakening of consciousness in order for us to survive on this magnificent planet we call home. A shift from aggression to compassion, from fact to truth, from fear to love, from separateness to oneness, from unquestioned dogma to faith, from left brain to right, from war to peace, from force to flow, from unconsciousness to consciousness, from fact to truth, and from unquestioned linear processes to lateral solutions.

We each have a light within us waiting to guide us home. Our Soul Purpose is to shine this unique light in a way that only we can. In doing so, we spark something in another and inspire them to do the same.

We are all being called to align our lives and answer the deep stirrings of our souls. I believe that through doing so, we can move into a new stage of Earth's history. It is a time when masculine and feminine energies swing back into balance, and when we acknowledge the inter-connectedness of all living beings.

As each one of us lights up, we will effortlessly spark something in another, and rise up together.

I believe that we can change the world, one conscious, authentic person at a time.

And I believe that you are here to lead the way.

Rise sister rise.

△

RISE SISTER RISE

When your plans and schemes and your hopes
and dreams beg for you to let them go.

Rise sister rise.

When the life you have so consciously
created all comes crumbling down.

Rise sister rise.

When your soul is heavy and your heart broken in two.

Rise sister rise.

When you gave it your best, and it wasn't quite enough.

Rise sister rise.

When you've been beaten and defeated,
and feel so far away from home.

Rise sister rise.

When you find yourself in a thousand pieces,
with no idea which bit goes where.

Rise sister rise.

When you have loved and lost. And then lost again.

Rise sister rise.

When your wings have been clipped, spirit

dampened, and all you hear is a whisper.

Rise sister rise.

When you finally beg mercy to your calling
but have no idea where to start.

Rise sister rise.

Rise for you. And rise for me.

For when you rise first you make the path brighter for She.

△

BASK IN THE LIGHT

I'm devoted to doing all I can to support your rising. My vision for *Light Is the New Black* has always been more than just these pages. Below are some ways that you can bask in the light some more while you read.

www.LightIsTheNewBlack.com

Get over to www.lightisthenewblack.com for free meditations, tools, interviews and gifts.

#LightIsTheNewBlack

Share the light while you read using #LightIsTheNewBlack.

Light Sourcing

Throughout this book I reference my Light Sourcing meditation. If you want to create huge shifts in your life, you can download it for free (*yay!*) at www.lightisthenewblack.com. Try it for 21 days and watch the Universe bend towards you.

Light Is The New Black Spotify Soundtrack

Get some light for your ears by listening along to the free playlist while you read at www.lightisthenewblack.com

Part I

LOSING EVERYTHING FINDING ME

One girl's journey

$\triangle$

CALL OFF THE SEARCH PARTY,
I WAS INSIDE ME ALL ALONG

We all have an inner light waiting to guide us home. But sometimes the Universe turns off all the lights, so we have no choice but to find our own. Perhaps that's been the case for you; it certainly has been for me.

For as long as I can remember, I had this inner knowing that I was here for a reason. I knew I had a purpose, a calling, but the whole thing stressed me out. It was like walking around with this huge weight of responsibility on my shoulders. It felt like I had this urgent thing to do and time was running out.

You know that feeling when you have an assignment or work to do on the weekend, and you can't relax until it's done?

Well, I had that feeling constantly. As if there was something that I was forgetting, a whisper that I couldn't quite make out. The feeling niggled me: there when I went to bed; there in the middle of the night; and there when I woke up in the morning.

I'd spent the majority of my life looking outside of myself for answers. Reaching for anything I could get my hands on, in order to soothe the subtle aching, longing, yearning, and calling deep within my soul, which said that there was something I was missing. There was something more.

I turned to relationships, career, travel, food, alcohol, and partying, but none of them quite hit the spot. I tried traveling to the ends of the planet, in search for something that I couldn't quite put my finger on...

I was pushing, striving, and controlling, instead of listening, trusting, and allowing. It took my whole life to come tumbling down for me to realize that everything I was searching for was inside me all along.

My soul was always calling. I was just facing the wrong way.

△
WHAT I THOUGHT WAS ROCK BOTTOM

By the time 2011 came along, it felt like my life was held together by a single thread, and at any moment the whole tower would come crashing down.

Originally from Australia, I'd just achieved my long-term career ambition of becoming the creative director of a London advertising agency by the age of 30. But the moment I got it, I felt nothing. Isn't this what I had worked so hard for? Why I had sacrificed so much? Overnight I knew that my career no longer fitted my soul.

My relationship of over 10 years was on its last legs, but I refused to admit it. Matt and I had met at university. Creative, sensitive, and hilarious, his cool nonchalance was ridiculously attractive and I fell for him immediately.

The first couple of years were wonderful, but as time went on we became more and more entangled, and more and more stuck. Matt had been suffering from chronic depression for several years. Living in London, far away from the support of our respective families, we ignored the reality of the situation.

I refused to admit that things were broken, throwing myself into a million-and-one ways to fix it, rather than surrender and accept. My gift of seeing the potential in people wasn't serving either of us one bit.

The worse everything seemed to get, the harder I tried to hold it all together. The harder I tried to hold it all together, the more I ignored the callings of my soul. The more I ignored the callings of my soul, the more out of flow with the Universe I got. The more out of flow with the Universe I got, the more alone I felt.

I hadn't felt real joy in my heart for years, but the thought of not being with Matt was too hard to bear. We loved each other with every ounce of our hearts, but in truth we had become best friends more than life partners. With every day, I felt more trapped and stuck in a life that I had worked so hard to create. The thought of saying goodbye to the one person who had been by my side through my entire adult life was too hard to comprehend. I was petrified of being alone and of nothing coming in to take its place.

My external world wasn't in alignment with my internal one. I was way out of flow with the Universe. I knew my soul was calling me to make a massive career change – to follow my passion for spiritual development, intuition, and the journey of the soul. But I was petrified of coming out of the spiritual closet, and turning my back on the great career and network I had worked so hard to create.

I began waking up at 3.13 a.m. each night, drenched in sweat, unable to catch my breath. Alone in bed, I could hear Matt down the hall still on his computer. My loneliness was palpable. Sometimes I would get onto my hands and knees and just sob, begging God to miraculously get me out of there because I lacked the courage to do it myself.

△

CRACKED OPEN

On April 15, 2011, I woke up to the news that Blair, one of my very best friends, had been diagnosed with acute myeloid leukemia. My heart fell through the bed, in a desperate attempt to get back to Australia. Blair held a part of my soul that no one else on the planet did. With him I could let my entire truest, biggest, most authentic self shine. He knew my secret dreams and held similar ones.

The moment we met it was an instant soul connection. I loved him immediately. Blair had a contagious charisma and he completely owned it. He wasn't afraid of being his biggest self and encouraged others to do the same: A lover of life, an exceptional human, and king of good times.

Blair was the only person my own age with whom I could talk candidly about my spiritual life. The first night we met, we discovered we were both reading the same book, Doreen Virtue's *The Lightworker's Way*. We planned to write books and 'change the world' together. But first we would become successful in our chosen fields (him as an actor and me as a creative director), and *then* we would use our power to change the world.

As the day progressed Blair's condition worsened. I prayed for a sign as to whether or not I should fly back to Australia. Two minutes later, as I was getting something out of my wardrobe, the whole thing fell flat to the floor, emptying out every single item of clothing in front of me. I took it as a sign and got on the next flight.

By the time I was on the plane, Blair's condition had rapidly declined and he was in a medically induced coma. During that long flight home, somewhere over Europe and the Middle East, I physically felt Blair's presence. I could feel the actual weight of his body pressing down on mine. I could smell his aftershave and the warmth of his lips kissing my forehead. His hand pressed down on my chest, soothing my aching heart. And in that moment, I knew he was gone.

Years earlier, we had made a pact that whoever died first had to visit the other immediately, so we knew they were OK and hanging out in the afterlife.

For someone relatively young, I had experienced a fair amount of death. But this was different. Blair was different. This was not part of the plan.

I fell into a deep, dark, regretful place, which no one could carry me out of.

A couple of months later we suddenly lost another dear friend from the same tightly knit friendship circle.

The Universe was not letting up.

I felt cheated, bitter and mad. I had no fight left. I wanted a refund from God.

Despite Matt and I supporting each other through the grief of losing our friends, one Sunday in October after celebrating my 30th birthday, we agreed to end our relationship. And before I knew it, I was watching a black cab disappear into the distance, taking away the person I had spent my whole adult life with – down the street to the other side of the globe and out of my life.

Winter was coming. I was alone, unreachable, and a long way from home.

△

FOUNDATIONS COME CRUMBLING

The only thing that got me through the months that followed was the work ethic my parents had instilled in me. I chose them well.

The grief would hit out of nowhere: at my desk, on the subway, in the grocery store aisle, while walking down the street.

My family and friends urged me to come back home to Australia, but deep down I had this inner knowing that this was something I needed to face alone. I needed to venture into the darkest caverns and try to find my own way out.

In an attempt to create a clean slate for myself, I moved into a studio apartment in the heart of London's Notting Hill. Within a week I discovered even that was falling apart. The foundations of the building were literally crumbling around me.

All the structures that stood before me had to be replaced. The irony was not lost on me. The world was my mirror.

One particular night it all got too much and I was near giving up. As tears streamed uncontrollably down my face, the water pipes exploded in unison, transforming my home into a stinking sea of watery despair.

Seriously Universe?

I found myself on the water-soaked carpet in complete surrender, praying (more like begging) for mercy. It wasn't the slightest bit graceful, and went something like this:

'God... Please help.

Please God help.

Seriously, I give up.

I GIVE UP.

I F*ING GIVE UP.

For F's sake I don't know what the F you want me to do.

I can't F*ing do this anymore.

PLEASE GOD F*ING HELP ME!

WHAT THE HELL DO YOU WANT ME TO DO?'

Then all of a sudden, I clearly heard the words, *Go to Chicago*.

Followed by a feeling of ultimate calm and relief.

I was like, 'Chicago? WTF is in Chicago?'

I racked my brains and the only person I knew in Chicago was my teacher Sonia Choquette whom I'd been training with in London for the past four years. Without giving my head a moment to butt in, I immediately looked up her website and emailed her assistant. He replied instantly saying there was a private teacher training in Chicago in a week's time. It was not available to the public, but there was one spot left and Sonia was happy for me to take it.

My mind said, *You've got a huge campaign launching in 14 days at work. You have no vacation left. Your house is falling apart. You are an emotional wreck – do you really want to let people see that? Pfffft teacher? Who do you think you are, training to be a spiritual teacher when you can't even get your life together?*

My soul whispered, *Go to Chicago*.

I knew my life wasn't worth living, unless something changed, so I asked, 'If I am really meant to go, prove it to me and prove it to me good.'

I turned off the water supply, sent a text to my landlord, changed my soaked pajamas, and went back to my semi-floating bed.

The next morning I woke up to a message from my landlord telling me that he'd found someone to fix the apartment, but I would have to move out for a week (*starting the date of the training in Chicago*). He apologized profusely and said I didn't need to pay rent for the next month (*the cost of the tuition and flight*), and he would pay for a hotel of my choice where I could stay while the work was getting done (*the cost of my hotel in Chicago*).

Well done, Universe!

But I still had a whopping big campaign launching...

An hour later, I arrived at work to discover the campaign had been delayed due to a PR scandal. And get this: The CEO then suggested that I take some time off while things were quiet, as I would need to be on standby after the PR scandal had died down in a month or so.

Well bloody done, Universe!

I took the blatant hint, booked my flight immediately, and for the first time in a long time, stepped onto the magic carpet and trusted the ride.

△

FINDING GRACE

From the moment I walked onto the plane, to sitting in front of the fire in Chicago drying out my waterlogged heart, I felt as though I was in exactly the right place. I could feel Blair cheering me on. It was like I was the main character of a movie that I had seen before. Déjà vu on steroids. As if I was being cradled by life. I slept the whole night through for the first time in forever and, while my heart was still heavy, I woke with a new light of hope.

The next evening, after a long day, I found myself sitting in front of devotional singer Gurunam Singh, and his seriously sexy drummer, Chris Maguire, who were there to play for us.

Having listened to a few songs and joined in with the chanting, my heart opened some more, and through the cracks my soul sheepishly edged forward. Gurunam's eyes caught mine and I could feel him holding my soul. I was about to have the most extreme healing of my life. (Go to www.lightisthenewblack.com to download this grace-filled song.) He sang:

Give up all your hopes and your dreams.
Give up all your plans and your schemes.
Give up the fear of darkness surrounded in the light.
Give up fear of being wrong and the need to be right.
Unto thee, unto thee, unto thee, unto thee.
Unto thee, unto thee, unto thee, unto thee.
Unto thee, unto thee, unto thee, unto thee.
I give everything I am... unto thee.

In that moment, I realized how much time I had wasted trying to control and force my life. I was absolutely exhausted from desperately trying to hold it all together for so long. I had no fight left and it was time to let go of the reins.

As Gurunam continued to sing, I mourned the loss of Blair. I grieved for the end of my relationship with Matt, the family that would never be, and the daughter I hadn't met (I'd had a miscarriage a year earlier). I cried for my inner voice that I had ignored for so long. I cried for all of the years I had spent in my masculine – pushing and striving instead of letting life support me. I wept for the exuberant woman inside me who longed to emerge. I mourned for all the time I had spent searching for things outside of myself, when really the only place I needed to look was within. I sobbed for the light deep within my heart, which no matter how hard I'd tried to snuff out, still shone bright.

Past, present, but mostly future, I mourned for it all. And during those 3 minutes and 39 seconds, my ego finally surrendered and asked my soul to lead.

In that short moment, I touched a space within me that can only be described as Grace. I surrendered. I touched God; or rather I received God to touching me. I came home. I realized that while I felt separate, I was actually part of a greater whole, or oneness, and thus never really separate or alone.

I realized the only reason I felt unsupported was because I wasn't supporting myself. The only reason I felt alone was because I had ignored the callings of my soul. And for the first time I was able to see beyond the devastation and truly feel the bountiful light of Grace.

I was learning, and yet also remembering who I truly was. Like the depths of me who already knew were saying, *Yes, yes, this way.*

I experienced a coming home to my authentic self, different from ever before, and felt my soul cheer.

While Gurunam sang his next song, *The Grace of God*, I had this big fat whopping mother of an 'aha' light-bulb moment, where I finally understood what I had been searching for all this time.

My entire life I'd had this weird fascination with a thing called 'nominative determinism' – when people's names fit their calling or purpose in life, like little clues from the heavens. For example, William Wordsworth was a writer, Larry Speakes is a White House speaker, Tracey Cox is a sex therapist, and Lisa Messenger is the founder of Collective Magazine. But I'd always felt a bit cheated by my name. In Hebrew, Rebecca means 'knotted cord,' or 'to bind.'

I didn't want to be a basket and I certainly didn't want to be a knotted cord. Then it hit me. Up until this point, I had spent my whole life searching for meaning, trying to unbind myself from the knotted bundle of thoughts that makes me, Me.

My last name, Campbell, is Scottish for 'crooked mouth' – inauthenticity at its best – which considering how long I had been ignoring my inner voice and hiding out in my spiritual closet, was pretty fitting. But then, right smack bang in the center of it all was my middle name... Grace.

Without even realizing it, Grace was the exact thing I had been searching for my entire life. And she was right there inside me all along. Searching north, south, east, and west trying to control, force and make it happen, when all I really needed to do was surrender to the gentle callings of my soul and allow the light of Grace to guide me.

$$\triangle$$

LIVING IN THE LIGHT

My inner light was burning bright. I was home. Now that I had found it, there was no way I was going to let it go. I vowed to say 'YES' to every little call from my soul, regardless of how much logical sense it made. I vowed to do everything I could never to turn my back on myself again.

Just as the old saying goes, 'When the student is ready the teacher will appear,' the very next day I was taught a form of meditation known as 'Sourcing' (which I'll share with you on page 182 and you can download at www.lightisthenewblack.com). Using this simple tool, I was able to fill myself up with Source energy (of which we are all a part), rather than turning to anything outside of myself.

I started Sourcing and listening to the callings of my soul every day without fail. I made it a non-negotiable part of my life.

I showed up every day.

Within a few months, my life was unrecognizable. I felt supported because I was supporting myself. My soul was content because I was acting on its callings. My foundations became strong because I was fuelling myself from within. Through the daily act of letting go, receiving, and allowing myself to be supported I was able to heal my aching heart and let my inner light lead the way.

I continued excavating my life, only letting the things that served me stay.

Alignment was key.

Replacing 'should' and 'could' with deep desires and 'why not?' I danced, breathed, shook off, and embraced. I only let in people, experiences, and things that filled me up, lit me up, and made me feel whole.

Consciously choosing not to enter a relationship until I was completely healed and whole, I discovered that I did not need someone else to be IN love. Instead it was possible to be IN LOVE (in the flow of love) all on my own.

By filling up myself first, I found I was able to show up to my relationships brighter and more whole than ever. Layer by layer, I allowed myself to get authentically naked and come out of the spiritual closet for real.

I quit my corporate job and my intuitive, spiritual mentoring practice took off, and my friend Robyn Silverton and I co-founded The Spirited Project and started teaching Spirited Sessions every month. New people (my kind of people) started arriving serendipitously on my doorstep.

Then I met someone who had been on his own journey home and I invited him to be in love (a space of love) with me. I don't *need* him in my life, but I sure as hell want and love him in it. Last September he asked me to marry him and I said a big fat YES.

My prayers were answered beyond anything that I could have imagined. All I ever needed to do was surrender and let my soul courageously lead.

Call off the search party. I was inside me all along.

△

WAKING UP

Rewind to the nineties.

Every now and then, the Universe conspires to cross our path with someone in a way that feels like they were put on this planet just for us. Had a particular meeting not taken place, perhaps you would have remained asleep? That was certainly the case the day I met Angela Wood.

Soon after starting high school aged 14, I began experiencing what I can only describe now as my first awakening. A natural empath, I would pass strangers on the street and feel their innermost thoughts and feelings.

All of this cracked wide open after I read an article in *Dolly* magazine about a teenage girl called Anna Wood who tragically died after taking the drug ecstasy. In the interview Anna's mother, Angela, openly shared the loss of her beautiful bright light of a daughter. This article touched my soul so deeply, and I remember sobbing myself to sleep from the sadness I felt for Anna's mother without really knowing why or being able to express my thoughts.

The next day I got the bus to the bookshop and bought *Anna's Story*, the biography of Anna Wood's life. The following day at school, I began passionately telling my friend how much Anna's story had touched my heart.

I turned to the page of the book where there was a picture of Anna and her mother and said, 'It's really weird, I can't explain why, but I just have this urge to find Angela and give her the hugest hug, and try to take away some of her pain.'

My friend said, 'That *is* really weird.' She then looked up, back down to the book and then back up again, and pointed, saying: 'That lady over there kinda looks like Anna's mother.'

I looked up at a tall blonde woman making her way across the school courtyard, and realized... IT WAS HER! It was Angela Wood!

I hesitated for a moment, unable to get my head around the weird serendipity of it all, but then, moved by a force bigger than my mind or body, I found myself running after her. The school vice Principal intercepted me with a question and mid-sentence, I turned back around to find that Angela was nowhere to be seen. Heart deflated I finished the conversation. As I turned around to head back to my friends, I found Anna's mum, Angela Wood, looking back at me.

Everything seemed to stand still and we had this weird moment of deep soul recognition... before I introduced myself and bumbled about doing my best to express how much her story impacted me, clutching the book in my hand. Angela then invited me to attend her talk that she was about to give to the senior year. Knowing I must be there, I skipped math and sneaked into Angela's talk – doing my best not to stand out. Afterwards, I waited sheepishly to talk to her and we made plans to stay in contact.

Angela later told me that it was her birthday the week we met. That morning she had asked Anna for a birthday present, and she knew our meeting was it.

We quickly became friends. Our families met and were generously understanding of our seemingly odd relationship.

We'd spend hours sipping coffee and deep in conversation about the meaning of life, the afterlife, grief, death, past lives, and angels. We'd trade dreams, poetry, books, and theories on life and the Universe. I learned firsthand about the power of the human heart and the courage of the human spirit. I'd listen for hour upon hour as Angela shared her stories about the life and death of her beautiful bright light of a daughter Anna. How she touched people's hearts more deeply in her 15 short years than most do in 80.

I pray to be able to do the same.

During those years I found myself getting off the school bus and walking up the steep hill in a sort of creative trance, words rushing through me that I had to get down. They would flow from my soul without effort and with a feeling of grace. I'd write about what was happening with the world, what happens when you die, that our loved ones lost never really leave us, and how we each have our own team of angels and spirit guides around us. Often I would wake the next morning not remembering what I had created.

Looking back, I see now that I was channeling – although, perhaps, all creativity is just that. Messages and ideas that are waiting to be born to people who are open enough to receive them.

During school vacations I would sometimes join Angela on the road at her speaking events as she spoke about how precious life is, how we must hold those we care about and tell them how much we love them. I watched in admiration as her message so effortlessly flowed from her heart.

I pray that one day I might do the same.

I'd been cracked open and all the other things in my life just didn't seem to matter. I'd spend all of my free time and money from my part-time jobs learning about the afterlife, Soul Purpose, past life regression, crystals, healing, and anything I could get my hands on. And all the time it was as if I were remembering things that were deeply engrained in my soul.

Desperately longing to meet other people who thought like me, I'd take two buses and a train to the other side of Sydney to have sessions with healers and psychics, inhaling it all with expanding pleasure. My appetite was insatiable. As I flicked through the pages and listened to the teachers, I experienced what could only be explained as a sense of remembering and homecoming. It felt as though I had found my calling and my true self. Yet, the more connected I felt on the inside, the more isolated I felt on the outside.

A few years later, just after I'd finished high school, Angela moved to the UK. I was devastated and felt like I lost the only person in my life that truly saw the real depths of me. At that stage she was.

I deeply longed to be surrounded by people my own age with whom I could share my innermost thoughts. I felt lost between two worlds – that of being a normal teenager and the expanding world of soul and spirit.

Even then I knew that I wanted to write books and create things to help people heal, but what could a young girl possibly know about healing people when she hadn't had anything significant to heal from herself?

So every night I would pray to God that something really bad would happen to me, so I had an external reason to feel all the things I was feeling and so I could help other people's hearts and souls – as I felt called to do. I figured if I had been through enough tragedy myself, then at least I could write about that. I'd wake up each day, wondering when the tragedy would hit. But it never did. Life was 'good' and I felt more alone than ever. So I ignored the callings of my soul and decided to dim to fit in.

I consciously went into what I now call my 'spiritual closet,' keeping my metaphysical studies a secret. I waited for the day when I would be justified to speak of the things that dwelled deep within me. Until that day came, I was determined to keep it all inside.

△
'F YOU GOD'

Fast forward to 2012.

Six months after returning from my grace-filled experience in Chicago I knew I needed to heal the lingering pieces of grief that remained, and my soul called me to go on silent retreat in Assisi with my friend Robyn.

We spent the mornings and evenings deep in meditation while our days were given over to walking the wildflower-filled trail of St. Francis, church hopping, and gorging on orgasmic Italian food – well, it would have been rude not to.

After meditation on the third night I was overcome with this unexpected and unrecognizable red-hot rage bubbling up from the depths of my core. Unable to talk (very frustrating!) I grabbed my Moleskine and headed for the hills.

On a bench in the middle of a field under a swollen Virgo moon, I started writing furiously what turned out to be a hate letter to God.

Through desperate sobs I let it all out. I ranted and raved to God, demanding to know, *What have I done to deserve all of this? Why no matter how hard I've tried to hold everything together and do the right thing, still nothing has worked out... Why do you expect me to believe in you, if you don't even have the balls to show your face?*

I was pissed off. Big time. Ever since I was a little girl I had this unwavering knowing that God/the Universe existed. And so, for a 'believer' I felt totally ripped off and unsupported. I held nothing back. Through angry sobs I ranted on for pages with my pen, at times piercing through to the next page.

When I had finally got it all out, I felt an overwhelming sense of calm and my sobbing ceased. All of a sudden, the energy around me shifted and I watched as my hand started moving on its own accord. As my hand moved across the page, I realized that God was writing her response.

You asked for this, don't you remember?

You said you weren't ready to answer your calling until you had some life experiences.

Well, you have your lessons and your stories, just like you asked.

Now, Rebecca, it's time to get to work.

In an instant I recalled all those pleas I'd made when I was younger. I understood that my suffering didn't happen *TO* me, it happened *FOR* me. I took a deep breath, gathered my notebook and marched myself back to my room.

I was ready.

Finally I was ready.

Tucked into bed, gazing out my window at the star-filled night sky, knowing that tomorrow was going to be a very new day.

I started writing this book the next day.

Part II

TURN YOUR LIGHT ON

Coming home to yourself

YOU WANDER
FROM ROOM TO
ROOM. HUNTING
FOR THE DIAMOND
NECKLACE. THAT IS
ALREADY AROUND
YOUR NECK.

RUMI

△

REMEMBERING

I believe that everyone has a calling and that deep down we all know why we are here. We might not consciously remember it, but our soul does. And every second of every day it's doing its best to call us towards it.

As our life unfolds bit by bit, our memory is sparked and we experience moments of *Ooh, this is familiar,* or *I feel drawn to do more of this,* or *I wish I could spend my life doing this.* It's almost as if we have been here before or have seen this part of the movie. Our soul might give us clues through our excitement or enthusiasm. Little butterflies in our stomach or an extra push towards something.

These little signs are always happening, but they are easy to miss. Our mind doesn't trust them, thinking that it needs to be much more complicated than simply following what lights us up.

In 2008, during a past-life regression session, I was taken back to the moment before this life where I received my own personal mission from the Councils of Light. I was taken to a massive, open, very bright, and white space where many other souls were gathering too. While I could not see other 'people,' I could see and feel their energy as balls of buzzing, glowing white light. It was hard to differentiate where one soul started and another began. It was like the best reunion you could possibly imagine. The atmosphere was electric – buzzing with total anticipation – like just before a Beyoncé, Kylie, or Lady Gaga concert. Some of the different souls' energies were familiar, as if I had incarnated with a few of them before.

As a group we were then given our brief for this lifetime on Earth. We were informed that in this incarnation we would use the interconnectedness of new media and communication to create a mass spiritual awakening in the Western world. Many of us would begin our careers in different fields of media where we would learn the skills to speak out, forming a sort of supportive sisterhood amongst like-hearted women and men – moved by Divine Feminine.

We were told that our missions would be deeply infused in us and we would be sent people and situations that would wake us up from our slumber early in life. As one of us woke up and chose to step out and work our light, it would spark a deep-seeded memory in another, regardless of how physically close we were to each other.

Once we were awake, it would change something in us and we were to follow what lit us up and, in doing so, light up the world around us. As we would do this, it would cause a chain reaction of mass-awakening. We all then received information on our choice of life and our own personal missions.

I couldn't tell you if there were 100 or 100,000 souls there with me, because in truth it felt like we were all one – which of course we were (and we are) – one big Army of Light. If you're reading this, perhaps you were there too?

WORK YOUR LIGHT

What does your soul want you to remember?

△

WELCOME TO THE AGE OF LIGHT

Welcome to the Age of Light

(It's safe to shine now.)

Can you imagine a part of you that yearns bravely to shine big and bright?

A part of you, which doesn't let fear override and knows exactly what it is here for?

A part of you that is so ready to step forward, to take the lead, to let itself be fully seen? Like really seen?

A part of you that is ready to stop striving and let the Universe support you wholly?

There's a unique spark within you, a spectrum so big and bright. An ultraviolet fire that has been pushed down, dismissed, abandoned, silenced, rejected. But still it burns.

With every new day, as we each light up, we leave the Dark Ages behind us and leap into the Age of Light. A time in history led by spirit not controlled by ego.

One by one, as we each light up, we remind others that it's safe now.

To come out of hiding. To break the silence.

To shine through the shadows, revealing our inner light in all its authentic glory.

Welcome to the Age of Light.

$\triangle$

YOU'RE HERE FOR A REASON

Never forget your real identity. You are a luminous cosmic stardust being forged into the crucible of cosmic fire.

We are part of a group of souls who agreed to be here at this time in history: a transition team intended to be beacons of light as we move from the shadow of patriarchy (enslaved by ego) to the Age of Light (lead by Source and Divine Feminine).

You are a highly conscious soul and not all souls on this Earth are. This doesn't mean you are better or worse than anyone else, just a different manifestation of energy and soul history. You may feel lonely at times because deep down you know that not everyone is like you. You may feel isolated because perhaps you hide your truest, biggest, brightest self from the world.

You have worked hard to raise your vibration and now you are being called to truly step into it. You have experienced different worlds than just this one. You have lived in different dimensions and on different planets, and incarnated as different expressions of your true essence. You are both infinite and one.

**You are both authentically unique and
part of the greater whole.**

You are here to remind people that it is OK to be whole. It is OK to shine your light. OK to be unapologetically you. In fact, it's more than OK, it's necessary in order to thrive. But you must go first.

The sooner you step up into the greater most authentic version of You, the sooner your fears will dissipate, the sooner your concerns will begin to fade, the sooner life will bend towards you. The more you will flow with life.

**You are already whole and complete,
why do you resist what you are?**

The more you lean into yourself and spend your time being rather than doing in order to be, the sooner you can be supported beyond your wildest dreams. And you will be supported.

△

YOU ARE LIGHT

Your soul is a unique expression of light from Source, carefully sculpted from your individual experiences from lifetime to lifetime. Arranged together in the most perfect way to make up the magnificent cluster of atoms that is You.

Your body is light too. Every cell in your body emits light every single second. Your unique consciousness emits bio-photons with every thought. No matter which way you look at it you are made of light.

You ARE light.

Shining our light is actually our most natural state. When we are connected to the inner light within us we are connected to the light of the Universe.

There is more than enough room for us all to expand and step into our bigness. We are all notes in the most amazing symphony. We were born to light up and expand together.

When we connect to Source we don't need to rely on any external thing to fill us up. The supply of Source energy (universal light) is unlimited. It never runs out. There is enough for us all. It's where we came from and it's where we will return. When you tap into this infinite power source, you slip into the harmonious flow of the Universe and raise the vibration of the planet. Like the morning sun, when you shine your light, you stir the sleepers and inspire them to wake up too.

I AM LIGHT.

Δ

YOUR AUTHENTIC SELF IS YOUR LIGHT

There is a shift happening right now where anything inauthentic can no longer survive. The things in our lives that don't serve us are crumbling. Relationships, jobs, social structures, or anything built on shaky ground is destined to tumble down. It's happening to bring us back home to who we truly are, so we can live a life that is in alignment with who we truly are, and who we came here to be. But when you're in the thick of it, it can feel like a personal attack from the Universe.

It seems as though we are being called to ensure that the lives that we build are true reflections of who we are called to be – vibrational matches at soul level. If they aren't, then the foundations will continue to come crashing down until we do.

Our soul is always waiting to guide us. Now more than ever it's so important to tune in and listen to its callings. And it is always calling. To come home to and connect within, rather than looking at people and things outside of us for fulfillment, love, meaning, joy, and to fill the gaping void.

Our authentic self is our light. Our Soul Purpose is to embrace it. But in order to do so it's not just about pretending everything is shiny and bright.

The brightest candle casts the biggest shadow.

Moving through the shadow can be hard, but it's so worth it in the end.

$\triangle$

LETTER TO A LIGHTWORKER

I believe that you came into this life with a deep
inner knowing of what you were here to do, and an
inner guidance system to make it happen.

I'm not talking about a carefully laid-out path, which comes with
an instruction manual, but rather an unshakable deep-seeded
knowing that you're here for a reason. That there is serious
work to do and the Universe will support you in doing it.

I believe that until you answer this calling, you will always feel
as though there is something missing and something you have
forgotten. No matter what you use to numb it out, it will be
there. The only way to stop the calling is to answer it.

I believe that your message is so deeply engrained
that sometimes it's hard to realize that everyone
else doesn't think like you. They don't.

I believe you chose your parents. No matter how hard or soft,
rich or poor, light or dark, old or young, present or not, kind or
troubled – you chose them. And with this simple selection you
were put in exactly the right place and given exactly what you
needed to inspire you to rise up, to rise up into yourself, to rise
up into your highest most authentic self. To take your position.

I believe that your tragedies, your losses, your sorrows, your hurt
happened for you, not to you. And I bless the thing that broke you
down and cracked you open because the world needs you open.

I believe that life lessons are less about getting it
right and more about getting it wrong.

I believe that you are more on track than you feel, even if you don't feel it – *especially if you don't feel it*. For the further you get off track, the closer you actually are to abandoning the wrong path and leaping onto the right one.

I believe that you are closer than you think and more qualified in your message than you could ever fathom.

I believe that the things that you are here to teach are the very things that you most need to learn, and that the best teachers are the ones that struggle the most because when they get it, they get it with a triple smackdown.

I believe that the darkness is a birthing process and that, in order to find your light, first you need to venture through the shadows of your ego.

I believe that in order to be a light in the world, you first need to come home to who you truly are and then bravely show it to all those around you.

I believe that you are surrounded by a personal team of angels, guides, and teachers, both in this world and beyond, who are so completely devoted to your growth that if you knew, you would not spend one more day worrying about things working out. And if you could see things from their viewpoint... each time you'd see a challenge, you would meet it with a cheer.

I believe in you. And us. And all of this.

And so it is.

$\triangle$

YOUR LIGHT IS CONTAGIOUS

You have an inner light within you that is craving to be shared by those around you, by the world at large – but mostly by you.

When you share your unique light, bit by bit, you light up the lives of those around you.

And, one by one, you inspire them to light up too.

It's a chain reaction.

And before long, the whole world lights up.

Your light is contagious.

△

WHAT THE *WHAT* IS A LIGHTWORKER?

A Lightworker is anyone who devotes their life to being a bright light in the world. They understand that their actions (no matter how big or small) have the potential to raise the vibration of the planet. A Lightworker soul is awake, conscious that their presence matters, and they are part of something that is bigger than them.

Lightworkers are not just tie-dye-wearing hippies and healers with dreads. Far from it. They are teachers and chefs, writers and singers, producers and cleaners, mothers and mediums, creative directors, and kaftan designers. They're at the country club and the nightclub, in the café and the classroom, the boardroom and the art room.

A Lightworker is someone who makes a conscious decision to answer the call of Source (light) over the call of the ego (fear).

There are two types of energy on this planet: light and dark.

Light energy is unlimited and comes from Source. It's high vibrational, expansive, positive, and full of love. Dark energy is much more dense. It's the manipulation, power struggle and fear. It sees us all as separate, rather than connected spiritual beings. It goes against the flow of the Universe.

Lightworkers turn their light on by following what lights them up and then effortlessly sharing that light with the world around them. They are in tune with the callings of their soul and act on its whispers regardless of fear. They do not need to convince anyone of anything, rather just *be the light*.

While some Lightworkers alive right now incarnated with a conscious mission to be of service (and have been doing so for lifetimes), there are countless souls awakening to the call to be of service.

Anyone who chooses to devote their life to being a bright light in the world IS a Lightworker.

There are no snobby spiritual tests to pass or assignments to hand in. The only requirement is a desire to connect with your own authentic light and a longing to serve their world.

I call it working your light.

Just by reading this book you are working your light. By following what you love, you are working your light. By choosing a higher thought when you find yourself in a bad mood, you are working your light. By encouraging someone instead of criticizing them, you are working your light. By sharing your unique gifts, you are working your light. By connecting to the unlimited supply of love in the Universe, you are working your light. By being true to yourself, you are working your light. By being kind and compassionate, you are working your light.

Definition of a Lightworker: Someone who wholeheartedly makes the decision to make the world a brighter place by being in it. The more conscious we get, the higher our vibration, and the more aligned to Source we become. The more conscious we are, the more we see how everything is connected and how we fit into a larger whole.

Many Lightworkers may find that as they raise their consciousness, they become more energetically sensitive, picking up other people's feelings, energy, and thoughts. You may find it hard to watch the news or violent films. You may also find that any old relationships that are built on manipulation, control, and fear, start to drop away as you are no longer an energetic match to them. In Part III, Living In The Light, you'll find lots of practical tools to protect your energy, and keep you grounded and supported.

For some time now, we have been living in a largely unconscious state. In order for Mother Earth to survive we need a global awakening. This awakening has already begun.

I believe that you are one of souls who chose to lead the way.

△
THE DOUBLE MISSION

Lightworkers have a double mission: To raise their consciousness and the consciousness of the planet.

Lightworker souls who aren't completely awake to this double mission (or calling) can have a niggling feeling that they can't quite shake. An odd inexplicable knowing that there is something that they are forgetting to do and time is running out.

Many Lightworkers are scared of coming out of the 'spiritual closet' and being seen. This may be because in the past (past lives) they have been rejected or punished for speaking their truth and rising up.

Once awake, most Lightworker souls find it hard to have meaningless conversations, jobs, and relationships. It's as if they innately know that there is much more to life and feel the constant nudge to surround them with this 'something more' and get to work. They will remain restless until they step into their calling and follow what lights them up, which is to shine their authentic light in their own unique way.

Many Lightworkers confuse their calling with their job or profession. It's actually much simpler than that. Our soul is always calling.

We follow our calling by following what lights us up.

Before incarnating on this planet you carefully chose your body, family, city, surroundings, and experiences to create a perfect environment. These conditions could have been fortunate or not so fortunate, but whatever they were, they were chosen to give you the perfect experience to eventually light up the world in your own unique way.

Lightworkers are scattered all over the planet in every single corner. Every single one, once awakened, serve the world by being them.

The city where you live, the suffering you've experienced, the education you received, the class system you were born into, the parents who conceived you, and the people who've touched your heart, this, all of this, creates the perfect conditions for you to light up the world around you in a way that only you can.

△

YOUR SOUL PURPOSE

The one thing in life you have to do.
Be the Lighthouse.
Yogi Bajan

For as long as I can remember, I was in a rush to grow up and get working on my Soul Purpose. When I was little my favorite question was, 'Where are we going today?' Even then I was searching for this thing that I knew I had to find. Eternally looking for the perfect black-and-white answer to the question, 'What is my purpose?'

To be honest, the whole Soul Purpose thing stressed me out. It felt like a big decision to make, the type that hangs over you until you do it. But I was petrified that I might miss my life, or get it wrong. The deeper I got into my career, the more trapped I felt.

I searched all corners of the world for the 'perfect thing' for me to do in order to play my part in leaving the world a little brighter with my presence. Spending many years waiting around for a perfectly plotted-out, single-minded plan to be miraculously revealed (in full) and land smack bang on my lap. And when I actually got pretty clear glimpses of what it could be, I longed for some external person to confirm that I had it right and to give me permission to get on with it.

I was *so* in my head... weighing up, pondering and questioning all the possible paths, petrified that I might choose the wrong one. I was stuck in inaction, waiting to be handed the map from the big G himself before I set off along my perfect path. I thought it was all about striving and doing, not being and embodying.

Through my own disillusion, time wasting, and working with loads of women who feel the same I have come to the conclusion that our Soul Purpose comes down to two things:

1. Be The Light

To 'be the light' you need to follow the things that light you up, so you can show up in life filled up and whole. You don't need a special job to 'be the light'; in fact you don't need any job at all. You can 'be the light' in the grocery store, you can 'be the light' while cooking dinner, you can 'be the light' on the world's most boring conference call, you can 'be the light' while updating your Facebook status, you can 'be the light' by being there for a friend or a stranger who needs a smile.

2. Be authentically you

There is no perfect path, only a perfectly authentic You – full of contradictions, uniqueness and gifts. It is your You-ness that allows you truly to light up the world with your presence. Your You-ness is lifetimes in the making. It is your flaws, your quirks, your weirdness, your ancestral history, your gifts, your humor, and your imperfections. Your light and message will come through you regardless of what path you choose. Your authentic self emerges when you follow what lights you up, or in other words, when you do what you love. And then do it in a way that only you can.

Our soul is always calling us towards what will light us up.

Our ego tries to trick us into thinking that it has to be more complicated. It cannot understand how it could be so simple as following what lights us up. But when we follow what we love over and over again, we stumble upon our calling without even realizing it. When we lose ourselves in the doing, we step out of the way and allow the light to flow through us.

And it feels freaking fantastic.

I've spent years trying to work out what my purpose is. Trying to fit it into a perfect little box with a step-by-step plan before I would even consider taking the leap. I looked at my strengths, listed my gifts, tried to work out the message my soul wanted to share, but still I held back because I couldn't see every single little step along the way. I wanted to know the final destination before I took the first step. All of the possibilities, purposes and callings would toss and turn in my head, but I was not acting on any one of them. I was waiting by the phone for the Universe to call saying, 'Hey guuuuurl, so this is your purpose.'

The amount of time I spent pondering whether I should be a writer, an actor, a life coach, a healer, an artist, a director, or a fashion designer is absolutely ridiculous. It doesn't matter if I write books, bake cakes, make movies, design cowboy boots, or tap dance on a piano.

It doesn't matter if I take photos, do speeches, run a country, teach kids, paint pictures, write comedy or host a TV show... As long as it lights me up, I will bring my own unique light to everything that I do. The only things that matters is doing the things that light you up over and over again and letting the light shine authentically through you.

Follow the trail of things that light you up and lose yourself in the doing. Before long you will find yourself right in the center of your purpose and the life you are called to live.

WORK YOUR LIGHT

Are you waiting for a perfect sign from the Universe
to tell you what your Soul Purpose is?

What can you lose yourself in because you love doing it so much?

PEOPLE CAME FROM AFAR TO **BASK IN HER LIGHT.**

△

YOU'VE BEEN WORKING ON
YOU FOR LIFETIMES

You're way more than the days that have breathed through you this life. You're also all of the lifetimes that came before. You're male and female, gay and straight, black and white, confident and shy, fat and thin, tall and small, a leader and a follower. And more. All of these experiences have polished your soul into the most magnificent expression that is your authentic self.

You = complete masterpiece.

Your soul has many facets. Imagine a fingerprint; your soul is a million times more intricate than that. If you put together all of the fingerprints of all of the people you have been, you would not even get close to fathoming how much of a unique masterpiece you are. You've been working on you for lifetimes.

It's why dogs seem to have a personality even when they are just small pups. The seeming personality is the light shining through their beautiful unique little soul. A part of them has experienced much more than the mere number of days since they were born.

You came in knowing. You came in with wisdom beyond your years, weeks, months, and days. This is the part of you that longs to be seen. This is the part of you that is ready right here and now to let the light shine through and emerge.

WORK YOUR LIGHT

Sitting comfortably, put your hand on your heart, and gently close your eyes. Breathe deeply and really sink into the space of your heart where your soul lives. Rest there awhile.

Imagine a multifaceted crystal in your heart center, slowly spinning. This is the eternal part of you, the fingerprint of your soul. As it spins around slowly, allow yourself to really absorb and embody all of the wisdom and all of the magnificent beauty that is You.

Ask your soul:

What wisdom do you have for me that can help right now?

What part longs to step forward right now?

What part is ready to emerge?

THE EGO TRUSTS THAT WE ARE SEPARATE AND GO THROUGH LIFE ALONE. **THE SOUL TRUSTS** THAT WE ARE ALL CONNECTED AND THUS NEVER REALLY ALONE. **THE UNIVERSE TRUSTS** THAT THE EGO WILL GET LONELY AND LISTEN TO THE SOUL.

△

THE EGO, THE SOUL, AND THE SPIRIT

We are divine beings having a human experience, here to grow, evolve and journey back to Source. Sometimes that human experience can be full of extreme joy and exhilaration. And sometimes being a spiritual being in a human body can be plain hard.

Getting to know the voices of our ego, soul, and spirit is extremely helpful when it comes to answering our highest callings.

The ego (our human self)

Our ego is the human part of us that sees itself as separate, as 'me' against 'them.' *A Course In Miracles* explains it 'like sunbeams thinking they are separate from the sun, or waves thinking they are separate from the ocean.' We are each sunbeams from the same sun and drops of water from the same ocean.

Often running off a program of fear, the ego is the inner critic, the judge, the victim, and the bully who thinks it is always right and has all the answers. Driven by a fear of 'everyone is out to get me' and 'there is not enough for everyone,' the ego sees the world as unfair and unsafe. It finds it hard to trust others, it lives in the past, it *loves* to create drama and feel sorry for itself (a lot). The ego tends to like things to be hard, believing that we need to 'work' to find our calling (if we are lucky enough to find it).

The ego is driven by a core fear, which colors the lens though which we see the world. When we are living in ego town, we are controlled by our fears. When we are living in a world of fear we are living in our shadow.

It's important to remember that we need our ego in order to survive on this planet. However, our life will flow more when our ego is serving and supporting the callings of our soul.

The soul (our ancient self)

The soul is the part of us that we carry from lifetime to lifetime. It is our ancient self. Both deep and hearty, it is a culmination of all the wisdom of the ages that you have trodden and the unique soul gifts that you have mastered over lifetimes.

Each life and experience adds to your authentic imprint. While it has wisdom through lessons learned, it can also carry trauma and patterns from past hurts. Lifetime after lifetime, we enhance our soul's growth, with the purpose of coming back home to our true essence (our divine self).

When a client comes to me in their dark night of the soul, I cannot help but celebrate. The extreme loss, heartbreak, or crumbling allows the ego to loosen its grip and admit it doesn't have all the answers, which leaves space for the light of the divine self (spirit) to come flooding in.

The spirit (our divine self)

The spirit is our divine connection to Source. It is the part of us that is connected to everything in the Universe. It is the spark in our eyes, the spring in our step, the sunshine on our face. It is the part of us that knows that we are whole and complete. It's grace. It's our higher self. It's God. It's pure light.

When our heart cracks open, a space is created for our soul to come through. When our soul cracks open, it allows the grace of spirit to come through. When our spirit, soul, and ego are working in harmony, the light of spirit (Source) is able to come flowing through our unique soul, body, and mind, and we are truly able to *work our light* in a way that only we can.

△
YOU ARE DIVINE

'Although you appear in earthly form, your essence is pure consciousness. You are the fearless guardian of divine light.'
Rumi

You are divine in every sense of the word: an expression of Source energy – light in human form. The ego leads us to believe we are separate from Source (and each other), and that we need to work to find our wholeness, love, and purpose. And if we are lucky enough to find it, we'd better cling onto it with all of our might for fear of losing it.

This denial of our divine nature leads us on endless searches outside of ourselves. We look to others to feel love. We look to something outside of ourselves to worship. We wait for people to give us permission to shine or feel whole and complete.

Whereas we already are all that we seek, we only have to turn our gaze in. Wholeness, happiness, and love are your birthright. As a baby there was no part of you that doubted your wholeness. As a result you lit up the world without even trying.

Love, light, wisdom, happiness, and wholeness are available to you 'on tap' at every moment because they are what you are at your core. And they're waiting for you to let them in.

MANTRA

I am connected to the never-ending flow of light. Everything I am searching for is ready to flow through me right now.

THE UNIVERSE IS
ALWAYS EXPANDING.
**YOU ARE PART
OF THE UNIVERSE.**
EXPANSION IS YOUR
NATURAL STATE.
IF YOU RESIST YOUR
EXPANSION, YOU
RESIST WHO YOU ARE.
**EXPAND INTO YOUR
BIGNESS NOW.**

△

ONENESS VS. ALONENESS

One of the most challenging things about being a spiritual being in a human body is the feeling of separation. Isolation.

Aloneness

While your soul is currently in a physical body (which is separate from others), you are part of a larger whole. A oneness beyond identity, body, and words. And somewhere deep down our soul remembers this. For souls who have experienced more than just the Earth plane, this Earth experience can feel horribly isolating. For our true essence knows that we are pure beings of light, love, and Oneness from Source having a human experience. You are divine.

While I have been blessed with a beautiful family and have always been surrounded by many friends, I have battled with this feeling of loneliness my whole life. It was like I had this distant memory that it wasn't meant to be like this. I had no idea that so many people felt the same.

From an early age I craved meaningfulness and couldn't stand conversations for the sake of it. You know the ones. Where people's mouths are moving but your heart is saying: *This whole thing is fake and a complete waste of both of our time, but let's keep talking because it's better than being alone.* I have felt more alone in some relationships than I have out of them.

This lingering feeling of aloneness has seen me hold on to relationships, friendships, and jobs longer than was in my best interest. It's also seen me gossip and stay at parties later than I wanted. And then there's the binge TV-watching and eating. It's as if I clung on to all these things, just so it could fill up the big gaping hole I felt deep within me. If only I had realized that this gaping hole was my invitation to go within.

During my own darkest hours, when I was truly alone and unreachable to those around me, I eventually discovered what I already knew intellectually. Sometimes we just need to clear out the space and let our aloneness take over to realize that we are never really alone. We are one. What we are seeking is actually what we already are. It's our denial of our own divine nature that makes us feel separate. It's our seeing ourselves as separate that makes us feel so alone.

There is a presence, which I call 'Grace' or 'Source', waiting for us behind the gates of aloneness. A presence so subtle yet palpable, that if we let ourselves feel it, it would bring us to tears. No words can do it justice, but once felt none are needed. A presence so supportive, loving, soothing, and familiar, that it feels like coming home. It feels like coming home because, when we feel it, we are actually tapping into the glorious Source energy, of which we are all a part. This presence of 'oneness' is available to us in every moment (and it's why I adore Sourcing so freaking much, see page 182).

Sometimes it takes everything to go wrong for us to give up the fight and give in to its warm embrace. Our soul knows the way. Listen to its whispers and follow the trail.

We are all bundles of divine cosmic Source energy buzzing around in human bodies. We see ourselves as separate, when really we are all going through the same thing. The same journey back home to oneness.

We are here to remember our divine nature and embody it in human form. We are not our body, our mind or our emotions. We are souls having an experience of body, emotion, and mind. The sooner we see ourselves as part of the greater whole and thus never really alone, the sooner we come home to the beautiful divine wonder that we naturally are (and the less alone we will feel).

We have chosen our bodies as perfect vehicles to express our divine light. Through these bodies, and the healing of our emotions, we express that light in our own way. The moment we try and be more like someone else, we get in the way and actually stop that effortless flow of light from streaming through.

You were not born to be like someone else. You were born to be like You. To remember that despite all of your experiences you are a Divine Being of Light, and to let that light flow through your unique soul, emotions, and body.

This is not about being perfect; the opposite is true.

It's about being real, true, transparent, and authentically You. Cracks, bumps, flaws, and all. When the light shines through our imperfections, that's when we are truly able to touch other people's hearts and souls.

MANTRA

I am a divine expression of light. I embrace
my flaws and shine anyway.

Th
ereis
nosepar
ationweare
onethereisno
separationweare
onethereisnoseparat
ionweareonethereisnose
parationweareonethereis
noseparationweareonetherei
snoseparationweareonethereisn
oseparationweareonethereisnosepa
rationweareonethereisnoseparation
weareonethereisnoseparationweareon
ethereisnoseparationweareonethereisnosep
arationweareonethereisnoseparationweareone

ALONE
OR
ALLONE?

△

WE CHOOSE OUR PARENTS

Before entering into this life, we chose our parents based on our own soul growth and the messages we're here to share. I chose my parents extremely well. But, like most people out there... I didn't always think so!

A non-traditional family where the roles were reversed, my mum, a fashion designer, was the primary breadwinner working long hours and traveling around the world a few times a year. My dad, a P.E. teacher at a local high school, would collect my brother and me from school, and also do all the domestic stuff like cooking dinner, ironing, and making sure we did our homework, because he had more time.

My parents taught me the importance of education; I can do anything I want to, if I put my mind to it; and how to work hard for the things I wanted.

When I experienced my first awakening aged 14, I wished that I had been born into a family that spoke of spiritual things around the dinner table. I was bursting to share my experiences and thought psychologist, philosopher, healer, or mind body spirit author parents would have been much better for me.

I first met Sheila Dickson after my mum suggested I babysit her children. Sheila had just moved in two doors down from my family home in Collaroy on Sydney's Northern Beaches. Eighteen years old, I bounced into Sheila's house and chatted with her and her four adorable children, swapping life stories and only pausing when we needed to take a breath.

Despite the huge age difference (she was 39 at the time) it was an instant connection and felt like coming home. Before we knew it, four hours had passed and the kids were asking if they could go to bed. As soon as I got home I called her on the phone and we spoke for a couple more hours before planning to meet the next day to do each other's tarot cards. We have been the best of friends ever since and consider each other family.

When I was 25, I visited Sheila and her family in Singapore, where she was living at the time, and she organized a past-life regression session for me. I had always been fascinated by the topic after reading books such as *Many Lives, Many Masters* by Brian Weiss and was excited to experience it for myself.

When I arrived, a lovely lady called Toni greeted me. She led me into a state of relaxation, and then regressed me from lifetime to lifetime. It was like traveling around the world, but without the jetlag.

I was then taken between lives to when I was getting ready for this life. *So cool!*

First, I was shown the experience of choosing my 'body' for this life, and presented with three different sets of potential parents, based on what I wanted to bring to the world and my soul growth.

The first were a lovely couple, Trevor and Julie from sunny Sydney (my parents). The mother was strong, kind, ambitious, and highly creative. The father was emotionally sensitive, big-hearted, easygoing, and ahead of his time in that he was able to be a rock and support his wife in an age when that was not the norm. I would be born the eldest child of two.

The second was a Russian woman, Olesya, who had migrated to America where she fell in love with an American businessman. Ancestrally her family line had endured a lot, so she would look to me to make the most of all of the opportunities I would be blessed with. An only child, I would be born male and go on to be an Olympic swimmer.

The third option was a Scottish couple. Andy and Sheila Dickson (my friend!). They were extremely young and I would be a surprise pregnancy. The early years would be tough, as they would have to adjust to being parents. An the child of an ex-pat family, I would live in many countries around the world. The mother would embark on a deep spiritual path paving the way for me, and encourage my spiritual work. I would be born the eldest child of five.

The concept of 'choosing your parents' had always resonated with me, but this experience took it to a whole other level. It helped me truly appreciate that I had made the right choice, and all of the gifts that my parents had given me.

When I told Sheila, she told me that her husband always referred to me as 'the fifth Dickson child.' And, one day, when the family was together, they played a game where they had to write down the name of their favorite person that felt most like family... And every single one of them said it was me.

There are things working on a different level that are impossible to see, but can be felt. For me, finding and answering my calling took a lot of courage, inner knowing and determination – which, considering my calling is to awaken Lightworkers to their authentic light and soul's callings, is a pretty good path to tread.

Regardless of whether you had a wonderful childhood or a terrible one, it was the perfect playground for your soul's growth.

WORK YOUR LIGHT

What things (good and bad) did your parents teach you?

Why do you think you chose them as parents?

How has this added to your soul's growth and path?

Δ

I'M TALKING TO THAT PART OF YOU

Today, I'm talking to that part of you who yearns for more.

The part of you who knows exactly what you want beyond all else.

To that part of you who effortlessly believes that anything
is possible, and that it's possible in an instant.

I'm talking to that part of you who longs to break right
on through that self-imposed ceiling your mind has
created out of fear, lack, should, and could.

To smash and shatter it into a billion little pieces.

I'm talking to that part of you who longs, who
dreams, who dances, who wishes.

To the part of you that cheers, that laughs, that leaps, that bounds.

To that part of you who truly wants the best for others because
it deeply knows that there is more than enough to go round.

I'm talking to that part of you who knows what you
want and the exact next step to take to get it.

To that part of you who knows you're not broken and isn't the
slightest bit interested in perpetuating the story that says it's so.

To that part of you who knows the way and longs
to guide the rest of you back home.

Today, that's the part of you I'm talking to.

And I'm asking it to step forward and lead the way.

△

YOUR INNER GURU KNOWS BEST

*'Come out of the masses. Stand alone like a lion
and live your life according to your own light.'*
OSHO

Your Inner Guru knows best. Better than even the most guru-like of teachers: the wise ones, the saints, the sages, and the swamis.

Sometimes it's just tricky to hear what is being said before your head comes in and doubts it all. To differentiate the crazy voice from the wholehearted, enlightened, centered voice of your soul. Then there's the times we wish it didn't know best, and so clutch outwards for another opinion to contradict our guidance and rest our fears, while secretly hoping it didn't know best in the first place. *Hello getting back with the ex, staying in a job we hate, or trusting someone we knew we shouldn't.*

Eventually we realize that our Inner Guru *DID* know best. Annoying but true. And if we had listened to that niggling little voice in the first place, we would have probably saved ourselves a heck of a lot of time/pain/money/pride.

It's comforting to realize that you have everything you could possibly need inside you to get through any obstacle. It doesn't mean it's going to be easy, but the more you nurture and listen to your Inner Guru, the clearer and louder the whisper gets.

Carve out a non-negotiable time every day and listen to that little voice inside you. Part III, Living in the Light, is packed full of ideas to help you connect with it.

You have everything you need inside you right now because your Inner Guru knows best.

WORK YOUR LIGHT

Put your hand on your heart, take a couple of deep breaths, and ask your Inner Guru to shed some light on your current situation.

My Inner Guru is telling me to...

△

INAUTHENTICITY NO LONGER STANDS A CHANCE

We are entering a time in history when we are moving from patriarchy to matriarchy: force to flow; masculine to masculine-and-feminine in balance. A time when inauthenticity no longer stands a chance. Gone are the days when we are rewarded for being good girls and boys, just because we stick things out, do our time, and live the life of a lemming.

Perhaps you've noticed it in your own life. Friendships that once felt like they'd last forever are drifting, relationships that you've been clinging to are hanging by a thread, it's becoming harder and harder to show up to that job every day without your heart in it, and perhaps it's getting impossible to put on that chirpy face and fake your way through the day. Or pretend to care about stuff that you don't.

Pretending takes effort. And effort leaves us depleted.

Life is throwing things at us to bring us back to the most authentic, fluid version of ourselves. Our foundations are being shaken, with only the parts of us rooted in authenticity able to survive. Relationships, jobs, friendships, things that we once took for granted are falling away.

It can be painful – change almost always is – especially when the change happens to impact the very foundations below us. The rug is being pulled and many of us have no choice but to find somewhere new to put down our roots. Somewhere the ground is fertile and the view is sweet.

The more we resist the ebbs and flows of change, the harder it gets. It's as if the tectonic plates of our lives will continue to shake until we loosen our grip, let go of the reins, and throw our hands up in the air and cry, 'I surrender.'

It's not until this moment that you can ask your soul to lead.

Amen.

WORK YOUR LIGHT

What is becoming harder and harder for you to hold on to?

What is the Universe trying to tell you?

YOUR **SOUL** KNOWS THE QUICKEST WAY **HOME**.

$\triangle$

LOOSEN YOUR GRIP

'You can only lose what you cling to.'
BUDDHA

You're either in flow with the Universe or you're not. If you're clinging to anything, you're resisting the natural flow of who you are.

The things we cling to are the things we most need to let go. The boyfriend, the coffee, the job, the friendship, the vino, the overworking, the people pleasing... whatever external thing you cling to, in an effort to feel whole or like you're enough.

The things we cling to often cover up our most vulnerable space – the one that is desperately scary to leave empty. But by keeping that space covered with something that doesn't serve us we prevent ourselves from receiving the things that will. And we cast a shadow on our light.

We cling on tightly because deep down we know that unless we control, cling to, and hold on, we feel that relationship, job, or [*insert your thing here*] might not stay on its own accord.

But in loosening our grip, we open space for the light to come in, and heal the part of us that doesn't feel whole. As *A Course In Miracles* tells us:

'Whatever we leave empty, grace will fill.'

If we can find the courage to surrender, then that thing we once clung to will either stay on its own accord or be replaced by something that is beyond any of our wildest dreams.

Loosen your grip. Grace is coming. It might be uncomfortable at first, but I promise it will be worth it in the end.

WORK YOUR LIGHT

What am I clinging to for fear of nothing coming to take its place?

△

THE WORLD NEEDS YOU CRACKED OPEN

'There's a crack in everything. That's how the light gets in.'
LEONARD COHEN

Be open to being cracked open. Wide open.

It is the difficult times that help us grow in leaps and bounds, and in ways we could only dream possible.

But first, they have to crack us open. And sometimes it hurts like hell. It's nature's way. And, whether you let it happen or not, it is going to happen. So surrender to the process and let life do its *thang*. It'll be worth it. It's how the light gets in.

△

I PRAY THAT YOU HIT ROCK BOTTOM

I pray that you hit rock bottom.

The most painful time of your life.

I pray that you feel alone. Isolated. Deserted.

And you discover that what you thought was rock bottom is
actually a ledge, so you come crashing down even further.

And as you land, you are cracked open into a million – no – a billion
pieces – and have no idea how to put them back together.

I pray that while you are down there in the depths, the
only person you have to keep you company is you.

I pray that you choose to gather up the pieces.

And with no idea how and in what order, then begin
putting them back together, one by one.

Just right.

I pray for foundations mightier than the acropolis.

And an inner light that shines so bright it dazzles the
corneas of anyone who cannot handle your bright.

I pray for skin as comfortable as a 10-year-old
tracksuit on a Saturday night.

And an inner light so bright that you can always find your way home.

I pray for the triumph of your soul.

And the return of You.

△

YOUR SUFFERING HAPPENED
FOR YOU, NOT TO YOU

As hard as it is, the things that almost break us apart are also the things that came to make us whole. To rejig things enough to get you back into alignment. To smash the pieces, which were stuck together in the first place. To shake your foundations so you build new ones that no situation or person could ever break.

So love your suffering and don't fight it. It's there to lead you back to your most authentic, biggest, brightest self.

Stand out of the way and let the Universe get to work.

WORK YOUR LIGHT

What have your greatest sufferings taught you about yourself?

△

YOU'VE BEEN TRAINING FOR THIS FOR LIFETIMES

If you don't feel ready, if you feel unprepared, I want you to know that:

**This moment right here, you've been
training for it for lifetimes.**

If you are faced with the unbearable and your heart feels like it might just rip in two, the thing I want you to know is:

**This moment right here, you've been
training for it for lifetimes.**

When your head is filled with 'Who am I to do this?' 'What happens if it doesn't work out?' and 'She's so much better than me,' the thing I want you to know is:

**This moment right here, you've been
training for it for lifetimes.**

You're more ready than you think and the sooner you act the sooner you will look back around and realize that:

**This moment right here, you've been
training for it for lifetimes.**

SHE LEFT THE OLD
STORY BEHIND
HER AND STEPPED
INTO A NEW ONCE
UPON A TIME.

△

DON'T LET IT DEFINE YOU

Don't let someone's unconscious acts define you. Chances are the healing journey spurred on by their actions will result in you being even more whole than before it happened in the first place. If it hurts like hell, take solace in knowing that any kind of cracking open is always a blessing in the end (sometimes it just takes time, if only you could see things from the view that we do).

We are all each other's mirrors, reflecting back the parts that are not whole. And, annoying as it may sound, the people who press your buttons the most are actually the ones who help you grow the most. They are a blessing. Or a curse. They can be the things that make you expand or contract. The choice is yours.

Soul mates are the people who spur on your growth like no other. Souls who agreed prior to this life to play a vital role in our expansion. When meeting a soul mate you may experience a sense of remembering or familiarity. Soul-mate relationships are not necessarily all sunshine and roses, in fact more often than not they can be extremely difficult, as sometimes, in order for us to grow, we need to experience pain.

Some are here for a moment, some for a chapter, and some for forever. Take the lesson and let go of the rest.

WORK YOUR LIGHT

What are your most difficult relationships?
Are you being called to let go of the relationship or hold on to it?
What have they taught you or are they trying to teach you?

HER INNER LIGHT ALWAYS CALLED HER HOME.

△

COME HOME TO YOURSELF

'The ache for home lives in all of us, the safe place where we can go as we are and not be questioned.'
Maya Angelou

We spend our lives searching, only to discover it was inside us all along. I'm a perpetual traveler. A searcher. Always looking for ways to grow, learn, ponder, and understand. The undercurrent of all my days on this planet has been filled with searching for that feeling of truly being at home, without even really knowing what I was searching for. I moved continents, countries, cities, and houses. To this day I have lived in over 30 homes!

I've journeyed to six out of seven continents (*Antarctica, I'm coming*) and had two jobs where traveling around the globe was my sole responsibility.

My heart has been touched by exquisite souls from many cultures and my lungs filled up with the most breathtaking views.

My spirit has flown with adventure and my mouth has dropped open in awe.

Still, despite all of these remarkable experiences, I always felt as though something was missing, that I was unable quite perfectly to find that place or person who would bring me that feeling of home.

Until I realized that the place wasn't physical and, while enhanced and made warmer by other people, it wasn't actually about anyone else in the least. It has nothing to do with bricks and mortar, beaches, mountains, forests, or skyscrapers. Like all things that truly matter, what I was searching for was within. Home is wherever I'm with me.

If you've been spending your life searching for your true home, know that it has been inside you all along.

AFFIRMATION

I am home.

△

WHEN DID YOU STOP BEING YOU?

Babies aren't afraid to shine their light and it's the reason why we can't take our eyes off them. However, as life goes on, we experience things that eventually lead us to retract or alter the way we show ourselves to the world – usually based on a belief that something must be wrong with us. We lose contact with the authentic spirit within us, which has been carefully sculpted over lifetimes, and keep our authentic light under a bushel.

WORK YOUR LIGHT

Think back to your childhood... What experiences can you remember that caused you to believe that something was wrong with you, or your authentic self was not enough? How old were you? What happened?

How did it make you feel?

Ask that younger version of you what they need to hear to feel loved and supported.

△

YOU ARE ALREADY DOING IT

The person you are trying to let go of.
That heartbreak that feels too big to bear.
You're already doing it,
And you are closer than you think.

The sadness that weighs on your shoulders.
The heaviness that sits like an elephant on your chest.
Breath by breath, you are moving through it,
And you are closer than you think.

The person you are praying to forgive.
That grief you are desperate to release.
You're already doing it,
And you're closer than you think.

The person you admire.
The woman you long to become.
You are her and she is you,
And you are closer than you think.

The vision you are striving towards.
That dream that feels out of reach.
You're already doing it,
And you're closer than you think.

The end will be unrecognizable from the picture in your head,
But you'll know it when you get there by the way you feel in your skin.

△

FILL YOURSELF UP

You are no use to anyone, if you are running on empty.

I used to feel guilty and selfish for putting myself first, and following those things that nourished my spirit. One day I remember working at home and my housemate Dana found me watching *Private Practice* while eating my lunch. *Addison Montgomery, I love you.*

Even though I had been working incredibly long days to get my business off the ground, I still felt guilty that I'd been 'caught' doing something that filled me up instead of working hard.

I didn't realize how much more I was able to give to others by filling up myself first. That little fact changed everything.

I've always known that fresh flowers light me up more than most things on the planet. But I spent many years waiting for someone else to buy them for me (how stupid was that). I got a bunch here and there, but on the whole the flowers didn't come.

Then I made a decision to give myself a weekly budget to buy the most gorgeous flowers I could find. So every Saturday I would take myself to the florist and pick my bunch. It felt fabulously extravagant.

At first I only let myself choose those that were good value. But then I stretched myself and bought the ones that lit me up the most. Before long, I had embarked on a deep love affair with the peony. Those flowers healed my heart more than anything else. The way they courageously open is breathtaking. And just when you think they can't open any further, they go and open some more.

Since making that simple decision to give my heart what it needs – beauty – my house has always been filled with the most beautiful flowers. It's a weekly ritual and worth every cent because when I look at them, my heart opens, my face softens, and light comes flooding in.

And the most fabulous thing is that once I started giving myself flowers I started receiving them too! The other day my fiancé, Craig, even surprised me with a subscription to Petalon, where they hand deliver a bunch of flowers, chosen especially for me, to my door every Wednesday!

Right now, as I sit writing this, I have a smile spread across my face because I'm sitting in the Queen's Rose Garden in Regent's Park in London surrounded by a kaleidoscope of thousands of beautiful roses inspiring me as I type. I am filled up and so my light effortlessly spills onto the pages.

The moment we stop nurturing and filling ourselves up, things just don't flow quite the same.

What nourishes you will be different from the next person. For my friend Amy Firth, it's knitting, Skyping her family, and playing music. For my Mum, it's walking along the beach, making things beautiful, and gardening. For my friend Jaqui Kolek, it's reading trashy magazines, getting a mani-pedi, and Vegemite on toast. The more you fill yourself up, the more you have to share with others

WORK YOUR LIGHT

Write a list of all the things that fill you up.

Pick one thing off the list that you can commit to giving yourself today.

△

WE ALL JUST WANT TO BE SEEN

We all just want to be seen, like really seen. Not glanced over and noticed, but for someone to take a moment and really witness the authentic light that flickers just beneath the surface. But we go about our lives, bumping into each other and not taking the time to stop and look.

The most intimate experience of my life was with a 50-year-old Croatian woman I had known for 5 minutes. I didn't even know her name. We met during a workshop led by Juilliard voice coach, Claude Stein. We were mostly a room full of strangers, and he instructed us to turn to the person next to us and look deeply into their eyes. *Like REALLY look into their eyes.* And witness the gorgeous soul standing directly in front of us. And at the same time, let that person truly see us. The real us. The deeper us. The us that we hadn't shown anyone before.

Before long, and without exchanging a word, my gorgeous partner and I began to sob. Deeply. It was unlike any other experience of my life. Precious. Sacred. A gift. It felt as though I was being truly seen for the first time in my life. I was humbled and overwhelmed by the beauty of the person before me, who until that point I hadn't even paused to notice. We carried on like this for 10 minutes. It was one of the best 10 minutes of my life.

After the exercise was over we hugged and looked around the room and there wasn't a dry eye in the house. I found out her name was Sanja, and she is now a true friend and part of my mastermind group.

This experience has been etched on my heart ever since, and made me understand that every human on the planet – no matter how soft or how hard, how open, or closed – just wants to be seen. *Like really seen.*

The greatest gift we can give another person is to witness truly their being here.

To see deeply and acknowledge the sacred soul that dwells within them and is longing to emerge.

After this, I came to realize how pretty much every problematic relationship I'd ever experienced was a result of either not being seen accurately or not seeing the other person accurately.

It brought to light how much of my life I'd spent holding back my biggest, truest, most authentic self, while secretly hoping someone else might see it. Spot it. Name it and call it forward. I'd spent so long keeping my light dimmed, while deep down hoping that someone would acknowledge all of the immense beauty that bubbled just below the surface. It dawned on me that I had spent too many years waiting for acknowledgment and permission for my brightest, most exuberant self to emerge.

That day marked the beginning of my conscious journey towards seeing the authentic light in other people and shining my own a little more brightly.

You have an authentic inner light, which has always been there and will never go away. An inner fire that no matter how dark it gets will continue flickering.

People can see it just by looking at you. It's that 'something special' that they see. It's that 'spark,' that 'twinkle' in your eyes.

Your light is your authentic self and you were born to shine it. You can't hide a light.

WORK YOUR LIGHT

Your presence is a gift. Rather than going through the motions, be truly present and let someone truly witness you today.

YOU CAN'T
HIDE A LIGHT.

△

SEE THE LIGHT IN OTHERS

'See the light in others, and treat them as if it's all you see.'
WAYNE DYER

One of the greatest offerings we can give another person is to witness truly their gifts. When we witness the gifts of another, we are actually witnessing the soul and light in them.

Such a simple and effortless act can have a life-changing impact. When we acknowledge the gifts of another, we raise them up and encourage them to shine a little bit brighter. This act not only feels wonderful, but it is impossible to do and not light up too.

WORK YOUR LIGHT

Light up someone's day today by truly witnessing them and acknowledging one of their gifts.

△

THE FEAR OF BEING SEEN

We have experiences, often stemming from childhood, where we decided that our authentic self was not enough. A significant moment when we decided that it was safer/easier/less painful to shine a little less. We decided to dim to fit in.

We don't need to have a conscious memory of these experiences for them still to affect us today. Our soul carries imprints from lifetime to lifetime, which hold wisdom gained from lessons learned, as well as past traumas that are waiting to be healed.

We are here to heal those traumas that are standing in our way and preventing us from stepping into our most authentic selves. When we step into our authentic power, we are unafraid of letting our biggest authentic self be seen, regardless of who is in front of us.

WORK YOUR LIGHT

Think back to a point in your life when you consciously decided that who you were wasn't enough. What happened? What does this younger version of you need to hear now?

△

DON'T DIM TO FIT IN

Don't dim your light to accommodate someone else's smallness. We are all born to shine big and bright. The Universe is expanding and you are part of the Universe, so expanding is part of your nature.

If someone makes you want to retract, notice, and slowly back away, they are not for you and you are not for them. Or better yet, find it within yourself to expand and shine your light anyway.

Flowers don't open and close according to who is walking by. They open and show their beauty regardless.

Light up no matter who is around you. When you do, you make it easier for your people to find you. And if others don't want to be around you, or you make them feel uncomfortable, it's because you are shining light on the fact that they are dimming to fit in themselves. And by you choosing to shine bright you may just inspire them to turn on their light too. Or not. Keep your light on anyway, and watch as life shines right back at you.

△

PEOPLE WHO CAN'T HANDLE
YOUR BRIGHT

If you have kept your bigness restrained and your light dimmed, chances are the people in your life have gotten used to that.

All relationships are essentially an energetic agreement. Some are built around one person shining, others around two people shining at the same level, and others around two people happy for the other freely to shine bright (*the best kind*).

The moment one person decides to start rising up and allowing their light to shine, it changes the energetic agreement and can create some waves. That's completely normal.

Choose to shine anyway.

The relationships that are meant to last will adapt to the change in energy. Others won't. But that's because they were likely born under the proviso of 'I love you as long as you don't shine more brightly than me.' That's OK, not all people are meant to be in your life forever. But the lessons they teach us can still live on.

WORK YOUR LIGHT

Who in your life raises you up, wants you to win
and is genuinely happy when you shine?

Who in your life can't hack it if you shine more brightly than them?

△

MIRRORS

In order for other people to acknowledge us, first we need to acknowledge ourselves. The people in our lives are merely mirrors reflecting back to us what we believe about the Universe and ourselves. Mirrors reflecting back to us our shadow and our light.

If you are not feeling supported, maybe you are not supporting yourself. If people are not recognizing the beauty in you, it's likely to be because you are not recognizing the beauty in yourself. If people are not acknowledging your musical talents, perhaps you are not acknowledging them yourself. If people are not giving you the time of day, it's because you are not giving it to yourself.

WORK YOUR LIGHT

Look in the mirror and really see yourself as if seeing yourself for the first time. Look deeply into your eyes and ask yourself:

What am I not seeing in myself that longs to be seen?

△

YOU ARE THE HEROINE OF YOUR LIFE

You are the heroine of your life. If not you, then who? We are each writing our own story with us as the lead character.

The moment we realize that we write our own story is the moment we realize that we have control to do a rewrite. And unlike most movies, with you, the sequel is likely to be even better than the first.

In the depths of moving out of the apartment I had shared with my ex, I played back-to-back movies on my laptop while I packed up the house. I was feeling very sorry for myself, and when my friend Sheila called I burst into tears. She asked what had brought it on.

I thought back and said, 'Well, I've been watching an awful lot of Meryl Streep and Susan Sarandon films, which I adore, but they are always quite emotional.'

We then dug deeper and deeper to realize that all of my favorite films have a strong independent female lead that gives and gives but still ends up alone: *Stepmom, Thelma and Louise, Sophie's Choice, It's Complicated...* BINGO! My favorite kind of film was how I was living my life. As hard as it was, I banned myself from watching strong female lead dramas and decided to write a new story for myself.

WORK YOUR LIGHT

Take note which films you choose to consume and what archetype the hero or heroine embodies, then ask:

What kind of movie am I currently starring in? Is it

a drama or an adventure? A musical or a comedy?
A saga or a life-affirming inspirational?

What kind of movie do I want to be starring in?

What qualities does the main character
of that movie need to possess?

△

WHO AM I?

'Beauty begins the moment you decide to be yourself.'
Coco Chanel

I'm a massive Oprah fan. When I first moved to London I lived with my friend Jaqui from university. We would spend our hangovers (*of which there were many*) watching Oprah's 25th Anniversary box set on repeat. We'd joke, 'Do you reckon Oprah and Gayle get hungover and question themselves like us?'

Jaqui would roll down the stairs in her favorite hangover T-shirt with 'Who am I?' splashed across the front. And that pretty much summed up how I felt during those years.

Back to the box set... The most moving moment for me was when Oprah told the story of a woman saying to her, 'Watching you be you makes me want to be more me.'

Those words continued to sit in my heart. Like many people in their twenties, I attached who I was to what I did, the roles I played, and the things I had learned to be good at, rather than following what lit me up (e.g. the hard worker, the ambitious creative, the daughter, the friend, the supportive girlfriend). But that wasn't who I really was... I could feel so much more inside of me that was bursting to come out.

Looking back I can join the dots and survey the signs of my life. But in those days (*especially the hungover ones*) I felt alone and lost. I was so attached to what other people thought that I didn't let my real self emerge.

The only thing missing was me.

PRAYER

Divine Mother, thank you for helping me remember the truth of who I am, especially when it is different from the truth of who I thought I was.

△

WHO ARE YOU?

Our instant response to this question is usually to list off name, age, sex, occupation, where we were born, where we live, relationship status, blah, blah, blah...

But that's not who we are. Not really. So we dig a little deeper and describe who we are based on our personality and things that the world has said about us: I'm a hard worker, I'm a good friend, I'm ambitious, I'm social, I'm creative, I'm a good cook....

But that's not who we are, or who we really came here to be. There's so much more to us than that. Secret parts that long to be expressed beyond the box that we have been put into or keep ourselves inside.

When we peel back the layers over and over again, we are able to find the wisdom and truth of our being, the essence that we are here to share. This is your magic, your gift to the world.

The part of you that is timeless and knows exactly what lights it up. The part of you that is expansive and waiting for you to remember, to discover, to unlock, and set it free.

WORK YOUR LIGHT

Standing in front of a mirror, look deeply into your eyes and ask the part of you that knows, 'Who am I?'

Allow it to answer. What you receive doesn't have to make sense as the purpose here is to peel back the layers and let your deeper self emerge. Keep repeating this question and response over and over again.

You may start by saying, 'I am a mother,' 'I am a daughter,' 'I am a hard worker,' 'I am a nurturer,' 'I am a fantastic listener,' 'I am wise,' 'I am love,' 'I am a tribal leader,' 'I am a mystic,' 'I am ready to rise up,' 'I am grace.'

Be open to being surprised. Peel back the layers and let your deepest self emerge.

Δ

ASK THE PART OF YOU THAT KNOWS

There's a part of you that knows the answer to everything you seek: your path, your purpose, which direction to move in, and exactly when to leap.

Before you incarnated, it received a mandate from spirit and, upon hearing this request, this part of you jumped right on in and couldn't wait to begin.

Willing to be ignored time and time again, the part of you that knows vowed never to give up, no matter how long it takes.

The part of you who knows, knows that you are in exactly the right place to do everything that you set out to do.

For the part of you who knows also knows that deep down you know too.

You're ready.

You know the next step.

The part of you who knows is calling you right now and wanting you to get ready to leap.

△

LEAP INTO YOURSELF

*'Don't dance around the perimeter of
the person you want to be.'*
GABRIELLE BERNSTEIN

Leap.

Take the plunge.

Don't waver.

Dive right in.

Into your wholeness.

Your You-ness.

Contradictions, imperfections, oddness, fabulousness, and all.

In doing so, sure you may find that you don't quite fit in, but that's just because in stepping into your bigness you might just need a little more room.

WORK YOUR LIGHT

How can you leap more into yourself?

THINK WITH
YOUR SOUL.

$\triangle$

FACE THE NIGGLE

That niggling feeling.

That annoying, niggling feeling.

That inconvenient, annoying, niggling feeling.

Try as you might, it's there. And it ain't going anywhere.

I spent years ignoring niggling feelings. Throwing my best dollops of stubbornness, ego, post-rationalization, and numbing-out at them. It's exhausting. And until you face it, life just throws you more bait to awaken the niggle. To draw your attention to the light within you that is bursting to come out.

Face the niggle now.

The niggle is your soul tugging at your sleeve, doing its best to get your attention before it has to turn up the heat. Listen now, if you don't face the niggle, the Universe will throw something in your path. And then you will regret that you didn't answer the niggle in the first place – *LOL*.

WORK YOUR LIGHT

What is your niggling feeling trying to tell you?

Who are you here to be?

FOLLOW YOUR INTUITION – ESPECIALLY WHEN IT DOESN'T MAKE SENSE.

△

ANSWER THE ACHE

We each have within us an aching that is craving to be met. It's not a physical ache and it isn't a mental one. It's much deeper than either of those.

We came into this life with it and, if it's not tended to, it will be right there when we die. It drives our deepest desires (our best decisions and our worst). It's lying beside us when we wake up in the night and while we make a cup of tea. It's there through the highs and all of the lows. The ache is your soul calling, and no matter what you do to ignore it, numb it out, or die it down, it will never go away.

Until we take the time to invite it to sit down and share with us, we will always feel a little uncomfortable. A touch off-kilter. Like something isn't quite right. Answer the ache.

WORK YOUR LIGHT

What is your soul aching for?

What is your soul trying to tell you?

What small thing can you do to answer that ache today?

△

YOU ARE NOT GOING TO MISS YOUR LIFE

The only way to miss your life is to spend it thinking that you are going to miss it. There is no right way, perfect answer, or correct road to take.

Work it out as you go and then you just dance extra quick.

It's just as important to get it wrong, as it is to get it right. In fact, getting it wrong is often a prerequisite for getting it right. Your stuff-ups, your fails, your confusion, your despair. All of these things make up *your* path less trodden.

Be OK with putting your hands up in the air and saying, 'I have no freaking idea where this is all leading.'

Take a deep, deep breath and walk ahead anyway.

WORK YOUR LIGHT

If you weren't afraid, what would you do?

Δ

MY SOUL IS CALLING ME TO...

Part III

WORK
YOUR
LIGHT

Answering your soul's callings

IF NOT YOU, WHO? IF NOT NOW, WHEN?

EMMA WATSON

△

YOUR SOUL IS ALWAYS CALLING

You're never too old to answer your calling and it can never be too late. For the truth of the matter is that your soul is always calling, it was calling yesterday, it is calling today, and it will be calling next week.

Answering the calling of your soul isn't a one-time act; it's a perpetual conversation. It's not actually about doing one big thing, or finding one single answer to the great big question: 'What is my purpose?' It's doing hundreds and thousands of little things in that direction, one after the other. It's through following each and every little call – a step here and a leap there – that we find ourselves living the life we are called to live.

Once we find this higher calling it seems like it 'just happened,' but in reality it has been in the process of happening for ages. Your soul knows your path.

Keep listening to, and acting on, the whispers each and every day and before you know it you'll be well on your way.

Your soul is always gently pointing you in the right direction, and subtly edging you closer towards the things that light you up. If you wait to find out exactly where your path is heading before you act, you will never experience the bliss of walking your path.

WHAT IS YOUR SOUL CALLING YOU TO DO RIGHT NOW?

Δ

IT'S HARDER TO IGNORE A
CALL THAN TO ANSWER IT

If this book has made its way into your hands, it's probably because your soul spoke and you responded. It doesn't matter if you bought it yourself, it fell off the shelf, or someone gave it to you.

The soul speaks in feelings, in longings, in yearnings, in deep knowing, in vibration, in signs, in nature, in people. It centers itself in the heart, and carries within it a blueprint for your life. You can't hear the calling of your soul if you don't create space in your day to listen to it.

The best way I've found to connect with the voice of the soul is regular meditation. I'm not talking just walking or doing something that is meditative, but rather sitting down and truly listening – every single day. Your soul has secrets to share, but you need to carve out the time and space to hear them before you can act on them.

Once the voice of the soul has been heard, it cannot be unheard. Try as you might, if you ignore the calling of your soul, life becomes uncomfortable. You may find that you try to soothe that aching feeling by things in the external world. This may work for a little while, but eventually that niggling feeling comes back, and each time it does, it needs more to turn it down.

Don't waste your effort trying to ignore the call; create the space in your life to hear the daily whispers. The more you listen the louder the calling will get.

WORK YOUR LIGHT

Are you carving out time every day to listen
to the callings of your soul?

Download the Light Sourcing meditation
at www.lightisthenewblack.com

△

SOUL CALLINGS VS. THE CALLINGS OF YOUR SOUL

There is no greater gift you can receive than
to honor your calling. It's why you were born.
And how you become most truly alive.
OPRAH WINFREY

Your soul is eternally calling you in the direction of your highest path. Answering your soul's callings is not about a single revelation; rather it is a lifelong dance.

Your soul knows the way and so is always calling you in the direction of your highest path. But in order for your highest calling to be revealed you first need to act on all of the little calls along the way. It's impossible to find the bigger calling without first answering the daily callings of your soul.

Have you been holding off answering the whispers of your soul because you are trying to work out your highest calling first? (In other words, wanting to know the end destination before taking the first steps?)

WORK YOUR LIGHT

What is one small practical thing that you can do in the
next 24 hours to answer the callings of your soul?

△
YOU WERE BORN KNOWING

I want to tell you right now that whatever you are called to do, that is your calling. Following whatever lights you up is how you will light up the world. How you will most light up the world is your calling.

The world needs you lit up.

Deep down, you already know what you long for. What your soul yearns for. What you came here to do. There is nothing for you to discover, rather more of You to uncover.

To remember. To recall. To call back home.

You are in exactly the right place to answer your calling now. You don't need to know the whole plan. You don't even need to know where it is leading. You just need to take the next step.

In my Soul Readings, I have found that deep down everyone knows what they came here for. Deep down they know exactly what they long to do. Deep down, their calling is actually clearer than they could ever imagine. But the things that trip most people up are:

- Wanting to label what it is, rather than just following what lights them up.

- Looking for some kind of approval that the thing that lights them up is actually the right thing, and that they are good enough for it.

- Feeling like they have a plan of exactly how it is going to work out before they consider leaping towards it.

- Comparing themselves to other people who are already doing their things (an overnight success is never an overnight success).

No one has ever had the complete, perfect plan. There is no end destination. There is no right or wrong way to do it and you do NOT need permission from anyone else. Don't put so much pressure on yourself. Forget about the outcome, the plan, and just start now by following one thing that fills you up, that gets you out of bed and you are enthusiastic about. And then reach for another. It doesn't have to make sense – the best things never do.

As Steve Jobs said, 'It's only in looking back that the dots begin to connect,' but first, you gotta get busy creating some dots.

△

EVERYONE'S GOT A SECRET DREAM, NOT MANY HAVE A PUBLIC ONE

There is insurmountable power in stating the biggest, brightest, most daring desires of our soul out loud. It tells the Universe that we are ready and gives people the gift of helping us make it happen.

For many years Jess went about her day with her dream of being an artist hidden underneath her pillow. Not feeling ready, good enough and fearing what people would think. The moment she started sharing it, the most miraculous thing happened, everyone around her said, 'Well, of course, it's about time you made that happen.'

The people who love you will love you regardless. Those who prefer you be small might fade away, but, hey, they're not company worth keeping anyway.

WORK YOUR LIGHT

If I knew I couldn't fail I would...

If I wasn't afraid of what people would think I would...

If I didn't have to get permission I would...

If money were no object I would...

My secret dream is...

YOUR SOUL HAS ALL THE **ANSWERS**. THE ONLY WAY TO HEAR THEM IS TO **GO WITHIN**.

△

CAREER VS. CALLING

'You can lose your job but you can't lose your calling.'
MARIANNE WILLIAMSON

A job is something that you show up to every day to get paid for. Whether or not you enjoy it, a job is seen as 'work.'

A calling is something that you do because you love it and can't imagine doing anything else. It's something that you would do for free for the joy of it and sometimes it feels like this is the exact reason you were put on Earth.

A job forces you to fit into a mold. A calling expands with you.

Your calling doesn't have to be big and lofty, and it doesn't have to be your job. It might be being a supportive mother or a peace activist for the UN.

▽

My whole life I knew I wanted to touch people's hearts through my creations. I didn't know how I was going to do it, but I knew I couldn't ignore that yearning deep in my soul. My work was always my number-one priority and I chose a hardworking mother to ingrain this into me further.

Torn between spirituality, healing, writing, creativity, and business, I went to art school and then took a degree in communications, while spending my free time and money learning as much as I could about soul growth, metaphysics, life purpose, intuition, and consciousness.

I pursued a career in advertising because I knew I wanted to my ideas to reach a mass audience. But, to be completely honest, I chose it because I thought it was the most socially accepted way for me to shine my light. I was an undercover Lightworker. I convinced myself that advertising would allow me to put my energy out there, and one day, when I had 'made it,' I would be able to really change things.

Naturally ambitious, I worked day and night on ideas to impress creative directors and get my first job. The day I got the phone call offering me the position of junior creative, I was over the moon. Thinking up ideas all day long, understanding the way people think, working with famous directors, going on shoots, and being taken out to lunch… There was so much about this job that I loved, but at the end of the day that niggling feeling was waiting for me, whispering that this job was not my highest path.

Six months into the job, the company merged with another global agency and I was made redundant. Without enough perspective or experience to realize that it wasn't personal, I felt completely devastated and ashamed. My inner voice was screaming that this was my out to follow my true calling, but my ego saw leaving as an act of defeat. A month later, I found a job at another ad agency.

About five years later, having moved to London and broken into the industry there, I was exhausted and depleted. I enjoyed so much of my job, but it was energetically draining. Endeavoring to fill the space inside, I turned to coffee, food, and social drinking to keep me going. The creative department ran on fear and everyone was constantly looking over their shoulders, worried that at any moment they'd lose their job if their last ideas were not good enough. While I knew I was good at my job, I also knew there was so much more of me that was not being used. Each night I'd arrive home completely exhausted, but still feeling like there was something in my heart that had not been expressed in my job.

When I heard Marianne Williamson say, 'You can lose your job but you can't lose your calling,' I realized that instead of forging my own path, I had been trying to fit into a job-shaped box. My job was on loan to me, but my calling was something that no one could ever take away.

I looked around but couldn't see any job that fitted the mold of what I was called to do. Knowing that whatever we leave empty God will fill, I quit my job and prayed. I updated my website so it boldly stated who I was and my unique and eclectic mix of passions and gifts. These included ambitious, big-hearted, creative, on a mission to change the world through my creations, big thinking, authentic writer, lover of travel (Romany spirit), excitable, hardworking, down to earth, believer, soulful. I affirmed over and over again:

My creations uplift and inspire people all around the world. I serve the world by being me.

I kid you not, the very next week I was head-hunted for the most amazing job ever – paid to travel the world making the gray spaces brighter – with the Let's Color Project.

I had leapt and the Universe caught me. A couple of weeks later I headed off on a world trip with an amazing team of big-hearted creatives filming, photographing, and documenting the journey. We brought color to orphanages, schools, community squares, and streets. I was getting paid amazing money (double my previous salary) to use my creativity, huge heart, and adventurous spirit to make the world a more colorful place.

I had listened to the callings of my soul and I felt more alive than ever.

WORK YOUR LIGHT

Do you currently have a job or a calling?

Do you have something more in you that longs to be shared with the world?

△

YOUR TREASURE CHEST OF GIFTS

You have more gifts than you could imagine. Thousands of them, all at your fingertips. Just waiting to be unwrapped. The things that come naturally to you, the things you might not even notice because they are so innate, so inbuilt, so effortless, and so abundant. And then there are the gifts that somewhere along the way you began to doubt. The ones you chose to put in the closet, thinking that you might not be enough. You are. More than enough.

Just because you are not using your gifts right now doesn't mean they aren't there: the musician, the comic, the poet, and the dancer, the listener, the optimist, the cook, and the nurturer. The more you remember and claim these parts of you, the more effortlessly your authentic self will emerge. Your authentic self is bountiful, it's magic.

They are the things that you love doing, many of which you probably already do for free. The things that people thank and compliment you for doing. The thing you can lose hours doing because it consumes you. And just because you're happy to do them for free, doesn't mean you have to. You deserve to be rewarded for doing what brings you joy. In fact, it's increasingly becoming the most abundant way forward.

In order to light up the world, we first need to acknowledge how much of a unique gift we are to it. It doesn't matter who you are, you have more gifts than there are minutes in the day. It is the wonderful mishmash of these gifts that makes you, YOU.

This may seem overwhelming and a bit uncomfortable, but it is true. As you recognize your gifts people around you begin to notice them too, and all of a sudden you start attracting opportunities, which bring these gifts to life.

**Don't squeeze your amazingness into
a square box. Take all the space you
need and spill over the sides.**

I'd been living in London for about six months, holding out for a job at one of the top ad agencies. I'd seen creative director after creative director and they all said the same thing, 'We love your work but we don't know where to put you.' The ad industry in Australia was quite different from London. As well as having TV, film, and print experience, I had also done online films and websites. What should have been my point of difference was actually working against me, and suddenly I realized that I had been trying to fit into a London-shaped box.

I was almost out of money, but refused to take a job that wasn't my dream job, and was too proud to go home. Then, when I thought about the people that I admired most, I discovered that they didn't try to fit in to succeed, they embraced their uniqueness and forged their own path. So I wrote down all the things that were unique about me and created an affirmation, which encapsulated it all: 'I have a job that only I can do and I am rewarded beyond my wildest dreams. My creative ideas spread all over the world.'

One month later, a creative director called me out of the blue. I hadn't worked with him directly, but I'd met him over a glass of bubbly while celebrating a new business win for the ad agency. We got talking and I told him about my love for travel and he made some Australian jokes and taught me what a Scotch egg was.

He explained that the job was unique, but he thought I would be perfect for it. Hearing those words, I gave myself a high five knowing that my affirmation had called this one in!

I was to travel around the world nonstop for Skype and share my journey through writing, photography, film, and social media: five continents in 33 days, meeting amazing people, and visiting 27 cities (*pretty much all of which were on my vision board*). The only catch was that I had to do all of this while in perpetual motion (including sleeping). Extremely challenging, it was also one of the most amazing experiences of my life.

In recognizing my own gifts, and choosing not to fit into a normal-shaped box, I had attracted a job that was not only perfect for me, but also I was perfect for it. I was out of my comfort zone a lot of the time, but as a result I realized I had more gifts that I hadn't even known were there.

The old way of put your head down and just fit in is coming to an end. When we truly embrace our gifts in an unapologetic way we create a special kind of magic that is impossible to mimic. As we acknowledge our gifts, the world acknowledges them too. In the Age of Light we will all be rewarded and supported for doing what comes naturally to us, for sharing our unique gifts.

You don't necessarily need to go out and quit your job to express your gifts. When you own your gifts, your life will expand with you. Don't fit into a box that already exists. Discover more, overspill and share them all now.

MANTRA

I have a job that only I can do and I am
rewarded beyond my wildest dreams.

△

THE NEVER-ENDING GIFT LIST

Name your gifts. There are no wrong answers. It could be anything from being a good listener, to having a great sense of humor. It could be the fact that you don't beat around the bush and have a special knack for saying what you mean. It could be that you have a huge heart or are an animal lover. It could be the fact that you have beautiful handwriting or that you feel what other people are feeling. It doesn't matter what your gifts are, just that you keep uncovering them. The more you name, the more will emerge.

WORK YOUR LIGHT

Write a list of 10 of your unique and eclectic mix
of gifts now. Keep this list going and add to it as
you uncover more and more every day.

1.

2.

3.

4.

5.

6.

7.

8.

9.

10.

△

YOU DON'T HAVE TO STICK AT IT

You don't have to stick at it just because you have been sticking at it for so long. The longer you stick at something the harder it can be to let go. But no matter how long you have been clinging, holding together, slogging away, it's still going to be easier to let go today than it will be tomorrow.

You can do this.

While you might feel like the years and the struggles and all the effort will have been for nothing, I promise you the opposite is true. You will not be left with nothing and nothing is ever wasted. That inner voice that is calling you, she has no plans to let up. Drown her out all you like, but there she'll be sitting on your chest the moment you wake up.

She wants the best for you.

Listen to her whispers, her gnawing and her cries. She can see the vista coming up ahead, and there's a reason she won't give you a reprieve. The only way to stop her nagging, her kicking, and her screaming is to loosen your grip.

Trust, surrender, let go, give in.

The lead-up to surrendering might take an awful long time. But once the act is done, what is meant for you will come to you immediately. And then you'll wonder why you didn't act sooner in the first place.

WORK YOUR LIGHT

What are you sticking at just because
you've been sticking at it so long?

△

A PRAYER FOR LETTING GO

Divine Mother,

May my soul be stubborn and my spirit fierce.

May I find the strength to let go when I have
nothing lined up to take its place.

May I find the courage to listen, especially
when I don't like what I hear.

And when I pretend I can't hear you, please
speak up louder than before...

For that is when I need you most.

Thank you. And so it is.

△

SHADOW CALLINGS

Everyone has a calling but not everyone has the courage to answer it. In fact, most people ignore their calling completely. The fact that you are reading this book is a pretty awesome feat.

Drawing inspiration from Julia Cameron's concept of the shadow artist, a 'shadow calling' is when we don't have the courage to answer our highest calling and so settle for something halfway. It's the managers who long to sing, the film producers who want to direct, the agents who were meant for the stage, the project managers who yearn to make art, the historians who are called to make history, and the copywriters who have 10 books in them.

**Only you know if you are in a
shadow career for your soul.**

Watching from the sidelines is agony. Your gifts are there to be expressed, and if you don't actively do something with them, the Universe will find a way to coax them out of you. But it might be in a way that doesn't serve you.

Deep down I always knew that I wanted to write, create, heal, and uplift. I found myself in my shadow calling working as a copywriter in advertising. There was a lot that I loved about that job because I was getting paid to write and create. But, at the end of each day, I felt dissatisfied because I was not consciously expressing my gifts as a healer and uplifter.

And so life demanded me to be the healer and the uplifter, regardless of my career. My boyfriend had chronic depression and so I was spending a lot of my energy looking at ways to get him through that. Several of my close friends were also suffering from depression.

At the time I was working in a creative team with a guy who was a quadriplegic. I chose to work with him because he inspired me so much. Unable to move from the neck down, his glasses had a laser chip in them that was connected to his computer and he would art direct in Photoshop by moving his head. We shared an office and had nurses in every hour to give him water, feed him, change his position, and take him to the bathroom. If they weren't available I would step in. While we were working together he had to have an emergency tracheotomy, which meant that he needed help clearing his chest every hour or so. Pretty much all parts of my life demanded that I be the uplifter. But I was running on empty, so it was exhausting.

Now I see that all of this was the Universe trying to wake me up to my path and this period of my life was a blessing.

The longer you stay in a situation that doesn't fit, the harder it is to take a leap towards your highest calling. I know it's difficult when you've worked so hard at something and how letting all of that go is a scary prospect. But in the end, it won't be as scary and hard as you think. Nothing is ever wasted. The sooner you leap, the sooner you will look back at this moment and say, 'I'm *so* glad that I found the courage to leap.'

WORK YOUR LIGHT

Are you in a shadow calling or your true calling?
What is your soul calling you to do?

△

SHAKE IT OFF

It's easy to get stuck in the trap of doing something just because you're good at it. Or just because you've spent a lot of time being good at it and are afraid of letting it go.

The more capable you are at doing things, the harder it is to differentiate your natural gifts from the ones that you've learned or forced yourself to be good at – especially if your motivation is approval.

WORK YOUR LIGHT

What have you learned to be good at that you don't enjoy?

△

MULTIPLE CALLINGS

'Where would you have me go?
What would you have me do?
What would you have me say, and to whom?'
A COURSE IN MIRACLES

We need more conscious people in power in all pockets of society. Perhaps you were called to work in one particular industry and then another. Don't be hard on yourself if you find that overnight you feel called to do something else. Nothing is ever wasted. Remember, your soul is always calling, every single moment of the day; it's not a one-time deal.

When we devote our lives to being of service, we will always be led. It doesn't mean that you had it wrong before. All that matters is that you listen, trust, and act on the call today. When you do that, all that has been held back will be delivered to you and you will be supported every step of the way.

WORK YOUR LIGHT

What do you feel called to do right now?

△

THE DOTS JOIN IN THE END

It wasn't till two weeks ago that the dots finally joined for me about being a writer. I was in Paris with my parents, who were visiting from Australia. Knowing that I was going to be writing this book, my mum brought over a children's book I wrote when I was 13 for a school assignment.

Later on, I eavesdropped as Mum told my fiancé how she always knew I would be a writer, as I was always really good at expressing my feelings in a way that I couldn't do out loud.

She spoke of how I was unable get the depths of my feelings out of my mouth, especially during an argument. Unable to find the words to explain how I was feeling I'd often end up in tears. I hated it and would run to my room, grab a pen and paper, and let my heart speak. Half an hour later my parents would get a 10-page letter slid under their door (or, if I was especially angry, slammed onto the kitchen counter) explaining what had gone on from all angles and how it made each of us feel. Mum laughed and said, 'We had no idea where she got such emotional understanding from or what to do with it. She thought about things a lot!'

The funny bit is that while Mum had always told me I was 'good with my words,' I didn't believe her. To me a writer was a good speller, a fast reader, top English student, enjoyed reading loads of different types of books, and used a vast vocabulary (*none of which are me*).

However, my whole life I've had a huge guided desire to let my heart speak. Looking back now, it's obvious that writing from my heart and experiencing feelings would be where my path would lead me. But at the time, I had no freaking idea. The dots only make sense when you can join them. But they always join in the end.

WORK YOUR LIGHT

What were you like as a child?

What came easily to you?

What did you struggle with?

How were you different from the other kids?

△

DEVOTE YOUR LIFE

What on earth would you devote your life to if you had the chance? (*You do*). A thing, a cause, lots of things, someone, something you believe in passionately, something that bugs you. Waking up every day. Long hours. Pushing through the hard. Flowing through the good.

What do you do tirelessly even when you're depleted? Especially when you're depleted. What brings you back to life?

What do you do when no one's looking? What do you want to be known for? What one thing do you want to change? What would you still do, if you were the only person left on the planet?

WORK YOUR LIGHT

If you had to devote your life to one thing, what would it be?

THE MEANING OF LIFE IS TO **FIND YOUR GIFT.** THE PURPOSE OF LIFE IS TO **GIVE IT AWAY.**

PABLO PICASSO

Δ

ASK THE PART OF YOU THAT KNOWS

Who are your heroes? What do they do for a living?

What topic can you never get enough information about?

What are you passionate about?

What comes naturally to you?

What do people thank you for?

What do you love doing more than anything else?

What is your favorite quote?

What annoys you most in the world?

What's your secret dream?

What could you talk about all night long without knowing where the time went?

What would you get out of bed for at 6 a.m. on a Sunday?

If you had to do a TED talk and you knew it would be an awesome success, what would it be about?

What are most of your books about?

If you didn't care what people thought, what would you do?

If you could start your career all over again, what would you do?

If you had five years left before you die, what would you do?

What would you like to be when you grow up?

If you could go back to the day you left school, what would you choose to do for a career?

If your 88-year-old self were giving you advice, what would they say?

If your eight-year-old self were giving you advice, what would they say?

What is your soul calling you to do right now?

What are you going to do about it?

Δ

WHAT LIGHTS YOU UP?

*'The things you are passionate about are
not random, they are your calling.'*
FABIENNE FREDRICKSON

We light up the world by following what lights us up. What lights you up will be completely different from what lights me up. There are no wrong paths, no whopping mistakes, no complete day-by-day life plan etched into stone by the big G. We are here to share the unique gifts that we all possess. There is no big secret to uncover, no contract which says 'You will do x, after that you will do y, and straight after that you will do z.' We don't discover our soul calling, we uncover it by following the trail of things that light us up and then lose ourselves in the doing.

If you love smelling flowers, smell flowers. If you love writing, start writing. If you love organizing events, put on a show. If you love making art, get out the pastels. If you love raw food, start chopping. If you love taking pictures, snap happy. If you love dancing to classical music with a beat, give me a high kick. Don't feel like you can only do one thing. Give your multi-dimensional soul what it craves. Do them all.

Don't do it for a reason or an end goal, do it because you love doing it. Follow it without knowing where it will lead.

When you follow what you love, the Universe will pick up on your expanded feelings and send you more things to match your newly found expansion.

Following the things that lit me up, I discovered that I loved taking photos, making things beautiful, surrounding myself with nature, but mostly sharing the whispers of my soul through writing. I wasn't writing to tell someone anything, I was writing to feel connected with my soul. I gave myself permission to play with these things every single day (not because I wanted to create something in particular but just because I let myself play).

One day, while walking in Holland Park, I heard my soul whisper and wrote it down in my Moleskine with my favorite black Sharpie. I then took a beautiful photo of me holding the notebook with my big turquoise ring in the shot, and some peonies in the background. I posted the pic onto Instagram along with a bunch of words that came flowing through me. I wasn't writing for someone else, I was writing for myself. I felt light, energized, expanded, and such joy.

So I did it again the next day. And then the next. And then the next. Before I knew it, I had stumbled upon what I now call #RebeccaThoughts, which I post regularly on my social media and blog. Writing these is such a huge pleasure; I could do it for hours and hours on end. When I write them I go into a place where time does not exist, I lose myself and a higher presence steps in. Anyway, #RebeccaThoughts then turned into my free 'Instant Guidance Oracle' on my website.

Over time, after showing up to this joyful practice every day, my own unique writing style started to emerge. And so I wrote every day, for 10 minutes at first, then 20, then 30, then for hours on end. I started getting paid to write channeled #RebeccaThoughts for other people.

I continued to show up and they turned into chapters of this book. What started as a 5-minute bit of play for the pure enjoyment of it is now a full-time job. And it only emerged because I kept following what lit me up without being attached to the outcome.

Start small and follow the invisible trail of the things you love; before you know it you will land smack bang in the middle of your calling.

WORK YOUR LIGHT

So, what lights you up? What do you love doing that
makes you feel joyful, inspired, enthusiastic and light?

1.

2.

3.

4.

5.

6.

7.

8.

9.

10.

Forge out a chunk of time every day to do one of these things, or
maybe even combine them. The trick is to play, don't be attached
to the end point, just enjoy the things that light you up.

FOLLOW WHAT **LIGHTS YOU UP** AND YOU'LL **LIGHT UP THE** WORLD.

△

WILL IT LIGHT YOU UP?

'Run my dear,
From anything
That may not strengthen
Your precious budding wings.'
HAFIZ

Every decision we make either takes us closer or further away from ourselves. Often it's hard to tune in to the subtle energy, but deep down everything is either a 'yes' or a 'no.' Feel good or feel not as good. Brightness or darkness. Avoidance or coming home.

WORK YOUR LIGHT

Next time you are faced with a decision
ask yourself the simple question:

Which solution lights me up?

△

YOU ARE YOUR HEROES

If there is anything that any human being in all of time has done, you have everything in you to do it too. You are drawn to the people you admire because you recognize something in them that is also in you. That thing you see in the people you admire most is the exact thing that your soul most wants you to express.

One of the biggest 'aha' moments of my life was when I heard Maya Angelou talk about Terence, a playwright from around 150 BC, who wrote.

I am a human being, I consider nothing that is human alien to me.

Up until then I had looked up to my teachers, my heroes, my bosses, and the leaders who came before me with what can only be described as unhealthy admiration. I put them on an unreachable pedestal as if they were above me, as if they had something that I aspired to have... And maybe just maybe if I worked hard enough at embodying the characteristics they had, then one day I might be as good.

But drinking in Maya Angelou's soothing voice I realized that my heroes, phenomenal women – such as Oprah, Sonia Choquette, Elizabeth Gilbert, Miranda MacPherson and Maya Angelou herself – were not separate from me. The reason I admired them was because they actually embodied some of the qualities that I already had deep within my being, I just hadn't allowed myself to express them yet.

They were devoted, courageous, authentic, empathetic, healers, resilient, full of grace, powerful, adventurous, artists, mystics, daring, strong, intuitive, wholehearted, leaders, motherly.

The only difference between them and me was experience and that they were bravely shining their unique light in their own unique way and their ego was not in the way. They owned the qualities that I was being called to start tapping into. The moment I realized that, the easier it was to get out of my own way, to start letting it flow through me and do it in a way that only I could.

WORK YOUR LIGHT

Write a list of the five people you admire most, your heroes.

1.

2.

3.

4.

5.

Now write down the three qualities you admire most about each of them.

1.

2.

3.

These qualities already exist within you.

How can you start expressing them in your life today?

THE WORLD
WILL ONLY
**ACKNOWLEDGE
YOU** TO THE
DEGREE THAT YOU
**ACKNOWLEDGE
YOURSELF**.

△

ACKNOWLEDGE YOU

'It's better to be in the arena, getting stomped by the bull,
than to be up in the stands or out in the parking lot.'
STEVEN PRESSFIELD

You are already all the things that you long to be. Until you stop and acknowledge all that you already are, the world will continue to match your longing for permission with circumstances that delay giving you the go-ahead. All that you dream of, all that you yearn for, and all that you long for, you already are. Sure, some of the things that come along with being that thing may not be present, but that's because we seek a power outside of ourselves to give us permission to be what we already are. Stop wishing, start believing. Live like you already are it (because you are).

If you long to be a writer, it's because you already are a writer. If you long to be an artist, it's because you already are an artist. If you long to be a mother, it's because you already are a mother (regardless of whether you have children or not). If you long to be a healer, it's because you already are a healer. If you long to be a singer, it's because you already are a singer.

Whatever you long for, you already are.

State out loud who you are today. And just show up. Write. Create. Nurture. Heal. Sing. By showing up every day the longing to be expressed will turn into claiming who you truly are, because what yearns to be expressed is who you truly are.

WORK YOUR LIGHT

What do you secretly long to be?
For example, I long to be an artist.

How can you start acting like you already are
it? For example, I will paint every day.

△

THERE'S NO PLACE LIKE HOME

Dorothy's journey in *The Wizard of Oz* is one we all take through life. We search north, south, east, and west only to discover that the very thing we were looking for was inside us all along. The same goes for searching for our callings.

The Scarecrow, the Tin Man, and the Lion all feel they are lacking the one thing that would make them feel whole and purposeful. Scarecrow thinks he doesn't have a brain, Tin Man struggles over his lack of heart, and the Lion believes he doesn't have courage. However, the Scarecrow is actually the smartest of them all, the Tin Man oozes compassion and the Lion has the most courageous heart.

They believe that they must ask the all-powerful Wizard how they can possess these qualities (seeking permission, approval, and validation from an external force). As the journey unfolds it's the exact quality in each of them that gets them to their destination. The Wizard then 'reveals' these traits and their true callings. Scarecrow becomes the wise ruler of The Emerald City, Tin Man a compassionate leader, and the Lion a courageous King.

Often the exact thing we feel we lack is the thing that we already have within us; it's our gift, but our fears are manning the gate.

WORK YOUR LIGHT

What do you think you lack?

Is that true?

△

YOUR GREATEST FEAR IS THE GATEKEEPER TO YOUR HIGHEST CALLING

'Rule of thumb: The more important a call
or action is to our soul's evolution, the more
Resistance we will feel toward pursuing it.'
STEVEN PRESSFIELD

Our highest calling is tightly nestled right behind our core fear. As Steven Pressfield says, 'The higher your calling, the more fear you probably have around it.' Annoying but true!

When we step into our biggest, brightest, most expanded self, our core fear is always triggered. Core fears are triggered by a childhood experience, and our ego uses these experiences as evidence that we are separate and alone in this world.

You are not separate. You are not alone.

The ego then creates a script, which plays round and round in our head. By understanding what our ego's script is telling us, we can stop the fear in its track and lessen the power it has over us. Some examples of ego scripts might be:

- 'I'm not good enough.'

- 'I'm bad.'

- 'I'm unworthy.'

- 'I'm all alone.'

- 'There's something wrong with me.'

- 'Everyone abandons me.'

- 'I should be ashamed.'

- 'I'm unlovable.'

- 'I'm nothing.'

- 'It's not safe to be me.'

Which one do you relate to most? Can you track it back to a childhood experience? What's the first time that you recall feeling like this?

The more conscious we are, the less power our core fear and ego's script have on us over time.

My core fear is around rejection with the scripts of 'I'm not good enough' and 'it's not safe to be me.' It was triggered when I was about eight years old after being kicked out of my friendship group at school. What was quite a normal childhood experience had a traumatic impact on me. All of a sudden, the way I saw the world changed and my ego script started playing. Looking back, it's this fear of rejection that caused me to go into my spiritual closet and hold off answering my calling.

And so, when I seriously decided to follow my calling, this fear raised its head – BIG TIME. In fact, any time I answer the call of my soul to expand, I can feel it coming, and a voice in my head saying, 'Hey guuuuurl, who do you think you are?'

But now when it comes I know I'm onto something good. So I let myself feel the fear, state it out loud (either to myself, or even better, a good friend). I then ask my younger self (who first experienced the trauma) what she needs to hear to feel supported.

If you notice your fear coming up, it's actually a good sign that you're stretching yourself in the right direction. If you were playing it safe and ignoring your calling, the ego would have nothing to lose. As you step into your bigness and make the choice to expand, your fears will raise their head.

Think of your fears as *opportunities* to expand, rather than things that are holding you back. If you look at your fears in this light then, as uncomfortable as it might feel, it's actually a sign that you are on the right track.

My teachers always taught me that if you're not uncomfortable, you're probably not growing. And the whole point of us being here is to grow. When fear comes up, give yourself a high five and say 'YES' to expansion.

WORK YOUR LIGHT

Look at the ego script examples (see pages 144–145), and ask, 'What is my core fear?'

Allow yourself to feel that feeling in your body and go back to your first memory of it. It doesn't have to be a conscious memory, it could just be a feeling and an age.

Ask your younger self, 'What do I need to hear to feel safe, loved, and supported?'

Now say this to yourself, as this is probably what you need to hear now.

The next time you feel fear coming up, give yourself a high five and then ask this younger version of you what it needs to feel safe, loved, and supported.

△

IF I WASN'T AFRAID I WOULD...

1.

2.

3.

4.

5.

6.

7.

8.

9.

10.

(See all those things? Do them, do them now.)

△

A PRAYER FOR EXPANSION

Beloved Council of Light,

Guide my hands, my heart, my mouth, and my feet.

When I start clinging, remind me to surrender.

When I ignore you, speak up louder than before.

When I make it about me, help me get out of my own way.

When I am fearful, let me see my fears as opportunities to expand.

Thank you for working through me throughout my day.

And so it is.

△

WHAT'S THE WORST THAT COULD HAPPEN?

It's scary to let go of all that we know against the hope of something we want to call in. And it's normal to feel anxious at the thought of letting go of what we know for sure.

So many of my clients tell me that they want to leave their corporate jobs, but are so petrified of leaping that they forget what they are leaping from. When asked, 'What's the worst-case scenario?' their response is generally, 'It won't work out and I will have to go back to this career.'

In other words, if, for some reason, their best possible outcome doesn't work out, the worst possible outcome would involve them being in the situation they're in right now.

They are so scared of the fear of the worst-case scenario that they don't realize that they are actually already in it.

Life bends for the courageous. The Universe wants to support you.

Take a deep breath and leap.

WORK YOUR LIGHT

What are you called to do that scares you?

If you don't do it will you regret it in 10 years?

What's the worst thing that could happen, if you leap?

What's the worst thing that could happen, if you stay put?

△

FIVE PEOPLE

Jim Rohn said, 'You are the average of the five people you spend the most time with.' Which is a pretty powerful statement when you think about it.

Vibrationally speaking, if you have a group of people, the highest vibration and the lowest vibration will always cancel each other out. So, if you are constantly spending time with people who bring you down, you will be brought down. If you are spending most of your waking hours with people who don't take your dreams and beliefs seriously, you are more likely to start doubting them too. Likewise, if you surround yourself with people who think anything is possible, it will rub off.

When we are on the spiritual path, we are in a constant state of growth. This can mean that we outgrow relationships that were once a big part of our lives. When this happens it's hard not to cling on. However, the tighter we try to hold on to people who are no longer an energetic match with the life we are called to live, the further away from our true path and our true selves we stray (and the further they stray from theirs).

Letting go of relationships that no longer serve us doesn't signify a lack of love, rather the opposite. There are times when we need to let go and leave space for new people to come in. Some people come into our lives for a moment, some for a chapter, and some for a lifetime.

If you follow your true path you will never be alone, for it will be filled with people who are walking right alongside you.

WORK YOUR LIGHT

Write down the names of the five people you
currently spend the most time with.

1.

2.

3.

4.

5.

Do these five people represent and encourage your biggest self?

Do they make you expand or contract?

Do they make you feel free or trapped?

Do they inspire you or bore you?

Do they challenge you to grow?

Do they support you?

Are they happy when you win?

Do they believe and value similar things?

Do they encourage you to shine?

Are they aligned with the life you are consciously creating?

△

ASK THE PART OF YOU THAT KNOWS

Right now, if you had to make five guesses as to what your highest calling is, what would you guess?

1.

2.

3.

4.

5.

Circle the one that excites you the most.

If you had to describe this calling in three words, what would they be?

1.

2.

3.

If you had to describe it in one word, what would it be?

△
BLING

If you had $1 million dollars to spend on your calling, what would you spend it on?

If you had $10,000 to spend on your calling, what would you spend it on?

If you had $1,000 to spend on your calling, what would you spend it on?

If you had $100 to spend on your calling, what would you spend it on?

If you had no money but all the time in the world to spend on your calling, what would you spend your time doing?

△

THE UNIVERSE WILL CATCH YOU

The Universe wants to support you, but first you need to leap.

I had known for a good 12 months that I was absolutely definitely going to leave my job in advertising to pursue my calling. I didn't feel ready and the whole thing scared me big time. I had spent way too many sleepless nights trying to work out how I would survive financially, and how I could come out of the spiritual closet in a way that didn't come across too crazy to my peers, who had never seen the complete six-dimensional me. It's not like I wasn't being me, I was just holding parts of myself back.

Being on a three-month notice period, I knew I had to quit my job first and then find part-time work closer to the time. After a couple of failed attempts (*read: chickening out*) I decided to bite the bullet and tell my boss.

I took a deep breath, consciously spoke from my heart to his, and broke the news to him. To my surprise, just five minutes later I walked out of his office with a whopping great grin spread right across my face. Somehow, in the process of following the calling of my soul, I had managed to reduce my working hours to three days a week, get a pay rise, and a promotion.

If that wasn't enough, I was also encouraged to bring my passion into work with possible speaking gigs on creativity and metaphysical marketing combined. So basically I would be paid more to work less and do more of what I loved.

Yes, the Universe has got you covered. It wants to support you. We just need to leap in order for it to catch us. Once landed, our life can become one big stream of flow.

WORK YOUR LIGHT

If you knew the Universe was looking out for you, what would you do differently?

△

START BEFORE YOU'RE READY

'Forever is composed of nows.'
Emily Dickinson

The thing about our calling is that it rarely relies on us taking a leap in a direction that feels a little (*or more likely, a lot*) unknown. It's scary seeing the big gaping hole from where you are and where you long to be, and it's rare to feel ready to leap over it.

I had known for a while that I wanted to teach workshops, but I was sh*t scared to do it. I had no idea where to start and was so afraid of being terrible that I didn't tell a soul about my longing. I prayed for a sign and the next day received a Facebook message from my friend Krish, asking me to take over his intuition workshops in London. I went along and he put me on the spot, leading the group in a meditation. I was nervous and sucked a bit. Something about taking over his workshops didn't feel right, but it was just the push I needed to entertain the idea of doing some myself for real.

A couple of nights later I was at my friend Robyn's house for dinner. An amazing roast chicken and a couple of glasses of wine later, we spoke about the potential of putting on monthly workshops in London. Both of us were craving a down-to-earth community of like-hearted people, so why not create our own!

The next day, we were both at a creativity workshop lead by Julia Cameron. She spoke about the relationship between intuition and creativity (one of my favorite topics) mentioning my mentor and teacher Sonia Choquette, who was coincidentally one of Julia's friends.

As the day progressed, audience members asked Julia to recommend workshops for developing intuition. The whole time Robyn and I were elbowing each other.

At lunchtime we decided that now was as good a time as any to launch our workshops. So we scribbled a note to Julia saying that we ran workshops on intuition and creativity. Julia read the notice out and that day 60 people signed up to attend our workshops. We were in business! (*Little did anyone else know that that was our very first day in business!*)

We put on our first workshop together a month later. One workshop turned into two, which turned into a company called The Spirited Project, which turned into monthly Spirited Sessions, which turned into Spirited Sundays and Spirited Meditation Circles, which turned into events in the UK and Australia, and now we have more planned for Asia and the USA.

What started as a great big fear turned into a wonderful creation, and a lot of fun too. During the first workshop, I was so nervous and afraid of what people were thinking about me that I got in the way of my message. But each time I taught one I became more confident. The more confident I became, the more I enjoyed it. Now I love teaching and leading meditation; thank God I acted before I felt ready and then stuck at it!

If you are called to do something, don't let a little detail like not feeling ready get in the way.

Nobody feels ready the first time they do something. Some people don't even feel ready the first 100 times they do something. Malcolm Gladwell says, 'It takes 10,000 hours to become a master at something.'

The trick is to spend those '10,000 hours' doing things that you feel called to do, rather than becoming brilliant at something you couldn't care less about. No matter in what direction you are being called, if you stick at it, before you know it you will be having the time of your life.

WORK YOUR LIGHT

What are you being called to do that you don't feel ready to do?

What would you be happy to devote
10,000 hours of your life towards doing?

△

JUMP RIGHT ON IN

If you've got a passion, a dream, a goal, some place that you want to leap towards, but are still looking on from afar... Don't freak out looking at all the distance between you and it. Don't wait for permission. Don't just dip your toe in. Instead, jump right on in.

Standing on the outside looking in, with your face all pressed up against the glass, is torture. It's also a waste of your gifts. If you're passionate enough to watch from the sidelines, you will love it even more when you're center stage. That's what you were born for. That's where *you* belong.

Start by making simple daily actions that take you one step closer to being part of the action. Fill your Twitter, Instagram, and Facebook feeds with people already living in that world. Join an online community or reach out to someone who shares the same interest and meet them in person for real. Engross yourself in it all. Start telling people in your life what you're up to, regardless of what you think their reaction might be. Don't hang by the edge. Instead, jump right on in.

WORK YOUR LIGHT

What can you do right now to jump in?

TO EVERYONE ELSE IT LOOKED LIKE A SINGLE LEAP. BUT IN REALITY IT WAS HUNDREDS OF **LITTLE BABY STEPS.**

△

DO ONE THING EVERY DAY

If you do one thing every day towards your calling....

In one year you will have done 365 things.

In two years you will have done 730 things.

In five years you will have done 1,825 things.

In 10 years you will have done 3,650 things.

In 20 years you will have done 7,300 things.

In 50 years you will have done 18,250 things.

Start before you feel ready.

You don't need to know where it's all going.

You'll work it out along the way.

△

JUST DANCE EXTRA QUICK

If you wait until you feel ready you will never ever act. Nobody who has ever done anything considerable waited until everything was perfectly lined up with a guarantee of smooth sailing ahead. That moment simply does not exist.

In 2011, I had just reached my goal of becoming a creative director, and a month later I was on a trip to San Francisco, where I was meant to be working with two terrifyingly senior tremendously talented creatives (who I deeply admired), and I was to direct them. I was way out of my comfort zone, trying to keep my cool while doing the *Wayne's World* 'I'm not worthy dance' in my head.

On my last night there I caught up with my old boss. He had moved from Australia to work for Apple in Silicon Valley. He asked me how it was going and I confessed, 'I have no idea what the hell I am doing and feel like a total imposter the whole time.'

He laughed and gave me the best career advice *ever*. He said, 'Bec, pretty much every day I drive into the car park at Apple I am scared. But then I remember that it's the fear and the challenge that make people great. No one who is doing anything new knows what they're doing. They just work it out along the way.'

Hearing those words from him was exactly what I needed. In one small moment I was able to realize that I wasn't the only one who felt like I didn't know what I was doing and that we are all just working it out as we go along. Even the people I admire most, in fact – especially the people I admire most.

WORK YOUR LIGHT

Pretend you are 88 years old. Write a letter from your 88-year-old self to your current self. What do they want you to go for, to give a shot, to take a big fat leap towards?

What advice do they have for you?

What are they most proud of?

What do they most regret?

LIVE YOUR LIFE TO BEYONCÉ DANCE MOVES.

△

DON'T BE ATTACHED TO THE OUTCOME

Don't be attached to the outcome. Your job is to work out the *what*. The Universe's job is to work out the *how*.

Don't worry about how it's going to pan out, just dive in, and do it with all the love and passion that you can conjure up.

Before you know it, the Universe will surprise you with an outcome that is beyond anything your mind could possibly imagine. But first you need to put your head down and lose yourself in the doing.

When you lose yourself in the doing you invite God in.

△

SHOW UP AND SHINE

From the moment I picked up my first Hay House book I knew I wanted to be an author, but it felt like such a big unachievable dream that I kept it hidden for more than 15 years. Year by year my soul called me more and more loudly. Eventually the nagging got too hard to keep numbing out, so I gave in and just started to write.

I put my heart and soul into a book proposal and sent it off to Hay House with a million prayers and then waited for a response. But I was so focused on the outcome of getting published that I let it paralyze me from actually writing. You see, I wasn't writing for me, I was writing for the approval of a publisher. Focusing on this external outcome stifled my creativity, my ability to write authentically, and share my message. Instead of getting on with writing my book regardless of who picked it up, I was frozen in time, waiting to hear the verdict.

My mentor Sonia said, 'The thing with you Rebecca is that you are waiting for some kind of approval and permission to share your message. You're waiting to be invited to some invisible table, to some imaginary club. There is no table, there is no club. The only approval you need to seek is your own. Don't assume your message isn't relevant until someone else says it is. Don't assume your message isn't relevant until someone else deems it to be. It is relevant. It needs to be told. Stop holding yourself back.'

Tears began streaming down my face as I realized that I had been holding myself back, waiting for some kind of external permission before I shared my gifts. I was seeking approval from an external force that didn't even exist. On the plane back to London, I made a pact with myself. I would stop focusing on getting published and instead focus on showing up to my writing every day.

After all, I love writing; it's what lights me up – why would I wait to do what lights me up? I vowed not to give a f**k what other people thought of my creations. If they didn't like it, well, I'm not for them and they're not for me. So I committed to allowing my message to flow through me as it always had without knowing where it would lead. Regardless of the fear. Especially because of the fear.

So I've decided that it's none of my business who reads my writing, only that I show up and write. It's none of my business, if Hay House publishes this book. Hay House is one path, another publisher is another, and self-publishing another. All I know is that if I don't show up and write, I will feel uncomfortable in my skin, and the niggling feeling and the ache will never let up.

Writing is how I unravel my thoughts. It's none of my business if it's a bestseller, or if only one person reads it. Only that I show up and shine my light. And so, now my affirmation of, 'I am a bestselling Hay House author' has changed to 'I show up and shine my light as far as God sees fit.'

This small shift has changed everything. Since then the writing process has been the most fulfilling experience of my life. I cannot wait to wake up every day, fire up my Mac, and let my soul sing.

It doesn't matter how far our light shines, only that we shine it.

Writing is what fills me up and (like meditation) I am certainly a much nicer person when I sit myself at my desk and do it.

If you have a message that you long to share, don't wait for permission before you act. Dare to follow your highest calling. Let the message in your heart come flooding out. When you devote your life to the things that fill you up and share your message, the Universe can't help but support you. You don't need to know how, just trust that it will.

OMFG!

As I typed the last sentences of the above paragraph, my phone rang. I almost didn't answer it because I was so enjoying writing and the words flowing down through me. When I picked up the phone, I was absolutely speechless to discover Michelle from freaking Hay House on the other end of the phone... offering me a book deal... *Holy sweet Jesus and Mary Magdalene*!

I am still pinching myself. I am humbled beyond measure and doing my best to accept the amazing support that the Universe has for me (and has for us all).

You have a special gift to share. You have a message to tell. You wouldn't be reading this book if you didn't. Don't worry about how. Just show up to it every day and lose yourself in the doing. The Universe *will* conspire to support you. This is something I know for sure.

WORK YOUR LIGHT

How can you show up and shine regardless of the outcome?

△

YOU'RE READY

You're ready.

That thing you're called to do.

Do it.

That place you're called to go.

Go there.

Those words you're bursting to say.

Say them.

That dream you've always had.

Live it.

That call deep within your soul.

Answer it.

That thing that lights you up.

Lose yourself in it.

Don't wait until all your ducks are in a row.

Go do it all now.

Don't wait to feel ready.

Just dance extra quick.

It's time.

You're ready.

Go do.

△

PERMISSION GRANTED

Permission granted. Go ahead. Please pass go. Start. Begin. Here's the ticket. It's time. We've been waiting. Welcome. Please proceed. Take a seat. Go do. Please progress. Advance. Continue. Enter. Commence. This way. Leap. Kick off. Commence. Do it. Take off. Come forth. Go on. It's about time. At long last. What are you waiting for? You're ready. Let's get this show on the road.

△

MY SOUL IS CALLING ME TO...

Part IV

LIVING IN THE LIGHT

Practical tools for shining your light

WALK WITH YOUR FEET ON EARTH, BUT YOUR HEART IN HEAVEN.

DON BOSCO

△

EMBODYING THE LIGHT

In my twenties, I mentally understood spiritual principles, could put my mind to most things, heard the callings of my soul, and was in touch with my emotions. But I was not embodying any of it. My mind, body, spirit, and soul were working in silos, not flowing in harmony. Like people who live in the same house, but never see each other or socialize, I was not grounding my beliefs in a disciplined way. I wasn't truly living in the flow of it. That was until one of my worst nightmares came true.

Ever since the day I pulled that first Hay House book off the shelf, Louise Hay became my Oprah, Madonna, Beyoncé, Stevie Nicks, and Tina Turner all rolled into one. It was the autumn of 2009 and I was at a Hay House event in London with my friend Julie-Ann Gledhill, who had flown in from Singapore. Reid Tracy (the CEO of Hay House) and Cheryl Richardson were speaking with surprise guest Louise Hay!

At that time in my life I had two feet in advertising, but deep down I knew I had a message to share. In one of the breaks, as everyone else was hanging around forming the 'I love you Louise' club, I was trying to look extremely cool by hanging back. Meanwhile, the whole time I was experiencing the most intense surge of energy racing through my body with a voice from the depths of my soul that beckoned, 'Go ask Louise for a job.' Not normally someone who does that kind of thing, I resisted it.

The next day, the same thing happened. It was as though I was being physically propelled forwards. Unable to resist it anymore, I took a breath, cringing on the inside, cursing my soul, spirit and guides all at once, and made my way to Louise.

Each time she became free, I held back and let someone else go ahead. It was as if my soul and spirit were pushing me, but my body and ego were resisting. The moment the final person started walking away, I took a deep breath and started walking towards Louise, but unable to control my energy literally bowled her over. *OH MY GOD!*

Regaining her balance, Louise then looked me right in the eye and said, 'Girl, don't attack people with your energy.'

I was mortified. My life was definitely over.

While wishing I could disappear off the face of the Earth, I made my way back to my seat and pretended like nothing happened. For the rest of the afternoon I played the situation over and over again in slow motion in my head...

'Was it really that bad?'

Yes, yes it was.

'Did I really bowl over Louise Hay?'

Yes, you did.

Cringe, cringe, cringe...

▽

Later at dinner, I confessed the story to Julie while holding back tears of horrification. Julie thought it was the funniest thing that she'd ever heard, and continues to tease me for it to this day.

Anyway, I tell you that story because it was actually a huge turning point in my journey. I had always been connected to my soul and spirit, received my creative ideas, intuition, and my soul's callings clearly – but I wasn't grounding any of it in my body with action. In other words, my very active mind, body, and spirit weren't talking to each other. So when I heard my soul callings, I didn't embody them with action. And when

I received guidance or creations, I didn't always let it flow through me.

I was receiving all this stuff from the higher realms, but had no idea what to do with it all, so I decided to ignore it. This caused a huge build-up of energy that needed to come out somehow. My mind, body, spirit and soul were not in union. I was out of the flow.

Louise's simple remark sparked a whole new path for me in embodying my spirit and the callings of my soul. Prior to this encounter I thought the mind, body, spirit connection was about strengthening these three parts of us. What this experience revealed is that it is impossible to follow our highest path without energetic integration. And it's difficult not only to hear but *act* on the callings of our soul if we haven't grounded ourselves in regular disciplined practice.

In this new chapter of my journey, I sought spiritual teachers to help me harness the subtle, yet powerful, energies of spirit and anchor them in my body. I have included the ones that work best for me in this section. Try them out and see which ones resonate with you.

SHE'S GOT A **LIGHT** AND SHE KNOWS HOW TO **USE IT**.

△

NON-NEGOTIABLE SPIRITUAL PRACTICE

You cannot hear the callings of your soul if you don't carve time out to listen to them with daily, non-negotiable spiritual practice.

It took me until 2012 to wholeheartedly show up to this practice every day without fail, and it was the best decision I have made. This one thing has created the biggest transformation in my life. Committing to showing up to your soul is like putting a message into the Universe saying, 'I'm serious about this and I'm ready to be supported.'

I used to be a total dabbler. I threw myself into loads of different practices, but I'd often feel overwhelmed with all of the stuff I 'should' be doing. Meditation, journaling, yoga, cutting cords – you name it, I tried it – it felt like I needed a whole extra life to get it all done. And because I didn't have a routine of showing up without fail every day, when I had a super crappy or busy day, my spiritual practice was the first thing to slide. But it was then that I needed my practice the most.

Committing to the discipline of a daily practice doesn't mean you have to meditate for hours or even one, it just means that you show up to something every day without fail. My basic practice takes no more than 20 minutes a day and consists of three things:

1. Light sourcing
2. Prayer
3. Chanting, dance or walking in nature

It is simple (and realistic) enough that no matter where I am or what I've got on, there's no excuse *not* to do it. The more I show up to it, the more my life turns into one big practice, into one big moving prayer.

Whenever a client comes to me wanting change, this is always the first thing I recommend. Your soul is waiting to guide you. The Universe is ready to support you every step along the way. But in order to connect to it, you need to show up.

WORK YOUR LIGHT

Do you currently have a daily spiritual practice
that you show up to every day?

THE QUIETER YOU BECOME, THE MORE YOU ARE ABLE TO HEAR.

RUMI

△
LIGHT SOURCING

My teacher, Sonia, introduced me to Sourcing. I loved it immediately because it is so easy and only took 10 minutes (*which, let's face it, helps*).

From the very first moment I Sourced, I had the most amazing feeling of coming home. It was so familiar. And the craziest thing: I had a sudden memory of Sourcing in bed, or at the beach when I was a little girl, but without even knowing I was doing it!

It's an ultimate prayer of surrender, where you connect back with the universal energy, called 'Source,' and allow yourself to rest, be filled up, and receive all of the gifts that the Universe has for you. Sourcing is a form of daily meditation in which you put yourself into receiving mode so that you can:

- Hear the callings of your soul.

- Remember all of the gifts that you already have within you.

- Connect with the amazing light energy that is on offer to us at all times (but often we look outside of ourselves to find it).

- Nurture your inner light and give it the fuel to shine as bright as humanly possible.

- Be fed by your higher self.

- Let the cosmic energy of the Universe in and surrender to the flow of your highest path.

- Loosen your control on life and let your soul lead the way.

All you need to Source is to open your heart, breathe, and receive. When we Source we open ourselves up to the universal energies of divine love, light, wisdom, and truth. You connect with your higher self and allow yourself to be filled up with whatever it is that you need. It's like taking a drink at the well of your unlimited boundless self. For 10 minutes, you hand over the things that you are striving for, struggling with, trying to heal, and allow yourself to be replenished by the never-ending supply of Source energy.

Let go and relax into the flow of the Universe.

I'm a big believer in morning practice because sleeping is one big meditation and by practicing as soon as we wake up, we maximize this high frequency (rather than reaching straight for our phones).

Most mornings, I walk up to Regent's Park and sit in the rose garden to Source. I love Sourcing in nature, but you can do it from anywhere you like – your bedroom, the bath, your car.

If I have an early morning reading or mentoring session, I light a candle at my altar (see page 208 for creating one of your own) then sit on my meditation stool and Source. But I've also done it on airplanes, trains, buses, even the bathroom, pretty much anywhere I can find to make sure I show up to it each day.

Sourcing is super simple, here's how you do it:

- Rub your hands together to open your heart (your palms are extensions of the heart chakra). Then, gently pull your hands apart and notice the subtle energy you have activated – this is your connection with Source. Rest your hands, palms upwards, on your lap, noticing the subtle pulse that has been activated in the center of your palms.

- Now close your eyes, and imagine a beautiful channel of white light streaming down from the heavens straight for you. Allow this bright supportive light to fill up your entire being and open your heart. Hand over all of your concerns, worries, struggles, goals, hopes, dreams, and any darkness to be replenished by the light.

- Breathe and allow yourself to be supported. Breathe and allow yourself to be filled up. Breathe and allow yourself to be nurtured. Breathe and allow yourself to come home. Breathe and listen to the callings of your soul. Breathe and allow yourself to light up.

- You don't need to worry about your mind being quiet or sitting still for hours, all you need to do is to open your heart, breathe and receive the beautiful energy washing over and into you from the heavens.

WORK YOUR LIGHT

If you haven't already, download the free Sourcing meditation at www.lightisthenewblack.com. Try it for 21 days and watch the transformation. And don't forget to send your Sourcing pics to me, using the hash tag #lightisthenewblack and tagging @rebeccathoughts.

△

LIGHT BATH

You can connect back to Source energy at any moment by giving yourself a light bath – a super quick way to connect and raise your vibration in an instant. Like a mini version of Sourcing (see page 182), a light bath is especially handy for those moments when you find yourself in a low vibe or depleted mood and only have a minute.

Here's how you do it:

- Rub your hands together and, as you do, visualize your heart opening. Then gently pull your hands apart and notice the subtle energy you have activated. This is your connection to Source. Place your hands with palms upwards (in receiving mode).

- Gently close your eyes and imagine a big ball of light from the heavens, shining down endless amounts of light just for you. Imagine the light coming down through the crown of your head straight for your heart and the palms of your hands.

- At the center of your heart, imagine a ball of light. As you receive the light from Source, imagine the ball of light in your heart getting bigger and bigger until it fills your entire being.

- Breathe and receive this beautiful unlimited light energy. Breathe and receive, as it fills you up, replacing any darkness with beautiful luminous light and bringing you back into flow with the Universe.

WORK YOUR LIGHT

Give yourself a light bath.

△

CALL YOURSELF HOME

As we move through our lives, we can leave parts of us behind through trauma, extreme anger, or heartache. The same can happen as we journey from lifetime to lifetime. However, we have the power to call these missing pieces back home, and this meditation is a great tool to do just that.

- Close your eyes and draw your attention to your breath.

- Breathe in for four counts, hold for four counts, and breathe out for eight. Repeat this process three times. Close your eyes and continue to breathe in and out really deeply.

- Now imagine an amazingly powerful magnet at the center of your heart. Breathing in and out, call all the lost parts of you back home. The parts of you lost through traumatic experiences. The parts of you lost through heartbreak, soul ache, and deep disappointment. The parts of you lost through not being truly seen, being under-estimated, and hurt.

- Continue breathing as all of these parts of you are effortlessly pulled back home.

AFFIRMATION

I call all lost parts of me home. I am home. I am home. I am home.

△

BACK TO CENTER

When we are in the flow our energy is balanced. We are not pushing or resisting, we are energetically centered. When we are energetically centered we are ready to receive. My friend Robyn Silverton taught me the following exercise, and it is perfect for getting your energy balanced in an instant. I love it because it takes less than 10 seconds and you can do it absolutely anywhere.

- Stand with your feet flat on the ground. Take a few deep breaths and draw your attention to the soles of your feet, noticing where your weight is. Is it forward in your toes? Or back in your heels?

- If your energy is forward, you are probably stuck in striving, pushing, forcing, controlling, and moving too fast (I used to live here). In this energetic state we are unable to let the Universe (or anyone) help us. We are controlling or giving rather than allowing and receiving.

- If your weight is back in your heels, then you are probably waiting around before you feel ready to act. In this energetic state you are lacking the fire to get up and go, to make stuff happen, to meet people halfway.

- Notice where your energy is without judgment and bring it back to center so that it is equally spread throughout the soles of your feet.

AFFIRMATION

Everything that is calling me is already on its way. I
trust that the Universe is doing its part in delivering
it all to me. I show up and receive it all.

△

DEAR GOD

'Every emotion that you feel, good or bad, is about
the relationship between your current thought and
understanding of the Source within you on the same topic'
ABRAHAM-HICKS

Perhaps you have a great relationship with God/Source/the Universe, or perhaps you were raised to fear God/Source/the Universe. Maybe you were taught that you needed to earn your love, or maybe you were brought up with the mantra that believing in a higher power is a bit airy-fairy.

Whether you have unwavering faith or are a flat-out non-believer, our relationship with, and beliefs about, God/Source/The Universe actually influence so much of how we live our life – especially the things that are left unsaid.

As I demonstrated in Part I with my 'F you God' letter (see page 20), opening up a real dialogue between you and the Source is an extremely powerful tool for interrogating your underlying beliefs and bringing your light into the world.

WORK YOUR LIGHT

Write a letter to God. It might be a F You letter,
a thank you letter, or a simple memo.

Simply write 'Dear God/Divine/the Universe' at
the top of the page and let yourself riff.

Once you're done, take a breath and let God/
the Divine/the Universe respond.

△

IMPROMPTU DANCE BREAKS

We all receive intuitive guidance, but most of us wait for that guidance to make sense before we act on it. Our mind, body, and soul are disconnected.

A wonderful way to embody your soul is through dance. Intuitive movement is the act of moving your body, however it feels like moving, letting your soul and spirit dance you. It might be gentle swaying, or some Sister Act style deep-shoulder action... Whatever your style, this simple act of letting your soul move you serves the following purpose:

- It strengthens the right hemisphere of the brain, which is linked to your subconscious, intuitive, and creative mind.

- It allows your body to process any stuck energy and emotions so you can get back in flow, and so is great if you're feeling stuck or down.

- It allows your soul to lead your body – physically rewiring your brain – so that you're more inclined to let the callings of your soul (your intuition) truly lead your life.

WORK YOUR LIGHT

Throw your own dance party for one. It need not take ages, one song will do. Close the door, crank up the music, close your eyes, and let your soul move your body. The more you move your body in ways it has never moved before, the more effective it will be in releasing old patterns.

△

TAKE A BREATH

'Fear is excitement without breath.'
Robert Heller

It's the easiest and most natural part of life. So many of us go about our day taking shallow sips without air even reaching our bellies. Take a moment now to notice what your breath is doing right now. Is your breathing deep or shallow? Take a huge breath in and let it fill the depths of your belly.

To breathe deeply is to gulp in life. To breathe consciously is to say to the Universe, 'I am here and I am ready to receive.'

Do not underestimate the healing potential of the simple action of taking a breath. My teacher Sonia stressed to me the importance of breath, but it wasn't until all I could do was breathe that I fully understood.

When I was at my lowest point, proper rock bottom, I went to a shamanic healer I had been seeing for a while. I was in such extreme grief that my body simply didn't want to breathe. My soul had almost given up. As I was lying there, she instructed me to take a breath. My brain was desperately instructing me to do it, but it was like my spirit had packed up shop and left. I would go about 20 seconds until I took a breath, and then it would be the shallowest of sips, just enough to survive until the next baby breath.

The truth was, I did not want to be here anymore. I was too tired and devastated to keep going. I had fought too hard for too long and I couldn't pretend any longer that everything was all right. So we spent the whole session literally trying to get me to breathe. Little by little

I could feel my spirit coming back home. After about 30 minutes my chest started to rise, and a week later I allowed air back into my belly.

But you don't have to be at rock bottom to notice the impact of your breathing. If you feel stuck, tired, stressed, or afraid... just change your breath. It brings in the life force and gets things moving. Just like a good spring clean does to your house, breathing in deeply can transform any stagnation or stuck energy.

WORK YOUR LIGHT

With your hand on your belly, take 60 seconds right now to pay attention to your breath.

Is it slow and deep, rapid and shallow, or perhaps you are holding it? Notice the difference between your inhalations and your exhalations.

Begin to take in more air, pulling it deep into the corners of your belly, right down into your feet.

△

WHO LIGHTS YOU UP?

You've worked hard to raise your vibration, so it's worth taking note who in your life raises you up energetically and who drains you.

This doesn't mean that you should only hang out with people who are committed to raising their frequency and in an optimistic place in their lives. Rather, it's about becoming aware of who has the tendency to drain you, so you can protect your energy and decide on how much time you spend with them.

Who makes you feel good and who makes you feel bad?

As we raise our vibration and shift energetically, we may find that we want to spend more time with people who are on a similar path. Or at least look at protecting our energy when hanging around those who drain us.

WORK YOUR LIGHT

Who in your life drains you and leaves you feeling depleted?

Is there anyone in your life that you take energy
from, instead of sourcing it from within?

△

WHERE'S YOUR ENERGY AT?

The higher your vibration, the more energetically sensitive you are likely to be. Protecting your energy is imperative to prevent yourself from being energetically depleted.

Here are some super, simple ways to protect, replenish and clear your energetic field.

Protect your energetic field

It is important to protect our energetic field in order to hear our intuitive voice clearly and prevent our vital energy from being drained by people and life in general. You can do this by imagining a protective energetic space about 1 metre (3 feet) around you, which nobody can penetrate without your permission. If you need more help, watch the 'how to' video over at www.lightisthenewblack.com.

Chakra shower

Chakras are wheels of energy in and outside the body. Each chakra point is associated with different emotions and bodily functions. As we go about life, our chakras can become blocked or stagnant. Giving yourself a chakra shower is a simple way of clearing your energy each morning while you are in the shower. Simply scan each of your chakras one by one, noticing anything that is blocked in each of them. As the water runs over your body imagine it cleansing away any energy that is stuck or stagnant in each of your chakras. At the end, call upon the light of Source energy to fill each of them up with luminous white light.

Cutting cords

Cords are the invisible energetic connection between two people. Attached to a chakra in each person, the cord feels more like a hook, and is generally controlling and manipulative. A healthy relationship is two whole people coming together, therefore it is important to cut the energetic cords that pop up as we move through life.

At the end of each day, tune in to your body and notice if there is anyone who is tugging at you energetically. In your mind's eye, scan each of your chakras and notice where the cord is attached to you and what the cord seems to be made of.

Perhaps it's a hook, a rope, a ribbon, or maybe even a steel cable. Imagine cutting this cord with a pair of scissors, or some other tool. If you need extra help doing this, call upon Archangel Michael with his big silver sword to do the cutting with you. At the end imagine a ball of white light protecting you.

Light bubble

Imagine your entire body being protected by a giant bubble of bright white light. This bubble is impenetrable by anyone or anything, protecting you every step of every day.

Earthing

Magic happens when we experience a complete union of mind, body and spirit. If we are not grounded and in our body, it is difficult to let our intuition move us, we are likely to feel unsupported by life and we run the risk of staying too much in thought rather than action. Earthing is a wonderful way to ground and embody our mind, body and spirit. It's super easy to do and can be done absolutely anywhere.

Find yourself a patch of earth (or if you can't find earth just imagine it) and stand with your shoes and socks off. Really feel the texture of the earth beneath your feet.

Send any blocked energy or emotions you are struggling with to the Earth through your right foot. Through your left foot, allow the healing frequency of the Earth to send you positive healing energy, and let it flow through your entire body.

High five a tree

Just like Earthing, you can transmute bad energy just by touching a tree. Place your hands on the trunk of a tree, and ask it to charge you up and help you dissolve any bad energy you may be holding.

Epsom salt baths

Soaking in an Epsom salt bath is not only a great way to protect and cleanse your energetic field, they're also brilliant for detoxifying your body and soothing your adrenal glands. I have one several times a week and feel so balanced after.

Note: If you have a heart condition, are pregnant, or are on any medication check with your medical practitioner before using Epsom salts.

LIGHTHOUSES DON'T GO RUNNING ALL OVER AN ISLAND LOOKING FOR BOATS TO SAVE; THEY JUST STAND THERE SHINING.

ANNIE LAMOTT

△

BE THE LIGHTHOUSE, NOT THE ELECTRICITY

As a Lightworker your purpose is to 'be the light.' Being the light does not mean that you become the light source for others by plugging yourself into them energetically.

Being the light means turning your light on, so that you can be the light, not be *their* light. Only they can be their light. As you connect with your own light source, you then effortlessly light up the way for others to connect with theirs.

You cannot fix or save anyone who doesn't want to be fixed or saved. If you assume other people are helpless, then you are actually doing them a disservice by taking away the opportunity for them to turn on their own light and be in flow with the Universe themselves.

WORK YOUR LIGHT

Are you running around 'looking for ships to save' or are you focusing your attention on simply shining bright like a lighthouse?

SHE LIT UP
EVERY ROOM.

$\triangle$

SACRED SOCIAL

How we interact on social media contributes to the future consciousness of the world. Our likes, shares, posts, pics, pins, and tweets; all of it is energy and it is being constantly cast out into the ether – and then multiplied over and over again at the speed of light.

In every moment, we can consciously choose what energy we contribute: The words don't matter, but the energetic intent behind them does. Just as your thoughts create your world, our collective energy creates THE world. Thanks to social media, this collective energy can now spread even more quickly – which is why it's important now more than ever to watch your thoughts and be intentional with the energy you bring.

Check in on the intent that you are putting out there as you post. Do you want to share your light, encourage the light in someone else, or is it coming from another place?

The more we put our physical energy toward the things that are in alignment, the more that vibration and level of consciousness will spread. So if you see a post that resonates with you, like or retweet it.

The magnificent thing about this period of history we are living in is that we can use the instant infinite power of social media to help us share and spread our messages. Regardless of whether you are using social media for your own personal use or for your business, it has the same power.

WORK YOUR LIGHT

Get sacred with social media by practicing intentional posting.

△

CHOOSE A HIGHER THOUGHT

We all have bad days and sometimes crap things just happen. You can't change the situation, but you can change the way that you think about it.

The worst thing you can possibly do, when you find yourself in a negative mood, is to berate yourself for being in a negative mood because you are meant to 'be the light.' We're human, human emotions are normal.

Let yourself feel whatever you need to feel, and then, when you're ready, choose a higher thought. It doesn't matter if it's only a teeny bit higher.

Baby steps are better than no movement at all.

WORK YOUR LIGHT

The next time you're feeling a bit meh, feel the feelings, breathe, and choose a higher thought.

△

CREATE A VIBRATION BOARD

In order to attract something into our lives, we need to be a vibrational match. If we continue to focus on it as something we want 'in the future,' that thing will always remain 'in the future.'

I've had success with vision boards, but there were always some things that I could never quite become a vibrational match for. Then I had an idea, to combine the following things together:

- The things we're calling in (what we want).

- The things we've already called in (what we've already attracted).

- The things that light us up (what we love).

When we bring our future wants into alignment with what currently is, our brain cannot distinguish between the two and so it's much easier to become a vibrational match, thus helping us attract it more quickly.

I call it a 'vibration board.' It's a vision board + a feel-good board.

So, alongside the convertible, the beach house, my affirmation – 'I shine my light as far as the Universe sees fit' – and meeting Oprah (of course), I have pictures of the people I love the most, pictures of me with my teachers, articles written about me, and a love letter from my fiancé. So my feel-good moments are mixed up with my future manifestations.

WORK YOUR LIGHT

Create your own vibration board filled with the things you are calling in, have already successfully called in, and that light you up!

△

MAKE YOUR LIFE A MOVING PRAYER

I've never been big on the formalities of going to church, but ever since I was a little girl I've had an unshakable knowing that God exists. I'm not talking about a big man in the clouds, rather an unknown presence that connects us all.

My mum taught me to pray at an early age, and I have done it ever since. I never really even knew who I was praying to, but I always felt I was being heard. The act of reaching out and connecting from my heart to the heart of the Universe made me feel more supported and connected to life as a whole. While my body was here on Earth, my heart was always in heaven and praying always reminded me of that.

Prayer and meditation go hand in hand. If you want to ask for something, pray. If you want to listen to the answer, meditate. There have been times in my life when my prayer and meditation practice dissipated. Looking back, these were the times that I felt most separate and alone in the world.

Nowadays I choose to keep the conversation (asking and listening) going at all times, so my life is one big moving prayer.

You don't need to get on your knees to pray, you can do it while you are walking down the street, washing the dishes, filing your nails, giving a presentation, or riding your bike. It can be a simple chat, a plea for help, an expression of gratitude, a request for guidance, or putting in your order for what you'd like to experience next.

Prayer doesn't have to be reciting words out loud. It can be thoughts and wishes, cries and silence, confessions and requests, gratitude and wonder. It is merely a reaching out to something beyond our separate human self.

In her book *Help, Thanks, Wow*, Annie Lamott speaks of the three main types of prayer.

1. **Help:** When we are brought to our knees and admit we need help.

2. **Thanks:** A moment of gratitude when we receive the help and realize that our prayers have been heard.

3. **Wow:** When the miraculous beauty of life takes our breath away.

When we make our life one big moving prayer, we move into a space of constant connection. There is no space that prayer begins and ends. We are in constant communion with life itself.

WORK YOUR LIGHT

Create your own prayer practice and make your life a moving conversation with something beyond your separate human self.

△

YOUR SPIRIT GUIDES ARE WAITING

You have a team of spirit guides waiting to support you. The only catch is that they cannot help you unless you ask them to. You can do this in an instant. You can do this right now.

Spirit guides are beings from the sixth dimension and above, and are completely devoted to your growth. Many have had lifetimes here on Earth and just like you they have their own eclectic bundle of gifts, wisdom, and experiences. They have been carefully chosen just for you. Perfectly suited to your highest calling, their only job is to support you and guide you as much or as little as you wish.

In giving soul readings, I have found that most people have approximately six guides in their inner circle and we call in new ones, as we need them.

We are born with spirit guides and we can also recruit them as we move through life. They can guide you through anything from finding a car park to healing your heart, from experiencing more joy to finding the right job, from meeting your future partner to getting through your darkest hour. No request is too big or too small, too specific or too broad.

If you are undertaking a particular creative endeavor, for example, you might recruit a spirit guide who has written books of their own during their time on Earth. If you are going through a particularly hard time you could call on a wise teacher guide to help you through it.

I have been working with my spirit guides half-heartedly for a number of years and the truth of the matter is that I spent a long time waiting for them to appear in black and white before I took them seriously.

I wanted a personal relationship, to see and feel them like I would a friend or family member. I wanted to know their age, their background, their personality, and hair color. I wanted them to pop over for dinner and share a bottle of red.

I would get hunches and the odd vision in my mind's eye, but would quickly dismiss it thinking I had no proof. After confessing this to my teacher a couple of years ago, I was guided into a meditation where I agreed to be open to experiencing them without any expectations. To my surprise, by letting go of what I thought this experience should look like, each of my spirit guides came to me.

One is a woman called Charlotte. She is a terribly English high-society lady from the 1920s, here to help me get my message and name spoken about in the right circles; a gifted gossip, with her fingers in all of the most influential of pies.

Knowing that I wanted some publicity to increase my chances of being published by Hay House, I asked my spirit guide Charlotte for help. That same day I was connected with a journalist called Anita Chaudhuri. One week after that a story landed on Anita's desk about British Spirituality for the *Sunday Times Style Magazine* (which also happened to feature several Hay House authors). Three days after that she got another feature story in *Psychologies* magazine. Anita interviewed me for both.

When I went to meet the Hay House team for the first time, they asked for the name of my publicist. Without thinking, I responded, 'My spirit guide Charlotte.' Everyone around the table burst into laughter. I've sat at a lot of boardroom tables in my life, but that was the first where I could have mentioned my spirit guides. How awesome is that?!

WORK YOUR LIGHT

Want to meet your spirit guides? Download my guided meditation at www.lightisthenewblack.com

△

INVEST IN YOUR SOUL'S GROWTH

Your soul is your most valuable asset. You can lose everything in a second, but nobody can take your soul growth away from you.

The biggest blessings you can share with the world are your light, your love, and your consciousness (*they're all the same thing to me*). You are here to grow as a soul and help the consciousness of the planet grow in the process. As you expand, so does the Universe. For whenever you are investing in your own expansion, you are investing in the expansion of the Universe. If you ask me, anything that can bring you closer to your potential, to your spirit, to your true essence, is priceless.

I have spent huge amounts of money, time, and effort on my personal soul growth. Books, courses, healers, training, retreats, trips, pilgrimages, mentoring, coaching, shamans, CDs, websites, making difficult decisions, taking leaps of faith, and more. But you know what? Each time I have invested in my soul's growth, I received that amount back plus tenfold more.

WORK YOUR LIGHT

How are you being called to invest more in your soul's growth?

△

ASSEMBLE YOUR SUPPORT TEAM

We are pack animals, we are not meant to go it alone. Everyone needs a support team, people who have your back no matter what and encourage you unconditionally. They're the ones who are genuinely as happy as you are when things go well. And feel it hard when things don't go quite to plan. They hold your vision and keep you on the right path. They are standing by, a phone call or a flight away ready to have your back the moment you say the word.

The space around you is sacred, so treat it accordingly. If you haven't already started, begin assembling your support team. Who you hire is completely up to you but it's the most important job spec you'll ever write.

The most amazing people in history have all had theirs: Jesus and his disciples, Obama and the White House, Kylie and her sexy back-up dancers.

It may consist of friends and family, teachers and healers, psychics and shamans, neighbors, peers and pets – it doesn't matter how many or how few. All that matters is that they are there to support you and, no matter how bright or how dark the day, they will be there to cheer you on.

WORK YOUR LIGHT

Assemble your support team. Write the names of five to 10 people who support your dreams unconditionally. If you can't think of that many people, then send a request out to the Universe to start sending them to you today.

△

MAKING AN ALTAR

Creating an altar in your home is a really effective tool for anchoring your spiritual energies into the physical. A sacred space filled with things that make you feel connected. Think of it as a little corner of the world where you can come to hope, dream, wish, pray, meditate, contemplate, and ask the Universe for support.

- Start by choosing a place for your altar. If you live with others and it's hard to find personal space, you can make yours a portable one consisting of just a candle and a special object, such as a crystal, which you keep on your bedside table. You can make your altar on a window ledge or it can take up the whole corner of a room. Size does not matter, intention does.

- Choose sacred items that make you feel connected and full of light. Consider what you want to call in. You might have a candle, a picture of a god, goddess, or guru that means something to you, incense, fresh flowers, a lucky charm, angel cards, artwork, magazine clippings, feathers, a champagne cork, a picture of a loved one. There are no rules, just choose whatever makes your soul feel good.

- Your altar is a place where you can go to pray, meditate, ask for support and set your intentions for the day. You might want to light a candle and say a prayer, such as 'Please Use Me' (see page 223) after Sourcing.

- The altar is an energetic portal for you to communicate with the Universe, so it's important to maintain it and keep it fresh. You may feel guided to replace things now and then, or even pick a flower each week to keep the energy clear and sacred. Don't overthink it; just go with what feels good.

WORK YOUR LIGHT

Make yourself an altar. If you've already got one, post your pics using #LightIsTheNewBlack.

△

LEAVE SPACE FOR GRACE

If we fill up our lives right to the brim, then there is no space for the new to come in. If your life is cluttered, the Universe has nowhere to deliver the new things that you are praying for.

Doing a regular physical de-clutter of your life can help let go of the things that no longer serve you, making way for the new. As you throw away old boxes from the past, you are also letting go of old thought patterns, and fears.

When we hold on tightly to the things around us, we are so busy clinging on that we are unable to catch the things that are coming straight for us.

Letting go and leaving a little bit of space wide open is scary, but that's why everyone doesn't do it.

You're not everyone. You are courageous.

And I reckon, there's something you're ready to let go of to make way for something even better that you truly deserve.

WORK YOUR LIGHT

If you weren't afraid of something not taking
its place, what would you let go of?

△

MY SOUL IS CALLING ME TO...

Part V

BE
THE
LIGHT

Serve the world by being you

TRAVEL LIGHT, LIVE LIGHT, SPREAD THE LIGHT, BE THE LIGHT.

YOGI BHAJAN

△

YOUR LIGHT IS NEEDED HERE

Do not underestimate the power your light has in creating change in the world. Your light shines brightest when you bravely step up into your biggest most authentic self. You will never know the true extent of your impact, but you can trust that it will be more than you could ever fathom. Your light is needed here.

△

YOU DO YOU (#YDY)

Don't waste your time striving to become the person you long to be, spend your time being the person you already are. The person you long to be is already inside you.

You do YOU.

Say you long to be a writer. If you long to be a writer it means you already are one. You don't need someone to come along and confirm it's true, grant your wish, or give you approval. It's who you are. Already, right now.

You do YOU.

When we spend our time being who we already are, the doing ends up being a byproduct of the being. So if you're a singer, go be that regardless of the outcome. It's who you are. You don't need to do anything in order to be it some day. She's in you. She wants to sing now.

You do YOU.

It's none of your business how many people read your books or download your songs or compliment your latest design, or buy your art or like your page or retweet your tweet. What is your business is showing up to what lights you up, to what makes you come alive, to that which makes your light shine even brighter. Let go of your attachment to the outcome. It's none of your business anyway.

You do YOU.

It's the most fantastic thing when you simply focus on the being and do from there. Any attachment to the outcome magically disappears and something very special happens... by allowing yourself to be filled up by the being, the Universe can't help but support you.

You do YOU.

So go be YOU, regardless of the outcome. Go do the things that you love, regardless of how good people think you are. Without even bothering your head about what others say.

You do YOU.

You already are all the things you strive for. And the more you show up to who you already are, the more filled up you become. The more filled up you become, the more YOU you become. The more YOU you become, the brighter you shine for all those around you.

You do YOU.

△

THE WORLD NEEDS YOU

If you follow what you love, while doing it in a way that only you can, you will serve the world by being you. If you spend your time trying to be like someone else, you will be holding back the unique gifts that only you can bring.

In her Dartmouth commencement address, Shonda Rhimes (writer of *Grey's Anatomy* and my all-time favorite TV writer) talked about how when she left college her dream was to BE Nobel Prize-winning author Toni Morrison. Eventually she realized that the role was already taken and the world certainly did not need another one. The only role available for her to be was Shonda Rhimes. So she followed what lit her up, went to film school, and wrote stories in a way that only she could.

Many years and Golden Globes later, in one of those glorious full-circle moments, Shonda Rhimes then finds herself sitting opposite Toni Morrison at dinner. And all her idol Toni Morrison wanted to talk about was what was happening in *Grey's Anatomy... I LOVE that!*

Shonda explained it so beautifully when she said, 'That never would have happened if I hadn't stopped dreaming of becoming her [Toni Morrison] and gotten busy becoming myself.'

Her dream didn't come true. Something even better did. She became herself instead.

The best possible outcome that the Universe has planned for you is way better than the biggest dream you could ever imagine. The trick is to lose yourself in following the things that light you up and do it in a way that only you can.

**The world needs your presence. Serve
the world by being you.**

WORK YOUR LIGHT

Are you striving to be like someone you admire, or more like you?

△

BEING OF SERVICE

'I've learned that people will forget what you said, people will forget what you did, but people will never forget how you made them feel.'
MAYA ANGELOU

Being of service means devoting your life to something greater than yourself, so that your presence can make a difference in the world.

Being of service doesn't have to be a humongous mission where you need to singlehandedly save the world, cure cancer, or run off to a Buddhist monastery. Making a difference in just one person's life can have immeasurable ripples.

My year seven English teacher Ms. Dorothy Bottrell served the world by embracing her eccentricity, open-heartedness, and presence, and by encouraging creative uniqueness in all of her students. Instead of wearing something plain and simple, like all the other teachers, every day her outfit was an expression of her spirit. When she spoke to her students, she spoke to their hearts and made them feel truly seen. From the first day that she took roll call, I felt both special and inspired all at once.

Ms. Bottrell turned a creative writing assignment into an inspiring adventure. She told us that there were stories waiting to be told and that we were the perfect people to tell them. She informed us that our assignment was not to write a piece of creative writing; it was to write our very first book. And the reward for writing the book was to be able to share our creations with the children at the local kindergarten.

She said that these children were waiting for us to tell them the story that only we could tell!

Ms. Bottrell inspired me to pour my heart and my soul into my book, *Where do Rainbows Come From?* In school vacations I went to secondhand bookstores looking for ancient inspiration from all of the ages and mystic traditions. I spent hours illustrating it with my favorite Derwent watercolor pencils. It was even 'published' by Tucker Glynn & Co. – my friend Terri's dad's accounting firm had a color printer and binding machine (*hey, it was the nineties*).

I will never forget the day when Ms. Bottrell handed back our books and congratulated us for being 'authors.' Enclosed with my book was a handwritten two-page letter straight from her heart with a carefully chosen wrapped present of a rainbow and dolphin window sticker and a poem written by her that she said was inspired by my story. I started crying from how special and loved I felt in that moment. I then looked around the room and discovered that she had written a letter and carefully chosen a present for every student in the class.

Ms. Bottrell had touched the hearts and encouraged the spirits of every single one of us. I still have my book and, in the process of writing this one, got my mum to bring it over to me when we met up in Paris.

Ms. Bottrell was completely unconventional, and unlike any other teacher I have ever known. Had she spent her years striving to be like someone else, the world would be a much less compassionate, creative, and bright place. My life for one would have been a little different and I have no doubt that there are hundreds if not thousands more who were touched by her spirit.

MANTRA

I light up the world by being me.

SERVE WHERE YOUR HEART SWELLS.

△

PLEASE USE ME

I request the Grace of the Universe to work through me
today so that I can serve the world by being me.

Let my light shine as bright as the Universe sees fit and
touch the hearts of those who need it most.

May my life be one big moving prayer.

Amen.

△

YOU©

You are like no other in this town, city, country, continent, planet, solar system, galaxy, Universe, Multiverse, and beyond. Way beyond. Through all the dimensions of space and time, there is, never has been and, never will be anyone quite like you. Not even close. Your hair color, your upbringing, your highs and your lows. Your accent, your nature, and all the lessons you've learned along the way. Your body size, your skin color, and all the learning from the lives that your soul has swum through before. You are a glorious tapestry that is being woven with every new breath. Evolving with every thought and every act and every moment.

Now, now, now.

In the entire existence of all the humans that ever were and ever will be, none will come close to possessing the same combination of amazingness that you have right now. You are the gift. You are the light. It's your You that lights up the world. Be like no other.

Be You©.

FORGE,
DON'T FOLLOW.

△

FORGE, DON'T FOLLOW

The age of worshiping and playing follow the leader is over.

Simon says You do You (#ydy).

There is also no one on this planet that comes even close to possessing the same combination of unique skills, gifts, life experience wrapped up in the same package as you. Fact.

If you spend your time striving to be like someone else five things will happen:

1. You will do a second-rate job doing what someone else will always do better, and more quickly, effortlessly, and naturally.

2. By the time you work out how to do it their way, they will have evolved and moved on to their next fabulous thing.

3. Your success will be limited because you will be out of flow with the Universe.

4. You miss creating your own unique masterpiece and lighting up the world with your presence.

5. Being out of flow with the Universe, things will always feel a little hard.

Don't look to the people who have come before you to work out your way, forge your own path. We do this by embracing our complete 360-degree self (*weirdness and contradictions are good things*).

It takes courage, but once you are on your way it feels absolutely fantastic because – everything works in perfect harmony – it fits, everything is built around your You. And before you know it, chances are, your path will roll up alongside those who you once admired and they will admire you for forging your own.

WORK YOUR LIGHT

What one thing can you do today to forge
your own path courageously?

△

EMBRACE YOUR WEIRD

*'You're mad, bonkers, completely off your head. But
I'll tell you a secret. All the best people are.'*

ALICE IN WONDERLAND, LEWIS CARROLL

The dictionary meaning for weird is 'extraordinary, out of this world.'
Don't know about you but I'm all in for that! Don't be normal. Embrace
your weird. Get naked. Release your inner oddball. Let your crazy out.
When you do, three amazing things happen.

1. The people in your life who don't really love you for you will drop
    away. This might feel like a loss but really it's a win.

2. You will feel a hell of a lot more fantastic and free. Oh, and you will
    be on your way to serving the world by being Y*O*U.

3. You will clear the space for your people to find you. The kinds of
    people who are actually looking for the exact thing that you already
    are.

By embracing my 'weirdness' – in other words coming full throttle out of
the spiritual closet and proudly owning it – I attracted my fiancé Craig.
He says that the moment he walked into my bedroom (full of crystals,
angel cards, sage sticks, pendulums, and books on the Akashic records)
he knew I was going to be his future wife.

I later found out that when he was growing up all his friends thought he
was 'weird' because instead of having a poster of Kylie Minogue above
his bed he had Sabrina the teenage witch!

Weird is the new normal. Let's weird it up!

△
MY WEIRDNESS LIST

1.

2.

3.

4.

5.

6.

7.

8.

9.

10.

△

CALL IN YOUR PEOPLE

*'We are all a little weird and life is a little weird, and when we
find someone whose weirdness is compatible with ours, we join
up with them and fall in mutual weirdness and call it love.'*
DR. SEUSS

Call in your people. They're out there.

The ones that get you.

The ones who are the same kind of bonkers as you, the same kind of
weird.

Those you don't need to explain anything to.

Who want you to win and feel it when you fall.

Who light up when they see you.

Who, no matter how long they've been on the planet, feel like they've
spent all of it looking for you.

They're out there. And they want to find you. But you gotta lean into
your weirdness, so they know it when they see you.

WORK YOUR LIGHT

Who do you already have in your life that is one
of your people, the same kind of weird?

How can you embrace your weirdness to
call in more of your people?

THEY WERE THE SAME KIND OF **WEIRD**.

△

LET YOUR SPIRIT BE YOUR BRAND™

I spent over a decade in advertising helping some of the world's biggest brands find their authentic voice. Brands throw millions into carefully curating what you have right now. What no person or thing can take away or come close to impersonating.

The whole process of branding is personification. Because brands aren't born with a unique spirit (unlike you), their spirit must be manufactured. Establishing a brand for a product is the process of quite literally creating a personality, set of beliefs, tone of voice, and visual style that did not exist prior to creating it.

You were born with your own personal brand; you might not have known it, but it existed in full the moment you took your first breath. But it didn't begin there. You've been curating it for maybe hundreds, thousands, perhaps even millions of years. It's living and breathing in a constant state of evolution. It's your essence, your spirit, your You-ness.

It's You©

It's in there. And it wants to come out. Now it's just a matter of identifying, remembering, and choosing to bring it out into the light of day. It's you at your most expansive. The You, which is bursting to be released. The shining, sparkling, powerful You.

We expand when we allow ourselves to embrace, own, and express the unique wonder of who we truly are. We retract when we turn our back on our magnificence by trying to be more like someone else. When we retract, we go against Source and the flow of the Universe.

Choose to expand and let your spirit be your brand.

WORK YOUR LIGHT

List ten words that describe You best. Your You-ness. Your You©. Beyond what society has said about you and the roles you play. Who you really are.

1.

2.

3.

4.

5.

6.

7.

8.

9.

10.

If you had to condense it down to five words, what would they be?

1.

2.

3.

4.

5.

If you had to condense it down to three words, what would they be?

1.

2.

3.

△

YOUR TRIBE'S WAITING FOR YOU

'We need you to lead us.'
SETH GODIN

The world needs more leaders. More people who can courageously step out, speak up, and guide the way. You don't need to have it all together to lead. In fact, it helps if you don't. No one wants a perfect angel who hasn't made any mistakes.

Let your life be your message. Don't underestimate the power of sharing your story. It's through hearing someone else's journey that we feel less alone. We can see that if there was a way out for them then there may be a way out for us too. We realize that we are actually all in this thing called life together.

We are not as alone as we feel.

The difference between a follower and a leader is that the leader has the courage to go first. In bravely stepping out, they shine a light on the path for others to venture forward, too. Don't fret too much about trying to work out who your tribe is. Don't get stuck in age, income level, hobbies, and occupation. The best way to discover your tribe is actually to look in the mirror. If you feel called to lead, chances are it is because at some point in your life you longed for someone to lead you. Your tribe is longing for exactly the same thing as you were (and are).

Your tribe might only be one step behind you. Hell, they might even be right alongside you. You don't need your ducks in a row or a special certificate to give you permission. The only thing you need is the courage to stand up. Embrace your struggles, the peaks, and the troughs. You don't need to know the way. Just that you believe that there might be a different one.

Your tribe is waiting for you. Step forward so they can find you.

WORK YOUR LIGHT

At what point in your life did you most long for someone to lead you?

Looking back, what did you most need to hear from someone then?

△

YOU ARE YOUR MESSAGE

Your message is your life. Your struggles and your triumphs. Your highs and your lows. Your start and your middle. There is no end.

It's the things you are most proud of and the ones you'd rather forget. And the more specific your story, the more universal your message.

Regardless of how you choose to spread your light, it will touch more people when you allow yourself to be transparent about your journey and the hardest lessons learned along the way. The good and the bad. The best teachers are eternal students; their message grows as they do.

Your message is the moral of your story. And there are people waiting to hear it. A story left unsaid is the saddest story of them all. Share yours now.

WORK YOUR LIGHT

A great way of getting clear on your message is to imagine it to be a Hollywood movie. It doesn't need to be your entire life story; it could just be a chapter. Ask yourself:

What would the movie be about?

What genre is it?

What would the main character be like?

What about the supporting roles?

Who/what is the antagonist?

What is the moral of the story?

What's the title?

△

CHOOSE YOUR OWN THEME SONG

Choosing your own theme song is an awesome way to stay connected to who you truly are. Think of it as a musical anchor to call yourself home, light you up, and give yourself a pep talk. You can play it every morning when you wake up, while you're strutting down the street, before an important meeting, or to bring you back on track when you're in a bad mood.

Your theme song can be absolutely anything you choose it to be. If you want to get creative you can even make up your own. I've been playing my own theme song (*She's a Rainbow* by the Rolling Stones) for a few years now. At first I chose it because it embodied everything that I longed to become (which was who I was at my core), but felt too self-conscious to reveal. Each time I played it, it was almost like calling the lost pieces of myself home.

First I started playing it while I walked down the street. Then I began having a little dance party each night in my apartment. Then I would play it in my head before a big creative presentation or before I taught a Spirited Session. Eventually I conjured up the courage to share it with Craig and now he sings it to me!

WORK YOUR LIGHT

Choose your own theme song. It can be any song in the entire world. Or if you feel the urge, create one yourself. Put it on your iPod, iTunes, or Spotify and listen to it daily.

△

WRITE YOUR OWN TAG LINE

If you had a legacy what would it be? The simple act of condensing yourself down into a tag line forces us to really get clear on what it is we most want to share with the world. It doesn't need to be world changing.

The tag line acts as a manifesto of who you are and what you stand for. It might sound silly, but the clarity that comes from having your own personal tag line is a Godsend when you're faced with a tricky decision. You can weigh up each option and see which fits your tag line. It's also a great measure for checking if your life is aligned.

My friend Blair Milan had his own tag line: 'Good Times.' Not someone who suffered from confidence issues, Blair used his tag line any chance he got. When signing off emails, when saying cheers, when someone was describing something that happened to them, when he was relaying a story. You name it he'd drop it in there.

Arriving in Sydney after his death we went straight into funeral organizational mode. The theme of the wake was 'Good Times' and it was the biggest extravaganza that The Sydney Theatre Company had ever seen: singing, comedy, speeches, videos, and montages of all things Blair. (*He would have adored the attention.*) There was even a 'Good Times Bar' as you walked in.

Blair lived his life so wholeheartedly in line with this manifesto that every single person knew what Blair had taught them about life. We got 'Good Times' badges made and everyone still wears them as a tribute to the way he lived his life.

Blair's whole life was a devotion to living, noticing, grabbing, and appreciating the 'Good Times' that life has to offer us all. People who barely even knew Blair were touched by the exuberant essence of his spirit. Because he was so clear on who he was and how he wanted to spread his light.

You are a rare gift. You have the ability to devote your life to whatever you wish. So what do you want your legacy to be? If you had to write one, what would your tag line be?

WORK YOUR LIGHT

My personal tag line is:

What in your life is not in alignment with your tag line?

COME OUT OF THE SPIRITUAL CLOSET

'Come out, come out wherever you are.'
GLINDA THE GOOD WITCH, *THE WIZARD OF OZ*

Come out of the spiritual closet, it's much better out here. With every day, it's becoming more and more socially acceptable to be openly 'spiritual.' But when you've been in the spiritual closet for some time, it can be pretty scary to reveal – particularly to the people who 'know you' best – that, actually, there's more to you than you've let them see.

I hid in my spiritual closet for over a decade. I would suss out people before I revealed just how 'spiritual' I really was with a whisper. But when my soul called me to align my life, I knew I needed to get naked. So little by little, I came out of the closet and timidly began to strip.

The biggest step was bringing my 'spiritual self' to my work. I started telling colleagues about weekend courses I was doing and leaving books I was reading on my desk (rather than hidden in my bag, so no one would see the covers). I shared my beliefs about the connection between creativity, spirituality, and ideas, which are waiting to be born. I then began dropping the 'S word' (spirit) in meetings, creating the phrase, 'Let your spirit be your brand.'

The more layers I shed, the more liberated I felt. The more of my authentic self I revealed, the more effortless work became because I was able to show up completely as me. Instead of fitting into a mold, I let myself overspill and expand. And then the overspilling bits became my 'thing.' I got pay rises, won awards, got promotions. The parts of me that I was trying to keep under control were the bits that everyone actually valued most. Getting naked was the most liberating and rewarding experience of my life.

We make the biggest impact in the world by sharing our full self. Are you bringing your full self to all areas of your life? The thing about getting naked is that you don't have to rip off your clothes all at once, so you're suddenly exposed in broad daylight for everyone to see and point. That's what nightmares are made of. The best stripteases leave you wanting more!

You might start by taking off your hat, then your scarf, and your gloves. Next might come your coat, followed by your heels. Eventually off comes your dress, bra, and the rest. The more layers that fall to the ground, the more people want to see.

The more of yourself you reveal, the easier it is for 'your people' to find you. It's much harder to spot someone when they are in a disguise.

WORK YOUR LIGHT

Are you in a spiritual closet? How can you start getting naked and align all areas of your life?

△

ALIGN YOUR LIFE

In order to thrive in a big way in (*we are all meant to thrive*), we must align our lives, so that all pieces flow in vibrational harmony. When we are in alignment everything in our life flows. When we are out of alignment, there's a feeling that something isn't quite right. If you understand the Law of Attraction you will know that in order to create what you desire, you must become an authentic vibrational match with what you want to attract. Just like a radio that is set to the wrong frequency, it is impossible to pick up the latest indie tunes when you are set to some boring talkback show.

Someone who is in complete alignment has aligned their energy, thoughts, actions, and words to be a vibrational match with what they want to attract. That is, it's not about longing to be something 'one day,' rather bringing your thoughts, actions, energy, and words into complete harmony so that you 'already are' all you are wishing to attract. If we manage to do this, it is impossible not to call in everything that you want. The catch, however, is being committed to make conscious daily actions that will bring you into alignment with that thing.

Just as I described in 'Show up and shine,' (see page 166), it wasn't until I was a 100 percent vibrational match with Hay House that I got the call. It took a while, but little by little – as my thoughts, words, energy, and actions came together into 100 per cent complete alignment – I became a vibrational match.

First was taking the leap from my career to throwing myself full-time into my intuitive coaching business, which I had been trained for, but never felt quite ready to start. Next was writing a little bit every day and putting together a book proposal. At this stage, I was given two opportunities to submit my proposal, but then it's no surprise that I didn't hear anything (because I still wasn't a vibrational match). A little disheartened, I scooped up my ego and committed to show up and write every day (just as I would if I was an author). Then came changing my thoughts around seeking approval from an external force before I felt legit, ready and deserving.

Finally, and most importantly, I found myself in a state of joy as I began to write for the love of it, rather than being attached to an outcome of being published. It became about answering the call for the joy of it rather than the end goal.

I lost myself in what lit me up, what happened, and the result of it was actually none of my business. Month by month, my thoughts, words, energy, and actions slowly but surely shifted into complete alignment with Hay House. On one hand, I worked extremely hard for a very long time (17 years, you could say) to get to that state of vibrational match, but the moment I was a complete vibrational match, it came without any effort, in an instant!

WORK YOUR LIGHT

What are you trying to call into or create in your life?

Are your thoughts, words, energy, and actions
in complete alignment with it?

Are you the same person in all areas of your life? (For
example, at work, at home, with friends, with strangers.)

$\triangle$

BE A YES

Be a yes. A full-blown, 100 percent, hands down, hell yeah we're doing this no matter what kinda YES.

The Universe does not dabble in 'maybe' or 'kind of' or 'yeah, but.' It's either an unwavering 100 percent or not at all.

When we hold an intention, every single thing in the Universe either resonates or 'disonates' with that. If something resonates it is a 100 percent yes and it's going to come straight at you like a magnet or a seagull after your chips at the beach. If it's not quite 100 percent, the manifestation is going to be not quite 100 percent.

**Every second of every day you are vibrating your
'yes,' 'no,' and 'maybe' thoughts and actions.**

The clearer you can get on what makes you say 'HELL YEAH' and what makes you say 'HELL NO,' the more YESSES will come flying straight for you, landing right on your lap.

WORK YOUR LIGHT

How can you be more of a HELL YEAH for the things you are calling into your life (which are also the things that are calling you)?

△

TWITTER BIOS AND FITTING IN

We live in an age where we are called to define who we are in 140 characters. The amount of time I've spent editing my Twitter profile description should be a jail-able offence. Everyone I know has no idea how to describe what they 'do' and who they 'are' in a sentence.

That's because defining who you are in 140 characters is impossible! And more than that, you are a work in progress, an ever-evolving work of art so 140 characters will never sum you up. Ever! And that is a good thing.

Chances are you've probably had more than 140 lives (that's a lot of soul history and soul gifts packed into one vessel)... how could you possibly fit all that you are into 140 characters?

So if you can't find the words, it's probably not necessarily due to not knowing who you are. Maybe it's because you know you are all that and more.

Let your vibration do the talking for you.

△

VIBRATION IS THE BEST MARKETING TOOL

Your vibration is more powerful than your words could ever be. More powerful than what you wear, say, or do. More powerful than the best marketing strategy, publicist, and PR darling all put together.

Like attracts like.

It doesn't matter how 'in tune' someone is, they will pick up your vibration a mile off and make a split decision or judgment about you without even thinking about it.

Vibration has nothing to do with thought; it has everything to do with feeling. People make a decision about you based on these feelings, and they don't need to be 'in tune' to do it. We may not be able to put it in words but we can spot if someone is authentic in a nanosecond, because their energy matches their words.

The best web, copy, and advertising campaign is worthless if it doesn't match the brand's vibrational truth. If your words say one thing and your energy another, people just won't buy it, either figuratively or literally.

Energy doesn't lie.

The best test to see if your words match your vibration is to say them out loud. If they make you feel strong and true, then it is a match. If they make you squirm and cringe then it's not an authentic representation of what you are saying.

Your body can also give you clues. When you say something out loud, notice where you feel it in your body when you say something that is true versus when you say something that is not.

DO IT IN
A WAY THAT
ONLY YOU CAN.

△

YOU© – YOUR AUTHENTIC VOICE

If you feel drawn to share your message by writing, finding your authentic tone of voice is an important part of the process.

My first job in advertising was as a copywriter. I then went on to become a creative director where I directed teams of writers in finding the authentic tone of voice for loads of big brands. Finding your authentic tone of voice can take time, but here are some tools to help you express yours.

Be You©

You cannot find your authentic voice unless you know who you are. Knowing who you are takes time. Looking at what other people are doing, in an effort to do the same, won't work. It will water down your voice and won't be in alignment with who you are. Write as you speak. Write as you feel. If you are optimistic, be optimistic. If you are passionate, be passionate. If you are a hippy who has a dark sense of humor and loves pandas, be a hippy with a dark side that loves pandas. Be You©.

Write from your soul

Don't write what you think you should write; write what your soul is calling you to share. When I am writing from my soul my writing is extremely different to when I am writing from my head: the words come flowing and have a deeper, RICHER feel to them; my pace changes; and it feels passionate and free. Sometimes I write something and then read it back and think, 'Wow, that's beautiful,' because my head could not have possibly put it quite like that, no matter how hard it tried. I know then that the writing has come through me. It's not of me. When I write from my head it takes a lot more effort and doesn't have the same authenticity to it. It feels considered and rigid. No one wants to read that! Before you sit down to write, put your hand on your heart, take a breath, and listen to what your soul has to share.

Start talking

The only way to find your voice is to start talking (and being willing to get it wrong!). When I directed teams of writers I would review at least 20 headlines to find *the* one. Finding your voice is a process, we are multifaceted beings and so there are different directions we can take our writing. You need to be willing to get it wrong in order to know when you've got it right. Getting it wrong is just as important as getting it right.

Write to yourself

If you don't know what to say, write what you most need to hear. Your tribe resonates with you because they are aligned with your message. More likely than not, the messages your soul has for you will strike a chord in them too. You don't need to overcomplicate it. Read the chapter 'Letters to self' (see page 260) for more information on how to do this.

Be willing to get it wrong

You can't find your authentic voice without getting it wrong. Be willing to try things, to find your flow. You will know when you have tapped into your authentic tone because it will resonate with you. You might feel warmth in your heart, an all-over feeling of expansion or lightness. If it isn't aligned with who you are you might feel a burning in your belly.

Share don't compare

Don't compare yourself to someone else who has been writing for years. Don't rush it. Stay true. Be you. Sometimes ideas and phrases that are meant to be born will come through different writers – which is a tricky thing to tackle when you've spent a lot of time creating it. If someone else's stuff is similar to yours, check in with yourself to ensure that what you created came from an authentic place (and not from being on their social media feed). Do your best to make it your own and ask your soul for guidance.

Don't write for likes

Don't get disheartened if no one 'likes' or praises your writing. You have no idea how many hearts it has actually touched. Just show up and trust that if you have a message to share, the people who need to hear it most will see it.

Sharing vs. selling

Don't write to sell, write to share. If you're sharing on Facebook, your message will be competing with people's best friends in their newsfeed. Share what will provide value to your readers, not you.

I read something a while back (on Facebook but can't remember who posted it!) that stuck with me, which went something like this:

'I don't share to teach or convince others, I share to make those who feel the same as me feel less alone.'

I adore this.

That's why we share our story, our message, and our soul.

A *freakin'* men.

△

YOU© – YOUR AUTHENTIC VISUAL STYLE

Part of shining your light is expressing your light in a way that is in visual alignment with who you are.

The way to shine your light the furthest is to do things in a way that is completely authentic to you, and a great way to explore your look and feel is to pin. I get everyone who does a 'Work Your Light Mentorship' or online course with me to start a personal brand pin board over at www.pinterest.com. You can keep it public or make it private. You could even name it, e.g. Amy©.

There are no rules to what you pin, but you might find the following guidance helpful in getting you started.

Pin what makes your heart expand

Don't analyze why you are pinning, just pin the things that make your heart expand. Pin what is a YES and scroll past what is a NO.

Find your own style

You want your brand to be a unique expression of you, not a second-rate version of someone else. Don't insult your authenticity by 'borrowing' someone else's look and feel. Draw your inspiration from your inner compass. These things take time so let it evolve. Let your inner light lead the way.

Don't feel guilty

If you have any feelings of 'this is a waste of time,' or 'I should be doing things that are more important,' shake those bad boys off.

Look for directions

After a little while (it might be a month or a couple of weeks), look at your board as a whole. You will begin to notice a couple of different directions starting to come through. Certain types of colors, photography styles, and typography will start bubbling up and a certain attitude will start to shine through. All of these things are priceless when it comes to finding your own authentic visual expression. Delete the things that don't resonate as much and keep the ones that do. What you want to get to is a consistent over-arching unique visual style that represents you.

Working with designers

If, at some stage, you plan to work with a designer to create a website, having a brand board is imperative. There are *so* many websites out there that look the same. One of the reasons this happens is not enough thought going into getting really clear on the unique brand, and so the creative direction the designer gets is 'make it like [*insert site name*] and [*insert site name*].'

Briefing a designer is really tricky because people respond subjectively to visuals. And as a designer, being briefed by someone who doesn't know what they are looking for is like designing in the dark. It is IMPOSSIBLE to describe visuals objectively.

I've worked with many designers and can't stress the importance of establishing a clear and unique visual direction before you jump into creating your site. For the cover of this book, I spent two days coming up with mood boards for all of the possible visual directions to brief the designer.

If you've done the groundwork on who you are and what type of visuals resonate with you, then you'll be well on your way to shining your light in a visually authentic way.

You are a work in progress

Be open to evolving your look and feel as you evolve as a person. Your style should always be anchored in who you are; however, as you grow, your design should too. THIS is what makes it impossible to mimic.

WORK YOUR LIGHT

If you don't have a Pinterest account already, sign up and start pinning. I'd recommend around 10 minutes a day for a period of a month to start seeing a nice visual style coming through. If you want extra guidance on developing your unique brand, I offer mentoring and online courses that will help you shine your light in a super authentic way.

$$\triangle$$

IT'S NOT ABOUT YOU

Living a life of service means showing up and shining our light regardless of what people think. If you dim your light because you feel inadequate, you are doing the world a disservice. The moment you bring your drama, fear or self-image into the picture you make it about you. It's not about you.

Recently I learned this one in a big way. I'm part of a Six Sensory Mastermind Skype support group of six intuitives from around the world. On a recent call one of them said, 'Rebecca has been a bit quiet today – so Rebecca, what's up?' (*Sometimes it's annoying having intuitives as friends!*). I told them that I was feeling nervous about a big speaking event I had coming up.

I told them, 'I know it's silly but I am feeling really nervous and am doubting myself because all the other speakers are much more experienced.'

Monika then firmly but lovingly replied, 'It sounds like that's Rebecca's ego talking. It's afraid of how she will be received. When really it's none of her business. She needs to trust that whoever booked her trusts that what she has to offer is exactly what the attendees need to hear. She needs to get out of the way and stop making it about her.'

Everyone agreed. Including me.

My ego was getting in the way; letting my fear of not being good enough prevent me from showing up and serving to the best of my ability. I was spending valuable time, which I could use to prepare, worrying. And had I gone on stage in a fear state then I wouldn't have been giving them the best, most present me. I heard the message loud and clear:

It's so not about me!

When I started giving intuitive readings and coaching, I used to do the same thing. I'd look to my clients for validation that I 'got it right,' that the information I was receiving resonated and was helpful. Now, I know that my job is more about holding space and being as present as I possibly can. I trust that I am the vehicle for the Universe to work through. And whatever words I have to share are exactly the ones they need to hear.

How people receive you is none of your business. You were given a unique set of gifts, life experiences, and passions. Your only job is to share them. Whatever experience you are facing right now

You are ready for it!

You would not have been given it, if you weren't. You do deserve to be here. Regardless of how nervous or unprepared you feel, suck it up and shine your light anyway. The world needs your light.

It doesn't mean that doubt doesn't exist. Doubt and fear are normal parts of being human. Admit your fears. My teachers taught me that if I am scared of something the best cure is saying it out loud; it makes it a little less scary.

WORK YOUR LIGHT

How is your fear getting in the way of you
stepping into your biggest self?

△
YOU ARE NOT FOR EVERYONE

The world is filled with people who, no matter what you do, will point blank not like you. But it is also filled with those who will love you fiercely. They are your people. You are not for everyone and that's OK. Talk to the people who can hear you.

Don't waste your precious time and gifts trying to convince them of your value, they won't ever want what you're selling. Don't convince them to walk alongside you. You'll be wasting both your time and theirs and will likely inflict unnecessary wounds, which will take precious time to heal. You are not for them and they are not for you; politely wave them on, and continue along your way. Sharing your path with someone is a sacred gift; don't cheapen this gift by rolling yours in the wrong direction.

Keep facing your true north.

△

BE OK WITH WHERE YOU ARE

Be OK with where you are and all that you are right now – especially the bits that you are working on. The people you are here to guide are the ones who are a few steps behind you. You don't need to have it all sorted, or be an expert...

It's your humanness that truly touches people, not your superhuman-ness.

When we first embark on our journey of spiritual awakening, we can find ourselves thinking that we 'get it' – as if there is a finite destination to arrive at. When the opposite is actually true. The more we know, the less we actually know.

You don't need to pretend or prove that you have it together, rather, just share what you have figured out so far. We are all in this school of life together. There is no final destination, no end point, just increased consciousness and a deeper understanding.

Every moment is an opportunity to deepen our learning about life and ourselves. When we resist saying, 'Oh this, I already know this,' we open the door for life to come in and touch our soul even more deeply than before.

We are all eternal students. I am so happy to have learned this recently, even more deeply than I knew it before. And I'm looking forward to learning it even more deeply than I think I know it now. Sometimes words get in the way of truth.

Soften your mind, and your soul will be touched.

△

CREATIVITY AND BEING
A CLEAR CHANNEL

When you tap into the flow of Source energy you are a clear channel for creations to flow through you. When you allow Source to flow through you, a beautiful thing happens – just like sunbeams shining through a stained-glass window: the light passes through your authentic self and creates something that no one else could have created.

Many of my clients fear that what they have to say isn't valid because:

1. It has already been said by someone else (who beat them to it and is already established);

2. Or, lots of other people have been through a similar experience, so what's so special about them?

As we allow the light to flow through the stained-glass windows of our soul, our vibration that the creation holds draws people in.

If there are people who have been through, or are going through, similar experiences as you, then all the more urgency for you to share your message and creations now. If you have heard the call (and I believe we all have) start creating now. Don't waste your time looking over your shoulder, do it in a way that only you can.

WORK YOUR LIGHT

What is stopping you from expressing your
message or creations more courageously?

△

INVOKING YOUR MUSE

Everyone on the planet has the ability to be creative and birth ideas. Creativity flows through us and while we might be there when the creation happens, there is a mysterious force that delivers it. This book has been written this way and many writers and artists admit to birthing their creations the same way. I call this creative force 'the muse.'

The muse is always on the lookout for people to receive creations that are waiting to be born. But if we don't show up every day, or only when we feel like it, the muse will move onto someone else. She's promiscuous like that. It's not personal. It's just the way of the muse.

The muse wants us to act on our ideas without delay. We are the vehicles for the creation to come into the world. Pretty much every time I have stalled on a big idea or acted a little slowly, someone else has come up with a similar phrase, creation, or idea in unison. When your muse speaks, act.

The more we show up every day to connect with our muse, the clearer the communication gets and the more effortlessly the creations start flowing.

When a muse chooses you, they choose you because you are the perfect vehicle for their message. It's that YOU-NESS they want, your unique creative fingerprint. A perfect concoction of life experience, upbringing, city, body type, and voice.

WORK YOUR LIGHT

What creations or ideas are waiting to be born by you?

△

LETTERS TO SELF

'A bird doesn't sing because it has the answers,
it sings because it has a song.'
MAYA ANGELOU

When embarking on writing this book, my teacher Sonia told me to 'write to your most interested reader... you.' I had heard this from her years earlier when she described the process of writing her first book, where her friend Julia Cameron had asked her to think of it as writing a letter every day. But to be honest I didn't know what she meant. Then it dawned on me, it's not because I'm my most interested reader (because I just love reading my own words), it's because at some point in my life these were the words I most needed to hear. Eureka!

Every day when I sit down to write, that is exactly what I do. It doesn't matter if it's a new chapter, a Facebook update, a tweet, a blog post, or scribbles in my notebook. I allow my fingers to be taken over by the energy of what my heart most needs to hear. It could be what it most needs to hear today, or it could be what I most needed to hear at a different moment of my life, a moment when I most needed to be shown the way, to be reassured, to be encouraged.

We are all linked through the most magnificent web of golden threads. What your heart needs to hear is what another does too.

If you are sharing your writing, don't write to teach or convince, write to soften your own heart. Allow each word that comes through you to be medicine for your soul. The people who need to hear it will be drawn by your words, by your message, by your truth, by your song. When you allow the wiser you to write to yourself, you allow your head to get out of the way and your wise higher self to take over.

Write to heal yourself. For as we heal ourselves, we can't help but heal the world at large.

WORK YOUR LIGHT

Write your own 'Letter to Self.' Get a blank piece of paper and write at the top, 'Dear [*insert your name*].'

Fill the page with the words you most need to hear. Maybe they're the words you most need to hear today, or maybe they're the words you most needed to hear five, 10, even 20 years ago. Without judgment let them come flowing.

If you feel inspired by what you have written, you might want to share your words on Facebook, in a blog, or wherever feels right.

We are all in this shared experience called life together. What is healing for you will likely be healing for someone else too. Serve the world by being you.

△

YOUR SOUL'S VOICE

'The planet needs your soul's unique tone to harmonise.'
SERA BEAK

We each hold a truth deep within us that longs to be expressed. Sculpted for lifetimes, the voice of your soul is like no other. It carries with it wisdom that can only be gained through soul growth. Through remembering, tapping into, and expressing this unique tone, we not only heal ourselves, we also heal the planet. Indeed, the world needs harmonizing drastically.

Our soul's voice is slightly different to the voice we are used to speaking with, and it can take a lot of courage to find and share it with the world.

My soul's voice comes through the most strongly when I write. It is deep and wise, it is compassionate and motherly, it is courageous and knowing, it is petrified and fierce. It is the result of lifetimes of speaking out and being silenced, of devastating grief and absolute devotion.

I know when I am writing from my soul as my whole energy changes, my writing style shifts slightly and it feels like I am being pulled by a gentle current in a deep, warm, ocean.

As we shed the layers of our personality and start letting our soul speak through us, we discover that we actually have a very clear message that longs to be shared. The more we speak it, the clearer it gets. However, more often than not, the message our soul truly longs to express can take extreme courage to share.

While I knew from an early age that my calling was to write, teach, and speak, I was petrified by the idea. I knew my soul had wisdom to share, but I kept making excuses for why I wasn't ready to step forward. When I was young, I rationalized that I didn't have any life experience to teach; once I had those extreme experiences I argued that I needed yet another modality to learn before I would feel 'ready.' I'd watch other people walking the path, knowing that it was similar to the one set out ahead of me, but I was paralyzed by an extreme fear that I just couldn't shake. It wasn't like normal fear, I felt as though if I spoke my truth I would risk my life.

One day, before attending a weekend workshop, I prayed to the Universe to help me release this fear for real. Sure enough, on the first day my teacher Sonia asked me to come to the front of the class to work on letting go of old energetic patterns from past lives. Held by the class, I journeyed from lifetime to lifetime where I was betrayed and killed for speaking my truth. A scholar in Ancient Greece, a witch in the Middle Ages, an Essene in the time of Jesus Christ, a priest in France, a mystic in Ancient Egypt.

Lifetime upon lifetime came flooding back and my soul showed me why I felt so much pain about speaking out and stepping forward. As Sonia and Shamanic healer Debra Grace guided me, I allowed myself to remember all of the pain and to release it through my tears and voice. I sobbed more than I ever had and surrendered the grief, anger, betrayal, and pain to the light.

Through tapping into this extreme grief, I was able to understand why I felt such extreme fear over stepping forward. Now when I feel the fear to speak out I remember all of these courageous men and women who my soul has embodied and I feel them standing alongside me. I see how all of these lives have led to the one I am living now, and how lucky I am to be living at a time in history in which it is easier to stand up than it ever has been before.

While my soul remembers the past pain, I choose to be strengthened by it. I allow these experiences to come through in my writing and I thank all of these amazing men and women for rising and rising. If you are having trouble stepping forward and sharing your soul's truth, it is likely that you have soul memory of being rejected in the past for doing just that.

There has never been a better time in history than right now to rise up and speak your truth. It is not only needed, it is necessary. If you feel fearful of speaking up and stepping out, know that you are not alone and, as Sera Beak so beautifully puts it, 'the world needs your unique tone in order to harmonize.' As we each rise up, we make it easier for the next to do the same.

WORK YOUR LIGHT

What fear do you have that is stopping you sharing your voice?

What is behind this fear?

How is your soul voice different to your normal speaking voice?

△

SPEAK UP, I CAN'T HEAR YOU

Speak up. I can't hear you.

I want to know how similar we are and that I am not actually alone.

Speak up. I can't hear you.

I want to be touched by your voice and raised up by your vibe.

Speak up. I can't hear you.

I want to hear how you struggled and how
after it all you still managed to rise.

Speak up. I can't hear you.

I want to be inspired by your journey and reminded
that, perhaps, one day soon I too can shine.

Speak up. I can't hear you.

Δ

RAISE THEM UP, DON'T CUT THEM DOWN

'Comparison is an act of violence against the self.'
Iyanla Vanzant

Raise them up, not cut them down.

The sign of true success is someone who enjoys raising up those around them. Let's all rise up together; let's encourage, not compete.

When one woman shines her light, she makes the path brighter for the next one to come. There are enough people asleep for us all to awaken with our light. Next time someone is rising, shine your light on them.

You'll shine all the more brightly for it.

WORK YOUR LIGHT

Who in your life do you feel competitive with?

What's behind the competitiveness?

△

IF YOU'RE COMPETING WITH SOMEONE...

That woman you're jealous of, envious, who has what you want.

They are you and you are them. And you're both doing your best.

That girl you're competing with, who presses your buttons, who doesn't deserve it as much as you.

They are you and you are them. And you're both doing your best.

That chick that annoys you, who beat you to it, who is doing what you were planning on doing and now it's too late.

They are you and you are them. And you're both doing your best

That lady who somehow got lucky and just landed on her feet.

They are you and you are them. And you're both doing your best.

That sister who courageously followed her calling, and is now bravely shining her light.

They are you and you are them. And you're both doing your best.

If you pay enough attention when you look in her eyes, you'll see your light reflected back.

For they are you and you are them. And you're both just doing your best.

MANTRA

I choose not to compare myself to others. I show
up and let the Universe work through me, knowing
that what I have to offer is enough.

△

BE AN ENCOURAGER

Be an encourager, not a discourager.

The one who wants the best for others and celebrates when they win.

Be an encourager, not a discourager.

The one who sees the light in those around them
and reminds them of it when they fall.

Be an encourager, not a discourager.

The one who acknowledges their jealous thoughts,
but chooses to replace them with others.

Be an encourager, not a discourager.

The one who admits when they are down but doesn't
demand that they take others with them.

Be an encourager, not a discourager.

The one who remembers that we are actually all on the same team.

△

THERE'S ROOM ENOUGH FOR EVERYONE

There is enough room for everyone. Your special unique bag of gifts, stories, struggles, triumphs, energy, and tools is like no one else's. The way you look, the city you're from, your voice, your body size, your smile... embrace it, don't change it. There is enough room for everyone.

In this social age, it's easy to see those who are walking a similar path as your competition. Don't let your ego see that person as separate, we're actually all on the same team, there's no need to compete.

There is enough room for everyone.

YOUR SOUL'S GOT THINGS TO SAY.

△
DEMYSTIFYING THE MYSTIC

The Ancient Egyptians believed that we have 360 senses all linked to the organs of our body (which coincides with the chakras, see page 193). While we may be more technologically advanced than the ancients, we are not as awake as they were.

Our wise sixth sense is not just reserved for the mystics and the psychics, it is available to us all. We just need to look within. The mystics knew this. But the sharing of this knowledge was not exactly convenient for those who were trying to control the masses.

As we move out of the shadow of the patriarchal system (where power and control reign supreme), light is being shed on this female archetype that is an embodiment of the Divine Feminine. I am she. You are she. We are all her. She was our grandmother's grandmother, our grandmother's grandmother's grandmother. She is all of the women who refused to stop rising up. And all of the men too.

If we all woke up to our intuitive nature, inner power, and authentic magic, the world would be a very different place. It's happening, slowly but surely, and you're at the forefront.

As more and more of us rise up to our inner wisdom and true authentic power, we embrace the authentic magic that dwells within. An era where it is safe for us all to shine as big and bright as humanly possible. An era where there is enough room for us all to follow our soul's callings and express our gifts freely. An era where we are all awake and living consciously.

My wish is that we all find the courage to lead the way. That we continue to rise up regardless of people who think that we are 'too much.' Now is the time we have been rising for. For centuries, for this moment.

**The Divine Feminine is within all of us
and she is ready to rise up.**

△
THE MYSTIC ALWAYS RISES

As she let her soul sing to her, she let go of lifetimes' worth of silenced truth missiles cemented in the deepest caverns of her soul. A voice snuffed out for centuries, for saying too much, for standing up too much, for being too much.

Her intuition and bigness restrained for centuries, but not any more. She could not be locked away, muted, or extinguished any longer. Not now. Not ever again.

As she let her spirit move her, she danced right through the flames. Resentment, anger, and memories stomped out with every blazing convulsion, sway, and kick. Sensing her in the distance, one by one her sisters joined her, knowing this dance by heart.

The movement created space for their tears, which flowed deeper than all of the rivers and lakes from all of the ages. Soothing and cooling the burning that once enveloped her entire being. Her whole body. All of her bodies. All of their bodies. All of our bodies.

Never forgetting. But still rising, just as she planned to. Just as we planned to. Rising and rising and rising and rising and rising. Standing taller than all the sisters who came before and will continue to come again.

The mystic always rises.

△

YOUR HEART IS ELASTIC

Your heart is elastic. It can grow or expand according to how much you are ready to receive. It can be stretched and filled up with all of the unlimited love and support that is flowing through the Universe.

If you've experienced real depths in your life, you'll know that just when you thought things couldn't get any worse, they sometimes do. The same goes for the good stuff too, though. The only limit to how much good you can receive is your perception of how much good you can receive. Your heart is elastic and your capacity for joy is as much as you say it is. Which is a lot. In fact, it's unlimited. So, how much good can you handle?

MANTRA

Every moment of every day, I am expecting
and welcoming good things.

△

LET THE UNIVERSE SUPPORT YOU

The Universe is here to support you as much as you let it.

Many of my Lightworker clients have a block around earning proper abundance for their soul work, particularly the healers (you don't need to be a healer to be a Lightworker). As if it is not quite fair to receive real prosperity for giving love, shining your light and being of service. I disagree.

Devoting your life to something bigger is not a small feat. There are many things you need in order to do your work; you deserve to be supported as you do it. Right now for me, I am spending most of my time writing and working with clients through giving Akashic record readings and mentoring.

In order for me to be of service for my clients I need to eat well, meditate, rest, and keep investing in my learning. If I have more than four clients a day my energy gets depleted (working in the subtle realms can be pretty tiring). I'm not soft or afraid of hard work (if anything I overwork), but I have found that I cannot be of service unless I listen to my body.

The work that you are called to do is priceless. As such, the people who choose to answer their highest calling and be of service should be bountifully supported. And you will be, if you allow it.

MANTRA

I let go of the outcome and I allow myself to be supported
by the Universe in ways that I could not even imagine.

△

EXPANSION AND
NEVER-ENDING GROWTH

'What is the difference
Between your experience of Existence
And that of a saint?
The saint knows
That the spiritual path is a sublime chess game with God
And that the Beloved
Has just made such a Fantastic Move
That the saint is now continually
Tripping over Joy
And bursting out in Laughter
And saying, "I Surrender!"
Whereas, my dear, I am afraid you still think
You have a thousand serious moves.'

TRIPPING OVER JOY, HAFIZ

We are all in this Earth school of life together; the learning never stops. Have you ever noticed how just after you have a spiritual breakthrough, the Universe sends something your way and it feels like you're at the beginning again?

It's so frustrating because our mind is so linear and likes to think that we are getting somewhere in particular – a definite end point or destination. But what I have come to realize is that really we are just deepening our learning, understanding, and remembering. We are all students and there's always more deepening to experience.

When we say to the Universe, 'Please use me,' or 'Let me be of service to the world,' it's as if the Universe cries, 'Hooray!' and then commits to sending things our way to make us better equipped to be of service.

These things, experiences, or people, then do their best to mirror back to us the part of our shadow that could do with a bit of work. Shining a light on all the things that you're facing that will make you even better equipped to serve in the highest capacity. If there are any healers or coaches out there you'll know what I am saying. I've had my most powerful sessions with clients who are dealing with the exact thing that I was struggling with the day before.

There is no end destination to get to, no time to arrive. Rather, more of yourself to embrace and expand into.

One of my friends reminded me of a cool fact about saints. She said, 'Why do you think that most saints are not deemed saints until after they have died? It's because all the people who were around to vouch for their humanness have passed away.'

I love that so much.

On our journey towards 'enlightenment' it's important to remember that we are human, and with being human comes having an ego. No matter how masterful we are, we are all students and the learning never ends. And that's a good thing. But as we begin to accept our challenging experiences as opportunities for growth, what would have previously felt like a tsunami crashing through our life can be reframed to be an opportunity to expand. Which is why we are here in the first place.

The amazing thing about this time we are living in is that there is a mass-awakening happening. In the past when people 'woke up' many would withdraw from society and go sit in a cave. But now, I believe that we are being called to integrate our awakened consciousness in all parts of society. With every new person who wakes up, the vibration of the planet also increases. With every conscious decision we each make (whether it's to meditate, follow a career that is calling us or going veggie) we add to the raised consciousness of the planet.

There is no right or wrong way to expand and grow, just many different paths.

Your inner guidance system knows what's the right one for you, don't let anyone tell you different.

$\triangle$

IT'S TIME TO STEP UP

The planet is beckoning. Coaxing. Calling you. To step into your wholeness. To step up and into all of you. The big you. The complete you. The one that's full of light. She's already in you. Give in to the stirring. Give in to the niggle. Answer the calling. You are the message. The time has come. You are needed here. Let's get to work.

△

YOU WEREN'T BORN FOR THE SIDELINES

You were not born for the sidelines, for the nose bleeders or the wings.

Raise the curtain, take the microphone, there's a song for you to sing.

You were born with a message; you have
something important to share.

Instead of resisting your soul's yearnings, make
your life one big moving prayer.

Stop waiting for permission, don't pretend to be blind.

Don't compare yourself to others; you are one of a very unique kind.

Your spot at the table is waiting; your seat has already been assigned.

Now take a breath, a good old leap and get ready to shine.

Come out from the sidelines, from the nose bleeders and the wings.

Raise the curtain, take the stage, it's your soul's song you need to sing.

LIGHT UP THE WAY.

△

YOU GO FIRST

You go first. It's time, you're ready, your soul is calling for you to lead the way.

If you can't quite find the courage to do it for you, then do it for:

Emma Ball, Ollie Neveu, Melanie Mackie, and Sanja Plavljanic-Sirola. Do it for Marlene Gourlay, Kirsty Hobbs, Jennifer Mole, and Bianca Young. Do it for Joanne Williams, Rosemarie St Louis, Bianca Filoteo, and Anne-Marie Tiller. Do it for Roz Grimble, Jen Bollands, Zoe Brewer, and Meghan Genge. Do it for Kay Blanchard, Brooke Steff, Vicky Maxwell, and Jane Wright. Do it for Natasha Van Staden, Michelle Van Caneghem, Alexis Williams, and Laura Paterson. Do it for Naomi Baird, Jessica Noyes, Narinder Bassan, and Emily Johnston. Do it for Libby Horsman, Bethany Love, Sheila Ann Lacey, and Suzan Ward. Do it for Victoria Cottle, Claire Ashman, Amelia Pearson, and Lizzie Houlbrooke. Do it for Kimberley Jones, Susannah Lee, Cath Dreamcatcher, Melissa LaJoie, and Louise Nyakoojo. Do it for Sonia Kaur, Jacquelyn Hayley, Tric Wright, and Helen Thomas. Do it for Hayley Wintermantle, Carolyn Sykes, Heather Burke, and Monika Laschkolnig. Do it for Renee Vos de Wael, Natalie Sneddon, Caya Munro, and Ruthie Kolle Hayes. Do it for Jacqueline Hulan, Giallian Marks, Lisa Barner, and Cornelia Blom. Do it for Laura Martin, Lesa Cochrane, Danielle Mercurio, and Rachel Whitehead. Do it for Juliana Ilieva, Karen Anderton, Aoife Anastasia, and Carol Harley. Do it for Viv Ferrari, Susanne Snellman, Kristy Blaikie, and Frankie Stone. Do it for Kay Jackson, Jett Black, Sarah Hook, and Susan Young. Do it for Lucy Paltnoi, Bill Gee, Louise Androlia, and Emily Riggs. Do it for Georgina Davis, Tania Constantini-Zimmermann, Shelly Drew, and Oeda O'Hara. Do it for Bekky May, Sarah Wilder, Lisa Caddick, and Lucy Milan Davis. Do it for Rachel Savage, Yolande Diver, Vienda Maria, and Carly Jennings. Do it for Annabelle Catherine Chambers, Nicola Phipard-Shears, Lisa Rose, and Keyon Bayani. Do it for Jen Claire Harrison, Emma Pedersen, Nathalie Hollywood, and Nicolle Smith. Do it for Gina Corneille Lilasong, Lizzie Bengal, Helen Hodgson, and Ailish Lucas. Do it for Jo Kilma, Kathryn Davy, Sonja Lockyer, and Alex Beadon. Do it for Kindra Murphy, Graciela Vega, Lauren Raso, and Helene Reinbolt. Do it for Martha Brown, Diana Sophie Walles, and Christina Walsh. Do it for Roslyn Tebble, Shelly Cameron, Debbie Bolton, and Lucy Sheridan-Wightman. Do it for Bea Bea's Baker, Lisa Marie Pittman, Renee de Villeneuve, and Amanda Emmett. Do it for Belinda Kerruish, Madalyn DeMolet, Zoe Wells, and Tiana-Marie Jones. Do it for Lily Holliday, Pauline Kehoe, Cllaire Brady, and Amy Davidson. Do it for Loren Honey, Julia Davis, Anne-Marie Williams, and Cassie Raine. Do it for Kate Sawyer, Marrsha Troyer Massino, Lindsay Pera, and Jennifer Caine. Do it for Jojo Williams, Jenifer Mole, Jayne Goldheart, and Lisa Crowned Jewelz Davis. Do it for Fiona Pearson, Gillian Marks, Jacqueline Haley, and Claire Maria Atkins. Do it for Marisa Madeline Beatey, Emma Pechey, Fiona Radman, and Betsy Bass. Do it for Jennifer Cainssino, Lindsay Perawyer, Julia Davis, Clare Sophia Voyant, and Katie Gee. Do it for Sheila Dickson, Dana May, Amy Firth, and Jaqueline Kolek. Do it for Cath Dreamdancer Gearing, Adriana Zooma, Zoe Caldwell, and Peg Watt.

Do it for your best friend and your sister, your aunt and your mother.

Do it for all the women who came before and all that will ever be.

Do it for all of these women, and all the rest.

For when they watch you go first, they'll find the courage to go next.

△

LETTER TO A LIGHTWORKER II

This is the dawn of a new day and the day of a new dawn.

You have the power to spark global change just by being you.

Every decision you make creates a ripple in the
interconnected sea that joins all life; there is nothing
too big or too small, every conscious act counts.

Follow what lights you up and what makes you feel
expansive. Don't worry about what it is, what people will
think, or the way it should be done. Just lose yourself in the
doing and invite the Universe to work through you.

Go 'in' every day. Sit down with yourself and listen. Your Inner Guru
should be the only authority of your life. Ask it to light your way.

Your soul knows the fastest way home. Act
on its whispers, especially when it's telling you
something that you don't want to hear.

Trade in controlling and forcing for allowing and trusting. The
Universe is waiting to support you. But first you've got to leap.

Breathe through your fear or speak it out loud but, whatever you
do, don't hide it away. Have a cup of tea with it and see it for
what it really is... an invitation to expand. Accept the invitation.

To expand doesn't mean you must push your energy onto
someone else. Shining can happen from a quiet space too,
you don't need to be an extrovert to do it. The Universe is
expanding every second. No matter how much you grow,
there is always going to be more than enough room.

To 'be the light' doesn't take strenuous effort, but it does require you to show up. Show up now. And now. And now. And now. And now. And now. And now. And now. And now.

You're not normal, you're extraordinary. Your attempt to fit in will never work. You were not born to live in a box. Overspill. Expand. Take up space. Anything less will be a tragic waste.

Embrace the energy that wants to come through you. There are books waiting to be written, speeches waiting to be given, mountains waiting to be climbed, and babies waiting to be birthed. Raise your hand, take a great big leap, and enjoy the ride.

This is the dawn of a new day and the day of a new dawn.

Thank you for lighting the way.

△

THE ARMY OF LIGHT IS ALWAYS RECRUITING

The Army of Light wants you! You are being recruited to light up the world by being you. In return for shining your light in a way that only you can and listening to the callings of your soul, the Universe will support you wholly.

Warning: Your dreams may not play out as you think they will. There is a considerable chance they will work out better than you could possibly imagine.

Name: ....

Signature: ....

Name: THE UNIVERSE ....

Signature: *The Universe* ....

I'M NOT AFRAID.
I WAS BORN
TO DO THIS.

JOAN OF ARC

△

THANK YOU

Here we are, at the end of these pages, but perhaps at just the beginning of a longer journey together.

From the bottom of my heart I hope that these words have in some way served you in coming back home to the wisdom of your soul.

Sometimes words cannot express all that our heart feels, but I trust that anything missed your heart and soul will catch.

Your being here matters, your rising up matters, your expansion matters, your courageousness matters, your consciousness matters, shining your light matters. No act is too big or too small. Keep rising up.

Thank you for your presence, for showing up, and your light.

Thank you for serving the world by being you.

I am so glad you are here.

Only love,

Rebecca

△
ONE THING

If you could take only one thing from this book, this is what I would choose it to be: Your soul is always calling you in the direction of your wholeness, flow, dreams, and purpose (and everything else). But you have to show up to it to hear it.

Non-negotiable daily spiritual practice is the only way that I have found to do this. Show up to the callings of your soul and the Universe will open its arms to support you.

In short: Meditate every day.

And wait for the magic to happen.

Δ

BASK IN THE LIGHT SOME MORE

Get on the list

Add some light to your inbox by signing up to my email at www.rebeccacampbell.me/signup

Ladies of the Light

Connect with other like-hearted soul sisters at www.ladiesofthelight.com

Instant Guidance Oracle

Get some guidance using my free Instant Guidance Oracle at www.rebeccacampbell.me/instant-guidance

Going deeper

If you dig this book and want to go deeper, check out my online courses and mentoring at www.rebeccacampbell.me

Connect

www.rebeccacampbell.me

www.facebook.com/rebeccathoughts

www.instagram.com/rebeccathoughts

www.twitter.com/rebeccathoughts

www.pinterest.com/campbellrebecca

△

I RECOMMEND

Books

The Artist's Way, Julia Cameron (Pan Books, 1995)

Ask and It Is Given, Abraham-Hicks (Hay House, 2008)

Boundless Love, Miranda Macpherson (Ebury Press, 2002)

Eat Pray Love, Elizabeth Gilbert (Bloomsbury, 2009)

I Remember Union, Flo Calhoun (All Worlds Pub, 1992)

The Lightworker's Way, Doreen Virtue (Hay House, 2005)

Reveal, Meggan Watterson (Hay House, 2013)

Tribes, Seth Godin (Piatkus, 2008)

Walking Home, Sonia Choquette (Hay House, 2014)

The War of Art, Steven Pressfield (Black Irish Entertainment LLC, 2012)

Wings of Forgiveness, Kyle Gray (Hay House, 2015)

Your Big Beautiful Book Plan, Danielle LaPorte and Linda Sivertsen

Music

Krishna Das: www.krishnadas.com

Chloë Goodchild: www.thenakedvoice.com

Baird Hersey: www.bairdhersey.com

Jai Jagdeesh: www.jai-jagdeesh.com

Light Is The New Black Playlist: www.lightisthenewblack.com

Gurunam Singh: www.gurunamsingh.com

Nikki Slade: www.freetheinnervoice.com

Events and courses

B School: http://marieforleobschool.com

Emerging Women: http://www.emergingwomen.com

Hay House Writer's Workshop: http://www.hayhouse.co.uk

School of the Modern Mystic: http://schoolofthemodernmystic.com

Six Sensory Living: http://www.soniachoquette.com

Spirit Junkie Masterclass: http://spiritjunkies.com

Spirited Sessions: http://www.thespiritedproject.com

△

ACKNOWLEDGMENTS

To my teacher and mentor, Sonia Choquette. For all of the teachings (even in my sleep!), for guiding the way through the crumbling of the past, for encouraging me to teach and write, and for handing this book to Michelle at Hay House.

To Craig Gourlay. For giving me the experience of rising in love, for riding the magic carpet, for your eight-ness, and for the limitless encouragement and support during the writing of these pages (and for putting up with my extreme messiness!).

To Trevor and Julie Campbell. For teaching me the importance of education, giving me every opportunity possible, supporting me every step of the way, and for giving me wings to fly on my own.

To Angela Wood. For your friendship, courage, huge heart, all of the D & M's, and for being such a huge catalyst in my awakening.

To Blair, Wildcat, and Adrian. For all of the good times, and for showing me how to truly live.

To Matt. For your unconditional encouragement, and for all of the growth made possible because of our relationship.

To Amy Firth. For your sisterhood and helping me edit my story in the best possible way. To Sheila Dickson for your friendship and being even more excited than me when great things happen.

To Chela Davidson for supporting me mid-leap. To Andrrea Hess for giving me insight into who I am at soul level and the work I am here to do. To Nikki Slade and Gail Larson for helping me free my soul's voice. To Miranda Macpherson for your powerful teachings and holding energy. To Gurunam Singh, Krishna Das, Baird Hersey, and Jai-Jagdeesh for your devotional music that touches my heart like no other.

To Jaqui Kolek, Louise Androlia, and my Six Sensory mastermind sisters (Betsy Bass, Monika Laschkolnig, Susanne Snellman, Fiona Radman, and Sanja

Plavljanic-Sirola) for your support, belief, and eternal encouragement. And to Robyn Silverton for our Spirited partnership.

To the entire team at Hay House UK, particularly Michelle Pilley. Thank you for welcoming me into the Hay House family and giving my work a home.

To my commissioning editor and friend, Amy Kiberd. Thank you for holding such a crystal clear vision for these pages and making the process such a sacred joy. I'm so proud of this co-creation!

To Julie Oughton and Sandy Draper for polishing this manuscript with a powerful mix of love and extreme attention to detail. To Jo Burgess, Ruth Tewkesbury, Jessica Crockett, Tom Cole, Leanne Siu Anastasi, and Diane Hill for always going beyond and being so supportive and skillful. It's a dream come true to work with each of you.

To Reid Tracy, Patty Gift, the team at Hay House USA, The Writer's Workshop, and to Leon Nacson and Rosie Barry at Hay House Australia, for giving *Light Is the New Black* wings. To Versha Jones (UK) and Michelle Polizzi (USA) for the beautiful cover designs.

To Louise Hay, Maya Angelou, and all of the women from all of the ages who have courageously risen before, regardless of the repercussions. Thank you for blazing such an epic trail and making it safer than ever for women like me to share what's in our souls.

To the Councils of Light, Divine Mother, Kali, Mary Magdalene, my spirit guides, ancestors, and Source. Thank you for your constant whispers, guidance, and support throughout my life, especially in the moments that I ignored it.

To all of my clients, students, and social media followers, thank you for showing up and letting me share what is in my heart.

And finally, but most importantly to you, dear reader. Thank you for answering my call and being so willing to shine your light. You are my blessing.

Love,

Rebecca x

ABOUT THE AUTHOR

Jamie Beadon

Rebecca Campbell is an author, inspirational motivational speaker, spiritual teacher, grounded intuitive mentor, and practical intuitive guide.

One of Hay House's freshest voices, Rebecca is passionate about helping people connect with their intuition in order to live wonderful lives both personally and professionally.

Drawing on her unique experience as an award-winning advertising creative director, Rebecca also guides her clients and students to light up the world with their authentic presence, to 'Let your spirit be your brand™'.

Co-creator of The Spirited Project, she teaches regularly and has been featured in several publications such as *The Sunday Times Style* magazine and *Psychologies*.

As a twentysomething jet-setter meets gypsy spirit, Rebecca blogged her way around the world as The Skype Nomad and shared her adventures in a regular column in *The Daily Telegraph*. She also spent a year of her life painting her way around the world with the Let's Colour Project.

Originally from the sunny shores of Sydney, Rebecca now lives in London but you can find her down under most summers getting her salt water and sunshine fix.

 /rebeccathoughts   @rebeccathoughts

www.rebeccacampbell.me
www.thespiritedproject.com

We hope you enjoyed this Hay House book. If you'd like to receive our online catalog featuring additional information on Hay House books and products, or if you'd like to find out more about the Hay Foundation, please contact:

Hay House, Inc., P.O. Box 5100, Carlsbad, CA 92018-5100
(760) 431-7695 or (800) 654-5126
(760) 431-6948 (fax) or (800) 650-5115 (fax)
www.hayhouse.com® • www.hayfoundation.org

———

Published in Australia by:
Hay House Australia Pty. Ltd., 18/36 Ralph St., Alexandria NSW 2015
Phone: 612-9669-4299 • *Fax:* 612-9669-4144 • www.hayhouse.com.au

Published in the United Kingdom by:
Hay House UK, Ltd., Astley House, 33 Notting Hill Gate, London W11 3JQ
Phone: 44-20-3675-2450 • *Fax:* 44-20-3675-2451 • www.hayhouse.co.uk

Published in India by: Hay House Publishers India,
Muskaan Complex, Plot No. 3, B-2, Vasant Kunj, New Delhi 110 070
Phone: 91-11-4176-1620 • *Fax:* 91-11-4176-1630 • www.hayhouse.co.in

———

Access New Knowledge.
Anytime. Anywhere.

Learn and evolve at your own pace
with the world's leading experts.

www.hayhouseU.com